MATES FOR MONSTERS

TAMSIN LEY

Twin Leaf Press

Print Version

ISBN-13: 978-1-950027-52-1

Copyright © 2017 Twin Leaf Press
Cover design by Tamsin Ley

Brimming with sexy mythical heroes who don't know they need a mate, Mates for Monsters will keep paranormal and fantasy romance fans reading long into the night. Find out for yourself why readers can't get enough of these sizzling hot happily-ever-afters. Set includes:

The Merman's Kiss

A finless female won't live long among the dangers of the sea, and our sexy merman must choose between keeping her at his side, and keeping her safe.

The Centaur's Bride

Half man, half beast, he can never run free with the shifter herd—until the ranch's heiress discovers his secret and wants to take him for a ride...

The Djinn's Desire

An ancient genie falls in love with a curvy human, but hers may be the one wish he can never fulfill.

Reader Promise: Steamy love scenes with dangerous mermaids, sexy centaur shifters, and beguiling genie magic. Intended for mature audiences.

THE MERMAN'S KISS

A STEAMY MYTHOLOGY ROMANCE

A sexy, sleek-tailed monster.

Zantu has evaded the mate-bond for thirty-five years, dodging promiscuous mermaids with vile intents. Unlike mermaids, mermen bond for life, and Zantu refuses to accept the heartbreak most mermen die of. That is, until the glint of gold catches his eye, and a simple salvage mission turns to passion. Now he's bonded to a human.

A woman looking for a reason to live.

Briana thinks her life is over after the loss of her child. Instead, she falls into the arms of a merman who is anything but cold-blooded. He's wild, seductive, and sets her blood on fire every time he touches her, and soon she begins to need him for more than his magic to breathe underwater. He might just give her a new purpose.

But as dangers encroach from every side, Zantu must choose; keep his new mate at his side or keep her safe.

Either way, he's sure he'll end up with a broken heart.

BRIANNA DROPPED THE pregnancy test into the bathroom trash and joined Eric in bed. He had his laptop across his knees, studying one of his corporate financial projection reports.

"Negative," she said, fighting the crack in her voice. The sheets felt frigid against her skin.

Without looking away from the screen, he reached over and patted her shoulder. "We'll try again next month."

After a stillborn baby girl almost two years ago, they'd followed the doctor's advice to wait a year before trying again. Now another year had passed without a ray of hope. What if she'd lost her only chance to be a mother? A tear leaked from the corner of her eye, soaking into the pillow. "Maybe we should stop trying."

"If that's what you want." He scrolled the mouse.

Brianna's chest ached. "Eric?"

"Mmm?" He tapped his finger against the mouse pad.

"Eric." Her voice did crack this time. At least he looked away from the computer. His eyes reminded her of the fish in the tank at his office, round and dark and emotionless. She swallowed her tears and slid her head forward to rest her cheek on his arm. "Make love to me."

His forearm bunched as he pulled it from beneath her. Her chest lightened for a single heartbeat, then his arm settled back down around the top of her pillow. He patted between her shoulder blades and returned his gaze to the computer. "It's late. We'll try again next cycle."

~

The salty breeze blowing across the pier tasted of tears. Behind her, a few scattered people went about their off-season business along the boardwalk. Ahead, only empty, colorless gray sky and water.

Brianna stepped off the pier.

The heavy fishing weights cinched around her waist did their job, pulling her toward the bottom quickly enough to make her ears pop.

She'd heard drowning wasn't a bad way to go, but the salty water stung her eyes and nose. And the water was cold. Really cold. As the light above faded to a murky blue, she watched the final pockets of air billow upward from her blouse. Who knew the bottom was this far down? A school of fish blocked the meager light a moment, and then they were gone.

Her chest burned with need, but she was afraid to take a breath. Was she sure she wanted to do this? She and Eric had been married three years before she'd realized he was such a cold fish and would never change. Even the stillbirth of little Pauline hadn't seemed to touch him. But he also wasn't the only fish in the sea. Would divorce be so bad? Just before he'd died, her father had made her swear never to divorce her husband. Her mother's abandonment had torn out a part of his soul. So she'd promised.

But he was gone now. This was her life.

Or her death.

This is stupid! She snatched at the rope belt weighing heavy against her hips. The entire thing was full of knots where she'd attached the five-pound weights. Which knot was holding it closed? Her loose blouse, useful to hide the weights on land, billowed in the current. She couldn't see the knots. With both hands, she lifted her shirt hem and pulled the garment over her head. The water's greedy clutches swept it away.

Her bottom bounced against the seafloor, sending up a cloud of silt. A surge of bubbles forced themselves from between her lips. She clamped her mouth shut. The air escaped from her nose instead. Her tortured lungs burned like they might explode.

Her left foot scraped stone, and she tried to stand. To push toward the surface. The rock slid out from under her as the tide carried her out to sea.

She was so stupid. Why had she thought she wanted to die? And like this, as fish food? Eyes burning in the salt water and straining in the light, she searched for the right knot. Her fingers were numb with cold. Tingly. More air trickled from her nose. Her lungs cried out for her to take a breath.

The light grew dimmer. With both hands, she pushed at the belt, trying to squeeze it down around her hips. The rope stretched a little. Maybe she could shimmy out of it. Except the waistband of her capri pants thwarted that idea. She flicked open the button and slid them down her legs, taking her panties with them. Kicking, she released the fabric to the tide.

Without her consent, her lungs sipped a draught of water, and she doubled over with a cough. Then her lungs were full. There was no air to cough. Her naked legs scraped along the rocky bottom.

Her vision was going dark from lack of oxygen. Or was the water getting deeper? A strange calm settled over her. Another school of fish blocked the murky light. She blinked. Maybe death wouldn't be so bad. Like falling asleep. And maybe her baby would be waiting for her on the other side.

Strong hands grabbed her arms above the elbows. A man with spiky hair and glinting eyes stared into her face. Someone had come to save her! She flung her arms about his neck. Or at least she tried. The water slowed her motion. Both her legs wrapped around his waist like she might climb him to the surface.

His eyes widened, metallic silver beneath a dark brow line. Smooth skin slid beneath her fingertips. His face drew closer, eyes boring into hers. A firm mouth found hers, and his tongue slid in.

She gasped, the lightheadedness of drowning turning into the twirling water-ballet of desire. Like a lure, the dancing tongue within her called on instincts she didn't know she possessed. Created a pulsing throb in her core, a need greater than air. She bent her head and matched the kiss, tangling her tongue with his and sending rockets of electricity straight to her core. Her entwined legs drew her hips against his. Ground against the hard line growing between them.

A drawn-out note—not quite a groan, not quite a song—surrounded her. Penetrated deep into her bones. He drew back, hands on her hips. The kiss continued in a teasing mockery of consummation.

For a split second, she wondered if this was the result of a final, dying fantasy. An attempt of her mind to protect her from the horror of death. But then the moment was gone, and all she knew was need. Need to be one with him. To feel him inside her. To cast away death with the very act that created life.

Legs still locked around him, she pulled him close again. Arched to meet him. Silently pleaded for more.

And as naturally as breathing, he filled her.

What...? The thought echoed in her brain, as if she were hearing his thoughts as well as her own.

Yet she had no time to pause and consider. His hands slithered down to cup her ass, drawing her closer. He undulated against her like a wave.

Dizzy with ecstasy, she bucked her hips in time to his rhythm. Threw her head back so the angle of their joining stroked her innermost ridges. Shivers rocketed down her thighs, pooled in the core of her belly. This was primal. A need greater than she'd known could exist. A demand blocking out all thoughts of anything but satisfaction.

All around them, the current swirled as he thrust. Pure instinct made her clamp her legs tighter about his waist. Nothing mattered now but the climax. The heady release of something larger than she'd ever experienced before. Heat flushed her, searing her from head to toe. Tumbling thoughts collided with each other inside her head. Sex. *Magic.* Heat. *Breath.* Life. *Yes!*

She screamed the last word, throwing her head back as her climax shook her.

The man's fingers dug deep into her buttocks as he joined her.

Eyes closed, chest heaving from exertion, she relaxed in his arms. Her heartbeat pulsed in her ears, and her limbs felt limp as jellyfish. Sex had always been bland with Eric. Clinical. She'd sought to please him but never found the ecstasy so many of her friends carried on about. Now she knew what the fuss was.

A muscular arm fastened about her waist, and a surge of water pushed her hair off her face. She opened her eyes, her breath catching in her throat. Then she stiffened. Breath? She was breathing. How was she breathing?

The weights she wore dug into her hip as he held her close against him. With amazing force, he propelled them through the water, focused on something ahead. Her gaze raked his spiked hair and naked shoulder. Down his back, his spine rose into a pronged fan. *A fin?*

She blinked, wondering if her eyes were playing tricks on her in the murky light. She was underwater. But breathing. She slid a hand across his shoulder blade and up the fin to the first bony prong. Craning her head, she looked down the length of his body. Salt water rose in her throat. Where legs should be, a silver tail ended in a billowing fin. *This guy has a tail.*

She'd just had sex with a merman. And now he was carrying her deeper into the sea.

2

*T*HE FEMALE'S WARMTH coursed through his bloodstream like a drug. Zantu had seen her struggling and had meant only to check her body for salvage, a weakness of his inherited from his father. The glint of gold around her throat had made him dare to approach. Then she'd wrapped herself around him like a squid. A very hot squid. His member had erupted from its sheath like a narwhal's horn through ice, ready to claim her heat before his brain even had time to process the act. The irrevocable act.

And now the green-eyed beauty owned him, body and soul.

Unlike the more promiscuous mer-females who would search out and copulate with anything with a penis, mermen bonded for life. A merman who bonded was doomed to a life of misery as his mate strayed again and again. He would raise the children, coddling them like a father sea horse until they, too, left him. Most mermen died of broken hearts.

Zantu gritted his teeth and tightened his grip around his new mate. He'd felt her stiffen, likely to flee into the arms of another man now that she'd taken what she wanted. But Zantu wasn't about to let that happen. He was determined to find a way to bond her to him as tightly as he was bonded to her.

He would find a way to harness this capricious female heart.

The woman struggled in his grip, flailing uselessly as he dove over the first chasm toward the nesting grounds. Her nails dug into the flesh on his shoulder, and her naked legs slid along his tail.

Legs.

He'd never imagined bonding to a human. Mermaids seduced men all the time, but mermen, lacking a female's seductive skills, avoided contact at all costs. Many a tale warned of humans hunting mermen for sport.

As the woman struggled, the bush covering her female parts brushed his hip, hot and inviting. His manhood stirred again at the invitation. He'd been told the bond would be strong when it happened, but the draw he felt was as inevitable as the tide. He adjusted his grip so she was beneath him, looking up, her eyes fixed on him. She opened her mouth as if to speak, but no sound emerged. Was she mute? Perhaps she was out of oxygen? The magic in his kiss should have enabled her to breathe as easily as a deep-sea dweller until the moon went dark. Then the magic would have to be renewed, or she would drown. At least that was what the mermaids said about the men they seduced. But perhaps a merman's kiss wasn't as strong?

After glancing forward to be sure he was on course, he dipped his head toward her and covered her mouth with his. Her lips were incredibly soft, working against his as she continued to try to speak. Her hands crept over his shoulders and slid along his dorsal, sending shivers across his skin.

Desire rose in him again, and he crushed her tighter against him, all thoughts of forward momentum banished as he plunged his tongue between her blunt teeth, twirled, and thrust. His shaft once again unsheathed itself, ready for another bonding.

Her legs fluttered, and he curled his tail up and between them, pressing his hips to hers. Her heat was waiting, slick and hot. Her legs around him tightened like a trap, and her soft breasts burned against his chest. Her mouth tasted like sunlight-dappled waves.

What am I doing? The thought wasn't his. Depths, he was truly done for. Only the strongest of bonds allowed a merman to hear his mate's thoughts. The only bond more rare was when the female could hear the male.

He opened his eyes. Maybe... Her lids were closed, her lips swollen with kisses. *Stay with me,* he thought. She threw back her head, mouth forming soundless words, but her hands kept tight hold against his shoulders. Maybe she heard him.

Maybe not. All he could do was hold her as close as he could as long as he could.

Crushing her against him, he trailed kisses down her throat. One hand found her breast and cupped it, teasing the tip into a coral nub. She shuddered, and her nails dug into his back as her depths tightened around him. He throbbed for release but refused to let the moment be over so soon. He drew back until the tip of his member just teased her folds. In his mind, he heard her whimper, plead for more.

Not yet. I'm not done with you.

She wriggled her hips against him, pressing herself along his waiting length. Her tongue roved her lips, inviting him to taste, but he resisted, simply gazing upon her, fighting his own desire. To exercise such control was as heady as mounting her. The drive was strong in him, but not overpowering. How was he doing this? A merman was supposed to be unable to resist his mate's lust, even for a moment, as doomed to her whims as a jellyfish to the tide. If he could hold off like this, perhaps there was hope for him.

Then she opened her eyes, and her lips mouthed, "Please." He was indeed doomed. With a shudder he sheathed himself inside her, slammed his hips against her. She matched his rhythm, throwing her head back and rocking with him until his tail curled in the ecstasy of release.

He sagged against her, holding her gently and allowing the current to carry them where it would. For thirty-five years he'd avoided his bond-fate, sidestepping many tempting offers in the process. Of late, his biology had nearly toppled him into the abyss on several occasions. A raven-haired seductress with a voice like an orca's. A green-tailed enchantress with a golden dorsal fin he later learned had been tipped with love toxin.

And yet, now that he was bonded, he was relieved. No longer would he need to live in terror of other mermaids. Of traps and subterfuge. And perhaps with a human, he would be able to maintain some control. Maybe even shrug off the curse of his bond-fate.

A war raged inside his chest as he held his mate close while some distant, protected part of his mind plotted a way to be free of her.

But for now, he'd do everything in his power to protect her.

3

*B*RIANNA FLOATED BONELESS as sea kelp, luxuriating in the afterglow of the merman's lovemaking. As primal as the act had been, she still thought of it as lovemaking. She could have sworn he'd whispered his devotion in her ear as they'd coupled. Or perhaps it was just her subconscious desire to be loved and cherished.

She opened heavy lids but could see nothing beyond the shoulders of the merman in the inky depths. Featureless. Maybe this was all a dream and she was dead. Could you dream when you were dead? Whatever the case, she never wanted to wake up. Not if death was like this. With a sigh, she wrapped her arms around the merman's waist and pressed her cheek against his shoulder. He smelled briny and herbal at the same time.

I wonder what his name is.

A voice like a song came to her. *Zantu.*

She giggled, bubbles tickling her nose. *Now I'm hearing voices. What kind of a name is Zantu?*

The palm he'd been stroking against the small of her back stopped. He thrust her away to look into her face, his hands like claws around her biceps. *You can hear me?*

His silver eyes flashed fiercely, and he grinned; every one of his pearly whites was sharp as a canine. How had she not noticed that while they'd kissed? For the first time, she was afraid.

Can you hear me? The sonorous voice again floated through her mind.

A shiver started in her chest and rattled outward through her bones. Her heart raced until her vision jostled with every pounding beat. She managed to nod at him.

He released one hand from her bicep and stroked her cheek.

She recoiled at the sight of the slight webbing between his fingers. A word formed in her mind as his gyrating tail caught her attention. *Monster.*

His hand hovered millimeters from her cheek, and she swung her gaze up to meet his, suddenly horrified that he'd heard. His mouth no longer smiled. His liquid-silver eyes gleamed like twin moons. *I'm sorry,* she thought, hoping he could hear her.

He sucked in his cheeks as if willing himself not to speak and dropped the hand from her face. *Come.*

His other hand slid down her arm to take her hand, and he turned away. With a powerful thrash of his tail, he pulled her along behind him, towing her like a bit of flotsam.

~

*Z*antu's joy about the discovery of the reciprocal, telepathic bond tasted like seagull spatter on his tongue. She thought him an abomination? A monster? Of course she did. Her kind hunted his. There could be no love between them.

I'm Brianna, she thought to him, but he didn't answer. He couldn't. He had to find a way to break this unholy bond before he revealed all the secrets of the mer-kingdom to an outsider. Before she could rally her people to hunt them down in their nests.

Pumping his tail muscles like he was fleeing an orca's teeth, he plunged them through the tidal current toward the deeper water where he could hold her until he'd formed a plan. The swim would normally take him less than a quarter tide, but with his mate's extra weight, he couldn't move nearly as fast. He surveyed the waters ahead, wary of sharks and other predators who might take advantage of his handicap.

A trill of laughter caught his attention, followed by three scale notes and the underlying vibrations of a fish-harp. His dorsal fin flattened against his back. Mermaids. Melody lilted through the water, a familiar cadence, a magic to incite desire.

He knew that voice. Loia. She'd tempted him before, nearly caught him in her net. But now he felt only the faintest acknowledgement of her song's power. His bond was set, and she could no longer influence him.

Fin flaring tall and straight, he readjusted his course to carry him directly toward the music. He couldn't wait to see her face when she realized she'd lost him.

In the center of a shoal of tiny, silver fish, he spotted the curvaceous indigo tail fin of the songstress. The fish darted and flashed in time to her voice, falling and rising and spinning around in a magical haze. Her hair billowed outward like a blueberry sea fan, while her breasts, pale as alabaster and tipped with violet-blue nipples, bobbed like lures. Luscious indigo lips sang promises of bliss.

His throat tightened. Her magic was strong. Even with his ties to his new mate, the mermaid's song pulled at him, burned through his blood, and made his sheath swell as his member surged in time with the dancing fish.

She spotted him. Her golden eyes narrowed and her lips curved into a predatory grin even as she continued her song. Her fingers caressed the tines of a fish-harp cradled in one arm, pulling notes from deep within each gold-tipped tine while she crooned of love and desire.

His mate's hand tightened around his fingers; for the barest moment he'd forgotten she was there. His heart thudded against his rib cage. He would be safe from the song because of his bond-mate. He pulled her up beside him and hooked an arm around her waist, delighting in the flicker of jealousy that crossed Loia's face.

"Zantu, what have you brought me?" she sang. "A pretty little feast?"

He held his woman tighter. "I've found my bond-mate. You have no more power over me, Loia."

The net of fish encircling the mermaid lost cohesion for a moment then re-formed, hovering like a million tiny blades ready to strike. "You cannot bond with a human. Their lives are over with a flick of the fin."

"Only because you abandon them to drown, Loia, lovesick and broken."

The mermaid undulated her tail and thrust forth her breasts suggestively. "Why would you even want her? She cannot play hide-and-seek with you among the kelp beds. Or race you along the canyon deeps. Or sing while you climax to your very bones. She can't even escape when a shark attacks. A human is no fit mate for our kind. They're barely useful as toys."

"You don't know that," he snapped. A tiny fish brushed his arm, and he shrugged it away. "Mermaids don't take mates." But her comments had him worried. How *would* he protect a human mate when predators invaded?

"We take plenty of mates, Zantu." Her grin exposed every one of her needle-sharp teeth, as if ready to devour him. "We just don't limit ourselves to one. A pity you will never experience a true lover's passion, only the clumsy limbs of a land-walker. Or... maybe she would like to play, too?" Loia spun in place, whipping her head around to find him again as she completed her turn. Her genital slit had pulsed open during her spin, exposing the pink invitation of her vulva. "Human men like to watch each other copulate. I could show her—and you—what a real female can do with a man."

Something caressed the opening of his sheath, and he looked down to find two tiny fish rubbing themselves against him. He looked back up and realized the rest of the school had engulfed them like a net.

Loia licked her lips and ran her hands up over her breasts to tweak her indigo nipples, arching her back. One hand traced lightly down her center line to massage the swollen folds of her slit. Her scent floated to him in the wake of her net of minions.

In spite of his bond to Brianna, Loia's overt sexuality was getting to him. The teasing at his groin had nearly burst his member from its protective sheath. His head spun, and all he could think about was letting his urges free.

Brianna batted at a fish near her face and pressed herself closer to him, turning her face into his shoulder. *I want to go home.*

Those words sobered him faster than the strike of a moray eel. She wanted to leave him. He wrapped both arms around her and began to back away from Loia's seductions. If he wanted to keep his mate, staying near Loia wasn't the way to do it. "Go find some other man to ruin," he called out.

Loia's pale skin went lurid. Her lips spread thin as she

bared every one of her shark-like teeth. "You cannot keep her," she shrilled.

Brianna wriggled in his grasp, her legs slapping his fin as if she wished to swim away. Her slender shoulders felt fragile in his grip, but he refused to let her go. The scent of blood reached his nose. Inside his head, he heard Brianna scream, *My legs!*

He loosed his hold and saw her lower extremities surrounded by Loia's net of fish. A trail of pink-clouded water floated in their wake. They were biting her. The blood would surely draw every predator within a league of them. Rage rose up inside him, and he opened his mouth wide to emit a deep, repelling sphere of sound.

The fish scattered.

4

*T*HE SUDDEN BARITONE note Zantu emitted, so different from the tenor opera he'd been singing to the mermaid, vibrated deep into Brianna's bones. He pumped his tail, and a sudden surge of water forced her to close her eyes as they left the singing mermaid and her biting pets far behind.

Brianna's skin itched and burned where the tiny fish had nibbled her with razor-sharp teeth, but he was moving too fast for her to check her wounds. She buried her face against his warm neck and hung on for dear life. The mermaid's mesmerizing performance had grown more bizarre with every note that passed the female's lips. The final lewd sexual display left no doubt in Brianna's mind about what the creature wanted. And the pesky, biting fish made it very clear she'd prefer Brianna out of the picture.

She'd been frightened by the merman's differences only a short time earlier; now what frightened her about him also made her believe he could protect her. She rubbed her thighs together in memory of him between them. Why did he want her, when he was pursued by a creature as alluring as that mermaid? Even Brianna had felt that pull, and she'd never been attracted to another female in her life. No wonder sailors were said to willingly plunge to their deaths in pursuit of the creatures.

Looking back over her shoulder, she sought the mermaid in the gloomy water, sure the fierce female would pursue, but her eyes were too weak to pierce the midnight depths. The world had lost its color and become murky shades of black and green. A school of small fish slithered past, spear-shaped sides seeming to turn as one. Ahead, filaments rose from the seafloor to create a shifting curtain patterned by other sea creatures darting to and fro among them.

Zantu readjusted his grip around her waist, the pressure of his muscular arms making her skin quiver. She could feel his heartbeat beneath her fingers as he carried her ever deeper into the water. The way his tail bumped her legs and pubic bone as he swam reminded her of their earlier coupling. Made her yearn for more. But he showed no intention of slowing for another dalliance.

Colorful sea stars and anemones passed by in a rainbow blur in the rocks below. He continued to shoot through the forest, past a big red-and-black fish with a gaping mouth, over an eel peeking from the rocks. The forest here seemed thinner, with more light reaching the seafloor. Or maybe they were in shallower water? She looked upward at the canopy of fronds swaying in the current but couldn't judge how far away they were.

Where are you taking me?

Where you'll be safe.

His words eased the tension in her chest. Until that moment, she'd harbored a fear that with his lust satiated he might develop another hunger. One that used his razor-like teeth.

He slowed and pushed her away to look at her. *I'm not a monster.*

Guilt flushed her from head to toe. This whole "hearing each other's thoughts" thing was weirding her out. *I'm... sorry. I just don't know anything about you or your kind.*

We stay away from humans. You're dangerous.

A chuckle of bubbles left her mouth as she thought of that. Here she was, who knew how many feet below the sea, held captive by a sharp-toothed, web-fingered, sleek-tailed merman, and he claimed to be afraid of her. Yet when she met his silver-eyed gaze, she realized he was completely serious.

antu clutched his new mate to his side and torpedoed toward the kelp beds where he and the other mermen maintained the nesting grounds. Brianna's unfiltered thoughts reached him in irregular and unpredictable waves, one minute with disconcerting openness, the next not at all. He had no idea why. Most clear was her terror. Her curiosity. Her sensual attention to his skin against hers. The connection was driving him mad yet reassuring him at the same time. Although she thought him a monster, she wanted him as badly as he wanted her—at least for now. Would her interest wane like the females of his kind?

Ahead, the kelp swayed rhythmically between glistening shafts of filtered sunlight. Zantu dragged her into the foliage without halting, sending sonic commands to the plants and the creatures among it to clear the way. Those unfamiliar with the forest would be quickly lost and confused among the stalks, but he knew the path as well as he did his own tail. Strands of kelp caressed his skin with familiarity, loosing bubbles in his wake. Brianna clutched his neck tight enough for him to feel her racing heartbeat.

The kelp opened up to reveal his small refuge beneath the sea. Like the others of his sex, he'd created a haven fit for a queen, in spite of his determination to remain free of a bondmate. Nesting was a biological imperative for his kind, mate or no mate.

His home had a floor of round, multicolored stones and wave-polished shells and glass. Items he'd salvaged from shipwrecks and lovingly restored filled the shallow depression: a rosewood table with three matching chairs, a vanity with a tall mirror still clear enough to see a reflection, a rocking chair inlaid with mother-of-pearl. A human bed with a fancy carved headboard rested in an alcove, mattress replaced by a soft garden of sponges. At the foot, an ancient ironbound chest held more treasures from his years of salvage. Around the clearing's edges, he'd cultivated a garden of fine, edible seaweed, decorative sea fans, and rock outcroppings covered with clusters of indigo and green mussels.

But his finest creation rested in the center of the nest, awaiting the day Zantu truly lost his freedom. Supported by living fingers of coral, a bassinet rocked evenly in the gentle ocean current.

In his mind, Brianna's thoughts swam with perceptions too jumbled for him to decipher. Or perhaps she was learning to guard her thoughts. There would eventually need to be a filter, if nothing else than to spare the other of the distraction of receiving every detailed impression.

He deposited her in the rocking chair, the fishing weights around her waist keeping her solidly planted against its seat, and pumped his tail once to back away from her. Spinning in a cautious circle, he surveyed the wall of kelp surrounding them. Loia's minions should have been blocked by the kelp forest, but he could take no chances they—and thereby she—might follow him to his refuge.

Satisfied they were alone, he faced his new mate, looking her over with what he hoped was an unbiased eye. Her hair, much shorter than any mermaid's and not nearly as colorful, floated in a dark halo about her face, and her speckled green eyes reminded him of sunlight through kelp fronds. Sun-kissed arms and legs transitioned to paler skin over her breasts and torso. Her deep-coral-peaked nipples bobbed lusciously above her smoothly muscled belly, and the tuft of hair between her legs made his groin stir as his eyes drifted over her hips and down her legs to her tiny painted toes.

A human.

He'd bonded with a human.

Had such a thing ever happened in the history of mer-kind? Certainly mermaids seduced human men, but never bonded. Not with mermen and certainly not with humans. The reclusive, emotionally susceptible mermen stayed far away from females of any kind—at least until a mermaid caught him. Just Zantu's luck to be seduced by a human. What was she doing in the ocean, anyway?

His gaze returned to the coarsely knotted belt around her hips. The weights he recognized as those used by fishermen seeking trophies. Such men were never gentle, and he'd helped many swordfish and tuna escape those deadly lines. The rope had marred her pale skin with angry-looking welts, and small blue bruises covered her hips.

Pointing a webbed finger at her waist, he sent, *Why do you wear this?*

Her face flushed crimson, and she tugged helplessly at one of the knots. *It was a mistake.*

Her efforts made her breasts bob more furiously, and he

fought to keep his cock contained within its sheath. *You wish it removed?*

Yes. She looked up at him with pleading eyes, and his attempt at cool objectivity melted.

Here. He located the knife he'd made from a large green piece of sea glass. Careful to face the razor-sharp edge away from her, he sawed the rope free and dropped it to the stony floor beneath the chair.

Freed of the device, she rose toward the sun-dappled canopy above them.

Snapping out a hand, he grabbed her wrist. He would not let her leave. Not so easily. She would abandon him eventually. That was inevitable. But before she did, he wanted to show her what it was to be a mate. What it was to be utterly controlled and owned, as he now was. He could control her but only beneath the water. As long as she was down here, she needed him.

He sent, *Why did you come to me?*

Her gaze returned to him, and once again a flush infused her cheeks. *It was an accident.*

This does not look like an accident. He pointed to the belt. *This was to tie you to the ocean. To bring you to me.*

She pressed her lips together, brow furrowing in pain. *No. That...* Her hands crept over her smooth belly to lace her fingers together. *I was trying to kill myself.*

He narrowed his eyes, gauging her sincerity. *Why would you want to die?*

Her shoulders slumped, her body sinking until her feet rested against the smooth stone floor. *It's a long story. A silly one. The weights were so I couldn't change my mind.*

Tell me.

I lost a baby.

Zantu's gills fluttered. Mermaids considered children a burden. Something to be abandoned along with their mates. Never did they grieve the loss of one. But Brianna wasn't a mermaid. Her thoughts pounded his mind in a wave of unfiltered longing.

He curled his tail around the back of her knees, drawing her toward him. *I'm sorry you are grieved.*

She brought her hands up between them to press stiffly against his chest, as if creating a wall, but didn't shove with any real force.

He embraced her, running his fingertips lightly up the smooth curve of her finless spine. Her heartbeat fluttered against his chest, and he was reminded of how fragile she was, especially here beneath the waves. *Please do not try to die again.*

Her stiffness eased. This close, he could smell her unique, sunshine-dappled-waves scent. Her skin slid like silk against his, and his sheath pulsed with his desire.

Closing his gills, he gathered air at the back of his throat and lowered his face toward her neck. He pursed his lips and gently blew a stream of bubbles against her collarbone. She shuddered, surprised enjoyment vibrating through their thought connection. Encouraged, he added sound, a baritone come-hither call that should penetrate her very bones.

She threw her head back, hips thrust forward, and he took the opportunity to slide his fingers over her folds, discovering her button waiting like a little clam. Her heat intensified at his touch, urging him to increase his rhythm. He pressed against her slickness and caressed the nub until it swelled and pulsed with fervent need.

Her hands slipped from his chest to wrap around his ribs. Nipples hard as tiny shells crushed against his flesh, and she bucked against his fingers. His shaft had sprung free now, bobbing in time to her rhythm, yearning for her each time her hip made contact with the tip. He gritted his teeth and continued rubbing, determined to make her come before he plunged himself into her heat.

A tiny squeak slipped past her lips in a stream of bubbles as her body shuddered in release.

I will make you mine. He thrust the thought into her mind even as he pulled her hips to him. Her legs spread wide, allowing him entry, and he pumped his tail to carry them both to the mossy bed. He wanted her beneath him, held in place so he could grind his hips against her. So he could know her full depths with every thrust.

She settled into the sponges and lifted her hips to meet his rhythm, tiny gasps sending bubbles from her mouth to tickle his cheeks. He dipped his head to claim her lips, his tongue probing one set of lips while his shaft probed the other. When she came again, he clutched her rounded buttocks and pumped one final thrust into her core. His shudders matched hers, leaving him exhausted.

Wrapping his arms around her, he allowed himself to fall into sleep.

5

*B*RIANNA WOKE TO groggy darkness. She stretched and rolled over to look for the bedside clock. Her movements were awkward, slow motion, unsupported. *What the...?*

Memories flooded back to her like a bore tide. The pier, the weighted belt, the water... the merman. *Merman?* That part must've been a dream, an escape for her mind before death took her. This must be death. She stared into the deep black, the weight of the entire ocean pressing against her. Nothingness. She hadn't thought it would feel so... alone.

A muscular arm snaked around her, and a voice sounded directly in her head. *Go back to sleep, my angelfish.*

She screamed—or squeaked, the sound muffled by water—and struggled free of the embrace. *Oh God, oh God, oh God.*

A short burst of sound, and the world ignited in lavender light. Zantu's webbed hands reached to still her. Blue-violet light reflected from his silver eyes and gilded his skin, accentuating the perfect muscles of his torso. *What's wrong?*

Her initial bout of terror was replaced by awe. The strange illumination came from everywhere and nowhere all at once, creating an eerie sort of moonlight without a source. And then there was the godlike form of the merman leaning over her, face creased with concern.

A soothing song pulsed from his throat, calming her nerves. Looking past him, she realized the water surrounding them was studded with what looked like tiny purple diamonds. *It's so beautiful.* She reached out to try to catch one of the motes, but it slipped through her fingers as if it were air. *What are they?*

Zantu wrapped his arms around her, nuzzling her neck and sending a stream of bubbles through her hair. *Humans call them plankton.*

Can you turn them on and off?

His chest vibrated with sound, and the water went black.

Oh, no, leave them on! She clawed forward, searching for him. Terror of the darkness, the unknown threatened to crush her.

You asked me to turn them off.

She located one of his biceps, wrapped both hands around it to pull him closer. *No, I wanted to know if you could.*

Again, he sang the motes awake, and Brianna looked up

into a face full of amused tenderness that made her heart skip a beat.

He leaned in to press his forehead to hers. The odd-colored light made his eyes hard to read, but his voice in her head was full of all the sincerity she needed. *I will keep you safe. Always.*

She reached up to caress his cheek, enjoying the smooth skin along his angular jaw. God help her, she believed him.

At that moment, her stomach growled.

And I'll keep you fed. His chuckle matched the curve of his lips.

A craving for nachos filled her. Or maybe fried chicken. She licked her lips. What did mermen eat? Raw fish? She'd never been a fan of sushi. Even rare steak made her queasy.

Don't worry, little angelfish. We're mostly vegetarians. Sit. He pulled a chair away from the rosewood table and gestured.

So far, she'd only moved through the water with his aid. Now, left to her own mobility, she floundered over and took a seat. Luckily, he wasn't watching.

He'd taken a knife to the edge of the clearing and was cutting seaweed and other unidentified items, placing them into a huge half-shell bowl. She watched him work, the muscles of his back and arms bulging and rippling with his movements. His powerful tail flexed with muscle as well, each move through the water accomplished with mere flickers of effort. This had been her first chance to really look at him without him looking back. She wanted to reach out and touch the delicate-looking fin at the end of his tail. Examine what she imagined were tiny scales covering his body. Find out exactly where he hid his cock when they weren't making love.

I can show you if you like.

Her skin heated with embarrassment even as her pussy tightened. She'd forgotten he could basically hear her every thought.

He looked over his shoulder at her and winked. *Don't be embarrassed, little angelfish. I like to know what you're thinking.* In a flash of movement, he somersaulted through the water to face her and set the half-shell down on the table. *What do men look like in your world?*

Not like you. The tremor in her thoughts embarrassed her even more, but she refused to look away from him.

What's so different? He moved closer, hovering mere inches away, six-pack abs flexing with the tiny circular movements of his tail. His webbed hands spread across his ribs and slowly made their way down over his hips, drawing her gaze like a lure to the place where his cock should be—a bulge, there beneath the skin, covered as if by well-fitted clothing.

His thought reached out and caressed her. Compelled her. *Touch me.*

Swallowing, she reached out a hand and brushed her fingertips across the bulge. A note like a sigh of pleasure coursed through the water. Emboldened, she placed her entire palm over the lump, surprised by his heat. By the softness of his skin. She'd expected scales, but he was as smooth here as he was on his torso.

Scales are for fish. Desire colored his thought.

What are you, then?

Am I not a man?

She caressed the throbbing bulge, the crevice between her thighs immediately hot and slick. Fish or man, she wanted him.

Like magic, the skin beneath her fingers bloomed open to reveal a dark, throbbing cock. Her fingers squeezed the velvety hot thickness of him, coaxing a glistening pearl from the tip. Without thinking, she leaned forward and took him into her mouth. He tasted of salt and musk and every bit as male as any man she'd known.

He groaned, hands settling on her shoulders. *What are you doing to me?* His thought was thick with lust.

Delighted with the ability to "speak" while pleasuring him, she circled her tongue around the head of his dick. *Making you mine.*

His hands on her shoulders tightened. *Do not mock me.*

The urgency of his emotions touched her through their link like never before. Exposed and raw. His desire shone bright and full but was shadowed with a mix of anger and resignation she didn't understand. She wrapped her hands around his hips and pulled him closer to her, tilting her chin to take him more deeply into her mouth.

He groaned, his fingers digging into her shoulders as she

sucked deeply. Against the back of her throat, she felt his release. After a shuddering moment, he disengaged and pulled her from the chair to squeeze her against his chest. *I will not let you leave me.*

The statement threw her off guard. Surprised her. She hadn't thought of escaping from Zantu, not since that awful episode with the mermaid. Despite the fact she was in the depths of the ocean. His promise to protect her made her feel safe. Nurtured.

He crushed his lips against hers. Her hands flattened against his ribs, her breasts tight against him, as he devoured her with deep, rolling thrusts of his tongue. If she'd been standing, she would've been weak at the knees. As it was, the water allowed them to twist and dance with each other without needing support.

His cock thrummed in a hard line against her belly, and she once again found his tail parting her legs. She slipped a hand between them, grabbed hold of him, and guided him inside her, yearning for the pressure of him, the fullness. The rippling muscles of his abs and the water slicking her skin ignited every nerve cell in her body with need.

Sliding a hand down her back to cup her ass, he pulled her firmly onto his rock-hard length and pressed himself into her core. He held there, deep and pulsing inside her while he ground against her clit. His tongue teased over her teeth and gums.

She wrapped her legs tightly around him, the edge of her climax rising above her like a wave about to engulf them both.

His teasing rhythm kept the wave hovering just out of reach. *You're mine.*

Please, please, she begged, unable to form a coherent thought.

Tell me you are. The hand on her ass squeezed, pressing him deeper into her folds with excruciating pleasure.

She threw back her head and bucked her hips against him, searching for release. *I'm yours. Please!*

Satisfaction dominated his thoughts, and he drew back only to pound immediately into her, again and again, until the wave broke and sent her spiraling into dizzying relief.

~

*B*rianna's head thrummed with what reminded her of morning birdsong: trills from her left, bass-throated hoots from high to the right, and an eerie rising and falling tenor undertone she realized was coming from Zantu.

He sat on the shell-strewn floor at the edge of the clearing, tail curled to one side, as he appeared to be tending the fine fronds of bright-green eelgrass growing there. Sunlight cut sharp angles in the kelp swaying above their heads, filtering gold light down into the clearing.

Still not believing everything that had happened yesterday, she sent a tentative thought. *What is that noise?*

The ocean's salute to the sun, my angelfish. Come, breakfast awaits you.

She sat up, realizing he'd moved her to the bed some time during the night. Tiny bubbles rose from the sponges and caressed her sides. She stretched and looked around.

Her gaze fell on the table, where two bone china plates had been set along with what looked like two solid-gold forks. A half-shell bowl waited in the center, brimming with seaweed and whatever else Zantu had deemed edible, much of it floating free of the bowl but enough remaining within to be considered a meal. Her stomach quivered, still nervous about what he might consider tasty. But by now she was hungry enough to eat almost anything.

She pushed herself from the bed, aiming for the table, and discovered if she relaxed, she could walk, albeit in slow motion. The stones and shells beneath her toes were surprisingly rough, but solid enough to give her purchase, and she made it to the chair without floundering too much. She sat and admired the place settings.

Are those real gold? She reached for a fork.

They were my father's. Zantu joined her, sliding himself into the chair next to her. *He found them in a sunken ship many years ago.*

You had a father? The thought was out before she could think about how stupid she sounded. She covered her mouth, even though the words hadn't come from her lips. What a rude question. She'd never thought of mermen having families.

Come to think of it, she'd never thought about mermen at all until yesterday.

Of course we have families. Well, fathers and siblings, at least.

Curiosity nibbled at her thoughts, and she fought to control it, but it was like only a sieve existed between their minds. *What about your mother?*

He used a smaller shell to scoop what looked like seaweed salad onto her plate, his thoughts obviously guarded. *Mermaids do not care for children.*

She frowned, unsure what to make of that bit of information. *So they have a baby and abandon it?*

He shrugged. *Fathers take care of the young.*

Are there a lot of other mermen? She looked around at the wall of kelp, as if the words might make one appear.

Zantu's hands paused briefly, then he pushed her plate in front of her, his silver eyes intensely regarding her. *Do not concern yourself with other merfolk.*

Brianna tilted her head, a small smile tugging the corner of her mouth. Was that jealousy she detected? *Afraid I'll run off with another merman? Or maybe a mer*maid—

Do not tease about such things.

The seriousness of his thought sobered her. Reminded her of her own vows of marriage, strengthened by her oath to her brokenhearted father to never follow in her mother's footsteps. She clenched her hands in her lap and stared at the seaweed salad. *I can't stay with you. I'm married.*

In your world, that means very little.

Her ire rose. *What do you know about our world? I take my vows very seriously.*

Even as she sent the thought, the hypocrisy of her words stopped her. The truth was, she'd abandoned her loyalty to Eric the moment she'd decided to jump. She'd chosen a coward's way out. And Eric was now as alone as her father had been. She might as well have divorced him.

Zantu placed a webbed hand over hers. *For a merman, a mate is for life.*

She looked at him out of the corner of her eye. *I thought you said mermaids didn't stick around.*

His jaw muscles twitched. *Even so, a merman will only ever take one mate.*

The way he thought *mate* held so much more meaning than could be put into words. Adoration. Certainty. Grief. And in spite of the contradictions, she knew exactly what it meant. The hopefulness of a word that could never truly be fulfilled. The inevitable loneliness of a life with the wrong person. Trapped in a marriage to a cold fish like Eric…

Her gaze shifted past Zantu's shoulder to the cradle resting in the middle of his nest. A baby cradle in a merman's lair. Had his mate left him with a child? Why else would he need a cradle? A twinge of jealousy invaded her as she pictured him with a gorgeous mermaid like the one they'd encountered yesterday. Then her gut squirmed. Why was she here? To raise a child in lieu of its missing mother?

A soothing series of notes permeated the water, stopping her thoughts. *Brianna, you are my mate.*

She met Zantu's gaze, blinking in confusion. *Me? What?*

You claimed me when you seduced me.

Seduced you? You're *the one who kissed* me.

The barbs of his dorsal fin darkened from blued silver to inky midnight. *I kissed you only to give you enough life to reach the surface. You're the one who... who... wrapped your legs around me and made me yours.*

Indignation drove her to her feet and sent her floating slowly upward. *Are you calling me a whore?*

He grabbed her wrist and pulled her back to the bottom beside him. His metallic-silver eyes bored into her with disconcerting intensity. *I don't know what a whore is, but from your tone, I believe it's a bad thing. So no, I will not call you a whore. But I don't want you to mistake my objective in saving you.*

Your objective? She tried to jab a finger toward him, her ire doubled by how slowly she was forced to move her hand. *You've made me a slave!*

We don't keep slaves. His grip on her wrist tightened, becoming almost painful. A series of deep clicks resonated through the water while his chest flexed widely like the hood of a cobra. *If anyone's a slave, it's me. I've avoided mermaid songs for thirty-five years, only to be captured by... by a human!*

She yanked her hand free of his grip. *If you feel that way*

42

about humans, why didn't you just let me die? Even as she said it, she regretted it.

He blew a violent string of bubbles and rose to hover above the table. *Maybe I should have. But now I am bound to protect you. I could no more let you die than I could kill our child.* With a flick from his tail, he was next to the coral-supported cradle. *A merman's driven to nest, mate or no mate. To prepare. To care for a baby in spite of overwhelming heartbreak. When you have our child, I'll be ready to care for it, whether you're here or not.*

His words hit her like a rock skipped over the water, only sinking in after the momentum had played out. He'd said "our child." Could a human and a merman…?

I don't know. He responded to her half-formed question. *Mermaids carry half-human children. Abandon them with one mate or another. I imagine our union will produce the same.*

He spoke as if a child were a foregone conclusion. Could it be? Her fingers strayed to her abdomen. She and Eric had tried so hard… Her hands hooked into claws. She knew that wasn't true. Over the last twenty-four hours, she and Zantu had coupled more times than she and Eric had in the last two months.

The real question was not if it was possible, but did she *want* it to be possible?

Her gaze returned to the man before her. His silver tail brushed the pebbled floor while his torso glinted in the filtered morning sunlight. He was her mate. A mate for life. A mate who wanted children, had sworn to protect her, and had created a love nest for her before he even knew who she was. Leaving him would be the biggest mistake of her life. She walked toward him, attempting to be graceful in spite of the water's resistance. *Do you want one or two?*

A jolt of elation reached her through their bond—a bond she now recognized as special. The kind mates should have. He drifted to meet her, his silver eyes alight with fire. *As many as you will give me.*

She threw her arms around him and kissed him.

6

ANTU CRADLED HIS mate in his arms after making love again, free-floating in the center of the clearing. She rolled over to snuggle her back against him, and he flexed his tail to maintain contact around her bottom and legs. *You've curled up like a little shrimp,* he teased.

Through the mental connection, she huffed indignantly. I'm not sure I'll ever get used to floating around all day. Can we go lie on the bed?

He pushed her hair aside to dot tiny kisses behind her ear. Mmmm, I just realized you have something to offer no mermaid does. He slid one hand along her spine and cupped her bottom, fingers following the crease to discover her still-slick opening. We can do it from behind.

Brianna stiffened, her skin trembling with tiny vibrations.

Fear, not excitement. He halted his caress. *Does that position offend you?*

Are you sure I shouldn't concern myself with other merpeople?

The worry he'd made a faux pas suggesting a new position was flushed away in a brine of adrenaline. Already she was thinking of other men. Yet her thoughts weren't full of lust... *Why do you ask?*

I think there's someone watching us.

Releasing his embrace, he whipped around in front of her, eyes scouring the kelp wall she'd been facing. Had Loia tracked them down after all? When his vision revealed nothing, he loosed a sonic query, reading the bounce-back for any irregularities. He knew this kelp forest like he knew his own fins.

A flash of turquoise silver caught the edge of his song. Familiar colors. Familiar shape. The tension in his shoulders and dorsal fin relaxed. He sang a playful coo, an invitation. "Ebby, come out."

From the floor between two crustacean-covered rocks, a tiny face appeared. "Hi, Uncle Zantu."

"What are you doing? Where's your father?" The sonic query should have revealed the larger shape of the merman or at least elicited an answering song. Perhaps his brother had spotted Brianna and fled.

The merchild remained partially hidden in the rocks, large

46

eyes even more gigantic as they rested on Brianna. "What's that?"

Of course the child would be frightened, and Brianna's thoughts weren't exactly calm at this moment, either. He pulled his mate from behind him by the hand, singing and thinking at the same time, "Ebby, this is Brianna, my mate. Brianna, meet my nibling, Ebby."

Ebby slithered out from between the rocks, mottled turquoise skin shifting to blend with the darker greens and purples of the mussels behind.

Oh my God. A baby. A real live mer... what are merchildren called?

That. Merchildren. Zantu smiled.

Snagging the bit of silk from the cradle and wrapping it about her hips, Brianna approached the child clumsily and settled to her knees against the stone-and-shell floor. *Is it a boy or a girl?*

Merchildren are sexless until puberty, Zantu sent, only half-listening to her. Ebby was far too young to be wandering the kelp alone. Where was Rubac? Had something attacked his brother's nest?

"Now you'll be broken like Dad?" A thumb crept into the child's mouth.

Zantu ignored the unintended barb. "Where's your dad?"

"With the new baby. I'm hungry."

What's it saying? Brianna's undercurrent of thoughts thrummed with eagerness to touch the child, but she held back. Which was good. Merchildren were wary of females. He didn't need Ebby fleeing into the kelp. He made the effort to think as well as sing his interactions with the child.

"New baby? So Didra's there?" Mermaids often arrived at a mate's nest pregnant, seeking a safe place to give birth before wandering off again in search of more lustful prey. And mermen, in spite of themselves, lived for those gestational interludes.

"No. She left." Ebby's song shifted to a higher key of worry. "Now Dad won't get up, and I'm hungry."

Dread filled Zantu's chest. Mermaids might not be the best mothers, but they stuck around to nurse their newborns for a few weeks, at least until their mates had lined up a local sea lion or otter mother to provide milk. If Didra had split early, Rubac would not only be fighting depression, but struggling to feed a new child. Entire merfamilies had met their end for this very reason.

"Brianna, Ebby's hungry," he both said and sent the thought. "Would you mind getting some food?"

While Ebby followed Brianna to the table, Zantu patrolled the edge of the clearing, sending a long-distance note to his brother to ask if he was okay. No answer echoed in return, so he called upon the nearest señorita fish to carry a message that Ebby was all right.

Ebby's high-pitched protest drew his attention to the table. "I said don't touch me!" The spines on the child's dorsal fin splayed like sharpened claws, and the mottled turquoise tail had darkened to gray.

Brianna held one hand out, thoughts full of curiosity, acting as if she hadn't heard. *Your tails can change color?*

The child's angry. Zantu propelled himself over and put a hand over Brianna's. He should have warned her to keep her distance. "Ebby, calm down. She didn't mean anything."

I didn't mean to cause trouble. Brianna clasped her hands in her lap.

"Is she deaf?" Ebby backed toward the kelp.

"No," Zantu made a point of both speaking and thinking the words. "She's a human and hasn't yet learned our language. Why don't you help me teach her? She won't touch you again, I promise."

Ebby paused.

"Let's start with your name." He looked at Brianna and pointed to the merchild, saying, "Ebby."

Brianna made a face and recoiled slightly. *You want me to sing?*

Like this. Taking her hand, he pressed it to his breastbone. The note vibrated from him once again.

Wrinkling her nose, Brianna opened her mouth and emitted a pathetic trickle of noise.

Ebby giggled.

I can't sing. Brianna crossed her arms and slumped in the chair.

Pull from here. His hand brushed Brianna's nipple as he sought a spot below her breastbone, and he had to forcefully redirect his thoughts to the task at hand. Her enjoyment of his touch filtering through their mental connection didn't help.

With an inner sigh, she sat up. This time her sound was a bit stronger but still pitiful and far off-key.

He joined Ebby in laughter while Brianna glowered. *You just asked a starfish to rub your belly.*

I told you, I can't sing.

You just need practice. Try to make it lower, he thought, again repeating Ebby's name.

Squaring her shoulders, she let out a long grunt that rose and fell.

"Oh!" Ebby dashed to the nearby rocks and disappeared.

Zantu swallowed back dismay. "You just tried to summon a school of barracuda."

Fear laced through the thought connection, and she clung to his arm, looking around. *I did?*

"There are none nearby, thankfully." How could this be so difficult? Ebby's name was an easy note. A baby name. He throttled his thoughts, hoping none of his frustration leaked through. "Ebby, come out. There's no danger."

"I want to go home."

"I know. I'll take you soon."

"I can go myself."

"I don't want you out there alone."

What's the child saying?

Ebby's small quick form was already darting away, keeping low to the rocks.

"Ebby!"

The child's trickle of sonic guidance clicks faded in the distance. The child should not be roaming the forest alone. And then there was Rubac's condition to consider. And a new baby. Zantu needed to be sure everyone was all right.

He turned to Brianna and caressed her cheek with his fingertips and leaned in to brush his lips against hers. *I need you to stay here. I must check on my brother.*

Can't I come? I'd love to meet him.

Mermen do not bring their mates to another's nest. It's forbidden.

Why?

I don't have time to explain. You must trust me.

Before she could argue more, he slithered between the kelp toward his brother's nest.

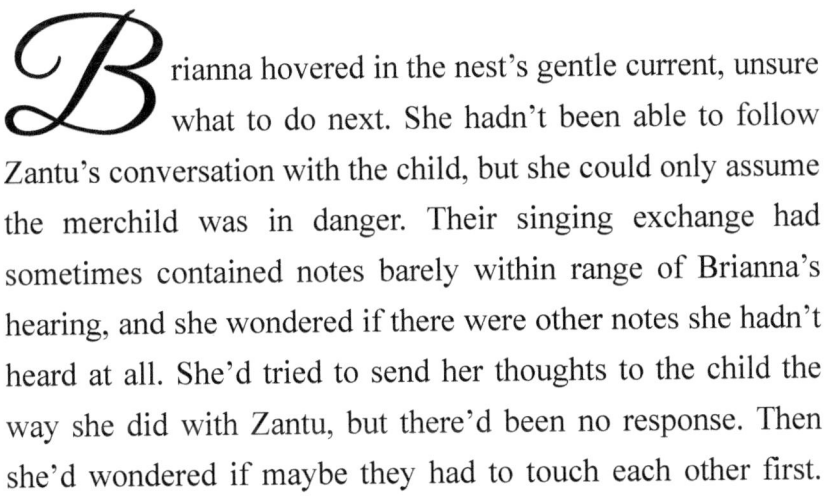

*B*rianna hovered in the nest's gentle current, unsure what to do next. She hadn't been able to follow Zantu's conversation with the child, but she could only assume the merchild was in danger. Their singing exchange had sometimes contained notes barely within range of Brianna's hearing, and she wondered if there were other notes she hadn't heard at all. She'd tried to send her thoughts to the child the way she did with Zantu, but there'd been no response. Then she'd wondered if maybe they had to touch each other first.

Bad idea, apparently. And now her tone-deaf singing had driven the child off for good. She prayed Zantu found Ebby before anything bad happened.

To kill time, she explored the clearing, admiring the way he'd integrated human items with ocean-based needs. The sea sponges for a mattress, the mother-of-pearl inlays on wood. When she bored of that, she tried to nap, but without Zantu to be her anchor, she felt exposed. Alone.

She was on the bottom of the ocean. Naked except for the scrap of silk she'd pulled from the cradle. At least she didn't need air. For how long? She wished she'd asked him.

From beyond the thick kelp wall, a constant humming and chirping reached her, as if she were in a forest full of birds and insects. She supposed the fish and crustaceans were the birds and insects of the ocean.

Curious, she put a hand through the fronds and pushed them aside, as if peering through curtains. A bright-orange fish met her gaze, seemingly as curious about her as she was of it. It wriggled there, looking at her expectantly. *I don't have any food for you, little guy.*

A mottled brown-and-white fish with a spiky dorsal darted up and nipped at the orange one.

Hey! Be nice!

The mottled fish darted side to side then hovered in front of her face, bulbous eyes moving independently of each other to look everywhere but at her.

The small orange fish returned, this time with a friend, and once again the brown fish shot out to attack it. The orange fish let out a pitiful cry, and Brianna found herself pushing through the kelp to come to its rescue. *Stop it!*

All the fish scattered.

Clear of the nest's confinement, she took the opportunity to survey the kelp forest. A rock wall covered with vibrant purple-and-pink mossy growth drew her attention. Unable to resist, she floundered forward to take a closer look. The wall teemed with fish and other creatures. A purple-speckled octopus bubbled out of a crack in the rock to slither down the wall and away as if indignant about her visit. A golden-shelled snail plodded a trail over an outcropping while small red shrimp darted across the surface around him. *You know how clumsy I feel in the water, I bet,* she thought at the snail.

Something stung her foot, and she jerked her knees up, realizing she'd stepped on an anemone. The sting burned like crazy. She grabbed her foot to look at the red welt striping her ankle. Twisting to keep from touching another anemone, she flapped her arms and legs and managed to gain some altitude. Without Zantu here, it seemed her body naturally wanted to be on solid ground rather than float. She'd have to pay better attention.

A small shark zigzagged by, startling her. She gulped, wondering if there were any larger ones lurking about. Putting her back to the wall, she decided she should return to the nest. Plus, her foot hurt like crazy.

She spun to retrace her steps and realized she wasn't

entirely sure how. Layer upon layer of kelp all looked alike. How far down the wall had she travelled? *Stupid Brianna. He told you to stay put.*

The mottled fish with the dorsal fin nudged her hand. She pulled away, regarding it. After the anemone, she was extra cautious. But it merely hovered there, eyes rolling every which way as if it were a sentinel tasked to guard her.

Maybe she could find the crack with the octopus again and go from there? She fluttered her legs in that direction, limbs growing tired from the effort of staying off the bottom. What she wouldn't give for a life vest right now.

She glanced at the canopy above. If she surfaced, would she be able to breathe air again? And if she did, would she lose her ability to breathe water? She could barely remember why she'd wanted to drown herself—was it only yesterday? Now she had a sea god for a lover. A mate. She could imagine eternity, safe in his arms. And why not? Eric already thought her dead. Going back would solve nothing. She'd been given a new chance at life. At love. And, perhaps, at motherhood.

She kicked her legs again, searching for a familiar landmark along the wall. What if he never came back?

She banished the thought. He had to come back. They were mates. Of one mind. The missing mental connection felt like a hole inside her. Out of curiosity, she mind-called, *Zantu?*

Only silence.

Overhead, the curious orange fish appeared again, as if

inviting her upward. Was it singing to her? Maybe she should swim up to the top of the wall and get a better vantage point.

She kicked her legs, propelling herself upwards with none of the grace Zantu could call upon. The mottled fish followed her, keeping close to her left ear, its song a funny little cicada buzz.

At the upper edge of the rock, the current grew stronger. She kicked harder, trying to keep close to the wall. The kelp forest up top was impossible to see through, but she thought she saw something move. Something large. Sharks returned to mind, and her heart accelerated to dizzying speed. She stopped kicking and allowed herself to sink again. She should just return to the seafloor and walk along it like before, sea anemones or not. Up here she felt out of control.

A broken leaf spun through the current and caught her across the cheek to flap over one eye. She clawed it away. When she could see again, the mottled fish was no longer in sight. Kelp fronds bumped her legs, grabbing her as she struggled against the current. The more she kicked, the more tangled she became.

Panic seized her. She thrashed against the restraining strands. While the kelp held her legs, the current continued to push against her torso, and she found herself lying on her back, staring at a wave-tossed slice of blue sky. Leaves covered her eyes, bound her right arm to her side, locked her legs in place.

What sounded like a laugh reached her, but she could no

longer see. Without thinking, she screamed, the sound rising from deep in her gut. She knew it was louder in her head than in the water, but what if she'd just called another school of barracuda? Or a shark?

She clamped her lips together and sent, *Help!* with all the force she could muster. *Zantu, help!* How was he going to find her, so far from where he'd left her?

Water stung her eyes and nose. The kelp felt like it was crushing the breath out of her. She struggled against her bonds, wondering if she'd die down here after all.

7

ANTU FOUND RUBAC lying on a mound of sea sponges, a newborn curled on his chest. The nest was a more traditional merman's nest, with none of the human detritus Zantu loved to collect, other than the toys he brought for Ebby. The merchild was already there, glowering from behind a dollhouse.

"Brother?" Zantu approached the prone merman through a seaweed garden eaten down to stubble.

Rubac opened his lime-green eyes. "You've come."

"Ebby showed up at my nest complaining about a new baby."

"Didra said she'd be back." His voice held a minor key that boded ill for any merman. "But I know she won't be."

Zantu wanted to find the golden-tailed mermaid and

strangle her with her own yellow hair. "Need help getting milk?"

Rubac waved a limp hand heavy with rings and what he called his prayer bracelet through the water. "There's no point."

Zantu took a closer look at the baby. The tiny nub of a tail lay limp across his brother's chest. A shock of ebony hair floated loosely in the current. But skin that should be mottled with newborn color remained pasty. Had Didra left because the baby was dead, or was it the other way around? His chest ached at the loss. "Rubac, I'm sorry."

"Will you take Ebby for me?"

Zantu's throat tightened. Mermen were very good at deluding themselves that their mates would be back any moment. Good at focusing on the children she brought them, in spite of a broken heart. Until his heart had enough. And once a broken heart fell apart, there'd be no return. Zantu couldn't allow his brother to just give up. "Remember when Dad left you in charge while he went to find medicine for that cut on his tail? How it felt to think he might not come back, and how we'd gone searching for him? Don't you think Ebby would do the same?"

"I knew he'd come back. I just wanted to go exploring." Rubac's mouth twitched upward, as if he wanted to smile but couldn't.

Sweeping the floor with his tail, Zantu kicked a flurry of

small shells and debris at the merman. "I'm serious. Think about how we felt. You want Ebby to feel like that?"

Rubac's reply held a key of despair. "I need you to help so I can try to elevate the baby's soul."

If Zantu's throat had been tight before, now his entire chest felt as if it were about to cave in. His brother's love of mer-myth and magic could sometimes be entertaining, but in this case, it would likely prove deadly. The myth of elevation said a great blue whale could free a mer-soul from the cycle of the sea. But blue whales only lived out in the wild deeps, far from the safety of the kelp forest. Zantu and his brother had braved it several times before Ebby was born, Zantu seeking salvage while Rubac spoke to the smaller whales and other creatures. Back then they'd had nothing to lose but themselves.

"Now's not the time to go chasing myths." He reached for the limp form on Rubac's chest. "Why don't I take care of the baby? You stay with Ebby."

Rubac's arm closed tighter about his dead child. "I have to try."

"A living child needs you. You can't take risks like we used to."

"That's why I need Ebby to stay with you."

"Ebby needs *you*, brother."

"You love Ebby, and you don't have a mate yet, so—"

"Uncle Zantu has a mate now," Ebby sang from behind the dollhouse.

The heart-wrenching drama with Rubac had almost made Zantu forget about Brianna. He hoped she wasn't too frightened. Although he'd verified no predators were near, every muscle in his body suddenly burned with the need to get back to her. Yet his brother needed him as well and just as badly. He was torn between two worlds.

Rubac rose from the mound of sponges and stared at Zantu. "You've been caught? When?"

"It's a long story, and I don't have time to tell it now. But I can't take Ebby. I need to know you won't abandon your child to pursue a myth."

"She's a human," Ebby threw out, holding up a long-legged, naked doll. "No tail."

Rubac blinked, frowned at the doll. He turned again to Zantu, his lime-green eyes now shrewd with curiosity. "Human?"

"I told you, it's a long story." Zantu pulled away, relieved by his brother's apparent return of clarity. "She's waiting for me at my nest."

"Waiting? Oh, you *have* been deluded." Rubac put a hand on Zantu's shoulder. "I'm so sorry. I thought you might be one of the lucky ones and escape the bond."

"Human women are different."

"You're serious." Rubac settled back onto the sponges. "You've bonded to a human."

"Indeed."

"I want to hear all about this."

His brother's innate curiosity gave Zantu a bargaining chip. "Promise you won't abandon Ebby and head off to the deeps, and I promise to come back in a day or two and tell you."

Rubac seemed to think for a moment then nodded his head. "I won't abandon Ebby."

Zantu blew out a string of relieved bubbles. Once he was more secure about leaving Brianna in the nest, he could come back to fulfill his promise. "Thank you. I need to get back to Brianna. She's never been alone." He pushed aside the screen of kelp to exit the clearing. "Remember your promise. I'll see you in a few days."

"You too, brother. Good luck."

Zantu slipped through the stalks, relieved by his brother's return to his senses. At least he hoped Rubac was okay and wouldn't abandon Ebby for a myth. But Zantu had other responsibilities than his brother right now.

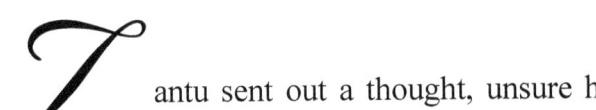

*Z*antu sent out a thought, unsure how far the link might travel. He'd lost contact not far from the nest.

Nothing.

The brown-spotted sculpin he'd left to watch her was

supposed to come find him if there was trouble. Not the best guard fish but more reliable than the capricious orange garibaldi fish who often served mermaids just for fun.

He jetted through the kelp, pulsing his sonic query ahead to clear the way. The kelp thinned as he exited Rubac's territory and reached the ledge down to his own. He jackknifed over a lip of rock, shooting straight for his nest.

Shoving through the thick wall of kelp into the clearing, he smiled in anticipation. He'd never had a mate to come home to before. Inside the nest, he looked around, and his smile faded. *Brianna?* She was nowhere in sight. He added a sonic query.

Gone.

Of course she'd left him. That was what women did. He'd hoped a human would be different, but obviously not. Why would he believe she was any different from any other female? Yet a dark cloud of doubt enshrouded his soul. His nest was far from land. How could she expect to strike out on her own and reach safety? There were predators, riptides, mermaids, and other dangers. Without fins or tail she'd be at the mercy of the current. He had to make sure she was safe, even if she had left him.

He slid out of the nest and searched for the sculpin guard. Missing, of course. Creating a song for the simple creatures in the area, he asked the whereabouts of the human. As one, the creatures pointed toward the rock wall nearby. An orange garibaldi giggled and darted away, trailing a few friends.

A flutter of panic leaked through Zantu's mind. He darted

after the garibaldi through the rocks and between kelp, calling ahead with both mind and sonar.

Even with the current, she shouldn't have drifted far. Where was she?

A brown-speckled sculpin poked its head from behind a sea fan on the floor, its mind relaying the feel of rising toward the surface and the pull of the stronger current. Sculpins were bottom dwellers, and the creature's own instincts had overridden the directive to watch Brianna.

Zantu should have known better than to trust a sculpin to report trouble. Cowards, every one.

Another panic wave rippled through Zantu. Was the feeling his own or something he was receiving from Brianna? Speeding toward the surface, he called with both voice and mind. *Brianna!*

The panic in his chest grew stronger, and now he recognized it wasn't all his. A word whispered through his mind. *Help!*

Brianna! Where are you?

As he entered a thick section of kelp, the words grew stronger. *I can't breathe. God, hurry!*

He spun in place, searching the surrounding forest. He could detect nothing awry. The mind connection gave him no sense of direction. *Can you sing to me? Call me!*

No! There's something nearby. I'm afraid. The kelp— her thoughts were muddy, but the panic remained sharp and clear.

Summoning a song deep in his core, Zantu formed a command to every creature within range. "Protect my mate!"

The water churned with activity as nearby creatures passed the message along: low foghorn calls from a nearby black jewfish, buzzing from a school of perches, and low against the ocean floor, the ba-ba-ba of a few sea bats. And then a high bark from a sea lion, a warning about invasion of territory. Zantu homed in on the call, racing between the stalks until he spotted the whiskered face of the local sea lion male. He'd interacted with the creature before, and it tolerated Zantu in what it considered its domain.

"What is it?"

The sea lion bared its teeth with unusual aggression and responded with the note sea lions used to warn competitors away.

Zantu tilted his head to look out of the corner of his eye submissively. "You know me, brother. I'm not here to hurt you or your family. I'm looking for a human."

The beast circled him, the whites of its eyes showing starkly against sleek brown fur. It grunted a story about a mermaid playing games, using the kelp to trap and drown his harem's babies.

Stomach churning, Zantu ground his teeth. A mermaid would find Brianna even more fun to toy with than baby sea lions. "Take me there."

The big animal somersaulted once and shot through the kelp to an area shorn from its holdfasts to create a floating mat of greenery. Thick stems tangled in the canopy, yanking more stalks loose as the current continued its relentless path. In the distance, the shouts of the sea lion's harem met the taunting giggles of a retreating mermaid. The big male bellowed and sped in that direction.

Zantu coiled himself to follow then spotted glints of skin amidst the tangle of kelp. A naked foot peeked from within the mat. Realigning his trajectory, he tore through the mass toward his mate.

I'm here, he thought as he yanked the stalks and debris free. Pushing aside mats of flat leaves, he searched for her face.

Her thoughts had drifted into a hazy calm. Almost nonexistent. He tore a leaf aside and found her eyes staring at him. Through him. *No!* Immediately, he placed his lips over hers and released a stream of bubbles into her mouth. *Brianna, breathe!*

Her body bucked, the kelp still binding her limbs. She couldn't die. Again he kissed her lips, trying to recall exactly how he'd done it when they'd first met. It was one thing for her to leave him, return to the surface. Go back to her life there. Knowing she lived, he, too, could live on. But if she died in his arms, he'd have nothing to live for. *Please, Brianna. I love you.*

Free me, she thought.

The ache in his gut twisted sharply. Wrenched him to the core. Reminded him she'd left the nest, swum to the surface to seek escape. Even now, she sought to be free of him. He wished he could mimic that desire. The bond he'd thought to find a way to break had only strengthened as time passed. He was as trapped by the bond as she was by the entangling kelp.

Clawing at a handful of stalks, he tore them loose. Another handful. Unleashing himself on the inanimate plant matter, he shredded away thick stems and fronds and let them drift away on the current. "You shouldn't have left me," he growled, his thoughts a boiling stew of emotion she probably couldn't decipher. He wasn't even entirely sure what he felt except that it hurt beyond anything he'd ever thought possible. He wanted to hurt her and hold her at the same time.

The moment he jerked the last bond free, she wrapped her arms around him and buried her face against his shoulder. *Oh, God, thank you.*

His frenzied emotions dissolved like salt in water. Embracing her, he savored the feel of her warmth against him, the sunshine scent of her skin that had so captivated him. How could she hold such control over him? It didn't matter. He was hers, now and forever. And she was alive.

Don't leave me again. She gripped him tighter.

She was toying with him, of course. Using him when she needed him only to throw him away the next chance she got. His chest ached, as if the mate-bond might squeeze the life out of him. He tried to read her thoughts, but his own were too stormy to see past. *I thought you wanted to be set free?*

I wanted free of the kelp. *Did you think I meant free of you?*

Why else would you have tried to reach the surface?

She pushed away from his chest to look into his face. *I didn't. You were gone so long, and I got bored. There were these fish fighting, and I thought I'd break it up. I know it was stupid. I should have stayed put. The current sucked me away. I couldn't find the nest again. Then I hit the kelp and, and—* Her thoughts catapulted over one another, saturated with raw terror. *I thought I was going to die.*

A wave of relief rolled over him. And guilt. The connection of their thoughts couldn't lie. *I promise never to leave you alone again.*

He curled his tail up to caress the sensual curve of her bottom with his fin. Her legs still fascinated him, and the way she could embrace him with both her arms and legs during lovemaking drove him mad with lust. She sighed within her mind at his caress and spread her thighs. Her mind radiated trust. Commitment. Love?

His cock bulged and thrummed against its sheath, demanding release, demanding the satiation of her heated core, but he held back. He wanted to savor every moment he could. To make her want him as badly as he wanted her. He roamed his hands along the curve of her hips, thumbs grazing the slight hollows of her hip bones until they found the downy mound of fur between her legs. So soft, so hot, the mound pulsed as he cupped his fingers over it, slipping between those sensual legs.

She traced her hands over his arms, up his biceps, around his neck. He dipped his head to kiss her, fingers massaging her labia even as his mouth plied her lips open to receive his tongue. Her fingers reached the top edge of his dorsal fin and traced both sides of it down his spine to his hips. His cock sprang free. Still he ignored it, enthralled by the erotic gyrations of her hips against his hand.

Leaving her lips, he found a breast, taking her nipple between his teeth to nibble gently. Her fingers clawed into him, her mind spiraling with both pleasure and pain. He'd need to be cautious using his pointed teeth against her tender skin. Still massaging her slick nub, he moved to the other breast and drew the nipple to a barnacle-hard peak before tracing kisses along her belly.

She bucked and strained against him. He wrapped his other hand around to cup her ass and dipped his head between her legs to replace his fingers with his tongue. She tasted as good as she smelled, and bucked harder against him, her thoughts yearning for penetration.

As you wish, he sent, and plunged a finger into her. Her interior ridges quivered around his finger. He slipped a second inside and discovered that crooking his fingers while plunging her depths sent her into a cascade of pleasure. The shared mental connection to her shuddering climax nearly had him spilling his seed into the surrounding water.

Keeping hold of her sides, he slid up her length to find her mouth with his again. His cock entered her core as easily as an eel returning to its den, smooth and graceful and a perfect fit. She sighed in mental satisfaction and lifted her face to kiss him.

I love you forever, he thought as he sent his seed deep within her.

8

*L*IKE A BABY otter, Brianna lay atop Zantu's chest, while yards below them the kelp canopy undulated in deceivingly benign patterns. She reached up and broke the water's surface with one hand, the droplets on her fingertips refracting the setting sun into tiny rainbows. Drawing her hand back into the ocean's embrace, she ran her fingertips along the rippled muscles of Zantu's abdomen. The thought of going back down through the kelp to his nest terrified her. Being apart from Zantu terrified her. Everything about this ocean terrified her. More than terrified her. As both adrenaline scare and coital passion subsided, she realized she was angry as hell. *How could you leave me alone like that?*

Zantu hugged her closer, his tail rhythmically sweeping the water. *I'm sorry—*

She shoved at him, flailed as he released her, then clung to him and pounded his rock-hard chest instead. *What if you hadn't made it back in time? Did you realize I'd stop breathing?*

I left a sculpin to watch over you—

A fish? You left me in the care of a fish?

A mistake, I admit. He grabbed hold of the fist she'd been pounding against his chest. *I don't know why you had trouble breathing. The breath bond is supposed to last until the new moon. Perhaps that mermaid broke it.*

A new fear took root in the pit of her stomach. *Breath bond? Is that a spell? What if it gets broken again?*

I won't leave you again. His face was hard with resolve. *Not until I know how to keep you safe.*

His evasive answer shifted her fright into suspicion. *That's not what I asked.*

As long as I'm near, I can renew the bond.

She stared upward at the darkening sky. *You can't possibly guarantee you'll be at my side every moment of every day.*

His mind was a maelstrom of ideas until he settled on a tentative thought. *My brother might know of deeper magic.*

Her fist tightened beneath his palm until her nails dug into her flesh. *I'm not letting you leave me alone again.*

No. I won't do that.

What then? she asked, hoping mermen had some way to communicate over long distances yet knowing they didn't. If they had, he could have simply called his brother the first time.

You'll come with me. In spite of the wall he'd tried to erect between their mind-connection, horrific images flashed across her vision. A frenzy of mermen tearing one of their own limb from limb. Blood filling the water. Horrific silence as they departed, leaving the dead to feed the fish.

She gasped, salt water catching in her throat. *Who are those mermen?*

Zantu's chest rose and fell in a sigh. *Remember I told you taking a mate to another's nest is forbidden? The punishment for breaking the pact is death.*

Her heart was beating so fast she thought it might explode. *But... even your brother?*

My brother's not like other mermen. He'll hear me out. The words he sent were steady, yet she could detect a falseness to his confidence.

Why such harsh punishment? she asked.

Most mermen are solitary creatures, avoiding both maids and men alike. His arms tightened around her. *Unfortunately, weaker mermen have been known to indulge a mate's desire and reveal the locations of fellow mermen's nests. Any merman not mate-bonded would likely be forced to mate, no better than a slave. Any who rejects her faces her wrath, not only toward himself but also his children. Entire families have been destroyed by a single mermaid. A nest is supposed to be a sanctuary. A safe place, hidden among the kelp away from predators and mermaids. Revealing a nest's location is one of the gravest sins. Carrying out punishment is one of the few times mermen will gather together.*

She swallowed, unable to erase the violent images from her mind. *I don't want you to get hurt.*

Rubac and I share a special bond, closer than other brothers. We spent many years together exploring the wild deeps for treasure and knowledge. When Didra caught him I thought our relationship would end, but he's strong. He trusts me to visit his nest. To care for his child.

What if you left me at the surface? She squeezed him tighter, pressing her face against his chest. *I could tread water there and breathe until you got back.*

His already-dark thoughts became stormy. *The surface is not safe. Predators can see you from below, waves can bury you from above.* And other humans could find you and take you away.

He didn't say the last part, but it carried across his thoughts unbidden. She stroked her fingers along his dorsal lovingly. *I do not want to leave you, my love.*

A shiver passed over his skin, and guilt soured the mind-connection. *I'm trying to trust you. But all I've ever learned of women tells me otherwise.*

From what little she'd learned—and seen—of mermaids, she knew he was fighting an uphill battle. She wanted him to trust her. Believed he would in time. And she had to admit, the idea of fending off sharks or trying to keep her head above crashing waves sounded as unlikely as surviving a journey to Rubac's nest. *If the surface is out, there must be another option. Where'd Rubac learn about the magic? Can we go there?*

Bubbles streamed from his nose. *The wild deeps would be more dangerous than taking you to Rubac's nest. I think Rubac will understand the special circumstances. Especially since you've already met Ebby.*

Her thoughts returned to the merchild and the reason Zantu had left the first time. *Is Ebby okay?*

Ebby's safe for now. My brother's the one who concerns me. Zantu's thoughts blurred and wavered with uncertainty.

Why?

His new baby is dead. Most likely stillborn. He's...

Stillborn? The mind-connection with Zantu popped and seemed to fizzle, as if shorted out. An unexpected tsunami of memory slammed into her. The first sound of her baby's heartbeat. The smell of new paint in the nursery. The sensation of that first fluttering kick from deep inside her. And then the day she'd realized the kicking had stopped. The pain of fruitless labor and delivery. Blessed unconsciousness from blood loss.

And finally, Eric standing in the hospital doorway telling her he'd already "taken care of things." She'd been unconscious five days, and the ashes had already been scattered.

The sting of water in her nose and throat yanked her back to the present. Water squeezed from every side, forcing the breath from her body. She realized she was gasping, and there was no air to be found.

Zantu's hands grasped her face, and she felt his mouth against hers. Her lungs eased immediately. His kiss was tender, gentle. Infused with love rather than lust. An anchor in her storm. He tilted his head and traced kisses along her jaw, his hands stroking her back as if gentling a horse. *I believe I understand now why you came to me,* his mind whispered to hers.

She might not have a physical voice, but her thought was choked with pain. *He took her from me. I never got to say goodbye.*

I'm so sorry. He gathered her in his arms.

Maybe it was because of the mind-connection, but the genuine shared grief flowing from Zantu's thoughts was stronger than all the combined words of comfort she'd received from family and friends. Definitely more than she'd received from Eric, who couldn't understand why she wasn't grateful to escape the chore of a funeral. She broke down and sobbed against her mate, truly cried as she never could with Eric. Zantu held her tight, saying nothing, because he didn't have to. It was enough that he was with her. Enough that he wanted with all his heart to make things better.

She cried from the pit of her soul, and the ocean accepted her tears as its own.

*A*fter comforting Brianna's grief, Zantu carried her through the night-dark kelp. Her thoughts were sorrowful but solid. Something inside her had changed, as if brackish water had been washed away by an incoming tide. She'd been through a lot—even before he'd met her. How lucky he was to have a mate who not only wanted to stay with him, but also wanted children. Children they would raise together. The anxiety he felt about approaching his brother's nest was caught up with a desire to share news of his lucky pairing. Who would have guessed a human would make such a perfect mate?

He pumped his tail and carried them toward Rubac's nest. Hopefully night would mask Brianna's proximity while he talked to his brother. Some silly part of him hoped he could get away without Rubac ever being the wiser about having his nest revealed. Another part hoped his brother noticed and wanted to meet his mate. He'd always wondered how a merman could be so weak as to take a mate to see other mermen, but now a part of him understood the draw of wanting to introduce your bond-mate to your brothers.

Brianna clung to his shoulders, thoughts numb with exhaustion. Adrenaline kept him moving. He sent sonic queries ahead to guide his path. A merman was never blind as long as there were landmarks for echolocation. One danger of the wild deeps was the vast expanse of water with nothing physical to orient himself with except the current. He prayed his brother had the answers they needed, because a trip to the wild deeps would be unthinkable with Brianna in tow.

He reached the thick wall of kelp surrounding Rubac's nest and unhooked Brianna's arms from his neck. Guiding her hands to a barnacle-rough stone, he thought, *Stay exactly here. I'll be just on the other side of this kelp. If I need to bring you into the nest, do not make eye contact. Do not interact. Most importantly, do not make physical contact of any sort. You saw what happened with Ebby. Pretend you're invisible, okay?*

She nodded into the darkness, which he felt as a slight ripple of water.

He stroked her cheek with his knuckles and then brushed her lips with his. She was too beautiful to ever be invisible, but his brother was already mated and should be immune to most female charms. Thinking of her charms ignited a fire low in his belly, and he had to rein back his desire. Now was not the time nor place.

Turning from her, he pushed aside the thickly woven kelp. Normally he'd have announced himself before entering, but he wanted to forestall Rubac's sonic query. Once Zantu was inside, Rubac's shorter query would hopefully miss Brianna's presence outside.

Moving past the kelp, he approached the mound of sponges Rubac normally rested on. He knew the layout from previous visits and moved with confidence to within an arm's length of the bed. "Rubac, it's Zantu."

No answer. Not even the shush of water against fin as Rubac or Ebby stirred.

"Rubac? Ebby?"

Still the clearing remained silent. He chirped another query and read the bounce-back. Nobody was home. He sent a louder query, verifying the other objects in the nest. Ebby's toys were right where the child always left them, and the mound of sea sponges was undisturbed. Nothing seemed out of place.

Zantu's heartbeat sped up until it pounded in his ears. Something wasn't right. He returned to where he'd left Brianna, relieved to find she was where he'd left her. *There's nobody home.*

Where do you think he went?

He rubbed a hand through his hair. All he could assume was that Rubac had taken the baby's body to inter it in the reef at the edge of the wild deeps. Why his brother had decided to do it at the edge of nightfall was a mystery. *Probably the baby's funeral.*

Oh. Her thoughts grew dark, her own loss a sharp background full of scars. *Shouldn't you be there, too?*

Her concern for his brother in spite of her own mental state touched him. *Funerals are rare, and very private when they happen. Most merfolk die in seclusion, and the dead are undiscovered until their bones have already scattered to the sea. When a loved one does find a body, it's taken to the edge of the reef and tucked into a crevice.*

The idea of Rubac at the edge of the reef, where the kelp dropped off and the wild deeps began, made Zantu nervous. Especially at night, when large predators rose to hunt. Ebby wouldn't be able to keep up the same pace Rubac did. The child would have to rest. Yet sleeping would be impossible with the current continually flowing out to the deeps.

He sent a long-range query through the kelp. A flutter of night-feeding damselfish but nothing else. The forest felt too quiet. He didn't like being outside the protection of a nest. *We'll wait inside. I imagine he'll be back in the morning.*

Won't he be angry to find us here?

Probably. But I'm not taking chances sleeping outside with you. He elbowed aside the kelp curtain and pulled her through. The current inside the nest was much weaker, and he relaxed his grip around her waist. *Do you want to rest on the bed, or would you prefer to float?*

Her fingers tightened around his forearm. *I can't see a thing.*

Exhaustion from the day's activities all seemed to drop on him at once, weighing him down like a bottle swamped with seawater. He could have called on the plankton to light the place, but it seemed easier to simply make the decision. *I think we'll rest on the bed tonight.*

He carried her to the tuft of sea sponges and relaxed, allowing their combined weight to settle them into the cushioning surface. Brianna turned to spoon herself into his embrace, her sleepy thoughts full of contentment, lulling him to sleep.

He murmured a lullaby into her hair, "You are my sunken treasure."

She sighed and snuggled closer. The gentle trickle of water over his skin soothed his sore muscles, and he fell into a deep sleep.

$\mathcal{B}$RIANNA BLINKED AWAKE in the darkness but this time with no confusion or fear. A predawn chorus of fish played a soothing background melody, and she snuggled closer into Zantu's warm embrace. She was delighted to feel his morning erection pressing against her bottom. His mind was blank with sleep, his body hers to explore, so she reached a slow hand around behind her and sought the throbbing shaft that'd woken her.

Sequestered in its sheath, his cock responded to a little coaxing from her hand. He flexed his hips toward her but didn't waken. Keeping her mind purposefully blank so as not to wake him, she wrapped her fingers around his heated shaft and pressed her thumb over the small slit at its head. Her pussy tightened with desire as she imagined his cock inside her. Seeking lower, she found his testicles hiding within the sheath. She massaged the tender sack, rolling the orbs between her fingers.

Zantu pressed his hips harder against her and crushed her in the circle of his arms, not enough to hurt but enough to immobilize her. A low growl rose from his throat against her ear. *Good morning, my little angelfish. Or should I say devilfish?*

The vibration sent shivers deep inside her, creating an ache that needed to be filled.

His hand sought hers still wrapped around his cock, encouraged her to squeeze and press his shaft downward. The tip grazed her ass, and she rubbed herself over it. *Depths, woman. We're on my brother's bed.*

So?

He slid her higher along his body until her opening was poised directly over his cock, the head teasing her lower lips. Both his hands found her breasts, fingertips pinching her nipples until they stiffened.

She arched her back, thrusting her hips against him to take him in, but he resisted, keeping the tantalizing head just at the opening. He sent, *I want to kiss your lips.*

She started to turn, but he held her facing away.

Not those lips. He lifted her farther up along his chest, skin sliding against skin, strong hands guiding her by her hips. His chin grazed her spine, making her back tingle. When he reached the top of her buttocks, she felt his tongue caress the upper edge of her crack. Both his hands encircled her ass cheeks, spreading her wide. One thumb crept inward to circle her anus. She puckered, yearning for more no matter his intent.

Thumb massaging with gentle pressure, he slid his face lower. She gasped as he thrust his mouth between her legs. His tongue slipped along her quivering folds, ending at the throbbing nub of her clit. The pressure of his mouth sent shudders of pleasure deep into her belly.

At some point they'd floated above the bed and now free-floated in the water. She flailed, seeking something to grip, something to ground her as he worked the sensitive button of flesh with his tongue and teeth.

Hold onto your breasts, he commanded. *Pinch them for me.*

She clutched her own flesh, pinching until the electric jolts of sensation from his mouth met the matching ones from her nipples.

His mouth covered her pussy, tongue circling every crevice before plunging deeply into her. She arched, aching for more. *I need you,* she thought.

And then he began to sing.

The deep vibrations worked into her bones, filled her as surely as if he were fucking her. The sensation grew to enormous proportions, demanding release, and yet she yearned for the moment to last forever. Every muscle tightened, unable to escape his song. The thrumming, pulsing cadence worked her very core until the crescendo rolled over her in a great spasming release.

With a single purposeful move, Zantu pulled her down, and his cock settled deep into her folds.

She moaned, rising through another crescendo toward climax. His hands on her hips held her tightly against him, his body rocking hard. She widened her thighs and wrapped her calves around behind him, straining to take him deeper. She wanted his cock to touch her soul. To make him come so deep he melded with her forever.

A gasp left him as he clutched her tightly, driving his seed deep inside her.

～

*Z*antu startled awake to early pink sunlight reflecting through the kelp foliage above the nest. He'd fallen asleep almost immediately after making love, arms cradling his mate like a precious pearl. Wondering what had woken him, he gently released her and slid from the sponge bed. Rubac would have taken refuge during the night, but with morning light, he could return at any moment. Zantu hoped his brother never found out they'd made love in his nest, but even if he did, that moment with Brianna had been worth it.

The usual fish song trickled through the water, nothing apparently amiss. He didn't want to send a sonic query to Rubac and risk waking Brianna, so he decided to gather breakfast instead. The overharvested seaweed gardens would offer little for a meal, but Zantu didn't want his angelfish to start the day hungry.

Rubac didn't utilize human artifacts much, and Zantu had to search among Ebby's toys to find a beautiful cobalt-rimmed bowl. Taking the bowl to the outer edges of the garden, he searched for edible leaves and pods, leaving the newest seedlings in place for future meals. The garden was in even worse shape than he'd originally thought. How long had Rubac lain here grieving, leaving poor Ebby to fend for food alone?

He decided to take a quick patrol of the outer nest, both for food and to scout out anything of concern. Perhaps he'd find a clue about where Rubac and Ebby had gone. Much as he told himself things were probably fine, his brother's state of mind hadn't been exactly stable when Zantu had left him.

Outside the nest, sunlight danced and glittered across the forest floor as the current tossed the canopy above. A nearby garibaldi let loose a string of notes that sounded like rain against the water's surface. Farther out, a moray eel clacked its teeth before retreating into its den. Zantu found a small patch of red dulse and bent to pick the fronds.

Something brushed against his dorsal fin. He turned to find a small yellow señorita fish looking at him, its tiny mouth pursed as if it had something to say. "What is it, little one?"

"Sorry, brother," the little fish recited—señorita fish were excellent at parroting back a song. "Elevation called. Sorry, brother. Elevation called."

Zantu stared at it in shock. His brother had gone to the wild deeps anyway? What about Ebby? Depths. He must've taken the merchild along. The fish had been left as a messenger to Zantu in case Rubac didn't return. The fish darted into the kelp, job apparently done.

Dropping the bowl, Zantu raced back to Rubac's nest. Brianna rolled over at his arrival, stretching in a languid arch he didn't have time to appreciate. *I have to go after my brother. He took Ebby to the deeps.*

Why? She sat up to look at him.

There is a myth, a type of funeral called an elevation which can free a soul from the cycle of the sea. It can only be done in the wild deeps with the aid of an ancient blue whale. He went to her, taking her in his arms. He realized he'd never told her about the deeps, only sought to protect her from them. *The deeps are past the kelp forest, where the sharks and squid and other predators live. There are no landmarks to guide by, only the strength of the current, which can challenge even a merman's stamina. I can't take you there. And I can't leave you here.*

She grabbed his arms and pushed away from him. *What the hell are you suggesting?*

It dawned on him that he was suggesting releasing her. Setting her free.

Oh, no you're not. We're mates, remember? Whatever we

do, we do together. Besides, land's in the opposite direction, and you don't have time to dawdle. I'm coming with you. Just give me a knife or something to help fend off the predators.

The determination in her thoughts about drowned him. He'd been trying to believe she wanted to be with him, but some part of him had been waiting to prove she was lying. That, like any mermaid, she'd leave him without looking back. But at this moment she was digging through Ebby's toys, looking for a weapon. Planning to accompany him on a journey that could kill them both.

Any reservations he may have had about her washed away.

Yet that knowledge didn't eliminate the problem at hand.

He searched through Rubac's small statues, jewelry, and other mythic artifacts but couldn't find anything that might serve as a weapon. Looking up, he saw Brianna brandishing a long pole with a net on it wider than his shoulders. *I can use this to push things away or tangle them up.*

In spite of the fear gripping his insides, he smiled. *My ferocious little angelfish.*

10

ANTU CLUTCHED BRIANNA tightly against his chest and exited the kelp forest. They'd been swimming for hours, heading toward the great chasm where predators hunted other predators, often merely for sport. The sudden lack of foliage, coupled with the immediate drop into nothingness, always made his stomach flip. His most recent trip to the deeps had been when he'd followed a trail of cargo containers washed overboard during the last autumn storm. Then, he'd run into a raven-haired seductress prowling the area and nearly lost his freedom. Now he'd be risking something much more precious.

He sent out a sonic query to test the dark waters. The song would not only provide him bounce-back information on what was ahead, but it would also frighten away any mindless hunting squid. Sharks and whales were another matter—much trickier to coerce—but he'd deal with them if the need arose.

How are we going to find them? Brianna asked.

He pointed to a dusky cloud of krill interrupting the milky light reaching from the surface. *See the krill? We look for that. Whales follow krill, and Rubac's looking for whales.*

He emitted a short burst of song, searching for the gigantic animals. Nothing.

I can't see anything. The tremor in her thought reflected his own nervous fear.

There's nothing to see. Whales haven't found this swarm yet. We'll keep looking.

He pressed onward, farther and farther from the safety of the kelp forest into ever deeper water. The true wild deeps didn't begin for another quarter league, where the colder waters from the north joined and pushed underneath the current coming off the kelp reef. He'd been down that current ages ago, when he and Rubac had first ventured out of their father's nest. They'd found their first sunken ship there, and Rubac had been introduced to the intelligent whales who carried the sea's myths.

"Sink you, Rubac," he muttered within his song. Would Ebby even be able to survive those cold depths? Would Brianna?

A drumbeat reached him from far ahead. Then a low moan dropped its pitch through the water.

Brianna's fingers dug into his shoulder. *What's that?*

He gave her a short squeeze of reassurance, his own pulse loud in his ears. *Blue whales.*

A warning thump beat the water as the whale sensed their presence. "Go play your games in another pool," the whale's ponderous voice cautioned. "You've caused enough trouble for one night."

Zantu slowed. "I'm not here for games. I'm seeking my brother and his child. Have you seen them?"

A dark form moved between them and the surface. Zantu kicked his tail to resist being thrust downward in its wake.

"Ah, merman," the whale grated, its barnacled body stretching forever into the darkness. "I thought you were a maid. Your females have delighted in inciting a frenzy among the nearby sharks."

Zantu resisted the urge to send a sonic query into their surroundings. Sharks were bad enough, but now he'd have to watch for mermaids as well. "Have you seen another male? He would have asked you to assist with an elevation."

The drumbeat sound approached again, and a great mouth, open as if to swallow them whole, appeared. "An elevation? How odd." The mouth brushed by, revealing the black orb of an eye, a dark moon to counter the pale sun outlined above the surface.

Brianna remained surprisingly calm in the midst of the inspection. Excited but not frightened, even daring to reach her hand out to brush the whale's scarred hide. *Can you understand it?*

The eye regarded them while the voice continued to groan through the water. "What's this? A human?"

Nerves jangling, Zantu thrust out his chest and swelled his song to potent volume. He wanted there to be no doubts about how far he'd go to protect the human at his side. "My mate."

The whale blinked and seemed to sigh. "I've not seen a mated human in over a century. You have much to learn. But now," the whale sang in a heavy tone, appropriate for a funeral, "I believe I hear your brother."

In the far-off distance, Zantu could barely detect the familiar notes of his brother's sonic query. The whale answered with a moan that seemed to shake the very ocean, and drifted off to swallow more krill.

"Rubac!" Zantu called, moving to intercept.

You've found him? Brianna clutched him with one hand, and the netted pole with the other, struggling to keep from losing it in the water's resistance.

Ahead.

They left the whale behind, Zantu querying madly to discover Rubac's location. His brother's song had stopped, but the higher, more uncertain chimes of Ebby's song grew louder. "Uncle Zantu!"

Zantu raced ahead, drawn to Ebby's voice. Finally, he saw Rubac's form.

Alongside the unmistakable curves of a mermaid.

Zantu halted his momentum. *The whale said there was a mermaid around.*

Oh shit. Brianna brandished her net in front of her, looking about. *I still can't see a thing.*

I don't see Ebby. A sonnet trilled to his left, accompanied by the notes from a fish-harp. He spun, only to spot the disappearing flash of an indigo tail. *Depths. There's more than one.*

He turned back toward Rubac and thrust forward, hoping to at least find safety in numbers. The mermaid teasing his brother had yellow hair and a golden tail. Didra.

"Oh, you've come to our party!" she chimed, clapping her hands. "Rubac's such a bore."

"Where's Ebby?" Zantu shouted. To his relief, the tiny figure materialized through the krill-speckled water. The child held back a distance, avoiding the mermaids and watching.

A duet behind him sent him spinning around in time to pull Brianna beyond the reach of a raven-haired mermaid. Her dark tail caught the light as she passed by, first iridescently green and then swirling violet. A section of her tail fin was missing, the jagged edge puckered with old scar tissue. She cooed, "I've heard about you, Zantu."

Her partner was familiar, nimble fingers plucking a fish-harp's tines. "Loia."

She laughed while her accompanying veil of fish shimmied and shifted around her in time to her harp. "I warned you a human was no fit mate for a merman. Especially a big strong merman like you. She'll never be able to keep up with our games."

Brianna's knuckles were white around the net pole, every muscle in her body tense. *What's she saying?*

Threats. Behind him, he heard the tiny susurration of skin against water as Didra shifted position. His brother remained eerily silent, eyes hooded, tail fin limp. There was no sign of the stillborn child. "Rubac? You okay?"

No answer.

The raven-haired mermaid swooped up from below, rubbing her scarlet nipples along Zantu's length. Brianna recoiled, arching away from the contact and throwing him off-balance, but he caught her and pulled her against him tightly.

An arm's length away, the mermaid backflipped to face them again and rolled a small dart between her fingers. Immediately, Zantu knew what was wrong with Rubac. Love toxin.

The mermaid's voice chimed with deceptive playfulness, her scarred tail fluttering with mesmerizing iridescence. "I wonder what would happen if I used this on her?"

He swelled his chest. "I will kill you if you touch her."

Brianna's thoughts spun like a water spout, her attention first on one mermaid then another. She poked the net at Loia. *We're surrounded.*

Fingertips tickled the tips of his dorsal fin, sending a shudder through his blood as Loia's lilting melody of desire began. "Oh, are we going to have fun now."

He twisted to bat the hand away. Loia's veil of fish enveloped them. Summoning his sonic blast, he sent them scattering. The scent of blood filled the water. Brianna's blood. He had to get her out of here. Get Ebby out of here. Fast. His brother… his brother would have to fend for himself. Coiling the muscles of his tail, he lurched forward between Rubac and his mate. "Ebby, swim home!"

Something nipped his side. For a moment he thought it was another of Loia's fish. He brushed a hand over the spot to flick it away and found the dart lodged there. Depths. He'd been hit with the toxin. Jerking it free, he continued his momentum, barely registering Ebby's tiny figure matching his pace several yards away. The fog of the poison was already taking hold. His muscles ached as he tried to force them to keep working. To get his mate to safety. The grip he held on Brianna slipped, her skin scraping along his side before he caught her again.

She clung painfully to his neck, her feet kicking in a pitiful attempt to help them swim. *Zantu, what's wrong?*

She hit me with a love toxin. Soon I'll be paralyzed. He didn't know what to do. His gaze scoured the blank expanse of water for anything, anywhere he could hide Brianna. His grip slipped again, and he realized his tail was twitching ineffectually against the current.

"Uncle Zantu, what about Dad?"

Sink it, Ebby was in danger here, too. Not from the mermaids—Didra wouldn't allow the others to harm her own blood. But she wouldn't ensure Ebby made it back to the safety of a nest, either. Ebby would be abandoned. "He'll be fine." He prayed he wasn't lying. "I'm going to be paralyzed soon, like him. You have to get back to the kelp forest. Take Brianna."

"I don't know the way."

He opened his mouth to tell the child how, but his voice had succumbed to the effects of the toxin. His arm now refused to keep hold of Brianna, and she clung to him as if he were a dead piece of coral.

Zantu?

You have to show Ebby how to get home. At least his mind-connection still worked.

How? I don't know the way, and I couldn't tell Ebby even if I did.

Keep the current to the right and in front of you. Stay out of the cold layer—it'll suck you to the bottom very quickly. If it does touch you, keep it hard to your right and swim upward as fast as you can. Ebby wriggled into view, turquoise eyes confused and frightened. He hoped somehow the merchild would trust Brianna.

The laughter of mermaids tinkled toward him like hail against the surface.

Kiss me, he thought.

What?

You have to let go now, and I want your breath-bond fresh. The thought of her drowning was almost as paralyzing as the toxin. All he could hope was that she broke the surface before the spell ended.

No! They'll rip you apart! The terror clawing through her mind was stronger than it had been while she'd been trapped by kelp.

If you don't, both you and Ebby will die.

Brianna's gaze cut to the merchild, then her lovely face crumpled in anguish. *I don't want to leave you.*

I know. He sought to make his thoughts calm. To reassure her. *But you have to. You have to save the child.*

She bit her lips together then nodded. Grief reddened her beautiful green eyes. Taking his face between her hands, she placed her soft lips against his. *I love you.*

The toxin didn't take away his ability to feel, only to move, and he was thankful in this instance to have one last memory of her. *And I love you, my angelfish. Now swim. Get back to shore if you can.*

She released him and turned to the merchild. Ebby's tail flashed with alarming colors, unable to settle on a single camouflage. The child's attention flicked to Brianna then back to Zantu. "I'll take care of her, Uncle Zantu."

Ebby reached out a tiny webbed hand and took Brianna's, pulling her away into the dark waters.

～

*B*rianna gripped Ebby's hand and kicked to assist their momentum. The mermaids' songs echoed through the water, trying to lure her back. She wondered if

Ebby felt the pull, too, or if merchildren—being sexless—were immune. The possible biological reason for a merchild's androgyny made a lot of sense right now.

The song's pull doubled her reluctance to leave Zantu and forced her to use every ounce of will to keep moving away. If it hadn't been for the merchild, she would have stayed by her mate's side, fought each murderous mermaid with every ounce of strength left in her body. She prayed he could find a way to escape. To find her again. He was stronger than any man she'd ever met.

Ebby dragged her along, using the current to aid their momentum. Now it was time to turn against it. To head back to the kelp beds. Brianna pulled against the child's grip and pointed with her free hand into the distance, keeping the water's flow slightly to her right as Zantu had instructed.

Ebby's eyebrows rose at Brianna's nonverbal instruction. The merchild blinked twice then nodded and changed direction.

Brianna let out a sigh of bubbles, grateful the child wasn't going to argue. Zantu's last wish had been for Ebby to reach safety, and Brianna would do everything she could to make that happen, even if she drowned in the process. She kicked with all the stamina she could muster. But exhaustion was already setting in. The drag created from the net was stronger than she'd previously realized, perhaps because they were now going against the water instead of with it. Poor little Ebby wriggled ferociously, but it didn't feel like they were making much progress.

A cramp seized her right calf, and she doubled over, awkwardly trying to massage it without letting go of the net. The tiny teeth marks left by the mermaid's swarm of fish continued to trail blood.

Swallowing, Brianna searched the surrounding waters. Hadn't Zantu said something about predators? Once, she'd watched a nature show about giant squid, with green-and-black video of a man-sized creature latching onto a diver's faceplate. The scrape and crunch of its beak biting the plastic still resonated in her memory. Zantu'd used his song to check for predators, yet Ebby moved through the water silently. Brianna hoped it was another survival trick, like the androgyny that made them immune to mermaid songs.

Overhead, the sun's orb seemed weaker, and the water had grown decidedly cooler against her skin. She reoriented toward the surface and aimed the net like a prow. Her leg threatened a new cramp, but she persisted in kicking until Ebby noticed and shifted direction. The downward pull was even more relentless than the outward current, and it seemed forever until a sudden flush of warmer water gave Brianna an extra burst of energy. She kicked like mad toward the sun.

Suddenly Ebby froze and spun to look behind them. A tremble passed between their connected hands, and Brianna squinted into the dark. Shadows. Moving shadows. Had the mermaids found them? The sharp curve of a dorsal fin cut through the waters.

Sharks.

Seriously? Sharks? She felt like she was playing a part in the worst horror movie ever. She clutched the net tighter, realizing how silly and useless a thing it would be.

The creatures moved sinuously toward her, toothy mouths open to taste the water. A large one was in the lead. When a smaller one moved abreast, the giant shot sideways to bite at it. Another midsized shark passed the fight, dead set on engaging its prey.

For the first time, Ebby let loose a wide arc of sound. It was nowhere near as authoritative as Zantu's thunderous voice, but it still had some effect. The sharks veered away, all but the largest one. The monster merely seemed pleased to ditch the competition.

Brianna released her grip on the child's hand. Tried to shake free so Ebby could escape. But the merchild didn't let go. Instead, Ebby gave Brianna a headshake to negate the idea. Did the little one have a plan?

The shark's mouth formed an oval of deadly teeth. Brianna pointed the net at it, hoping to at least force it to keep its distance. The shark was more agile and intelligent than she imagined, nosing the net aside so it could slide along the pole. At the last moment, Ebby jerked Brianna away. The beast's sandpapery side grazed Brianna's foot, leaving a burning welt in its wake.

Ebby turned, little tail churning water, and emitted another blast of song. The shark ignored it and circled back. The merchild's hold on Brianna tightened, shaking wildly. Brianna realized the child was no match for this beast, no matter how brave.

Gathering her strength, she jerked her hand free of the merchild's. She grasped her net with both hands and swung it down between her and the shark in a maddeningly slow arc. If she could lodge it in the creature's mouth, at least Ebby might be able to get away.

Ebby cried out again, and the shark twitched to the right.

Directly into the loop of the net.

The creature bolted forward, face in the net, and the hoop caught against its dorsal fin. Brianna's head rocked back at the sudden speed, her grip on the pole slipping slightly. The net seemed to both anger and confuse the beast. It twisted and rolled, trying to free itself. Brianna hung on like she held a tiger by the tail.

Ebby darted in front of the shark's nose, luring it along. The creature pulled determinedly, slowed by Brianna's weight. At first Brianna thought the merchild meant to use the shark to head home. Instead, Ebby turned into the current.

Back toward Zantu and the mermaids.

It appeared they really were going to take the tiger by the tail.

11

*Z*ANTU CLOSED HIS eyes and tried to ward off the effects of Loia's song. Her hands caressed his chest and arms, her endless song complimenting his physique, promising pleasures untold. One hand found his sheath, attempting to lure his cock free.

Then a second voice joined hers, battling for supremacy. He opened his eyes a slit. The raven-haired mermaid undulated in the filtered light, her iridescent skin shifting with mesmerizing color. Her crimson nipples pointed as sharply as the dart she'd hit him with. Her genital slit gaped suggestively, and he felt his cock respond with a will of its own.

Loia screeched in complaint, sending her veil of fish at the newcomer.

The dark one screeched back, "It was my dart that felled him!"

The water churned with foam and bits of slaughtered fish as the two engaged in a physical competition. The iridescent one spun and smacked Loia in the face with her scarred tail fin, drawing blood. Loia's hand flew to her mouth, and she reeled backward, her fish-harp sinking from sight.

The dark one rippled toward Zantu, a predatory grin on her lips.

Loia recovered and shot forward, mouth open to bury her pointed teeth in the other's shoulder.

And then a flash of gold as Didra slipped past the fight to press her coral-brown nipples against Zantu's chest. Her song in his ear was subtle, quiet, and deliciously inviting.

His cock surged against her genital slit. The helplessness from the love toxin clawed at his soul. Burned through his blood. Raged against the injustice of one sex that held so much power over the other. His fingernails bit into his palm as he commanded every muscle to fight the promise of pleasure.

Another angry screech, and Didra was ripped from him. Flashes of indigo, gold, and iridescent-black fins created an intoxicating dance. The water grew cloudy with fish parts and blood. Furious mer-song escalated as each mermaid attempted to outdo the other, their notes coalescing into a single, primal melody of lust.

His racing heart pulsed in his head, the tempo overriding the music in the churning water. He clenched his fists, focusing on the sensation of his fingernails biting into his palm. Perhaps the toxin was wearing off. If only he could slip away now, while they were busy competing with each other.

Out of nowhere, something slammed into the midst of the brawl. He barely had time to register the predatory shape of a massive shark—with a human trailing it like a lamprey...

Brianna? he sent.

There was too much chaos for him to sense anything in return. The cloudy water reddened with more than fish blood, and the mermaid's screams no longer carried a hint of seduction. *Brianna!* he sent. Surely he'd been imagining things? How could she be controlling a shark? Under the best circumstances, even mer-song couldn't exert much control over the beasts other than inciting them against each other. Brianna couldn't even sing.

He twitched his tail, pulling forth every bit of strength he had to fight off the waning toxin and regain mobility.

A voice reached him. Not through the water, but in his mind. *Zantu!*

Brianna? Where are you? I told you to run!

Out of the gory cloud emerged a small merchild followed by a clumsy, flailing human. The ravenous crunch of bones from within confirmed the shark was otherwise occupied.

Brianna's thought echoed with feverish energy. *We're here to save you.*

"Where's my dad?" Ebby cried.

Zantu was gaining strength by the moment and turned to point in the direction he remembered leaving Rubac. Ebby took his hand and began hauling both him and Brianna that way. As the toxin left his system, he joined the child's efforts.

He sent out a query and was answered by a weak version of Rubac's familiar song. Ebby released them and darted forward. Zantu took the moment to draw Brianna against his side. *You should not have come back.*

She wrapped her legs around him and buried her face against his neck. *I thought I'd lost you.*

How the depths did you wrangle a shark?

All I did was hang on. Ebby's quite the little scrapper. Her trembling body told him a bigger story.

He embraced her, savoring the scent of her hair and skin. His imagination churned with other more likely outcomes. *You got lucky this time.*

Rubac appeared through the hazy water, tail movements still uncoordinated from the effects of the toxin. Ebby held his hand, leading the way.

Zantu looked over Brianna's head to greet his brother. "What were you thinking, Rubac? The deeps are no place for a youngling."

"You refused to help." Rubac hung his head. "And Father used to bring us out here. Ebby wanted to come."

"I wanted to see a whale." Ebby looked into Rubac's face with a youth's oblivion to mortality. "But we lost the baby."

A part of Zantu felt sorry for his brother. "What happened?"

Rubac covered his face with both hands. Ebby wriggled up

to give him a hug. The child answered for him. "Didra dropped it into the deeps."

The pity in Zantu's soul intensified, but there was nothing to be done. "The child is at one with the sea again. That's all anyone can ask for."

Gripping Brianna tight against him, he led the way back to the kelp forest.

∼

Zantu carried a sleeping Brianna back to his nest and laid her on the sponge bed. He spent the night holding her, stroking her, making love with her, etching each moment into his memory so it would last a lifetime. He wanted her at his side forever, but if today's incident had taught him anything, it was that Brianna didn't belong in the ocean. She couldn't sing. She couldn't even hear the full range of notes the ocean carried. And even if the breath-bond could be made permanent, she couldn't defend herself; the net had been a lucky moment, one not likely to be repeated.

She belonged on land.

If she stayed with him in the ocean, it only meant death for them both. And while he'd die for her in a heartbeat, the thought of her dying because of his selfish need to keep her close was unacceptable. The only place she'd be safe was back among her kind.

He knew she would fight his decision. Resist his plan to

send her back. How odd that he was about to execute the very thing he'd feared from the outset of his mate-bond.

At the first notes of the morning chorus, he lifted her gently and carried her out of the nest. Each coral-covered stone they passed on the way toward the shore felt like an added weight to Zantu's soul. He broke the surface as golden fingers of light glinted across the wavelets of the cove he'd chosen for her. His lungs felt tight with more than unaccustomed air as grief threatened to turn him back. He forced himself onward, knowing this was the only way to keep his mate safe. The pebbled beach was vacant in the morning light, but a small boat rested on the shore, and a house stood in sight of the water among wind-twisted trees on a rocky hill.

She roused as his tail scraped the rocky bottom, her sleepy thoughts reaching for him, seeking comfort.

Zantu? Where are we?

He set her feet against the floor. *You must go home, my angelfish.*

She groped for him, fingers slipping against his shoulders. *Wait! I don't understand!*

He gritted his teeth and dove beneath the waves, swimming fast and far out to sea.

Don't leave me! Zantu!

Her cries followed him clear to the edge of the wild deeps.

*Z*antu cruised the watery interface where the cold northern waters met the current off the kelp beds. Since abandoning Brianna, the dark waters of the wild deeps seemed to call his soul. He'd spent the last four moons scouring the bottom for treasure. His nest was crowded with human items, from gilded picture frames to unidentifiable plastic machines.

But none of it was the human thing he wanted.

He circled the long metal box from a cargo ship that had lodged on a ledge. This one appeared undamaged. The lower current's cold water had seeped into his bones, and his fingers were stiff as he lifted a chunk of basalt to bash the lock. Merpeople didn't have the layer of blubber that kept whales and other sea mammals warm in northern waters, and he'd already been down here past his usual endurance. But finding human artifacts was the only thing that interested him since leaving Brianna, so he kept at it.

The rusty metal lock crumbled under the impact. Once it was removed, he put a shoulder beneath the bar securing the door and pushed. The latch gave with a rusty, hollow grating sound, as did the hinges as he opened the door. He squinted and sent forth a sonic query to judge the contents.

Mounds of rotted textiles.

Disappointment sank him to the stony outcropping. Ruined by the sea. That seemed to be the story of most things human down here. Broken. Decayed. Unable to survive.

The familiar drumbeat of a whale reached him, and he realized he'd been resting too long. His joints were stiff with cold, and his heart seemed to struggle to beat. Going to sleep seemed like a good idea.

The whale thumped the water, calling to the krill it sought to consume. Whales were one of the few creatures, fish or mammal, to have words in its song. Rubac swore they were the keepers of myth and still grieved over the lost opportunity to elevate his child.

Zantu thought about his last meeting with one, when Brianna had been by his side. The creature hadn't denied the magic of elevation, so maybe the myth had some truth.

But it had said something else, too. Something just now returning to his memory. *I've not seen a mated human in over a century. You have much to learn.*

Zantu frowned, blood pumping a little harder. What was there to learn? Was there something he'd missed? Gathering his strength, he forced his cold muscles to carry him upward toward the whale's song.

He found the whale circling near the surface, its massive, scarred body black against the light.

"Great whale," Zantu called. The frigid waters had sapped him of his voice, and the whale took no notice of the small visitor, continuing its wide-mouthed sweep through the clouds of krill. He tried again. "Great whale, I have a question."

The whale continued to ignore him, thumping the water.

Zantu bolstered his song. "Please, I have a human bond-mate. I need your help."

The whale's thumping paused, its barnacled body slowing its loop through the swarm. It turned its great black eye upon him. "Bond-mate?" the creature grated. "How did this happen?"

The story flowed out like a riptide, of how he'd happened upon her, how she'd proven herself loyal, how he'd been forced to set her free. The retelling left Zantu mentally exhausted.

The whale resumed its circle through the krill. "If she cannot be with you, why do you not join her?"

Zantu's mind spun. "Join her? How would I do that?"

"Humans and merfolk separated ways not so very long ago in the timeline of the world. You can breathe air, can you not?"

Although mermen avoided the surface, Zantu had indeed breathed air a handful of times and knew that to be true. "Yes, but breathing air is only one piece of things. She lives on land. With legs."

The whale's drumbeat call sounded like laughter. "Have the merfolk truly lost all knowledge of their magic? As you can give the gift of the ocean with water breathing to her, she can give the gift of land to you."

Zantu's mind reeled. "Do you mean legs?"

"True bond-mates compromise to be together. Sometimes one gives more, sometimes another. It is the way of things if they wish to be together."

"I could live on land," Zantu said, rolling the words around as if tasting the idea.

"Indeed," the whale sang and swiped its tail to pursue the retreating cloud of krill.

"Wait! How?"

But the whale didn't stop. Its words floated back in an echo of song. "If you're bonded, you already know."

Zantu wasn't sure what that meant. But he meant to find out. Reenergized with new hope, he aimed himself for the surface.

12

SURROUNDED BY THE scent of rotting seaweed and salt, Brianna rose from the damp stone and snapped shut the picnic basket that'd held her lunch. Facing the sea, she brushed bits of sand from her cotton capri pants. As always, the slate-gray ocean whispered to her, waves kissing the shore with promises never kept. Sometimes the water cleared the beach, leaving pristine pebbles glinting in the sun. Sometimes it left lines of garbage. Today the beach was clear.

She called with her mind as she did every time before she left the cove, *Zantu!*

As usual, only silence in return.

Perhaps her therapist was correct. Her time in the ocean had been a hallucination. Her mate a myth.

As if in disagreement, the child within her rolled, a

sensation like tiny bubbles. She placed her hand over her barely rounded belly. "Don't worry, little one. I know I'm not crazy."

Upon her forced return to land, she'd climbed the stairs to the small house. The driftwood-gray structure had obviously been vacant for a long time, but the door was unlocked, and inside she'd found some old clothes. After a short walk down the dirt lane, she'd reached the highway, flagged down a car, and made it back to town.

Within the week, Eric had signed her divorce paperwork without question. Soon after, she'd discovered she was pregnant. The idea of raising a child alone broke her heart, but she knew there'd never be another man in her life. Zantu was her mate and always would be.

She'd bought the small cliff house overlooking Zantu's beach and taken a position at the nearby marine research center. Granted, she was only a bookkeeper, but being near the fish and other creatures felt like home.

And, sometimes, she swore she could hear them singing.

Placing her sandaled feet carefully over the uneven beach stones, she headed toward the stairs up to the house. The tide was coming in, and although she sometimes dreamed of throwing herself back into the ocean's embrace, she knew better than to hope to be saved a second time. Plus she now had another life to consider.

The brisk breeze at her back seemed to call her name as she walked, stones crunching beneath her feet. *Brianna...*

She paused, cocking her head and closing her eyes to accept the wind's caress. She often dreamed like this, her name upon her lover's lips, the sensation of the word along her skin.

Brianna...

She opened her eyes. This wasn't the wind. *Zantu?*

The baby rolled again, fluttering within her as if dancing to a song.

Brianna, I need you.

She spun to face the sea, nearly turning an ankle on the uneven stones. A silver tail splashed the water near the cliff.

"Zantu," she whispered, the air in her lungs refusing to move. Then, full force, she screamed, "Zantu!"

Heedless of her shoes, her clothes, her footing, she flung the picnic basket aside and ran into the waves. "Zantu, I'm here!"

A head appeared above the surface a little closer than before, silver hair blending with the gray-clouded horizon, then was gone.

She stopped as the water reached her waist, sandals slipping over the lumpy bottom. Waves lifted and dropped her. Had she imagined him? She watched the water, every ounce of her being calling to him. *I'm here!*

A length of silver materialized beneath the mirrored water in front of her, and then Zantu's naked gleaming torso rose.

"Oh my God." She stepped forward, slipped, fell into his

arms. She threw kisses across his face, gulped water as they both went under, found his mouth to kiss.

He pushed her away, upward to the surface. *No.*

Gasping and choking, she clawed her hands against his shoulders, feet scrabbling to find the bottom. *Why are you here then? Please don't leave me again.*

He rose to face her, helping her stand. She gripped him tightly around the neck. Wrapped her legs around his hips. *I won't let you go. You have to take me with you.*

Chuckling against her hair, he shifted his hands down around to support her bottom and began moving to shore. He stumbled once but caught himself. He was *walking* to shore.

Brianna nearly let go. "*What...*"

I'm here for you, angelfish. It's your time to share magic with me.

Rising out of the water like an ancient god, he carried her toward the cliff.

"*You're human!*" She found herself speaking the words as she thought them. Still in shock, she lowered her feet to the ground to make him stop. "*Are you really here to stay?*"

"*Yes.*" He used his real voice this time instead of only his mind. The word, although accented, was clear and deep and sexy as hell.

She stepped back, her gaze roving over his broad shoulders to his well-muscled stomach and lower, to where his member stood at half-mast amid sparse silver curls. Where his tail had been he now had perfect, athletic legs. Her attention returned to his cock. "You're naked! And you're a man."

His cock twitched in response, rising to attention. "Yes, I am."

Tempting as he was, she forced her gaze back to his eyes. They were as silver as she remembered, his lips just as luscious. She raised one hand to trace a finger over the soft skin.

From down the beach, a child's voice snapped Brianna out of her lust. While her little cove was generally secluded, it was by no means private. There'd be time to explore Zantu later. Lots of time.

"You're going to need some clothes." She shrugged out of her windbreaker and wrapped it around his hips. It didn't cover everything, to her chagrin and delight, so she had to skew it sideways to hide the most important parts.

"Why do you get to undress and I have to dress?" He tugged at the knotted fabric, and she slapped his hand gently.

"You've got a lot to learn about humans."

"I'm looking forward to it."

She took his hand and led him past the curious stares of two children toting kites along the windswept beach. *Well, you're going to get to learn from the ground up—Daddy.*

His moment of confusion was followed by a joyful shout that echoed from the rocky cliffs and drew giggles from the nearby children. He swept her into his arms and spun her as she giggled.

Together they climbed the stairs to their nest overlooking the ocean. She'd found her mate. Her true love. The father of her children.

I hope you enjoyed reading about Zantu and Brianna. Before you turn the page to the next book in the collection, would you like an exclusive deleted scene from The Merman's Kiss? Join my VIP Club and download it now! Members get special giveaways, sneak peeks of future books, and bonus scenes. Join here >
https://books.bookfunnel.com/m4m-deleted-scenes
Now turn the page for sexy centaur secrets!

THE CENTAUR'S BRIDE

A STEAMY SHAPESHIFTER ROMANCE

THE CENTAUR'S BRIDE

Riding a cowboy never sounded so good...

City-girl Renee plans to take one last look at the sage-covered hills before she sells her late grandfather's ranch. When she meets a shirtless cowboy with abs of steel and a soft spot for horses she decides a little time on the range may be just the vacation she needs. But the ranch workers are acting mighty strange, and her sexy cowboy has a secret she never expected...

Black Stevens has always been an outsider. To the herd he's defective, unable to shift to full equine form, and to humans he's a monster found only in myth. When the herd's leader offers him a chance to earn a position among his people, he can't say no. Now he only has to get the ranch's sexy young heiress to say yes...

Can he convince Renee to leave the life she's always known behind and give herself over to a monster like him? More important, can he protect her from the rest of the shifter herd?

1

*B*lack Stevens pushed the brim of his cowboy hat up off his forehead with the back of a wrist and stepped aside to allow the newborn foal room to stand. Dim florescent bulbs hanging from the barn's rafters fought back the night with tenacious insistence. The delivery had gone smoothly, in spite of the herd's concern that Millie was too old for another pregnancy.

Beside him, Millie's oldest daughter, Su, let out a sigh of relief. "She looks okay?"

"Right as rain," he said, meeting her gaze.

Su quickly looked away. In her human form, Su was even more mousy than her horse form, with nondescript dark hair and sallow skin that matched her mare coat. She was one of the few herd members subordinate to Black.

Millie, a bay, bumped her gray-haired muzzle against the newborn, encouraging her to stand.

"What're you going to name her?" Black asked.

Millie snorted and rolled an eye, unable to answer in horse form, while Su held out a hand to the filly, sharing her smell. "We'll probably let Lori decide."

Now it was Black's turn to snort and roll his eyes. He hooked his thumbs into the front loops of his jeans rather than ball his hands into fists like he wanted to. Since his grandmother's death, Lori had taken over as Lead Mare and had all but declared martial law over the herd.

"Let me decide what?" Lori's sultry voice filled the barn. Black ducked around the stall corner to find the blonde-haired herd leader approaching, decked in what she called her human bling—lacy black bra peeking above the plunge of her red button-down shirt, tight jeans with bright rivets along the pockets, and a big silver belt buckle shaped like the state of Montana. Her shiny New Helens cowboy boots brought her almost eye-to-eye with Black's six-foot-three frame.

"Hey, soldier." She sauntered past him, keeping her gaze locked with his until he looked away like a good herd member. A lifetime of ingrained respect for rank warred with his urge to buck the new Lead Mare's authority. Stallions protected the herd physically, while mares guided policy, and the lead mare's word was law once she was voted in. Only the strongest herd members might dare to challenge her. His grandmother had demanded respect during her leadership, but she'd also given it in return. Lori was just a bully.

Inside the birthing stall, Lori took a wide stance, hands on her hips. "Well she's a plain-Jane little thing, isn't she? Let's call her Jane, shall we?"

Su kept her chin down and nodded, while Millie turned her head aside submissively.

Black's nostrils flared, but he kept his posture relaxed. "I thought we might name her Ivy because of those lovely stripes wrapping her hocks."

The herd leader flicked her manicured fingers dismissively. "Ivy's for greener pastures. We'll stick with Jane. Come on, ladies. We're heading out." She snaked her belt off and hung it from a peg near the entrance as if staking territory with a flag, then pulled off her boots. She shoved them at Black. "Put these in my locker."

Before he could blink, Lori and Su were naked, Lori's upright breasts and perfectly manicured pubic area a complete opposite to Su's natural sags and bulges. Lori slipped into the darkness outside. Su followed close behind, casting a concerned glance over her shoulder at Millie. The light spilling from the open door caught a flash of Lori's golden palomino coat as she shifted.

Millie nudged her new foal toward the exit.

"You don't need to go. Let Ivy-Jane get her legs and nurse." Black refused to call the baby plain Jane. "She should meet your human form, too." Black put a hand on Millie's bony whither, self-conscious about giving a seasoned mother advice, but his veterinary training wouldn't allow him to remain silent. Not only were there dangers like mountain lions out there, but the first few hours of a foal's life were critical for imprinting, especially for shifter young, who had to acquaint themselves with what amounted to two mothers. The foal wouldn't be capable of shifting for a few years, but she'd have to learn both equine and human communication right away.

The mare's scarred flank flinched at his touch. She turned her head to bump against him with her cheek, telling him she appreciated his concern, but to mind his own.

He sighed and stepped back, listening as the sound of hooves striking packed dirt faded into the night. Stuffing Lori's clothes into a cubby, he looked around for any spectators before he stripped down himself. As a centaur, he'd never be a true part of the herd, and had to guard his secret more diligently than the other shifters, but tonight he had a foal to protect.

Taking a breath, he faced the door and allowed the pressure of the shift to take hold.

~

*R*enee angled the rented Ford Escape up the dirt hill toward the ranch's gate, air conditioner running full blast against the dry Montana heat.

Her best friend, Steph, sat in the passenger seat, scrolling through her phone, already bored with the sagebrush-covered hills and stark rock formations rimming the plateau. Decades-old memories tumbled over Renee as they drove: Mom and Grandfather and even Dad watching her ride her black-and-white spotted pony, Cookies; stormy nights when Grandfather would sneak her out of bed to watch the lightning from the covered porch; Mom showing her a nest of kittens in the barn. Happy memories that filled her with regret the closer they got to the ranch.

Grandfather had died, and she'd never gone back to see him. He'd been gone two years and she hadn't even known. The news had arrived with the detective hired to track her down and deliver the will. Now the ranch was hers, at least for a short while. This would be her last visit. Best to be rid of it along with all the memories, she told herself. Keeping up with Steph's rock-star lifestyle cost a lot of money, and the realtor had offered a nice sum for the property. What did Renee know about running a ranch, anyway?

The final message in Grandfather's will looped through Renee's mind as she drove.

The ranch holds a treasure deep under cover
Toliman's secrets are yours to discover
Guard it with care, and love it with spirit
Once you gain their trust, you'll no longer fear it.

Her father would've said it was more of the old man's voodoo or something, putting a poem in a will. But then, Dad hadn't been invited to the reading, had he? An age-old bitterness rose in Renee's throat. After Mom had died, Dad had shunned Grandfather's "heathen" ways. Something or other about shaman ceremonies and cloven-hoofed devils causing Mom's cancer. The moment Renee'd turned eighteen and inherited Mom's trust fund, she'd run away, thinking only of escaping her father's hysterical recriminations.

Steph thought the poem meant there was buried treasure, and insisted they go check it out before Renee got rid of the place. She'd booked the first available tickets out of La Guardia on Renee's behalf, posting memes about treasure hunting to Instagram and posing for lurking paparazzi with a tiny shovel from one of her previous escapades. "Does it look like I'm ready to dig? Maybe I should shoot a music video while I'm there."

Glancing in the rearview mirror at what was obviously a reporter's car keeping a discreet distance, Renee wondered what fodder they'd end up feeding the ever-hungry press this time. Sometimes she felt like no more than a fictional character of her own life, following Steph around. But living in the rock-star's shadow at least provided an itinerary in Renee's discontented life.

Beneath a gnarled tree in the distance, a herd of dun-colored animals lifted their heads at the SUVs approach.

Renee nudged Steph. "Look, elk." At least, she thought they were elk. Maybe deer?

Steph glanced up from her phone, then back down. "Cool. Are we almost there?"

"Soon, I think." Every fencepost they passed along the sage-dotted plateau made Renee's stomach grow tighter and tighter. Why was she so nervous? She felt like something huge was looming on the horizon, a choice she wasn't prepared for, even though her decision to sell had already been made.

The arch of the head gate came into view, Toliman Ranch scrolled in wrought iron along the lintel. She pulled to a stop and opened the car door. A blast of dry heat flooded the air-conditioned cab, along with the far away scent of horses and sunbaked sage brush. She took a deep, appreciative breath, noting the guy behind them hanging from his car window snapping pictures with a telephoto lens. Quickly opening the gate, Renee returned to the cab and the relief of the air conditioner.

"How rustic," Steph said, eyeing the gate as they drove through. "I suppose we have to do that every time we come or go?"

Renee shrugged. "Not so bad. Gave your paparazzi boyfriend an opportunity to flirt with me."

As if in territorial response, Steph rolled down the window and stuck her torso through, offering the cameraman a shot of her ample cleavage. Renee calmly drove past the gate and then hopped back out to shut it behind them. Steph could keep the limelight for all she cared. Renee was a nobody anyway.

She drove another several hundred feet around a hill that blocked most of the house from view of the road. Sunlight danced through motes of dust as they pulled to a stop in front of the wide covered porch. Almost expecting Grandfather to emerge from the house to greet them, she cut the engine.

Steph flung open her door and glanced at Renee with her nose wrinkled. "Whew, what's that smell?"

"Horses," Renee replied, recalling a younger self who'd also wrinkled her nose. Today the smell stirred something in her, as if a trembling bud was about to bloom in her chest. She squashed it down, reminding herself she was only here to hand everything over to the real estate agent. Hopping out, she gazed at the fancy log-frame house with its high windows and country décor. An old rusty wagon wheel hung from the wood shake siding, and the front door fixtures were made of black wrought iron, right down to the old-fashioned knocker shaped like a horse shoe. Two square planter boxes on either edge of the porch steps held nothing but wisps of dry brown grass.

Behind her, the metallic rattle of the barn's bay door opening made her turn. A very tall blonde woman emerged, pointed toes of her cowboy boots impossibly shiny for a ranch worker. The woman raised her chin, as if smelling them as she approached. "Which one of you is Renee?"

Renee stuck out a hand to the giant of a woman, at least giant compared to Renee's five-foot-one frame. "I am."

The woman gripped Renee's knuckles with uncomfortable firmness. "Name's Lori. I've been running the place since your grandfather's death. Sorry for your loss, by the way."

Steph pushed forward, her hand out. "Good to meet you, Lori."

Lori took her hand, eyebrows high. "And you are?"

A look of irritation passed over Steph's features. "Oh, sorry. I'm just so used to being recognized. Steph Bilmore." She cocked her head coyly. "You might have seen one of my music videos?"

"Ah. That would explain the fellow at the gate taking pictures. Hope he knows people in Montana carry guns." The woman turned back to Renee. "How long you planning on staying?"

"Uh," Renee automatically glanced at Steph for validation. "A few days, probably? I've got a realtor coming out tomorrow."

"We're on a treasure hunt," Steph added. "Plus I want to ride a cowboy. I mean a horse." She held up her camera for a selfie next to the wagon wheel on the siding.

Lori's nose flared. "A realtor? I see. Well. The housekeeper's inside. He'll show you your rooms. I'll be in the barn." She spun and strode off without looking back.

Steph sniffed as if unimpressed. "Amazon woman there acts like she owns the place. I suppose we have to get our own luggage, huh?"

"You were a little bold with that cowboy thing," Renee

said, feeling strengthened by the Montana air. "We don't even know her."

"This is your property. You can do what you want. She needs to get over herself."

Self-assurance dwindling, Renee nodded and wandered to the fence near the barn, allowing Steph time to sort through her usual mountain of luggage. Leaning against the rough wood rail, Renee surveyed the pasture. Beyond the green, irrigated section within the fence, the rolling hills were calico-spotted with patches of yellow broom and silver-green sagebrush. A shirtless man in a cowboy hat knelt next to one of the sprinkler boxes inside the fence. She admired his broad, tanned back as he picked up and discarded tools and parts. A baby horse with zebra-striped legs pranced around him while its mother grazed placidly nearby.

The man reached a hand behind him while he continued working, wiggling his fingers until the baby nosed them and darted away in delight. The pit of Renee's stomach danced with butterflies watching his obvious affection. The man's throaty laughter floated across the field as he rose and dusted his hands against the front of his jeans. He crouched and did a playful football shuffle, taunting the tiny horse, who kicked up its heels and ran back to its mother.

Momma horse flicked her black tail and continued grazing without concern.

Gathering up his toolbox, the man glanced in Renee's direction, sending the butterflies in her stomach into overdrive. He adjusted his hat off his forehead, letting the sun hit a fine, straight jaw with a haze of stubble. She fluttered her fingers at him, a little thrill chasing down her spine when he lifted a well-muscled arm in a reciprocal greeting. *God, he's hot.* Looking over her shoulder, she realized Steph hadn't yet spotted him. Renee never got the jump on her, often due to her own hesitancy. Well, not today. This was her ranch, and she was going to own it for as long as she could. Heart beating in her throat at her own boldness, she called, "Dibs."

"What?" Steph abandoned the luggage and crunched across the gravel to stand beside her. "Aw, not fair! There'd better be more delicious cowboys around."

Renee grinned. Wow, that felt good. Most of the time, Steph picked the targets and left Renee to play wingman, which meant spending the night fending off the target's wingman. Not this time.

Setting her chin atop her forearms, Renee leaned into the fence, watching the rancher stroll toward the barn. His jeans hugged his lean hips and muscular thighs in exactly the right places, and his muscled abdomen flexed with his gait. He didn't look at her directly, but she could feel his attention igniting her core.

Face heating, she looked away.

Steph turned back to the car. "If you don't seal the deal before tomorrow, all dibs are off."

Her previous thrill of confidence crumbled. "Hey! I called dibs!"

"Dibs are first shot, not exclusive. So don't screw it up. Just screw." Steph smirked and rattled her wheeled suitcase across the gravel into the house.

Yanking her own suitcase from the jumbled pile of Steph's castoffs, Renee scurried after her.

2

*B*lack's ears rang from the conversation between the two women as he entered the barn. They had no way of knowing he could hear them that far away—no human could, at least not clearly. The tiny brunette with the pixie face looked damned sexy peeking over the top fence rail at him, and she smelled amazing even at this distance, like wind coming off a cherry orchard in bloom. The other one wasn't bad, either, but she had a hard scent about her that reminded him of a predator.

He set his toolbox just inside the barn, safely away from little Ivy-Jane's curious mouth, and, now that he was out of sight of the ladies, he adjusted his fly. How long had it been since he'd had a woman? According to his hardening dick, too long. There weren't a lot of options for a centaur living on a remote ranch. To the herd he was a misshapen monster, unable to assume full equine form, and to humans, a monster of myth. Centaurs had no place in either world.

He headed to the back corner stall where they stored extra parts and equipment for the hinky water system that served the ranch. Parts of the system dated back over a hundred years. The water outlet had been clogged with rust, and he hoped they had a spare O-ring.

Should he approach the brunette or let her come to him? Young stallions from the herd hooked up with humans at the local bar occasionally, but that outlet had been quashed when Lori took over. She enforced strict rules over who left the ranch and for what purpose, minimizing what she called "frivolous" interactions with humans.

The image of the little pixie, small breasts pressed against the middle fence rung while she watched him, wouldn't leave him. Oh, how he'd love to get frivolous with that. To nuzzle into the warm curve of her neck while she wrapped both legs around him. His dick hardened even more at the thought. Good thing there was no one around right now.

He dug through a plastic bucket of miscellaneous-sized O-rings, comparing the old one from the spigot for size. Lori wanted the ranch—the entire plateau, for that matter—as a haven for shifters. No humans at all, even though Old Man Toliman had known about the herd and provided things like medical assistance and winter forage. With him gone, the herd was on shaky ground.

The scuffing of feet against the dirt floor behind him made him look over his shoulder. The Lead Mare leaned against the doorway, one boot crossed over the other. "I have a job for you, soldier."

He went back to digging through the bucket, dick thankfully shriveling at her presence. He hated her nickname for him, as if he only lived to follow her orders, not be part of the herd he protected. "I'm already working on something."

"You heard we have visitors."

He shrugged one shoulder noncommittally.

"The midget is Toliman's heir. I need you to marry her. The sooner the better."

Bristling, he shoved the parts bucket back onto its shelf and turned. "Marry her? I thought you wanted nothing to do with humans?"

Lori lowered her chin, brown eyes flashing with authority. Sometimes he wondered if her sire had been a wild cat instead of a stallion to give her the kind of command she seemed to wield. She spoke in a sultry tenor that brooked no argument. "She's got a realtor coming. One of us needs to marry in, take ownership. Keep her from selling the place or turning it into a tourist trap."

"Why me?" He exited the storage stall, brushing uncomfortably close to her when she refused to step aside.

"You're here at the barn more than any of the others. And it's not like you fucking a human could pollute the bloodlines any worse than you already have." She followed at his heels, her voice close to his ear. His skin crawled as if she might nip his flank any moment. He hated it when she tried to pull herd rank on him in human form. "You're probably already half-hard thinking about mounting her, anyway. Do it. I'll tell the other stallions to back off. Just watch out for that friend of hers. She's a piece of work."

"Mounting's one thing. Marrying's another."

Did she think Toliman's granddaughter would simply marry a strange ranch hand and sign things over? He bent to pick up the toolbox. "Old Man Toliman kept our secret for decades. Why don't we just tell his granddaughter?"

Lori stepped so close to him, their boots touched. "Not one word. Our secret died with that old man and it better stay that way."

A direct order? How was he supposed to build trust strong enough to propose marriage to a human, yet keep that kind of secret? He dropped his gaze, lip curling with distaste at Lori's nearness, and backed up a step. "You expect me to just drop to one knee and propose out of the blue? I have a feeling she's smarter than that."

"I've seen you in action at the bar, soldier. I know you'll make her swoon. Convince her to be your bride, and I'll ensure you have a place in the herd. A real place, running the wind with the rest of us."

The idea took hold of him like a lover's hand cupping his balls. He'd dreamed of running with the herd since before his first shift at seventeen. Unlike other equine shifters, he'd been born to his mother while she was in human form—a human baby—and had endured his long childhood waiting for his first shift to join his grandmother's herd. As time wore on, and he'd shown no sign of the ability, everyone assumed it would never happen. He'd tried so hard to make it happen, when it finally did... Well, he'd nearly killed himself shifting over and over in an attempt to "get it right."

He never could.

The herd hadn't exactly shunned him—they didn't dare when his grandmother was the Lead Mare. But the indulgence they'd once shown the poor human boy, like bareback rides across the plateau, had quickly turned to disdain and dismissal. The entire reason he'd gone to vet school was to give himself worth to the herd. But even that hadn't increased his rank. Being a vet was a human thing.

He licked his lips, regarding Lori warily. "How do you propose to make the herd take me in when I can't even run with them?"

She lowered her chin to stare him down. "What I say, goes. You know that. Once we own the ranch, you'll be free to roam like never before. And if you don't do it, I can find someone who will."

His heart palpitated in an uncomfortable rhythm. He'd never considered himself marriageable. But to belong to a herd, he'd do almost anything. And either way, Toliman's granddaughter was a tempting treat. "If I pull this off, and she becomes my little ranch wife, how're you going to hide our secret then?"

Lori's grin was feral as she retreated into the barn. "Believe me, she won't stick around."

Black was suddenly sick to his stomach as he considered what Lori might mean.

3

*R*enee stared at the huge barn door and swallowed. Steph was in the house, tied to a wall phone so she could talk to her agent. Cell service apparently didn't reach the ranch. But this gave Renee an opportunity to find that cowboy without Steph's watchful judgment or a teasing recap of her clumsy flirting later.

Why does it have to be so damn hot? She held her arms away from her body, hoping for a cooling breeze. Despite a reapplication of antiperspirant, her underarms were already stained with sweat.

Taking a deep breath, she ventured into the barn, hoping she'd find him there. She peered down the length of stalls, refamiliarizing herself with a layout she faintly remembered from childhood. The stalls to the right were simple, chain-link cubicles, while the ones to the left were enclosed in solid wood. The empty barn echoed, the sweet scent of warm hay and dust permeating the air. A bare-bones wooden stairway climbed into the hay loft, while several bales of straw formed a more solid looking stairway of their own at the other end of the building.

What if he's not here? Or worse, what if he's already involved with that Lori chick? She clutched what little confidence she had left tightly within her and ventured into the barn's cool, dim interior. "Hello?"

The man in the cowboy hat appeared from behind the straw stairway, now wearing a dark, form-fitting tee shirt. *What a shame.* At least his shoulders and biceps stretched the fabric in all the right places. An arrow of sweat darkened the shirt's neckline, pointing down between his sculpted pecs.

He strolled toward her, well-worn cowboy boots scuffing against the hay-strewn floor, each step sending quivers through her core. He had a strong jaw dusted with five o'clock shadow, dusky blond hair curled slightly over his ears, strong, straight nose, and sensual lips. Under his mahogany gaze, her pussy felt anxious, hot, and undeniably wet.

"You must be the new owner." His voice was as low and sexy as she'd imagined.

If she wanted to beat Steph at dibs, she'd need to play like Steph. *Say something sexy.* But all she could think of was riding a cowboy. Totally inappropriate. Instead, she smiled and stuck out a hand. "Howdy partner!"

Howdy partner? Really? That was the best she could come

up with? She shook her head and said a small prayer that her blush was invisible in the dim light of the barn. He accepted her handshake, his large, work-calloused grip firm but in no way uncomfortable. In fact, the contact sent a delightful shiver up her arm as she imagined that hand touching other parts of her skin.

She cleared her throat and tried again. "My name's Renee. What's yours?"

A tiny smile twitched at one corner of his mouth, and she was drawn into his warm brown gaze. "Black."

"Black? That's your first name?"

"Yep." His gaze flicked down to their still-clasped hands.

She scrambled for a Steph-like quip to keep the ball rolling. "Let me guess. Black Beauty?" *Oh, God, what was she doing? A little girl's book? Come on, Renee.* "No, too girly. Black Jack? No, that's a pirate." *Bad to worse...* "Oh, wait, Black Stallion!" Her blush built to an almost intolerable heat, and she was dying to cover her face with both hands. Then she realized she was still clutching his hand. She jerked free, trying to stand tall when all she wanted to do was cringe.

The twitch at the corner of his mouth rose to a full smile. "Close. Black Stevens."

Before he could say more, Lori emerged from one of the wood stalls behind him. The tall woman clapped a hand to his shoulder, but not with what Renee would call affection. More like possessiveness. "I see you've met our ranch-hand. Black here's been assigned to show you around."

Rats. He *was* taken. It figured that the one time Renee'd claimed dibs on a hot guy, she'd choose one who was already hitched.

Shrugging off Lori's grip, Black scowled and turned to look at her. "You and I need to talk about that."

"You can always go back to mucking out stalls." Lori's smile was tight.

Renee held both palms out. There was some serious tension going on, and she did not want to get in the middle of it. "Hey, I don't want to interrupt a lover's quarrel. I can come back later."

Black let out a rough laugh. "Lori and I are not, and never will be, lovers."

The tall woman's haughty expression confirmed his words. Whatever was going on between these two had nothing to do with sex. Unsure what to make of things, Renee looked around to find a new subject. "I don't suppose Cookies is still here? Grandfather used to keep a pony for me."

Lori laughed. "No Cookies for you, my dear." She shot a strange glance toward Black. "I'll arrange to saddle our stallion, Saul for you."

Black seemed to stiffen. "Saddle Saul? What's Saul think of that?"

With a disdainful look, Lori moved past him toward Renee. "He's eager to please."

Black turned as she walked by. Cleared his throat. Shifted to address Renee. "A stallion might be a bit much for you."

"Nonsense." Lori flicked a hand dismissively, sending lazy dust motes into a swirling frenzy. "She's Toliman's granddaughter. I mean, look at her. She's got the curve-less physique of a jockey. Plus, I hear she and her friend are thrill-seekers. Saul's going to love her."

Tension permeated the barn, loaded with a subtext Renee couldn't fathom. Steph loved the hype of thrill-seeking for her paparazzi, but in truth, the things Steph did scared the bejesus out of Renee. Riding a stallion sounded like it might be right up there with swimming in a shark cage. Besides, Grandfather had died riding a horse, and she was nowhere near as skilled as he'd been. "Er, I haven't been on a horse since I was eight."

Black grabbed Renee's arm and turned her firmly toward one of the stalls open to the pasture. "Why don't I show you around before you decide anything? Let's save the riding for later, when it's not so hot." He shot a look over his shoulder but didn't slow down. "We have a new foal. She was just born a few days ago."

"Sounds good," Renee said breathlessly, dodging a drying pile of manure.

"Let me know how you enjoy riding!" Lori's voice floated after them, followed by a laugh.

Now that they were away from Lori, Renee tilted her head to check out Black's jeans-covered ass. Not too baggy, not too full. *Nice.* She trailed her gaze up his broad back to the sexy muss of hair peeking from beneath his cowboy hat. Were all cowboy hats called Stetsons, or was that a specific brand?

A loose rock twisted under her foot, causing her to lurch forward. He spun and caught her by both arms before she fell. *Ohh, quick* and *strong.* She smiled coyly up into his face, pleased at the startled blink he gave her before he looked away. *See, this Steph thing's not so hard. Well, as long as no talking was required...*

"Careful," he said. "These rocks seem to appear out of nowhere." He turned and continued walking, no longer holding Renee's arm. *Shucks.* She closed her eyes and inhaled the lingering scent of him. Sweet hay and leather and sexy, sexy man.

Opening her eyes again, she was abashed to see him looking at her from a few steps away, near the mare. A smirk tweaked his sensual lips. "This is Millie."

The mare cocked her ears toward Renee curiously.

Cheeks burning, Renee straightened her spine and held out a hand to the horse as if to shake. "Good to meet you, Millie. I'm Renee." *There, that was cute, right?* The beast bobbed her head as if in greeting, and Renee giggled and curtsied back, pleased by Black's approving smile. "So polite!"

"Millie, Renee's the new owner of the ranch, and she'd like to meet Ivy-Jane if you don't mind."

The tiny foal peeked out from behind its mom's hindquarters, nose too big for her body and dainty feet ringed with stripes. Renee let out a gust of air. "Oh, my, God, she's adorable."

The foal startled back into hiding. Momma horse flicked

her tail and turned around to continue grazing, as if shrugging in acquiescence.

Black crouched and leaned forward, offering one hand toward where the foal had disappeared. "It's okay, Ivy-Jane. Come meet the human."

Renee admired his wide chest as he stretched his arm. "I like how you talk to them."

He rose without looking at her. "It's about respect, that's all. Isn't it, Millie?" He scratched the mare's neck where her dark mane emerged. "And with the little ones, you need to allow them to come to you. They can sense who to trust."

The foal peeked at them again, this time from around the mare's front end, dark ears back. Renee averted her eyes, keeping focus on Black. Not difficult to do. The muscles in his forearm rippled as he scratched the mare, and the tiny gold hairs on his skin caught the sun. Remembering how he'd stretched a teasing hand out to the foal while he was working on the sprinkler box, Renee held her palm up and wiggled her fingers at the foal.

To her delight, the little creature approached to sniff, velvet muzzle brushing the backs of Renee's fingers.

"Seems you pass muster." Black watched with a hooded gaze and easy smile. Damn, he had a sexy smile.

"How old are they when you start breaking them?"

Millie nickered and swished her tail, sending the little foal skittering away before turning and plodding slowly after. Renee let her arm drop in disappointment.

"We don't break horses here." Black's voice held a low growl of irritation. The hooded smile had transformed to stone. "Besides, Millie's... from the wild herd."

"Sorry. I meant tame." Renee raised her brows, but his face didn't soften. "Work with? I don't know horse lingo. Besides, I thought wild horses would run away. Why's she in your pasture?"

Black removed his hat and ran a hand over his dusty blond curls. "Old Man Toliman—your grandfather—always helped horses. Didn't matter if they were his, the neighbors', or from the wild herd. He offered protection for new foals. Provided forage during hard winters. Medical help when needed." He shrugged. "We try to honor his methods."

More of that wistful sensation that had captured her on the drive here, that sense of something lost, took hold of her. She had a vivid image of her grandfather's broad smile whenever he took her out to the barn or pasture. "He used to pull me around in a little wagon to see all the horses. He'd say we were going visiting," she said, tears filming her eyes. Why had she never come back here to visit? Just because Dad was worried about voodoo or some such? "Grandfather loved horses."

A breeze passed between her and Black like a ghost, and she wiped her eyes with the backs of her hands. She tried to laugh. "Sorry."

Black's rich mahogany gaze sought hers. The stony face he'd worn earlier had softened yet remained serious, like he was expecting something of her. "Maybe you can love horses, too."

She laughed again, heart pounding like a flighty bird in her chest. Mr. Intense was one compelling fellow. She shifted her gaze back toward the barn. If anyone could make her love horses again, it would be Black Stevens.

"Maybe you can take me riding and show me how?" She tilted her head and shot him that same shy, coy look she had when she'd tripped on the rock. Her nethers tingled with the desire to ride, and not necessarily a horse.

He breathed in deeply, as if absorbing her. "Sure."

"Oh!" She remembered Grandfather's poem. "And Grandfather's will said something about buried treasure. You heard anything about that?"

"Uh... nope."

"Well, you're officially recruited to help look for it." She took his work-calloused hand and pulled him back toward the barn to saddle some horses, her forced boldness making her heart flutter.

4

*W*ith utter bemusement, Black allowed the pixie to lead him back to the barn. He was supposed to be seducing her, not the other way around. How the hell was he supposed to think straight when he was continually fighting a hard-on near her? He'd never had this kind of physical reaction around anyone. It was as if his body was hyper aware of her every move. When she'd stumbled on that rock, that look she'd given him, electric and inviting, had just about knocked him flat on his back.

Just because she's flirting doesn't mean she's looking for anything permanent.

She was likely after a vacation fling. Which he'd be happy to oblige, except for Lori's scheme. And threats. First of all, it didn't sound like she intended there to be a happily-ever-after marriage, which is why Black had hesitated during Renee's introduction. Then there was the other threat, almost as sour as the first. *If you don't do it, I can find someone who will.* Someone like Saul, who was more than a stallion—he was Black's Uncle Saul, the leader of the Bachelor herd.

The idea of Saul mounting Renee—or the other way around, for that matter—made Black's hands curl into fists. Not that Uncle Saul was a bad guy, but the thought of anyone besides himself riding that sweet little filly made him want to punch someone.

The barn's cool shadow enveloped them and Renee let out an audible breath. She plucked at her tee shirt, exposing a glimpse of her lacy pink bra and sending out wafts of her amazing cherry-blossom scent, like a cool spring breeze on a sweltering summer day. *Get it together, Black. You're acting like a yearling around a mare in heat.*

"Damn, that sun's hot," Renee said in a breathy voice, sexy as hell. "I don't know how you work in it all day."

He let his gaze wander from her face to her breasts and lower, then back up to meet her eyes, nostrils twitching with her intoxicating aroma. "What's that perfume you're wearing?"

She flushed. "Just deodorant."

He liked the way he could make her blush. She was a good girl trying to be bad, and he had to admit it was appealing as hell. Wanting to see just how pink she could get, he took a deep, purposeful breath. "You smell delicious."

Her flush deepened and she shifted her gaze away shyly.

The strength of his cock surged against the hard zipper on

his jeans. He stepped forward until he was sure she could feel his breath on her skin. He was sure he smelled of horse and sweat, but Renee didn't seem to mind. In fact, she seemed drawn to it, if her earlier nose-to-the-wind moment was any indication.

She tilted her chin to look up at him, the flush of embarrassment melting into an aroused glow. Her lashes fluttered closed, lips parted slightly, ready for him to taste.

Much as he wanted to throw her into the hay and sink himself inside her, he knew he had to do more. He had to win her heart. He'd never played at courting before, because no mare would ever choose a centaur. His previous sexual encounters had always been with humans, quick and dirty, no tethers attached. And now here was Renee, offering him the usual steamy interlude, and he was thinking about bonding.

"You ever been in love?" His voice was husky in his own ears.

Her eyes popped open. A flash of something vulnerable passed through her gaze. Then the wild filly was back. She reached up to run her index finger from his throat down his chest. "What a silly question."

He reached up and grabbed her hand, stilling it against his breastbone. Her heated skin was soft. Looking deeply into her eyes, he said, "I take that to mean 'no.'"

There it was again, that vulnerable flash behind her eyes. She straightened her spine. "This doesn't have to be about love. We can just have some fun."

He frowned back. Behind her clumsy attempts at flirting he'd glimpsed someone worthy of being Toliman's granddaughter. Someone capable of love. Not a woman on the prowl. He rubbed his thumb across the soft skin of her palm. "You don't want more?"

She shook her head. "Love's just a way to get yourself killed, if not in body, then in spirit. I watched my dad turn into a stranger after Mom died." She shook her head, as if flinging away memories. "I'm not looking for love."

Black raised a brow at her, knowing he was about to push some buttons. But he wanted to know who he was really dealing with. "So you decided to become a player, instead? A predator?"

She blinked. Pulled her hand free. But he caught it and brought it back to his chest. She glared up at him. "I'm not a player."

In that moment, something about her posture, the way she defended herself, grabbed hold of his heart's reins. This little blushing filly was definitely not a predator. Pretending to be, maybe, but when push came to shove, she wasn't the type to leave a string of broken hearts behind her. No, this one was playing a game, like a yearling flirting with a new herd.

He gave her a wry smile. "If you're not a player, then you're a tease."

She gasped and jerked her hand free. "I'm not a tease!"

"No?" He stepped closer, pressing his chest against hers,

forcing her to back up. One step, two, until she bumped the post he'd been aiming her toward. "Prove it."

He looked down into her wide eyes, and when she didn't push him away, he ducked his head to meet her lips. Cupping one side of her head, he threaded his fingers into her pixie hair. The softness of her mouth, the sweet flavor as she opened to him, made his head reel. She seemed to melt beneath him, opening up like petals to the sun. Her hands slipped to his hipbones, sending shivers across his skin, igniting his already rock-hard cock. Damn, this woman was like a drug.

He found himself kissing her harder, slipping his tongue between her teeth. Exploring her mouth. Inhaling her breath as his own.

She arched her breasts against him, throwing her head back and exposing her neck. He nibbled along her jawline, his hat bumping her cheek. She reached up and knocked it tumbling to the floor. Freed, he pulled her tightly against him and dropped his mouth to the sensitive skin at the curve of her neck. Her warm scent engulfed him, deeply female and exciting. Her nipples had risen like little buttons through her shirt, prodding him through the fabric. God, he wanted to taste those breasts.

She set both hands at the back of his hips and rolled herself against him, grinding his erection into her. He reached down and cupped her backside, lifting her slightly, fitting her to him. She made a tiny noise at the back of her throat that about sent him over the edge. Her hands roamed his back, his sides, swept down to rummage for the hem of his shirt and slide beneath, burn trails across his skin as she stroked his abs and sought his own hardened nipples.

"Woohoo, you go girl!" A flash penetrated his closed eyelids, and a familiar, predatory scent intruded on the moment. "This is so going on your Instagram page."

Renee stiffened, her fingers ceasing their caress. He loosed his grip, turning to face their peeping Tom while stepping between Renee and the camera. Her friend stood there in a low-cut tanktop, Daisy-Dukes, and flip flops, her frosted hair falling in two short braids to either side of her face. He growled, "What are you doing?"

"Capturing the moment." Steph didn't look up from her phone as she typed something to go with the photo.

He lowered his chin to glare at her. Photos were something he avoided, for obvious reasons. "You shouldn't publicize pictures of people you don't know."

She looked up to meet his gaze with artful innocence. "Oh, we're definitely getting to know you. Aren't we, Renee? Besides, I told that fellow out at the gate he could come inside with his camera."

"You did what?" His hands balled into fists. His head felt naked without his hat, and he searched the dirt floor until he found it. Dusting it against his knee, he glared at her. "We tend to be private here at the ranch."

"You have nothing to be ashamed of, stud muffin. You are

one gorgeous hunk of man!" She grinned and snapped another photo of him.

Gritting his teeth, he slapped his hat back onto his head, taking one step toward her. He was going to yank the phone right out of her grasp and—

Renee's soft touch on his arm reined him in. He crossed his arms and waited to see what his little filly would do.

~

*R*enee stepped out from behind Black, trying to calm her racing pulse. Steph was just being Steph, taking over like she owned the place. Only this time, Renee actually did own the place. This was Renee's territory, and for once she had no patience for Steph's disrespect. "Steph, not everyone wants their life out in the open."

"Don't worry, the photos didn't post. I don't have cell service here. This place is so backwater." She shoved the phone into her back pocket. "I came to tell you we've been invited to go base jumping! We're leaving for Dubai in the morning. Let's get this treasure hunting thing out of the way and move on." She looked around as if the treasure might pop out of hiding any moment.

"Base jumping?" Renee's step faltered. Steph had been talking about base jumping for almost a year. She'd even convinced Renee to do a tandem parachute jump in "preparation." Renee had sprained an ankle and been laid up for over a week.

"There's this building there, like, a million miles high. People do it all the time. And if we get caught, we could end up in prison." Steph squealed and made a little mock face of excited fear.

Black's deep voice rumbled at Renee's back. "You're excited to go to prison in Dubai?"

"Oh, we won't end up in prison. At least not for long. I've got people to get me out."

"And what about Renee?" His voice was hard as iron. Renee wasn't sure if that made her feel worried or safe. He was looking out for her, but his animosity toward Steph was almost physical.

Steph moved around Renee toward him, a familiar hungry glint in her eye. "Aw, that's so sweet, I love a man who's protective."

"Dibs, remember?" Renee gritted softly between her teeth.

Huffing, Steph spun and flounced toward the bay doors. "We don't have time, anyway. We have to be in Dubai day after tomorrow. Jamison has it all arranged."

"That's not enough time." Renee swallowed, trying to find some courage—not courage to base jump. No way in hell she was doing that. She needed courage to tell Steph no.

"You haven't signed the papers yet, so everything'll still be here when we get back. Maybe your lover-boy can find a friend for me while we're gone?" Steph shot a look over her shoulder at Black, pursing her lips in a playful kiss. "Come on, Renee."

Renee gave Black a tight smile. The set of his shoulders told her his hackles were still up. Best she step away and deal with Steph now. "I'll have to take you up on that ride later."

Scurrying after her friend, she caught up in the gravel lot where they'd parked the Ford. Steph had the back end open and was digging through one of the suitcases. "I'm sure I packed my Louis Vuitton flats in here. I want to wear them on the plane."

"We just got here, Steph. I want to stay a few days." Renee paused beside the SUV to watch Steph unfold and refold several stacks of clothing, all too fancy for the ranch.

"This jump is a once in a lifetime chance." Steph didn't look up. "You don't want to miss it."

Renee swallowed, her stomach churning. "I have an appointment with the realtor. Why don't you go on without me? Maybe I can catch up?"

"Is this about the money?" Steph scowled. "You know I'll cover you until you can pay me back."

"No, it's not that. I just want to get this ranch thing handled."

Steph paused her assessment of a navy blue sleeveless blouse dotted with sequins and looked at Renee. "Renee." She tossed the blouse on top of the open suitcase. "Are you really going to flake on me now, when I've finally lined this up? You know I've been waiting months for this."

At the edge of the barn, Renee spotted the glint of a camera lens as the paparazzi took his opportunity. Rolling her eyes, she redirected her attention to Steph. "You'll have Jamison. Anyway, three's a crowd."

"He has a friend for you, too. Not like here, where *I'm* the third wheel." She wrinkled her nose like a petulant child.

"I haven't been here since I was eight, and I've barely had a look around—"

"Come on! It'll be a blast! The shopping in Dubai is crazy."

Renee shrugged one shoulder, trying to keep the acid in her stomach from rising any farther into her throat. "I think I'm going to stay here." There. She'd said it.

Steph squinted at her, her lash extensions shading her flecked green eyes. Her scrutiny shifted to the barn and back again, not even acknowledging the camera guy there. "I see. Thrown over for a penis."

"What? I would never—"

"What do you call it, then?"

Renee swallowed back the sour taste filling her mouth, her blood pumping as hard now as it had while kissing Black. Truth was, she *did* want to stay and see where things went with him. Plus, the ranch was bringing back so many memories, she felt she needed some time to absorb them before the ranch was no longer hers. Black was helping her do that in a way that felt safe. Like she could be herself instead of the player she had to act like in Steph's shadow. Renee dug her nails into her palms. "I don't want to go base jumping. Not now, not ever."

Her friend's eyes widened and she took a half step back, as if she'd been slapped. "Oh. Well, why didn't you say so?"

Eyes burning with angry tears, Renee shook her head. "I— you—" The words were choking her, too many held back for too long.

Steph reached out to pull Renee into a hug. "I know, I know. You just did." She squeezed until Renee's hands rose to hug her back. "Fine. I'll go by myself. I already told my fans. But don't sell this place until I get back. We have a treasure to find."

Renee slumped against Steph in relief, guilt already sprouting in her chest, urging her to relent. To pack up and go back to being Steph's shadow. Instead, she simply said, "Thank you."

Planting a big kiss on Renee's cheek, Steph said, "Make sure to take notes on that juicy cowboy. I'm going to want all the deets."

Renee gave her a wry grin. Then she pointed to the paparazzi skulking beside the barn. "Meanwhile, can you get rid of your boyfriend over there?"

5

*B*lack stomped back to the barn to grab a bridle for Petunia, resenting the need to rely on a normal horse's legs to carry him, but he couldn't shift with all these humans about. And the herd needed to know right away about the photographer before one of them got careless and shifted near the barn. On top of that, the mention of a realtor proved Lori really did have a reason for him to move fast with Renee. Developers had been hounding Toliman to sell for years, but the old man had held out, mostly because of the herd. Without the ranch, they'd no longer be able to *be* a herd.

Whether Black married Renee or found another way to convince her to keep the property, he had to do it soon.

A thump from the stall where they stored grain and medical supplies drew his attention. *Too loud to be a barn cat.* Had one of the ranch's yearlings snuck in to get into the grain again? He didn't need a colicky horse added to his list of worries. It didn't rain, it poured, as the saying went. He sighed and grabbed the nearest bridle before going to check it out.

Around the corner, near the shelves of vet supplies, stood a man with his back to the door. His shirtless torso showed the many years of tiny scars his position as Lead Bachelor had gained him from nips and kicks as he jostled for dominance.

"Uncle Saul?"

The dark-haired man swung around, holding a bloody swath of gauze. A fresh magenta bruise stained his cheekbone.

"What happened?" Black moved forward.

"Eh, I'm fine. Lori caught me with a hoof, that's all." He was favoring his right arm, and blood smeared his ribs.

"She do this to you before or after she volunteered you as a steed?" Rage burned the back of Black's throat. Shifters only offered that honor to very special humans. Like his grandma and Old Man Toliman. They'd run the ranch together as if they were an old married couple, and she'd often served as his steed. But that was her choice. Not even the Lead Mare had a right to force another herd member to serve as a mount.

"This had nothing to do with that." Still favoring his arm, Saul grabbed a shirt from one of the wall pegs and started to put it on.

"Wait. Let me take a look." Black strode forward to examine the laceration on his uncle's ribs. The sharp edge of an unshod hoof had left a gash surrounded by bruising that might hint at broken bones. "How's your breathing?"

"I'll recover." Saul's voice carried a thread of pain that showed even through his gruffness. He tended to overdo the alpha posturing, especially in human form. After a decade leading the other bachelors, his position had become a point of pride for him. "Just have to take it easy."

"You're Lead Bachelor, not some gelding." Black searched for a bottle of antiseptic spray on the shelves. "She had no right to do this."

"She caught Grant in the canyon after she told everyone to stay out. Went after him like she does. He's just a kid, so I stepped in. Things got a little rough."

Black frowned. "Grant's okay?"

Saul nodded tersely.

"Why's she keeping the herd out of the canyon?" The canyon provided shade and sometimes pockets of water or green grass during the drought of summer. It was also a nice place to hide from tourist eyes and allow young shifters a chance to master their human form. Black had enjoyed the relative solitude many times in his centaur form.

"Says it's cursed ground since we lost both Gloryanna and Old Man Toliman there."

"I see." Black located the bottle and leveled the nozzle at Saul's wound. Toliman had been riding Black's grandmother— Saul's mother—when the accident happened. The official report said icy rocks and a trail too close to the edge had fouled up the older horse's footing and plummeted both horse and rider to their deaths. Lori declared it'd been the old mare giving her human one last ride. Black still had difficulty believing his grandma would've been on that trail under those conditions.

He finished cleaning the blood from Saul's side and reached for a laceration kit. "You're going to need a couple stitches."

"Naw, it's okay." Saul stuffed an arm into his sleeve.

"I insist." Black glowered at his uncle. "You may outrank me on the range, but in here, I'm the vet. You need stitches."

Saul paused, eyes swinging to meet Black's. After one blink, he dropped his gaze in acquiescence. He pulled his shirt loose and exposed his side once again. "All right, then."

Black's heartbeat slowed a little. He hated these battles for hierarchy. He'd prefer a more democratic way of interacting with his brethren. But instincts ran strong, and traditions were hard to overcome. He broke out a sterile needle and pinched the gaping skin together to begin the first stitch. "Uncle Saul, you ever hear anything about a buried treasure around here?"

Saul twitched as the needle entered his skin. "Buried treasure? Like pirates or something?"

"Not sure. Renee—Toliman's granddaughter—said there was something in the will about a buried treasure."

Saul's laugh forced Black to pause or risk skewering his uncle in the wrong spot. "I don't think your grandmother expected that one."

"Huh?"

"Toliman wanted to tell his granddaughter about us, but

the girl never came to visit. And you know our policy about putting any of our history in writing. Gloryanna convinced the herd advisors to let him put a cutesy poem in the will."

"So the treasure is... the herd?"

"Hidden, not buried. And yes, I believe so."

Black tugged the stitch tight and tied it off. "Renee's in for a surprise, then."

"Only if she discovers us."

"If Toliman wanted her to know, we should tell her."

Saul turned to face his nephew. "Lori wants to keep humans out of herd business."

Black surveyed his uncle's swollen eye. "You're head of the Bachelor Herd. What do you think about it?"

Shoving his head into his shirt, Saul grunted. "Doesn't matter what I think. It's a herd thing."

The underlying subtext—that Black wasn't part of the herd and couldn't understand—stung. Lori's promise to give Black a place in the hierarchy felt like an impossible dream when even his own uncle couldn't accept him. Black held up the needle. "You need one more stitch."

"Not unless you want me to kick you." With that, Saul stalked out the door.

~

That night Renee and Steph had a bonfire, staying up far too late and drinking far too much tequila.

She glimpsed Black watching from the barn door, but he chose not to join the bonfire, and she was grateful. She didn't want to share him with Steph. There would be plenty of time tomorrow to flirt with her cowboy.

Steph stumbled to bed slobbery and emotional about leaving Renee behind. Renee fell asleep dreaming about cowboys and adventures that were all her own. The next morning she woke woefully hung over, but managed to see Steph off before stumbling back to bed. Around noon she woke again, suddenly alert to the fact she was on her own. No one else was going to decide where to go or what to do. It was all up to her. Today was going to be fantastic. She just knew it.

Jumping out of bed, she stretched and smiled, gazing from her second story window across the rolling grasslands. Heat waves shimmered the air outside, giving the day a dream-like quality. After showering, Renee dressed in light capris and a strappy tank-top with a forget-me-not appliqué and matching sandals. She blotted her face, and applied a light coat of lipstick, then headed into the afternoon sunlight to find her sexy cowboy. Flirting with Black felt like uncharted territory without Steph's looming presence.

She found Black in the pasture once again working on the sprinkler head, this time with a shirt on. He looked up as she crossed the gravel parking area. Putting on what she thought was a sassy smile, she opened the gate and entered, keeping an eye out for rocks. A slight breeze had picked up, and the sun cast long golden shadows through the tufts of grass.

"I'm ready for a ride." She immediately kicked herself. *Stop trying so hard.*

He looked her head to toe with an appreciative gaze, lingering on her breasts and hips in a way that heated her already-flushed skin. His attention drifted back down to her strappy little sandals. "You planning to ride in those?"

"Why not? They're cute, right?" She stopped a few feet away and wiggled her sparkly red toenails at him. She knew riding in sandals was a bad idea, but she wasn't trying to impress a horse.

"At least you're not in Daisy Dukes." He rose. "Not that I'd mind ogling your legs. But that'd be begging for saddle burn. C'mon, I have a spare set of boots in the barn."

He put a familiar hand at the small of her back and led her to the barn. The contact seemed to draw energy from his hand, sending tingles over her hips and spine as they walked. He ducked into a stall holding odds and ends and reappeared with a dusty pair of leather cowboy boots.

Nerve endings crying out at the break in contact, she eyed the footwear. Steph had a policy about sharing footwear; shoes carried toenail fungus. Renee didn't know if that was true, but why risk it? "I'm not wearing used boots."

"You need heels to stick in the stirrups." He thrust the boots forward.

What would he do if she put her foot down? She didn't really care about riding a horse at the moment. Trying to be cute, she pursed her lips. "I have a pair of stilettos in my suitcase. I could wear those."

His eyes narrowed and his mouth quirked into a smile. "You can wear those with your Daisy Dukes later."

She blushed, legs going rubbery, the churning sensation low in her belly distracting her. *You walked right into that one.* He was good at putting images in her head. Her, in stilettos, backed against the barn post while he pushed aside the crotch of her short shorts to...

Black's nostrils flared slightly, and his playful expression shifted intensity. He advanced, and her heart kicked up a notch, his leather and sweet-hay scent filling her senses. Heat flooded her panties. She backed up a step, wad of hay catching the lip of one sandal and making her wobble. His arm shot out to steady her. A nuclear jolt of energy coursed up her arm. She closed her eyes and leaned into him, allowing the sensation to wash over her.

To her surprise, he pressed the boots into her grip and backed away. "If you want to ride, you need to wear boots."

She opened her eyes, her gaze on the worn leather in her hands. "Even for a short ride?"

"You wanted to look for buried treasure, so we're going camping."

Another memory of her grandfather surfaced, of nights sleeping under a sky milky with stars, crickets singing her to sleep. "I haven't been camping in ages."

"I've got the gear all packed." He turned toward the length of stalls.

Her excitement twisted into a new kind of anticipation, rapid heartbeat making her dizzy. "You know where the treasure is?"

"I have some ideas." He clicked his tongue and a dark speckled muzzle appeared over the stall door. "This is Petunia. She'll be your mount today."

Thinking back to Lori's earlier offer, she teased, "I'll be riding a stallion in no time."

Black turned toward her slowly, his eyes narrowed to mahogany slits and a wicked smile curving his lips. "You will. And I'm going to make sure you're good and ready."

All rational thought flooded from her head and pooled with scorching intensity at the apex of her thighs. *Good God, how'd he do that?* She'd been offering crappy innuendos all day, and here he'd thrown her off balance with a single zinger. *What would Steph do?* She widened her stance and lifted her chin. "I make that decision."

His voice went silken, deep with promise. "And how will you decide which stallion to ride?"

She swallowed as he paced forward, his gaze boring into her. The swell in his jeans told her he was ready, even if she was now weak in the knees. When he reached her, he paused, eyes shifting downward to her lips, throat, then breasts. She could scarcely breathe. He eased sideways, eyes devouring her.

Maintaining that intangible connection, he moved around her, so close she could feel his breath on her skin. She craned her neck to follow him, keeping the rest of her body frozen in place.

His warmth stopped moving behind her. A hand gripped her neck, fingers threading into the hair at the base of her skull. Pressing slightly, he drew her head down and to the side. Breath heated her neck as he grazed his chin over the curve of her shoulder, trailing his mouth over her sensitive flesh. He paused, sucking at the curve between her neck and shoulder. Her back arched involuntarily, thrusting her ass against his bulging cock. She'd never wanted anybody this much in her entire life.

Black turned her in his arms, still gripping the back of her neck with one hand. His other came to rest lightly on her hip. He dipped down to nuzzle against her ear, each scrape of his rough stubble sending tendrils of desire quaking down into her belly.

She whimpered in response. Why were her legs going numb?

Black chuckled close to her ear, the rumble vibrating through his chest and into hers. Her hand was splayed between the perfect lines of his pecs, and the desire to feel his skin overwhelmed her. She lowered her palm and let her fingers slide beneath the hem of his shirt. He twitched, his breath leaving him in a hiss when her fingers made contact with his skin. His abs were like ripples of stone, his skin smooth and hot. She let her fingers play up over the ridges until she reached his chest, coming to settle right over his heart. The beat thudding beneath her palm threatened to melt her knees completely.

With a groan, he released her, stepping backward, his smoldering gaze locked with hers. "We need to get moving if we're going to make camp before dark. Go pack an overnight bag."

The break in contact made it feel like all the air had left the room. She leaned forward even as he backed away. Her palm tingled, remembering the beat of his heart. She could sense it was taking a lot for him to hold back. His obvious erection told her he was no more finished than she was, and yet he maintained his distance.

Renee cleared her throat. "Now who's the tease?"

He looked over his shoulder at her, features shadowed by the brim of his hat. "Oh, I promise I'm not teasing. But I'd prefer not to have an audience. We ride in five minutes."

Audience? She looked around the barn in confusion. There was no one in sight, not even Petunia, who'd retreated into her stall. Only a gorgeously blonde palomino stood watching them from the paddock outside. The horse flicked its tail, gaze disconcertingly intense, and Renee decided she might agree with Black in this instance. That horse was beautiful, but it gave her the creeps.

Breaking eye contact, Renee headed toward the house to gather her toothbrush.

6

*B*lack kept his gelding abreast of Renee and Petunia wherever the trail would allow as he guided them up the plateau. The sensation of Lori watching him seduce Renee had set him on edge, and he was working hard to leave the leader's scrutiny behind.

Ahead, the sun sat low on the horizon. They'd been riding almost an hour, climbing a gradual rise toward one of his favorite camping spots. Renee swung her head to scan the dry landscape, orange sunlight illuminating the tips of her hair with fire. "Where did my grandfather die?"

The question caught him off guard. He'd been to the spot many times since the accident, trying to picture how his grandma could've fallen. The path was narrow, but even with Toliman on her back, it wasn't dangerous, and there were plenty of wide spots to pause and rest. He sometimes wondered if she'd been running for some reason. To or from something, he'd probably never know for sure. Clearing his throat, he pointed to his left toward the canyon. He couldn't see the sharp drop, but he knew it was there. "Over there."

She reined back, bringing Petunia to a halt. "Who found him?"

"Lori." He stopped a few paces ahead. "The medical examiner determined he died on impact. No suffering." His voice sounded a scratch too high in his ears. There'd been no exam on Gloryanna. As the ranch vet, he could've done a post-mortem himself, but he couldn't bring himself to cut open his already mangled grandmother. And no one seemed concerned enough to ask.

"What was he doing there?" she asked.

"Someone said there was a yearling stranded over at Pearson's Point. He and my...Gloryanna went to help."

"Gloryanna?" Renee shaded her eyes against the low sun. "Someone else was with him?"

"His horse. She was special to him. A very special lady to all of us." Black's stomach felt sour talking about this. The herd had mourned the loss of the Lead Mare in their own way, assembling for a gallop from east to west across the plateau to follow the sun. He'd only been able to join them as a rider, not a runner. Remote as the ranch was, tourists still drove a rutted trail over the reserve's northern ridge to view the wild horses.

Governmental wild-herd managers came to count heads and do roundups. Even airplanes flying over could notice the misshapen figure of a centaur. As a result, he was constrained to joining the herd at night, lingering on the outskirts of the family units while they slept, routing away any would-be predators.

Renee blessed him with a soft smile. "You're very much like my grandfather, I think. You love horses."

He adjusted his hat and looked out over the horizon. "They're my life."

"I wish I'd come back to see him." Her voice was high and light, like she was fighting back tears, and he regretted they were on horseback so he couldn't reach out and comfort her.

"He'd be glad you're here now, looking after his horses."

They stood a few minutes in silence, looking toward the canyon and allowing the horses to snatch mouthfuls of grass. The sun painted vibrant colors across the horizon, and the evening breeze carried a dusty, resinous scent only a hot day could leave behind. Renee nudged Petunia forward, and the tension left Black's shoulders. He hadn't realized how much the area still bothered him.

He directed the horses off trail, up a gradual incline that would lead them to a spot protected by ponderosas and a cluster of giant boulders he'd played around as a child. As if sensing the end of the journey, Petunia bumped up to a trot, jouncing Renee in the saddle. "How much longer until we reach camp? I think I'm getting saddle burn."

He laughed. "Regret not running away with your friend?"

"I've done some crazy stuff, but jumping off a building in a wing suit? No thanks."

"Not to mention the whole going to jail thing." His heart thudded a little harder at the thought of her in prison.

"Yeah, prison in Dubai doesn't sound like a good idea. Thanks for sticking up for me on that, by the way." She grinned at him.

"I'm a regular knight in shining armor." He tipped his hat, then pointed to several dark figures outlined against the horizon. His wild kin were less skittish than shifters. "Wild horses."

"Are they all wild out here?"

"Pretty much. Your land borders the Reserve. We can camp over there." He gestured with a nod toward a jumble of rocks not too far off where he'd spent the night many times before.

She guided Petunia that direction. "How much of this belongs to the ranch?"

"Around a hundred and eighty acres. Your granddad refused to fence it. He wanted it left open to the wild horses." *And the herd.* He was aching to tell her. To show her. But he was trapped here on this gelding instead of his own legs. His mind wandered to what it might feel like to have her legs clutched tightly against his centaur's withers, her breasts pressing into his bare shoulder blades as she held on from behind. His human body tingled with a desire to shift, and the gelding beneath him danced sideways as if sensing an imminent change.

"Whoa, there." He used the pressure of his knees to calm the creature and shoved the shifter magic down.

Petunia had continued without him, her head bobbing in time to her stride. She was an unimaginative beast, but that was a good thing for inexperienced riders. Like Renee and her glorious backside straddling the lucky horse. The boots sticking out of her capris looked ridiculous, but he wasn't going to tell her that after the struggle they'd had over wearing them. The curve of her bare shoulders and neck beckoned to him to kiss her there, nip her gently as a lover does. Pull her hips against him and make her moan as she rode his cock. He had an entire night with her under the stars ahead. Nudging the gelding, he caught up and passed her at a canter. Petunia knew the way from here.

Drawing up next to a ponderosa pine, he dismounted, tied his gelding to one of the branches, and began to unpack the saddle bags. The sky had turned lavender overhead, and beams of light poked through the dusty motes above the sagebrush. By the time Renee arrived, he'd thrown down a picnic blanket and popped open a bottle of wine.

He reached up to help her dismount, running a hand from her knee, up her thigh to her hip, ending with a cheeky pat against her bottom. "You've got a nice seat on a horse."

She grinned down at him. "You're the expert."

"Indeed I am." He kept his hand on the swell of her ass, maintaining eye contact like he never would with a herd member. He loved that he felt no need to look away, no need to play the ranking game. In fact, it felt like she was inviting him to take charge.

Renee made a face and swung her leg over the saddle. "I don't remember Cookies hurting my ass like this."

Her ass hovering at face level made his jeans feel tight, and he kept his hands on her hips a bit longer than necessary to help her down. She turned in his grasp, looking up at him with an impish smile. "Have any cowboy remedies for me?"

He brushed a strand of hair from her forehead, letting his fingertip trail around the curve of her ear and down the side of her neck. "'Fraid you're just going to have to ride this one out."

She trembled beneath his touch, closing her eyes and lifting her chin in invitation. Much as he wanted to kiss her right now, he knew better than to start down that path before setting up camp. He wanted to take his time with her, not be fumbling in the dark with a tent.

He brushed his lips across hers in a feather-light caress. "How about you scout for firewood while I finish setting up? Then we can talk some more about my cowboy remedies."

She opened her eyes, her pupils taking up most of her irises, lips in a playful pout. "Work, work, work."

He stepped back and allowed her to pass, swatting her butt

cheek lightly. She squeaked and hop-skipped a step forward. "All right, all right. Firewood."

He gave himself the briefest moment to appreciate her swinging hips before tending to Petunia, thankful she was a normal horse instead of a shifter.

7

*R*enee held out the wine bottle to offer Black the last few drops. She'd been ready to pounce on him all night, but he seemed to want to take things slow. To savor her. The anticipation only made her hotter for him. Everything from a palm pressed to her lower back as she bent to spread out her bedding to the way he let his smoldering gaze linger on her in the dusky light made her panties dampen and heat creep up her thighs.

She held up the last triangle of goat cheese and arugula sandwich. "This is fancier than I imagined for a cowboy camping trip."

He surveyed the fire through the contents of his wine glass. "I roomed with a culinary student while I was at vet school. He was always bringing home weird leftovers, and I was a starving student. Guess I developed a taste."

"You went to vet school? So, are you a vet?" She'd thought him a simple creature, a one-note kind of flavor. But she was slowly discovering Black had many layers. Maybe that's why he was taking things so slow.

"You find that hard to believe?" He raised an eyebrow at her.

"No. I mean yes. I mean…" She licked her lips. "For some reason I never pictured a cowboy vet before. I thought vets were all doctory, with white coats and stethoscopes and stuff." She'd actually never met a vet, not that she could remember.

"I've used my share of stethoscopes. But it's kind of hard to keep that white coat clean when you're mucking out horse stalls."

She laughed. "But you grew up here on the ranch?"

"I was born in the city. My mom died when I was a baby and my grandmother brought me here. I've called it home ever since."

"Is your grandma still around?" So far she'd only met Black, Lori, and the housekeeper, Emile, but she knew there were about a dozen employees on the ranch, most of whom had worked for her grandfather for decades.

Black shook his head, looking down at his lap. "She died about the same time as your granddad."

Renee's heart twinged and she took a breath. Here she'd been playing up the pity card with a deceased grandfather and didn't even know Black's wound was just as fresh. Actually fresher, since his grandmother had actually been a part of his life. "I'm sorry. I didn't realize."

He looked up, a half smile lighting his features. "I remember you from when you were little, you know."

"You do?" She tried to dredge up his face in her memories. "Why don't I remember you?"

"I was a cocky teenager." He took a sip of wine and winked at her. "Too proud to talk to an eight-year-old girl who only wanted to chase barn kittens."

"Oh!" She laughed. "You can't be that much older than me!"

"Five or six years is a lot when you're that age. Not so much now." He set his wine aside on the blanket they shared. "I was sorry when your mom passed. She was good to me."

Renee felt tears prick her eyes. "It happened so fast. One minute she was helping me with homework, and the next I was sitting at a funeral. It was confusing. Dad called her cancer a curse."

"Cancer is an evil thing." His eyes were soft in the firelight.

She grit her teeth, remembering her dad's ranting against evil curses, searching for anyone, anything to blame for his wife's death. As a terrified little girl, she'd bought into the frenzy and fear. But later she began to wonder if the true evil wasn't Mom's death, but how Dad had let the loss affect him. "Do you believe in evil? I mean real evil?"

Black took a deep breath and lay back against the blankets, staring up at the stars. "Not to be trite, but there's a little bit of evil in all of us."

"Dad claimed the cancer was punishment for Grandfather's evil spells." She watched closely to see what Black thought of that bit of mysticism.

He snorted. "Your granddad didn't have an evil bone in his body."

She raised her brows at him. "I thought there was a little evil in all of us?"

He turned to look at her, throwing out one arm like an invitation.

Her insides quivered, the anticipation that had been bubbling through her all night shooting straight to the juncture of her thighs. Yet he'd taken things so slow, she didn't want to just dive right in. Not yet. She leaned forward on hands and knees and scooted toward him, stopping to stare down into his face.

He curled his hand around her knees on the blanket, like a half-circle of protection. His voice was soft as he said, "Well, if he had any, I never saw it. He was a good man. Can I tell you a secret?"

She nodded. She wanted to know every deep, dark thing this man held dear. To tighten the heartstrings that had wrapped themselves around her without her even realizing they were there.

"Your grandfather's treasure's part of this ranch. You can't separate the two."

Goosebumps pimpled her flesh. She whispered, "What is it?"

His hand tightened against her hip. "The horses here. The horses are the treasure."

She frowned. "I know Grandfather loved his horses, but how can they be a buried treasure?"

Black's eyes darkened and he dropped his hold. "I've said too much. More than I'm allowed."

"Allowed? Why are you not allowed?"

He turned his gaze from her face to the stars. "Go back to the will. Read it closely. Consider before you sell the ranch. That's all I can give you."

What the hell was going on around here? She and Black had gone from butting heads about footwear to molten lust to a connection she couldn't begin to explain in the course of a single evening. And now there was some sort of weird Nancy Drew secret going on. Was her father right about the black voodoo and midnight spells? "If there's something valuable here, why didn't he just tell me? Why leave a cryptic poem?"

"I can't say for sure. I only know he cherished each and every living being on this ranch. He wanted them taken care of. You should think about that before you make any decisions."

Her throat swelled, making it hard to speak. The longer

she was here, the less she wanted to part with her inheritance. And with the cowboy who was part of it. In spite of Black holding back right now, Renee felt closer to him than she'd felt to any human being since the death of her mother.

"I can't afford it."

"The ranch won't cost you anything," he said earnestly. "We've always made do."

"That's great, but I need the cash." She gulped, thinking about how quickly the trust fund Mom had left her had disappeared.

"Are you in trouble?" His hand tightened on her leg.

"No," she said. "I'm just... out of money. These adventures with Steph cost a lot."

For a few heartbeats, he studied her, firelight wavering over his face. "Seems to me you might not actually like the adventures in the first place."

She flushed. He hardly knew her, yet he seemed to be able to read her soul. Lately the adventures had become burdensome. Renee thought more and more often of settling down in one spot. Selling the ranch would buy her a few more years, but then what?

He put a hand on her shoulder and guided her to lie beside him, pillowing her cheek in the hollow where his pec met his shoulder. Wrapping his arm behind her, he fitted her body against his and asked, "What do you do for a living, anyway?"

The question embarrassed her. At twenty-five years old,

she'd never worked a day in her life. Mom's trust fund was supposed to have set her up as an adult; paid for school, bought a house, whatever. Instead, she'd squandered it on things like paragliding, swimming in shark cages, and chickening out of running with the bulls not once, but twice. "I'm between jobs."

"What do you *want* to do for a living?" His fingertips played delightful tickles up and down her spine, making it difficult to think.

"I like to cook." Not that her adventures with Steph left much time for cooking. "And I like to read." Not much time for that, either, come to think of it. "I used to really like riding horses."

He stiffened. "You didn't today?"

She traced her fingertips over the ridges of his chest. "Oh, I did. Although my backside might disagree."

Lowering his hand to cup her ass, he spoke into her hair. "You just need to re-train your muscles. I could help you."

The embers simmering in her core flamed to life once again. The heat seemed to burn away all her witty responses. "I'm sure."

He took a deep breath of her hair. "You smell delicious," he said, voice low and gravelly.

"Like what?" Her gaze was fixed on the growing lump in his jeans.

He rolled toward her, hoisting up on his elbow to stare

down into her face. "Spring orchards and hot-blooded female."

Gulping, she lifted a hand to trace the stubbled line of his jaw. "That's quite a combination."

His free hand slid down her ribcage and over her hip, coming to rest over her sex. She inhaled sharply, her back arching against the hard ground. The heat of his hand through her capris made her flood her panties with moisture. He eased a fingertip between her thighs.

"I can smell when you want me."

"Like now?" she murmured mindlessly, lifting herself to meet the pressure of that finger.

Dipping his face to hers, he blotted out the starlight, capturing her lips. It wasn't a gentle or questioning kiss. It was demanding. Hard and focused. Chills raced across her skin as he thrust his tongue between her lips and claimed her. His fingers maintained pressure against her sex, and the weight of his body over her overwhelmed her senses. She wanted this, wanted him. No fooling around this time. She wanted every inch of him.

She fumbled at his waist for the tongue of his belt. God, she was bad at this. When was the last time she'd had sex, anyway? It didn't matter. She wanted this man, and she wanted him now.

He let out a soft, sexy noise deep in his throat and let her fumble a moment more before reaching down and flicking the belt loose. She yanked his zipper down and thrust her fingertips into the gap, locating the firm rounded head of his cock. He let out another soft groan, and nipped against her lower lip. His abs went rigid while he shoved his pants down his thighs.

He eased himself against her, and the hard length of his erection threatened to burn through the thin material of her capris. Cupping a hand behind her neck, he used the other hand to drag her waist hard against him. His tongue stroked her mouth rhythmically, spiraling the kiss into new heights of pleasure. He ran his hand up her ribs, dragging the thin material of her tank top with it. She raised her arms above her head so he could pull the garment free. He flung the flimsy material somewhere into the darkness and then was back on her, kissing her as he reached around to unsnap the clasp of her bra.

Cool night air hardened her nipples, followed by the hot wet heat of his mouth. Before she could exhale, he had the waistband of her capris undone and was peeling both them and her panties down her legs, her bare feet kicking the fabric free. She lay there naked in the firelight, him on his knees above her, as he stared down, drinking in her body with his eyes. His jeans hung part way down his thighs, allowing his massive erection free, but the rest of him was still covered, which seemed wrong on this glorious, sex-scented evening. Renee bolted upright, shoving his tee shirt up his torso. Her palms skimmed the hard ridges of his muscles before he reached down and grasped the hem, nearly ripping the material off his body before flinging it into the night to join her tank top and capris.

He grabbed her and flung her back to the blankets, one hand beneath her hips. She wrapped her legs around him, urging him closer. His mouth found hers again, sucking the breath from her with his impassioned kiss. He ground his hips, hitting her in exactly the right spot, his erection rolling against her slick folds and leaving her trembling.

His body was shaking now, too, a low noise rumbling deep in his throat. He grabbed her wrists in one hand and pushed them over her head, nipping kisses down her throat to the hollow of her neck and shoulder. God, was he a forceful, sexy man.

The dying embers of the fire cast shadows within shadows. Black lifted himself into a pushup above her, allowing her to view his incredible body, his incredible strength. Chest heaving with passion, deep ridges outlined every one of his muscles. His eyes seemed to have an almost feral glow. He dragged his hungry gaze from hers and traced his attention almost tangibly across her lips, down her throat, to the electrified peaks of her nipples. The head of his cock waited directly against her entrance, pressing only hard enough to tease her with his girth.

She let out an incomprehensible murmur, arching her back, trying to take him in.

With infuriating slowness he pushed into her, millimeter by millimeter, stretching her.

"Ride me," she whimpered, too trembly inside to scream. Then louder, "Hard!"

The sexy noise in his throat vibrated louder and he thrust downward, burying himself, crushing himself against her. She bucked against him, yearning for a second stroke.

He held the grind, his hand still holding both of hers trapped above her head. She wriggled beneath him, driving herself mad. When she sought his face, she found a smirk there. The naughty cowboy was teasing her, tormenting her. And she loved it. Loved being at his mercy.

"More," she said on a breath.

He pulled back only to dip into her shallowly again, another kind of tease, another kind of pleasure. "Tell me what you want."

"You. Please. All of you. Give me everything."

Black thrust forward, hard and deep, and she cried out in pleasure. Oh God, this was perfect. So right, and he was sliding in and out of her hard and fast. He pounded against her clit with excruciating skill, over and over, filling her with a tingling she hadn't experienced in so long.

He released her wrists and lowered himself against her, flesh to flesh, belly to belly. His hard muscles slipped against her skin, the friction adding yet another layer of sensation. Had sex ever felt like this? A desperate need to go farther, faster, deeper. To envelop every bit of him, not just his cock.

Something blossomed in her chest, radiating outward like a glowing wave. This was mystical. This was unique. Like every cell in her body had come alive at once, and every pump of his cock made the wave rise higher.

He spread her legs wider, thrusting into her, pounding her, and she was ready. The wave crested, and she had no control over what was happening. She cried out and grabbed the back of his hair, clutching on for dear life.

The deep-voiced vibration in his throat erupted into something primal and wild. The sound tightened her core around the orgasm ripping through her, sent her into an explosion of pleasure that nearly made her lose consciousness. Black buried his face against her neck, his teeth against her skin as he rammed her, rode her, every muscle coiled. Pulsing ripples sent a second wave of pleasure through her as he shot his warmth into her. He reared back and bucked one last time, filling her with pleasure bordering on pain as flooding heat emptied inside her.

He collapsed on top of her, weight mostly on his elbows as his cock throbbed in time with her own aftershocks. Resting his forehead against hers, he hugged her tightly. "What just happened?" he asked.

She could barely catch her breath. "You've never had an orgasm before?"

He pulled back only enough to look into her eyes. "You're saying it's like that for you every time?"

If her heated skin could have flushed any more, she would have. But he was right. Two people couldn't get any closer than they were right now, connected at the hips, him buried deep inside her. And yet it felt like they'd just shared more. It felt like their souls had met.

Black rolled to the side, bringing her with him. She cuddled into his warmth, surprised at how cool the night air felt against her skin. "I don't... I know I talk a big game, but I don't just jump into bed with anyone. What we just did, that was... I don't know what that was. That was special."

"It's not fair," he said, his heart beating too fast under her cheek.

"What isn't?"

He swallowed audibly. "Relationships."

Renee sat up, her heartbeat matching his. Was that what this was? Were they in a relationship? If she was honest, she felt more vulnerable now than she ever had in her life. Her playful flirting had turned into something deeper than she'd anticipated. She craved him for more than just sex. They'd connected on a level she'd never thought possible. His touch made her feel alive again. She wasn't merely someone else's shadow waiting for that someone to make the next move so she could follow. This man made her feel tall. Like he understood what it was like to need to fit in, no matter the cost, and he didn't expect her to act like someone else to make him like her.

She covered her breasts, suddenly self-conscious under his gaze, fighting the feeling deep inside her. *Get a grip, Renee. It's not like he said he loves you.* Yet how was she supposed to respond?

Before she could form the words, Black bolted upright. His attention seemed to be focused on the darkness outside camp, like he'd heard something.

"What is it?" she asked.

Then a woman's scream pierced the night.

8

*B*lack was on his feet in an instant, ears alert. He'd heard the horses shifting uncomfortably, but had ignored it. Now he wanted to kick himself for growing careless. For losing himself so completely in the mind-blowing sex. He bent to help Renee to her feet.

She rose, pressing herself against him, her sweet scent mingling with the night air. Her voice trembled. "Was that a woman?"

"Mountain lion." Giving her a reassuring squeeze, he let go and moved to stoke the fire back to life. "It won't come near the fire."

Renee scrambled to find her clothes, pulling her tank over her head. Black dug in their gear and pulled out the .45 he carried for protection. He'd only had to use it once before, to warn off a bear that had been coming too close to the barn. "I'd better bring the horses in."

As he reached for his jeans, terrified whinnies from the wild herd cut through the night. The distinctive high pitched cry of a foal set Black's limbs trembling. *No.* Shifter herd or wild brethren, it didn't matter, he had a driving need to protect, especially the young.

He thrust the gun toward Renee. "You know how to use a gun?"

She stared at the weapon as if it might bite her. "N-no."

Still holding the pistol, he spun toward the herd's cries. His centaur form was stretching the seams of his control, bucking to be released. He took Renee by one shoulder and turned her toward the blaze, thinking fleetingly about leaving the gun. *Better not.* A gun in inexperienced hands could be more dangerous than helpful. "You'll be safe here. Keep the flames high. I'll be back."

"Wait! You're going out there naked?"

The power of the shift vibrated uncontrollably inside him. He called over his shoulder, "I'll be fine!"

Bounding from the camp, he held the change at bay until he was clear of the firelight. He couldn't allow Renee to see, not only because Lori forbade it, but also because he wasn't ready to expose himself. She'd think he was a monster.

The wildcat screeched again, the echo tapering to nothing as it routed its prey. Black's shift seized his muscles and bones, splitting his legs and shifting his elongating spine backward. He paused only long enough to stabilize his new footing, then galloped across the moonlit sagebrush, hooves thundering against the dry ground. His blood burned with the need to protect. He let his ears guide him. The wildcat had gone silent. It'd made its mark.

Heading for the pocket of unnatural silence, Black galloped forward. The sky outlined several horses in starlight. Millie's familiar slumped back stood at the outer edge, bravely facing into the night. He'd assumed the nearby group was a herd of wild cousins. If he'd known it was shifters, he might not have so readily made camp nearby.

Millie nickered in his direction, calling for aid. He drew close, scanning the group. Millie's baby was nowhere in sight. "Where's Ivy-Jane?"

The mare nickered again, hopping her front hooves up and down anxiously. If it hadn't been more dangerous to be in human form, she'd likely have shifted back. But a naked human would be just as tasty to a mountain lion as a helpless foal. He forced thoughts of Renee, alone at the camp, from his mind. The fire would keep her safe. Right now he needed to find Ivy-Jane. How had the foal gotten separated from her mother?

He clutched the gun in his right hand, glad for the extra protection. His centaur blood commanded every nerve in his body, seeming to grant his senses extra power as he scanned the night.

A terrified squeal split the darkness from the direction of

the camp. He must've passed Ivy-Jane on his way to the herd. Spinning, he leapt over a tall clump of sagebrush and barreled toward the cries, adding his own voice to the night in hope of driving the predator away. "Ivy-Jane!"

The foal's pitiful cries grew louder as he approached. A frantic rattle of branches to his right slowed his approach. In a pit of darkness next to the rocks, the tiny foal struggled within a mat of brush. Atop the nearest boulder, a pair of glowing cat eyes caught the moonlight, and Black could make out the hunched shoulders of a big cat against the midnight sky. He raised his gun, straining to aim in the darkness.

And then a pinprick of fire rounded the stone.

A single stick of firewood held high above her head, Renee crept past the lion without even seeing it. The lion shifted its gaze to the helpless woman, and Black's chest felt like it was about to explode. "Renee, watch out!"

She whirled, facing the rock, her face a mask of terror in the flickering light of her makeshift torch. A scream as fierce as the wildcat's echoed from her throat, and she shoved the torch upward toward the coiled beast.

The cat drew back, one paw poised as if to ward off the attack. Then it turned and sprang off the far side of the stone, disappearing into the night.

Black's protective instincts spurred him on. He reached Renee's side without thinking. "Are you all right? I told you to stay by the fire!"

She stumbled back a few steps, staring up at him. Her

mouth was a perfect circle of shock as her gaze traveled across his chest and over his heaving flanks.

Heat flooded his skin as he realized what she saw. A monster. *Him* as a monster. Gritting his teeth, Black shoved his emotions down. There was no way to undo the damage. He'd deal with the repercussions later. Right now he had to keep both Renee and Ivy-Jane out of the mountain lion's jaws. He shoved the gun into Renee's hand. "Hold this." Plunging through the wiry branches ensnaring the foal, he snapped limbs and plowed through leaves. "It's okay, darling. I'm here. You're all right."

He reached the little horse and knelt to slip his arms beneath her belly, untwining her gangly legs from the grasping branches. Backing out of the mat of foliage, he was relieved to see Renee still waiting, her make-shift torch flickering down to a glowing red coal. He set Ivy-Jane on her feet, but the foal cried out and immediately collapsed.

Black felt sick to his stomach. "She may have a broken leg."

"What do we do?" Renee's voice cracked and wavered, and her eyes locked on the foal. At least she wasn't freaking out completely.

He needed to get everyone back to the fire before the mountain lion regained its courage, and the fastest way to do that was to carry them. He knelt to scoop the foal into his arms again and shot a sideways look at Renee. He'd never had a rider before, but how hard could it be? "Get on."

Even through the darkness, he could feel the weight of her shocked stare. "Wh-what?"

"That cat may return at any moment, and I have two easy meals in my charge. Now get on."

For a moment, she seemed undecided. Then she dropped her torch and ground it into the dirt, stabbing it deeply to ensure it was extinguished. Shifting the gun to her right hand, she used her left to steady herself against his shoulder and swung a leg over his back. As her weight settled against his spine, his hide shivered in a strange sort of pleasure. But he didn't have time to contemplate that now.

"Ready?" he asked.

He felt her nod, and lurched to his feet.

~

*R*enee clung to Black's shoulders and concentrated on the man in front of her rather than the horse beneath her. What the hell was he? She thought back to her semester of Greek mythology in high school. A satyr? No, she seemed to recall that was a goat-man. *Centaur*. That was it. She gripped her knees against his sides as he trotted back toward camp. The ride was less jarring than on Petunia, and she didn't know if that was because he made the effort for her, or if centaurs just naturally had a smoother gait.

Centaur. How could such a thing be possible? The thought flitted through her mind that perhaps he'd brought her out here camping and drugged the wine or something. She had to be experiencing a vivid hallucination. But his shoulder beneath her hand, not to mention his rippling flanks now between her legs felt very real.

And there was another thought. Between her legs. She'd just had sex with this man, this creature. A man with a stallion for an alter ego. And how could he be a man one minute and a centaur the next?

They reached the camp and Black lay the foal down next to the fire. The poor little thing curled up in a heap and closed her eyes, obviously exhausted. Once again Black knelt, his head drooping as he waited for Renee to dismount. She slid free, breaking contact reluctantly, despite her confusion.

Black's not human. The concept made her legs weak. But the magnificent creature kneeling before her was real.

She didn't understand any of this. But she liked Black. He was sexy and protective and... really good in bed. At a complete loss on how to address anything that had just happened, Renee said, "Well, tonight was... exciting."

Chest heaving from the effort of carrying both her and the foal, he gritted, "Why didn't you stay put like I asked you?"

"Our horses got loose." She pointed into the darkness, heart racing as she recalled the thundering hoofbeats coming out of the darkness. "They ran right through our camp and almost on top of me. And then I heard what turns out to be Ivy-Jane crying for help. You said the mountain lion didn't like fire, so I thought maybe I could scare it off and save what sounded like a baby."

He lurched to his feet, hooves striking the dirt with purposeful intensity as he turned to face her. "You could have gotten yourself killed."

She threw back her shoulders, her blood boiling. How dare he be angry at *her*? "I was worried for you. You ran out there all alone! How was I supposed to know you had a secret superpower?"

He stopped his advance, mouth twitching as if fighting back a smile. "Secret superpower?"

She flung out a hand to gesture at his sleek legs. "What do you call it? I didn't even know there was such a thing as a centaur-horse-shapeshifter whatever you're called. I've heard of werewolves, but a were-horse? Is that what you are?"

His eyes danced with amusement, and his mouth looked a little less glum. "Not exactly. But there are horse shapeshifters. And I wasn't supposed to tell you."

"Well, you didn't exactly tell me, did you?" She made a sweeping gesture, telling him to look at himself.

Black broke into a resigned laugh.

Her irritation ebbed a fraction. He was sexy when he laughed. "Are there more of you?"

He pressed his lips together and looked away.

He said he couldn't talk about it. She wondered why, but didn't prod him again. What did she know of the magic or whatever it was that allowed him to do this, to be this mythical creature? Maybe he'd turn into a pile of ash if he talked about it. Her gaze shot to the exhausted foal. "Is she going to be okay?"

"I don't know." He shifted his weight uncomfortably.

"Well aren't you a vet or something? Can't you tell?"

"I need to examine her more closely, but it's difficult in this form."

She frowned, confused. "Can't you change back?"

"I… can. I just… I don't shift in front of people. Not even my herd."

"Oh." For some reason that statement hurt. They'd just made the most impassioned, intense love she'd ever experienced in her life, and now he didn't want to show her this part of himself? "I can turn my back."

She spun, crossing her arms and staring into the darkness, her heart shriveling a little at the way he shut her out. She shouldn't care. It was only sex, right? But she'd believed Black was letting her in, and in accepting that from him, she'd become vulnerable herself. Her head told her to let it go, but her heart wanted to cling to him, like she'd found a perfect mate in a man of a different … species? Was this even okay? He wasn't human. Could something like this even work? Her vagina certainly seemed to think so. Stupid vagina.

A warm hand captured her shoulder and tugged her around to face him. He was still a four-legged fiend, towering over her with that sexy, sweaty chest all glistening in the firelight. She licked her lips, her own chest tight with anxious thoughts.

"I thought you were going to change—shift—whatever you call it?"

Ribbons of dust and electricity surrounded her, stinging her eyes and prickling against her skin like lightning about to strike. She threw up a hand to shield herself. Through her teary vision, the shadow against the fire shrank from massive equine height to Black's only slightly-less-massive human height. She rubbed her eyes with the backs of her wrists and found herself looking at a butt-naked Black, standing square before her, his eyes glittering in the firelight.

The hardened shell she'd been building around her heart crumbled. He'd let her in after all. Shown her what he claimed he showed no one, not even his own kind. She wanted to laugh. She wanted to cry. She wanted to pound her fists against him with helpless abandon. Helpless because she'd never felt so close, so vulnerable to anyone in her life.

Black turned away, his attention now on the injured foal. She let her gaze linger on his naked back. Caring for the helpless foal, he looked so sure, so powerful and confident, so beautiful all at once. She could almost convince herself the centaur had been a hallucination. How could it possibly be real? The only explanation was magic, and she'd never believed in magic. In fact, she'd rejected it, leaving it to her father's ranting.

Everything she knew about the world had just crashed into itself, leaving her reeling and confused.

Renee moved toward the flames, thinking at least she

might be able to lend a hand with the foal. The sound of hooves in the darkness once again drew her up short. The pounding stopped, and two shadowy figures emerged into the flickering firelight, a slightly older man with deep-set midnight eyes and tattoos down both arms, and Lori, her blonde hair mussed as if she'd just been on a joyride in a convertible. Both were stark naked.

Renee's gaze flicked between Black and the newcomers. Did this mean Lori was a centaur-shifter, too? How many of them were there?

Black rose to face Lori. "I didn't tell her."

The blonde smiled and shook her head, holding her hands up palm out as if to settle him. "Of course not, Black. But the cat's out of the bag now, isn't it?"

He edged toward Renee, placing himself between her and the visitors. "Her granddad knew and kept our secret. Give her a chance."

Renee shook her head. "Grandfather knew? Is everybody on the ranch a centaur?"

Lori let out a low chuckle, her too-perky breasts bobbing with the sound. "Of course not, honey. Only Black here is burdened with that deformity. The rest of us are purebreds through and through."

"Deformity?" Renee's mind swam. "He looked rather magnificent to me."

"Never mind, Renee." Black kept his eyes on Lori and the other man. "We can talk about all that later. Ivy-Jane's hurt. I need to carry her back to the ranch where I can take care of her."

"Then go. Survival of the fittest, they say." Lori's gaze wasn't on Black or the foal. It was on Renee.

Ice crept up Renee's spine.

The strange man stepped gracefully into the circle of firelight. Something about him reminded her of Black. The light caught his eyes with a reflective glow that reinforced these people weren't human. His voice was gruff, nostrils flaring. "I'll carry the human for you, Black."

Behind him, a look of annoyance crossed Lori's gaze. Then her smirk returned. "I knew I'd make a mount out of you, Saul. Go on, then."

Black's jaw muscles visibly bunched in the firelight, and Renee flushed, remembering Lori's offer to saddle a stallion this afternoon. "This is Saul? The stallion you didn't want me to ride?"

Casting an apologetic glance her way, Black said, "Saul's my uncle. He'll take care of you."

Renee raised her brows. "You didn't seem to think so earlier."

"It's different now," Black said.

"How?"

Saul crossed his arms, orange flickers glinting off hard lines of muscles. The guy was built like a brick house. "Well, you smell like sex, for one. Sex with my nephew. I'm not going to touch that."

Horror filled Renee's mind. First of all that she stank like sex. Second, that there seemed to be some sort of unspoken agenda among these horse people. Why had Lori offered to saddle Saul for her earlier? "Do I get a say in all this?"

Lori pursed her lips in a coy sort of tease. "Unless you want to stay behind and face the lion on your own, honey, I suggest you ride whichever stallion is willing to get between your legs.

Renee's heart threatened to jump from her chest it was beating so hard. Lori put her nerves on edge. But then, riding a strange stallion shifter didn't sound much better. What should she do? Their mounts had run away, and she had no idea how to get back on her own, let alone in the dark. "Can Ivy-Jane wait until morning?"

Black shook his head. "She needs medical attention."

A glance at the foal told Renee it was true. The baby horse's dun-colored flanks were shivering in spite of the warm night and the heat from the fire. Renee took a deep breath. "All right, Saul. Show me what you've got."

*a*fter setting Renee down just outside the barn, the shifters had almost seemed to forget about her as they hurried to tend the foal. She'd slipped away to her room to find some time to think, away from mountain lion screams, thundering hooves, and magical creatures beyond any girl's wildest dreams for a pony. Now in the early morning light, Renee stumbled out of the house with a travel-mug of coffee in one hand and her phone in the other. Her inner thighs ached from the unaccustomed riding yesterday—both kinds. The yard was quiet this morning, the tension from the previous night dampened by the dewy air.

Gravel crunching loud beneath her borrowed boots, she approached the barn. A quaking desire to see Black twisted her stomach, and not just to have her questions answered. She was afraid of him, but not for the reasons others might think.

Centaurs and shape shifters? Those were cool. Her fear went deeper. Black had touched something inside her. He didn't play games like the men she met with Steph, and he seemed to understand what losing her grandfather meant to her. She'd even flirted with the idea what they had was something unique. Love was one thrill she'd avoided with a passion, and yet here she was, facing a fall if she took a single step forward.

But Black was a mythical creature. Did he even think like a human? She'd tried to Google information on centaurs and shape shifters, but cell service was spotty at the ranch and she couldn't get many web pages to load. Grandfather apparently hadn't owned a computer, let alone wi-fi.

Black seemed to think he was some sort of deformed monster. All Renee could see was a man with a superpower he used to protect her and a baby horse from an awful predator. The connection they'd shared last night lingered in her blood like a drug. Her inner thighs tingled with memory, the bones down there aching from more than the extended horseback ride. *I want to ride a cowboy...*

She froze in front of the open bay door, steam from her coffee hitting her face like a wake up call. She obviously needed some space or else she might just let her hormones forget all the craziness from last night. If she went to town, she could find a coffee shop with wi-fi and do a little research. Think this through before she got any deeper.

Turning, she stared at the empty gravel parking area between the house and the barn. Steph had taken the rental when she'd left. Renee hadn't worried then, figuring Black or someone could get her to Missoula to catch a flight home. Now she was stranded here alone, surrounded by who-knew how many shapeshifters, with no transportation of her own.

Her gaze drifted to a smaller building she remembered as a machine shed from her younger days. Grandfather kept a tractor in there for hauling hay and raking pasture. *You going to drive a tractor to town?* She smirked at the idea. But maybe he had a car or something in there to haul supplies from town.

She shoved against the side door to get it open and entered. The dark building smelled of stale oil, metal filings, and dust. She left the door ajar to let in light and moved past an ancient John Deere tractor and a well-ordered workbench. In the far bay sat a beat-up Chevy pickup with the keys in the ignition. *Score.*

Setting her coffee on the hood, Renee wrestled with the garage door, realized it was latched, and finally got it open. Morning air rushed in like the building had been holding its breath. She took a deep taste, savoring the sunlight painting the far-away tops of trees and the faint singing of birds. In spite of the excitement from last night, this place felt peaceful. Protected. Special. She could see making a home here. Maybe with Black.

"You're up early." Lori's voice startled her from the barn's side door. Her bling was back in place, right down to the Montana belt buckle covering most of her flat stomach.

The icy shiver Renee'd felt last night returned to the base of her spine. "So are you."

Lori sauntered over, coming to rest at the open garage door and leaning one shoulder against the frame. She crossed one boot over the other, thumbs hooked into her belt. Her gaze reminded Renee of a housecat watching a bird. *That makes me the bird...*

After a heartbeat of uncomfortable silence, Renee asked, "How's Ivy-Jane?"

Lori waved a manicured hand. "Black has it under control. He has the touch. But then, you already know that."

Heat flooded Renee's face, and she turned to retrieve her coffee mug. Sex with Black had been mind-blowing, satisfying in a way she'd never expected or experienced before, and a big part of her resented that others seemed to want to belittle it—first Saul, and now Lori. She decided to play innocent. "He seems like a really good vet."

As if she hadn't heard, Lori continued. "Women like you come and go. But Black's special. I can't have you breaking his heart."

Renee's desire to play nice burned away like a flash of gunpowder. She spun, her chest tight. What right did this woman have to judge her? "I didn't exactly get the impression you liked Black all that much."

Lori shrugged. "I have a duty to protect my herd. Whether I like them or not."

"Well, I *do* happen to like him, so you can just bugger off and mind your own business." Renee's blood boiled. Partly because Lori rubbed her the wrong way, and partly because she didn't want to face that she really did like Black. A lot.

Lori's hands rose in front of her, palm out. "No need to attack me. I'm only looking out for my own. Your grandfather understood."

Renee's urge to jump in the Chevy and drive right over this bitch warred with her need to have answers. "If Grandfather knew about shifters, why didn't he tell me?"

"The herd's only refuge is this ranch, and your grandfather used our dependence to his advantage. How do you think he kept this place running without paying a dime in wages? Though I have to give him credit for keeping his promise to Gloryanna."

Frowning, Renee looked out over the empty parking area and silent morning pastures as if she might find the answer there. She hadn't considered how everything had continued running in the time since her grandfather's death. Finances had never been her thing. "What are you saying? That you're slaves?"

A smirk twisted Lori's face. "What do you call a worker who doesn't get paid?"

Renee grit her teeth, refusing to take Lori's bait. "Volunteers. No one's forcing you to stick around."

"Ah, there she is. Old Toliman's granddaughter." Lori's lip curled. "Deluding yourself that keeping the herd's secret justifies the exploitation of its members."

"I never said that." Renee clenched her hands into fists at her sides.

Lori's face sobered. "Then prove it. Join us."

"How?"

"Marry Black."

Taking a step back, Renee shook her head, unsure she'd just heard correctly. Marriage? In what kind of fantasy world was this woman living? But then, in what kind of fantasy world were centaurs and shapeshifters real? Black was something other than human, something more. Who knew what the rules were in this crazy version of reality? And she *had* been fantasizing about making a home on the ranch with him. "We just met two days ago."

"Time's meaningless." Lori arched an eyebrow. "Prove you consider us equal."

"I don't have to marry someone to consider them equal."

Lori smiled. "Look, I know you like Black. And he obviously likes you. The truth is, he'll never really be part of this herd, in spite of being Gloryanna's grandson. I'm trying to look out for him."

Renee frowned, not appreciating Lori's subtext. "Why? Because he's different? What I'm hearing is that *you* don't consider *him* equal."

Confusion brushed across Lori's face, but she recovered with a look of pity. "I respect his dedication to the herd. It's just that the herd's very particular about bloodlines. There are so few of us left, we have to be choosy about our breeding partners."

"First of all, I'm not a *breeding partner*." Renee advanced on the tall woman, even though she had to look up into her face. "And second of all, there's nothing at all wrong with Black. He's perfect just the way he is, and you're a fool if you can't recognize that. Now if you'll excuse me, I'm going to check on Ivy-Jane."

Brushing past the woman, Renee stomped out of the garage, all thoughts of leaving the ranch gone.

10

*B*lack bolted awake to the slam of the barn's side door. Small, angry footsteps made a beeline for Ivy-Jane's hospital area. He sat on a straw bale just outside the open stall door with his back propped against the wall, eyes closed. He'd been unable to keep Renee out of his mind, even as he'd tended Ivy-Jane and withstood Lori's recriminations for revealing himself.

Renee's cherry-blossom scent filled the air, and the footsteps silenced. He could feel her energy while she stood there watching him. Was she frightened of him? He didn't blame her. Yet he didn't smell fear as the silence stretched longer and longer. He smelled the rich scent of arousal. He let her continue to look a good sixty seconds before drawling, "Morning, sunshine."

She released a startled squeak, then whispered, "Is that

some sort of shifter sixth sense, knowing when someone's watching you?"

He sat up, a bleary smirk on his lips. Millie and the foal were asleep just inside the stall, so he kept his voice low as he rose. "You weren't exactly treading lightly when you came in here."

"Oh. Yeah." Renee cleared her throat and shifted her gaze toward the open door. Her face was flushed, and her shoulders heaved as if she'd been running. "How's the little one?"

He dusted hay from his jeans while he stepped away from the stall. He still wasn't wearing a shirt, but what he felt most naked without was his hat, which was still at the camp site. "Her leg's only sprained. She'll be up and around in a day or two." He plucked a tickling thread of hay out of the hair at the nape of his neck. "I'm more worried about her mental trauma."

"I can relate." Renee bit her lip.

Black felt himself frown, and tried to smooth his face without much success. There was so much to say now that the secret was out. But he didn't know where to begin. "This isn't the way I wanted you to find out."

Renee shook her head. "I still don't understand why Grandfather couldn't tell me."

Black glanced behind him toward Millie. She lay beneath a chevron blanket in human form next to Ivy-Jane, one hand resting on the foal's shoulder, her long, dull gray braid lying limp on the hay behind her. Her chest moved in the steady rhythm of sleep, but he wouldn't be surprised if she was listening. Lori hadn't lifted the ban on talking about the herd, but Renee already knew so much. *Enough to be dangerous,* as Lori had put it last night. Well, there was no going back. The secret was out. The only direction now was forward, right? With or without Lori's approval. Besides, this secret was Black's as much as hers. More so, maybe, because he had even more to hide.

Moving forward, he took Renee's arm and led her from the stall toward the pyramid of bales at the end of the barn. The loose straw on the floor prickled his bare feet. He headed toward an alcove where he sometimes retreated to satiate his un-herd-like desire for privacy. "Ask me whatever you want."

She glanced around, but didn't resist his guiding hand. He sat on a platform of bales he'd covered with a horse blanket, pulling her gently down next to him and trying to hide his disappointment when she chose to keep several hand-widths of space between them.

She twisted her fingers in her lap, her gaze on him guarded. "Lori wants me to prove I don't mean you harm."

His eye twitched. Of course Lori'd been on the prowl to catch Renee before he could this morning. Who knew what kind of lies that witch had already fed Renee about the herd? "Stay away from her, all right?"

"Why?"

"She bites. For real. Please, just stay away."

To his relief, Renee nodded. "All right, I'll try. But she's an in-your-face kind of person, isn't she?"

That made him chuckle. "That's one way to put it."

"She said you're Gloryanna's grandson. Wasn't that the last herd leader?"

He nodded.

"So, I take it she hates you because you're, like, a prince or something? A threat to her leadership?"

"A prince? No, we don't have royalty. I'm just a half-breed stallion. And besides, the Lead Mare's chosen by vote."

Her nose wrinkled in an adorable frown. "And they chose Lori? Why?"

"The herd respects Lori's knowledge of the outside world." His carefully phrased answer was the product of a lifetime of ingrained respect for rank, but left a bitter taste in his mouth.

Renee rolled her eyes. "I don't think she knows as much as you give her credit for."

"Lori was captured as a foal and broken to ride like other domestic horses, which is humiliating for a shifter. When her first shift came over her, she escaped and lived on the streets until she found us. She spent years hiding among humans, hiding her shifter nature, learning about their ways."

"She didn't know how to get back to her family? How sad."

"The way she tells it, you wouldn't feel pity. She's tough —tougher than most equines—and not afraid to stand up for what she wants." Or to force her will on others, he thought. "The herd was in chaos after Grandma died. Lori stepped in and took over and no one ever complained."

"So if Lori's not worried about you taking over her leadership, why's she treat you so badly?"

Black shrugged. "The herd always tolerated me for Grandma's sake. But I'm different. Deformed."

"You're not deformed." She pulled herself back to look at him, one eyebrow raised. "I've heard of centaurs in Greek mythology. I've never heard of horse shape shifters. They're the deformed ones. Besides, aren't you all the same in human form?"

He smiled, appreciating her spunk. "Yes, but horse form is how we determine rank. While the rest of the herd can exist together day and night, horse and human, I can't because an outsider might see me. I never get a chance to fight for rank."

"But you could rank as a human. You're even a vet. That has to give you as much street cred as Lori. How come they didn't choose you?"

He shook his head. "Besides being a centaur, I'm male. Stallions can't lead the herd, not like the Lead Mare does."

"Why not?"

"Biology, I guess." Sighing, he tried to formulate how to describe herd hierarchy. "Herd society is sort of like a game of chess. The queen is the most powerful piece. The Herd Stallion—the king piece—has limited power."

Renee looked at her hands a few heartbeats before she met

his gaze again. "You said you're a half-breed. Does that mean you're half human?"

He should have known she'd ask, but for some reason he wasn't ready. Most of the time there were hidden barbs when someone brought up his heritage, and he found it difficult to rein in his knee-jerk response to her perfectly innocent question.

"I'm sorry." She scooted closer and leaned her cheek against his biceps. "That was rude. I shouldn't have asked."

The contact dissipated his instinctive shield, replacing it with a surge of feeling in his chest he couldn't define, but that made him want to nuzzle against her neck and breathe deeply of her essence, preferably with his cock embedded in her wet heat. He settled for putting one arm around her, pulling her close to his bare chest. "Don't be sorry. It's a perfectly honest question. And I want to tell you." He put his chin atop her head and rested there a moment. "I'm... I need to start at the beginning. With my mother. Grandma said my mom wanted more than a podunk ranch could give her. She wanted to go back to the herd's nomadic roots. So she left. The herd hadn't been here at the ranch very long at that point, but that's a different story."

Renee readjusted her position, turning her cheek so she could gaze up into his face while he spoke. One hand slid up to rest palm-down over his heart. The contact of her smooth skin may as well have been a lasso around his soul.

He covered her hand with his free one, wrapping his

fingers around hers, and continued talking. "My mom kept in touch, sent postcards from cities across the country, even made it to Alaska. The letters stopped suddenly without reason. Your grandfather helped search, I guess, hired an investigator to track her down. No luck. My mother had disappeared. Then, a couple of years later, a hospital in Chicago called with bad news. Or as Grandma liked to say, miraculous news." His chest ached with the memory of his grandma's voice in his ear while he sat on her lap as a child, and he clutched Renee's hand all the tighter against him. "Mom had given birth to a healthy baby boy. She'd told doctors the name of the ranch on her dying breath."

"Oh, Black!" Renee pulled her hand free and wrapped both arms around his waist, squeezing.

"That was the one and only time Grandma ever left the ranch. To retrieve me." He cleared his throat. "But to bring this story back to your question—we have no record of who my father is. The logical assumption is that I'm half-human."

Renee's shoulders rose and fell in a deep breath, her voracious hug remaining firmly in place around his waist. "I can say from personal experience that there's nothing wrong with you being human." Her breath was hot against his chest. "You're sexy as hell."

A laugh crawled up his chest and rolled from his mouth in an unexpected release. How could she make him feel whole in so few words? "Sexy, huh?"

Renee eased up on the embrace, fingers tickling over his bare skin, and murmured against his chest. "Incredibly."

"You're not put off by my centaur?"

She pushed him back against the blanket. "Mmm. That only makes you more sexy. I like to ride."

The rough blanket sank into the straw beneath his shoulder blades. He reached around and stroked the small of her back, letting his fingers slip into the gap between her shirt and her jeans. Her heart-shaped face had an impish grin while her palm skimmed his stomach, downward to his fly. His cock leapt to life at her touch, the scent of her arousal mingling with the smell of clean straw. He curled his fingers around the back of her neck and pulled her down into a kiss. Her mouth opened to him, and he rolled his tongue in a twining dance with hers.

Her hand over his fly cupped and massaged his balls while her mouth fired his blood. He reached around behind her and grabbed her jeans-covered ass, fingers dipping into the hollow between her legs as he palmed her backside. She moaned and clenched her butt, grinding her hips against him. His cock surged again in response. He growled, wanting to be in control. In one easy sweep he lifted her off him and rolled to bring himself on top, resting on his elbows above her. He didn't give her a chance to complain, but claimed her mouth again, crushing his lips against hers and plunging his tongue within her, tasting her sweet breath with every inhale.

He wanted to feel her skin, to explore every inch of her exquisite body. He thrust one hand beneath the hem of her shirt. Her skin glided like satin beneath his rough palm until he reached her bra and cupped the padding there. That had to go. He expertly slid his hand around her back and flicked the undergarment open, retracing his trail underneath the elastic to her waiting breast. Her nipple was hard and waiting for him. Kneading the soft flesh, he rolled the bud between his fingers.

With tiny, panting breaths, she fumbled at his waistline, trying to unfasten the button. "No," he said against her lips, catching her hand with his free one and pinning it to the blanket. He wanted to make her come with his hands and mouth alone. He wanted to make her yield to him and beg for him before he mounted her. He wanted to really believe she wanted him.

He caught her other wrist and brought both her hands above her head. Her wrists were so tiny and delicate, he could hold both in one hand. Keeping her trapped, he used his free hand to trace a teasing line across her lips and down her chin and neck to settle between her breasts over her heart. She arched her back, her ribs heaving with passion.

"You are so sexy," he whispered.

She licked her lips, and he wondered what it would be like to fuck that mouth. *Whoa, boy.* Right now this was all about her. He dropped his trailing finger beneath the partially-raised edge of her shirt and eased both it and her bra up, exposing her breasts. Her pert nipples jutted toward the rafters like a pair of spurs urging him onward. He dipped his head to one, tongue flicking out to sample the very tip. She whimpered, and he relented, taking the nipple into his mouth to tug and suck it into a tight peak. Then he nipped his way across her chest to give the other equal treatment.

She squirmed beneath him, but he held her hands firmly above her head. While he paid homage to her second nipple, he ran his palm over her belly to her sex, cupping the warmth there. Wet heat had soaked through her jeans, and he massaged her with the flat of his hand. She lifted her hips to grind against him, and he increased his speed until he sensed she was ready for the next level. Flicking open the top button, he slid his hand down the front and over her curls. His middle finger found her slit wet and ready, her clit throbbing beneath the pressure of his touch.

Sliding his finger in and out along the slit, he teased more moisture from her, plunging deeper with each stroke until his finger curled and found her opening. Her tight ridges clamped around his finger as he dipped inside.

She struggled against his grasp, her hips bucking in time to his thrusting fingers, searching for more. He continued to tease her opening, sliding over her clit with each stroke. Wetness soaked his hand. She wriggled beneath him, gasping for breath, words nearly incoherent. "I need more. Please."

He decided to oblige, freeing her hands so he could shimmy the fabric off her legs. Her scent filled the air with the heady flavor of her arousal and he sucked air into his mouth and over his palate, absorbing every juicy nuance. She groped for the buttons on his jeans. He cupped her face and kissed her deeply while she fumbled, each butterfly brush of her hands against his fly nearly sending him over the edge. The release of the buttons eased the pressure his cock had been exerting against his fly, and he had to remind himself to please her first. He grabbed her hands before she could expose him. "Not yet."

Getting to his knees, he reared back to look at her, drinking her in. Her flushed skin and gentle curves made him want to bite her, to nip her flanks and rub his face against her before he covered her with his body. He placed his hands on her breasts, kneading gently before sliding lower to mold against her ribs, thumbs tracing down her center line toward her belly button. There, he paused to circle her navel before continuing downward, thumbs leading the way into her curls. She gasped, hips flexing upward to meet him and her small hands flew to his wrists, urging him downward. Inward. He lifted his eyes to meet hers, the light of her passion burning bright as their gazes connected.

He slid along her lower lips, easing them open, spreading her legs with his palms at the same time. She blossomed like a flower, and he lowered his face to her folds. Her flesh quivered. He sucked gently, pressing his lips against her and probing his tongue into her heat while he continued the massage of her outer lips. Her fingers wove through his hair and she let out a moan that made his blood sizzle. He plunged his tongue hard into her opening once, twice, three times. She cried out, bucking upward against him, and her heated flesh pulsed and contracted with her orgasm, flooding his tongue with her juices.

He drank her up until he was sure she was finished, then he reared back up on his knees. Her chest heaved, hands fluttering weakly against the blanket. His cock could wait no longer. Shoving his jeans down around his hips, he freed himself and lifted her hips up and onto his waiting shaft. Again she cried out, calling his name, and he thrust into her, her circles of heat tightening around him in ecstatic embrace. With blinding fury, his release overtook him, and he buried himself inside her, pulsing into her core.

Shuddering, he dropped to his elbow over her and whispered, "I think I love you."

"I think I love you, too." She murmured.

11

*R*enee clutched weakly at Black's shoulders. Had she really just reciprocated the "L" word? Her blood pounded in her ears. It had to be hormones making her stupid. She couldn't be in love. Love was dangerous. To be avoided at all costs. Especially since she hardly knew the guy. Right?

Yet she knew more about him than she'd ever imagined possible.

Love for Black somehow felt empowering. Like acknowledging it would not just free her, it would make her whole. Complete her. And she hadn't even known she was in pieces. Well, some part of her had. Why else had she been drifting around after Steph, searching for that ever-elusive thrill that would somehow give meaning to her life?

She opened her mouth against his skin, circling her tongue

to taste his earthy scent, scraping her teeth lightly across his flesh. He shuddered and turned his face to nuzzle against her ear, his breath hot. Black was amazing. Heart-throbbingly, knee-meltingly, amazing. Worthy of love.

No. No! She placed her palms flat against his chest, trying to push him away.

He rose only far enough to look down into her eyes. "Am I too heavy?"

"I need to get out of here." And yet everything important suddenly felt like it was right here, right now, and the thought of leaving made her want to plant her feet and stay.

Black rolled off her with graceful ease and rose to his feet. The air felt suddenly cold, and she jerked her shirt down over her torso. The small effort seemed to sap her willpower. The beautiful man back-lit by dusky light mesmerized her. She wanted to burrow into his arms. To wrap herself around him and never let him go.

What if she gave the relationship a go? She risked herself all the time at these stunts Steph arranged. Why not choose a stunt of her own? She might actually be good at this one. Might actually be able to have a white-picket-fence kind of life on the ranch, married to a real-life cowboy stud. She rolled over and reached for her pants. "Did you know Lori asked me to marry you?"

"No." He focused unwarranted intensity on fastening the buttons of his fly. "What'd you tell her?" His arms and chest flexed in sexy ripples of muscle. How could anyone think him anything but perfect?

She thrust her legs into her pants. "That what happens between you and I is our business. She can just get over herself."

He jerked his gaze to her, teeth flashing in a grin. "You'd make a fantastic Lead Mare."

She scowled and awkwardly scooted off the makeshift bench, looking for her shoes. "Yeah, no. Your herd is not my circus or my monkeys. Why they follow a narcissistic bitch like Lori is beyond me. How does marriage even work in the herd, anyway?"

Black held out a hand and pulled her to her feet. "There's a lot of dating around, I guess you'd say. Finding a life-mate is rare."

That answer made her chest feel like it had been stepped on. He'd said he loved her, but that apparently didn't have the same meaning for him as it did for her. Renee felt sick to her stomach. Blinking to keep her burning eyes from spilling tears, she elbowed past him. She would not let him see her cry. No, no, no. She'd wanted to ride a cowboy, and that's what she'd done. End of story.

Striding purposefully toward the door, she spoke without looking behind her. "I'm running to town. Text me if you need anything."

"Renee, wait. Is something wrong?"

She walked faster, pleased he was forced to mince across

the sharp gravel driveway in his bare feet. Stupid Black. Making her love him when she'd been completely honest at the start that she wasn't interested in love. She reached the beat up Chevy and jerked the door open. The engine complained when she turned the key, but chugged to an uneven start, rattling her forgotten coffee cup off the hood.

He reached the garage and stood blocking her way. "Renee!"

Unable to hear him over the engine, she revved it louder, hoping the growl told him to get out of the way.

He moved toward the driver's side door and she threw the pickup into gear.

Nothing happened.

Black reached the window, making a rolling motion with one hand. Reluctantly, she rolled down the window. He leaned against the frame. "The transmission went out on this a while back."

Well, hell. She thumped the wheel with both hands in frustration, then turned the engine off.

Black remained leaning on the window frame. "Mind telling me what's wrong?"

The burning in her eyes was worse, tears clouding her vision. But she couldn't escape unless she slid across the bench seat to the other door.

As if sensing her thought, he looked down and took a step back. Her flight instinct eased a fraction. Taking a breath, she stared at him, this beautiful man who she wanted to punch in the face. Her heart hurt way more than it should. She'd only known him one day, and he was way out of her league. She should have let Steph have him.

"Renee, I don't know what I said or did wrong back there, but I wish you'd tell me."

"I'm not your wife or your life-mate or whatever. I don't have to tell you anything."

An infuriating smile curved his lips. "You're cute when you're jealous."

"I'm not jealous. I'm just... I don't sleep around. You... what we did was kind of special to me. Even if it wasn't to you."

Black's eyes glittered and he leaned forward, close enough for her to smell his hay and leather scent. "It was—is—special to me. I said life-mates were rare. Not impossible. And when a bond does happen, there is no going back."

Renee swallowed, lost in the depths of his gaze. It was like an electric field bound them together as they stared at each other. She wanted to love him more than anything in the world at that moment in time. "What are you saying?"

"I'm saying I've never shared myself with anyone like I've shared myself with you. When you saw me in my centaur form, I was terrified, but now I'm glad you did. It's a relief. I don't have to hide from you. I finally have someone I can trust."

"You trust me?" Her voice came out as a squeak.

Black reached into the cab and slid his hand around the

back of her head, his thumb caressing the cup of her ear. "I showed you my shift. If that's not trust, I don't know what is. Plus you're fun to do naughty things to."

She flushed, the butterflies in her stomach sending a giggle up her throat. "But what about life-mates and all that?"

His teasing smile grew serious. He leaned in to brush his lips against hers, and his breath was warm and sweet. "This centaur's found his."

～

*B*lack hung a new IV from the barn rafter above Ivy-Jane, feeling the weight of Lori's gaze on his back. The foal lay with three legs curled beneath her, the fourth, wrapped in a bandage, stuck out straight in front of her. The sprain would be fine in a few days if he could keep her off her feet. But right now the foal was the least of his worries.

Renee had returned to the house, needing rest after all she'd learned, and he was glad she wasn't around to overhear Lori's hateful words. Black turned to face the herd leader, her heeled boots bringing her to eye level. Saul sat on a nearby straw bale his face an emotionless mask.

"The deal was I'd marry her. " Black clenched his fists to keep his anger under control. "And I will. Just give me more than two days to do it, for Christ's sake."

He wanted nothing more than to build a life with Renee. She said she needed time to think, and he could give her that. After all, she'd been hit with a lot of new information in a short period of time. Hell, so had he. Being with her had made him reconsider his life goals. He didn't need rank in the herd anymore, as long as he could have Renee. The relief he'd felt showing her his shift had almost been as satisfying as the ecstasy he'd felt buried in her pussy. Almost. The idea of having a life-mate, having someone he didn't have to hide from or pretend to be someone else around, made his blood sing. For the first time since discovering he'd never be able to fully shift, he felt alive. If it took him an entire lifetime, he'd use it to make Renee his.

"It's too late for that." Lori stood wide, hands on hips.

He blinked, coming back to reality. "She's not going to expose us."

"Oh, after two sweaty interludes you know her so well?" Lori cocked one manicured eyebrow.

Black glared at the barn wall where he pictured Millie on the other side, skulking like a little rat. The mare had obviously told Lori about this morning. "I do—"

"She's here to sell the place," Lori interrupted. "She told me so the first day she arrived."

Refusing to back down, Black stalked past her and Saul toward the cubbies where spare boots and clothes were kept. "She might've intended to sell when she first got here, but I bet she doesn't now."

"That girl is out for money. I've seen her kind before. If she doesn't sell the place, she'll certainly exploit us."

"Just because you would, doesn't mean Renee will." He could trust Renee—the herd could trust her—just as his grandma had trusted Toliman.

"We're out of time, soldier. And protecting the herd is paramount. We've got enough witnesses to forge the marriage documents." Lori's voice dropped to a threatening purr. "And once we get her to sign them, we'll take her out for one last ride."

Shock froze Black in place. Lori hadn't said it directly, but the meaning was clear. The words reminded him of the way she'd pretended to grieve her predecessor's death. *Gloryanna died giving her human one last ride.* Lori was proposing murder. The murder of his mate. Slowly, Black turned to face the herd leader, mind still trying to accept the truth.

Saul rose ponderously, shaking his head. "Her family will protest. We'd likely lose the ranch in probate."

Lori rolled her eyes. "The only family she has left is her religious-fanatic father, and he thinks this place is cursed. Believe me, I've thought this through."

Saul scrubbed both hands through his wild, black hair. "Killing her seems a little extreme."

"No one's killing anyone." Black's voice was a low growl, as if his animal nature was more bear-like than equine.

"Keep your voice down," Lori warned. "It's the perfect plan. And I don't care which one of you is the groom. I just need an extra witness signature on the papers. Saul, you on board?"

Saul hesitated a moment, then asked, "Millie and Su are in agreement?"

Black stiffened. "You can't be considering this?"

Saul refused to meet his gaze. "She's just a human."

"She's not just a human. She's my mate. And she's Toliman's granddaughter," Black gestured toward the direction of the house. "Is this how you repay him for years of protecting the herd? By murdering his only grandchild and stealing his ranch?"

At least Saul had the grace to blush. Lori stepped between Black and his uncle, shimmering as if on the verge of a shift. "Don't be stupid. Humans can't be mates. The herd comes first. I should've known better than to expect you to understand that."

Her words stung like the lash of a whip. But Black'd had enough. Shifter magic tingled across his skin. "I look out for this herd just as much or more than you do. My grandmother was Lead Mare, and one thing I know is Renee is my life-mate. I'm calling a herd meeting."

She scowled. "You can't call a herd meeting. You barely even have rank."

Saul's gaze shifted between Lori and Black. "Any shifter can call a herd meeting."

"Like they'll listen to a centaur." She snorted derisively. "Besides, it's almost daylight. You might be seen."

The tingle subsided as Black realized she was right. He couldn't go out as a centaur.

Crackling tires on gravel cut short the conversation. Lori bared her teeth. "Fuck. She said she had a realtor coming today. We need to get rid of him."

She spun toward the door and stalked out. Black and Saul followed close behind. In the heavy sunshine, a shiny new Dodge Ram with a Wright Minerals Co. logo on the door was rolling to a stop in front of the house, heat waves warping the air over its hood.

Lori slowed her pace, and Black spared her a glance as he passed her. Usually she insisted on being the face of the ranch, but maybe she was too angry and flustered to deal with it right now.

The engine silenced, and a man slid from the cab, adjusting a black Stetson over his balding head. He gave Black a thousand-watt smile. "Afternoon. I'm looking for Lori Sandvur."

"Lori?" Black glanced at her, confused.

Lori had her hands on her hips, glowering. "You're not supposed to be here until next week."

"I'm in the area and thought I'd take a quick look," the guy said.

She stepped forward, stopping abreast of Black. "Turn around and leave. Now."

The man held his palms up, looking from Lori to Black to Saul. Uncle Saul just stood there, thumbs in the loops of his jeans. Black narrowed his eyes at Lori. Why'd she contacted a mining company?

"I apologize, ma'am." The man backed to his truck. "I'll be in contact next week."

Quick as an arrow, Black was at the truck door, hand flat against the window frame to keep it closed. He wanted this story straight from the source, not Lori's convoluted version. "Why don't you tell us what you'll be in contact about?"

Scratching the back of his neck, the man glanced at Lori, then back to Black. "Ms. Sandvur sent in a rock sample several months back. Seems there's gold on the property, and she has some questions about getting it out of the ground."

Black dropped his hand and spun toward the lead mare. Gold? When had that happened? News of gold would bring a lot of attention to the ranch. Human attention. What was the lead mare thinking? Behind her, Saul's mouth hung open.

Lori crossed her arms and settled her weight on one leg, gaze still on the visitor. "I told you to leave, mister."

The guy shook his head and jerked open the truck door. "Next time I'm bringing backup," he muttered as he slammed the door shut. The engine rumbled to life and the man gunned the truck into reverse down the driveway.

Black let him go. The man wasn't the issue. In silence, he watched the truck round the base of the hill before speaking again. This time he turned to Saul. "You said the buried treasure was the herd."

Saul shook his head. "It was. At least as far as I

understood." He moved up to stand next to Lori, his brows drawn into a frown. "What's this about gold?"

Lori shot a look toward the house and spun, boots crunching over the gravel as she bee-lined toward the barn. "The ranch can't sustain itself without income. I'm trying to see to the herd's future."

"Wait, there really is gold?" Black lengthened his stride to keep up, a twitch irritating his left eye. Why hadn't Lori mentioned the find before?

Inside the barn, Lori entered the nearest stall. She spun to face the men, her voice a whisper. "In the canyon where Toliman died."

"Did he know about it?" Black didn't bother to keep quiet.

She bared her teeth at him and focused on Saul, as if Black didn't matter. "The gold will give us freedom like the herd's never known, not since before the settlers fenced everything off. Once we've secured the land deed—"

The soft tread of feet outside was followed by, "Black?"

Lori hissed, her fingernails biting into his arm. "Don't you dare say a thing, Black."

"It's her land. Her gold." He jerked free, Lori's nails leaving long welts on his skin. Turning, he strode toward the bay door.

Within three steps, he felt the air behind him swirl and condense with shifter magic. Lori's pale palomino form bowled past him, knocking him to the side. He tripped over a stall rake leaning against the wall, the handle tangling his legs.

He fell to his hands and knees, palms jarring against the gravel. Saul's bulky equine shape followed close behind Lori, disappearing out the barn door.

Black struggled to his feet, his shift grabbing hold of every muscle in his body, straining the seams of his clothing and boots as he shouted, "Renee, look out!"

12

A sleek blonde palomino careened out of the barn toward Renee, a terrifying scream issuing from between its bared teeth. Startled, Renee fell backward, landing with a painful thump on her backside. Head lowered, the horse churned up bits of gravel, charging straight at her. Renee rolled, flinging herself out of the way. Hooves streaked within a hair's breadth of her shoulder. The beast's momentum slowed as it rounded the driveway. It then faced her again, ears pinned, and reared.

A bolt of fear ricocheted through Renee's blood. *Is it angry at me?*

Before she could react, a familiar charcoal-gray stallion barreled out the door. *Uncle Saul?* Renee clambered to her feet, palms stinging from the gravel. The stallion drew up facing the mare, neck arched and teeth bared. *Were they fighting? What was going on?*

Yet another form exited the barn. Renee let out a breath of relief to see Black's centaur shape gleaming magnificently in the sun, bare torso rippling with muscle. He pounded toward Renee, and she backed up a step, uncertain. Thrusting a hand toward her, he commanded, "Get on."

The seriousness of his gaze gave her strength, and she gripped his hand. He lifted her with a powerful flex of his arm, settling her into the curve where horse met man.

"Hold tight," he said, and spun toward the fence gate.

"Is that Lori?" Renee wrapped her arms around his chest, glancing at the gaping barn door in case any more rabid horses decided to emerge.

"Yes," he gritted between clenched teeth, freeing the gate latch.

Glancing over her shoulder, Renee sucked in a breath as the palomino reared back, front hooves churning the air. The stallion reared in return. They clashed, teeth gnashing and front legs flailing.

Black lurched forward, and Renee was forced to face front again, wrapping both arms tightly around his ribcage. *I'm riding a centaur. Again.* The thought would have made her giddy if she wasn't already dizzy with confusion. Pressing her cheek to his shoulder blade, she squeezed her knees around his withers to hold herself steady. Within moments, he was at a canter, headed for the road toward town, and Renee found herself easily adjusting to the rhythm of his gait. The combination of man and beast felt so natural, she closed her eyes, enjoying the passing air, the feel of his muscles flexing beneath her, the warm scent of his skin.

Her brief dip into sensuality was broken by pounding hooves approaching on the left. Her eyes popped open to see the palomino giving chase. Even more horrifying, the beast's pale muzzle was flecked with blood.

"Black!" Renee cried.

Leaning forward, Black increased speed, but the palomino continued to gain. The mare reached his hind quarters, neck stretching forward and lips drawn back in almost predatory ferocity. Renee could swear the horse's eyes glowed with demonic light.

At that moment, Black grabbed painfully tight to Renee's thighs, and it felt like his hind legs went out from under him. Turning sharply, he skidded to a stop.

Too terrified to even scream, Renee hung on for dear life.

The palomino overshot them, hooves scrambling against the parched grass. Black looked over his shoulder into Renee's eyes. "You okay?"

She nodded, her voice still caught in her throat.

"This might get ugly. Whatever happens, get as far away from Lori as you can, okay?"

Renee watched the mare paw the ground. Lori was

horrible in human form. As a horse, she seemed possessed. "What's wrong with her?"

Black shook his head, dancing sideways as the mare stalked toward them with her neck arched menacingly. Renee locked her hands around his chest as he angled his upper body to shield her from the mare. Lori tossed her head, white mane flaring wildly. Then she lunged, that awful sound screeching from her throat.

Black grasped Renee's thighs like before and reared, pummeling Lori with his front hooves.

Clinging to him for dear life, Renee pressed her cheek flat against his shoulder blade, heartbeat racing ahead of her breathing. With every ounce of strength, she squeezed her knees to keep her seat. Black's muscles rippled and flexed between her legs, and she felt herself sliding loose in spite of his added grip on her thighs.

The mare backed away, and Black dropped back to all fours with a jarring thud. Renee wriggled to regain her seat.

Then the mare twisted, ninja fast, lashing out with her back legs.

Black dodged right.

Deadly hooves cut the air where Renee's thigh had been.

With lightning speed, Lori sprang forward again, sending Black into a backward leap. Renee wobbled precariously. Black threw a hand back to steady her, and Lori took advantage of the distraction, lunging again.

This time, teeth bit into Renee's leg just above the knee.

Renee cried out in pain, muscle bruised against bone. The next thing she knew, her grip tore free of Black's chest and she was flying through the air. She landed hard on the dirt, her left shoulder taking the brunt of the impact.

Dust-choked air burning her lungs, she rolled to her knees. The ground shook with beating hooves while Lori and Black continued their battle. Black kept himself between Renee and the mare, but Lori was ferocious, biting and kicking until blood streaked Black's bare chest and arms.

Another twisting kick caught Black's cheek. He reeled, hooves stuttering unevenly across the ground. Lori broke away, and a horrific realization struck Renee. This fight wasn't between herd members. It wasn't about Lori and Black. *He's protecting* me.

Renee hopped sideways, trying to get away. Her bitten knee throbbed. Her left arm tingled from her fall. She couldn't get away, but she could fight back. Searching the ground, she located a stone the size of a softball. She hurled it at the oncoming mare as hard as she could.

The palomino shied away, bucking her hind legs as if to kick the stone from the air. In one fluid movement, she rounded on Renee again, whites of her eyes gleaming. Both front hooves pawed the air.

Black threw himself into Lori's path. "Run, Renee!"

Renee limped back another step while the mare snapped her teeth. Black caught the bite with his forearm, shoving the palomino's bulk backward. His front hooves slashed the palomino's chest, drawing bloody grooves into her pale hide.

Renee scoured the ground for another rock. No way was she leaving Black to fight this bitch alone. The pasture here was frustratingly clear of stones. Several yards to her left, a handful of horses had appeared. They stood watching curiously, tails swishing the dusty air. Were they shifters? Why were they just standing around?

Black threw his arms around the palomino's throat. His biceps bulged as their horse bodies scrambled for dominance. Lori managed a well-aimed kick against his hind leg and he went down, dragging her head along with him. The mare's neck muscles stood out as she tried bucking off his added weight.

A chocolate brown horse in the nearby herd tossed its head and whinnied, looking at the nearby lane. The other horses nickered and looked that direction. A second later Renee heard it, too—the thrum of an approaching engine. *Oh, God, the realtor.* She'd never canceled the appointment.

A small white sedan appeared around the hill, moving slowly toward the house. It disappeared at a low spot in the road, but within seconds it would appear again, in full view of the fight.

"Black!" Renee cried. "A car's coming!"

He'd wrestled Lori to the ground and knelt with both forelegs against her neck, his hands on her head. He couldn't hear her.

TAMSIN LEY

She had to stop that car. Lurching toward the fence, she shimmied between the rails. Maybe she could stop the realtor before he saw anything. Block his view. Distract him. Anything. After a few steps, her injured knee gave out. She landed with both palms on the gravel, fire lancing through her wrists. Refusing to stop, she scrambled upright and limped down the gravel lane.

The car skidded to a stop amidst clouds of dust. Through the windshield, Renee watched the young man's mouth form a perfect circle, his gaze focused past her on Black and Lori. *Shit shit shit!* She reached the car door, and the realtor rolled the window down a crack. His voice tremored. "Is everything all right?"

Shooting a glance toward the fight, Renee was surprised to see six or eight naked people in a circle around Black. He knelt on the mare's neck in human form. "Uh," she said, unsure how to respond. Like a lightbulb, her father's accusations about dark rituals and voodoo came to her. She smiled and leaned toward the window. "It's a spiritual ceremony. Religious. Everything's fine."

"Oh." The realtor cleared his throat, his gaze flicking down to Renee's bleeding hands. "How about I come back later?"

Renee shook her head, closing her fingers over the stinging wounds. "I've changed my mind about selling the place. Sorry you drove all the way out here."

240

The man nodded, already shifting into reverse. "Not a problem. Really. I'm... you... have a great day."

She stood up, allowing the man to escape the unnaturally still scene outside. He gunned the accelerator all the way back down the driveway. Once the car had disappeared around the hill, she returned her attention to the herd of people assembled around Black. This was her ranch, and she was done being pushed around.

13

*B*lack gulped air, kneeling with his full weight on Lori's carotid artery. Renee's voice only reached him through a fog. His full attention remained on the twitching horse. He'd made it into human form in time to avoid being seen, but without his centaur's weight bearing her down, Lori would regain control any moment. Sure enough, she rolled, forcing him to scramble away from her crushing weight.

The car's retreating engine hadn't yet reached the road as Lori regained her feet, eyes rolling with fury. Immediately she reared, razor sharp hooves churning the air. Although Renee was on the other side of the fence, Lori could clear that in mere steps.

Fuck this, Black thought. He no longer cared if he was seen. No longer cared if the herd saw him shift. His life-mate was in danger. Still in human form, he charged, tightening the shifter magic into a ball inside him then letting it flash outward in an explosion of change.

He reached the fence in centaur form at almost the same moment as Lori, his full weight tackling her off balance. Her front legs cleared the rail, but her back legs hit hard, knocking the wood beam loose. She and the rail tumbled head over feet into the gravel, raising a choking cloud of dust.

Renee had retreated to the other side of the lane and now stood with her back pressed to the fence on that side.

Black cleared the damaged fence, shooting past Lori and skidding to a halt between his mate and the mare.

Lori writhed in the gravel, her high-pitched screeching putting his teeth on edge. Glinting white bone poked like a spear from her right hind leg. Black's vet instincts reared up, but he resisted the urge to help. If this was what it took to stop Lori, so be it. A break that bad would likely cripple her for life, since pins and other hardware used to fix broken limbs didn't play well with shifter physiology.

The rest of the herd, still in human form, ducked through the fence and approached, gazes flickering between Black and their lead mare.

All Black could think about was getting Renee out of here, to safety, even if that meant parading his centaur form straight into town. He knelt on the gravel next to Renee. "Can you ride?"

She crossed her arms. "I could. But I won't. This is my ranch, and I'm not being chased off." Putting a hand on his wither, she nudged him aside and stepped out to face the oncoming shifters. "As the new owner of this ranch, I call a herd meeting."

Black watched her in astonishment, a proud smile tugging the corners of his lips. The shifters slowed, standing in a line on the opposite side of their lead mare. Lori's shrieking stopped, and her golden body shimmered and shrank, hooves becoming feet and hands, mane transforming into mussed blonde hair. Bone still poked from her bloody shin, and her face was a rictus of pain. Through gritted teeth, she yelled, "This human can't call a herd meeting."

More shifters arrived, still in horse form. The ones in human form murmured among themselves as the newcomers shifted. This was a good sign. For once they weren't obeying Lori on pure fear and instinct. Black squared his shoulders. What he was about to do was more nerve wracking than showing Renee his shift. "Renee's my life-mate. I demand the protection of the herd."

The word "life-mate" whispered through the crowd. Black watched Renee out of the corner of his eye, unsure what her reaction might be to this announcement. She gawked at him, a huge question behind her eyes. But he didn't have time to get down on one knee and ask if she felt the same.

Lori had bared her teeth, lips quivering. "She's a danger to the herd."

Renee placed her hands on her hips, her stance wide and assured. "I'm not the one who started this fight. And I'd appreciate someone telling me what the hell is going on." She looked up at Black. "Why's she trying to kill me?"

He glared at Lori as he answered. "The treasure in your grandfather's will is real."

"I thought you said the treasure was the horses?" Renee waved at the surrounding crowd of shifters. "And by that, I assume you meant the shifter herd."

"I did. And I think your grandfather thought they were, too." He curled his lip in disgust at Lori. "But apparently Lori found gold in the canyon."

Renee's eyes widened. "Really? I'm... I still don't understand, though. Why attack me?"

Black's eyes were drawn to Renee's blood-flecked pant-leg, and his pulse thundered again. He shifted to human form and knelt beside her. "Let me look at that. Are you all right?"

"Unless she has rabies or something, I'll be fine." Renee batted at his hand. "Tell me why she wants me dead."

Black refused to let go of her leg, examining the wound. Let Lori try to defend herself. "Care to share your plans with the herd, Lori?"

The blonde curled her lips in a feral snarl. Even though Lori couldn't possibly stand on a broken leg and attack, a few of the nearby onlookers backed away a step. "You can't trust a human."

Millie ducked her head from between two of the men and raised her hand. She didn't say anything, just stood there with her hand up. Black narrowed his eyes, uncertain about her sudden boldness. But she wasn't looking at Black. She was looking at Renee.

"What's your name?" Renee asked.

"Millie," the woman rasped.

"Ivy-Jane's mother?" Renee glanced at Black, who nodded.

Satisfied Renee's wound wasn't critical, he rose and asked, "Millie, what do you know about this?"

"Lori murdered Toliman and Gloryanna." Millie ducked back between the men as if expecting a blow.

A collective gasp rose among the group. Lori glowered but said nothing.

Black's blood turned cold. *Murdered?* The air had become too thick to breathe. He'd always suspected foul play, but by one of his own herd-mates? Poor Grandma probably never saw anything coming. His throat tightened. "Why?"

Lori snarled. "I'm the one who found the gold. I begged Toliman to have the ore tested. He just wanted to let it sit there while we slaved away keeping his precious ranch running. I would have used the money for the herd. We'd never worry about our security again."

"So you killed him?" Renee's voice came out an octave too high. "How did you think killing him—killing me—would make the gold yours?"

An evil look entered Lori's eyes. "Ask your so-called life-mate." She smirked at Black. "You don't have to play the part anymore, Black. The cat's out of the bag."

Black glowered at Lori, nostrils flaring, heart thumping hard against his ribs. Of course she'd try to get in one final blow.

"What's she talking about?" Renee asked.

Lori's voice dripped saccharine-laced poison. "Black was going to convince you to marry him, sweetie."

The full weight of what he stood to lose by telling Renee the truth slammed into him. A life-mate was a rare gift, one not many shifters found. But he couldn't lie to her, even if it meant losing her forever. Renee's eyes glittered with pain, but he pressed on. "When you first arrived, I agreed to marry you in return for a rank in the herd."

"You'll never have that now." Lori interjected. "You know that, don't you?"

Black ignored her, his eyes only for Renee, pleading for her to understand. "The plan wasn't to hurt you. Only to keep you from selling the ranch. And you're so beautiful, it was easy to pursue you. But then you saw me. You saw my... monster." The words felt thick in Black's throat, but he kept on. "And you accepted me."

"You're not a monster," Renee said softly.

He grit his teeth, refusing to look away from Renee's trusting gaze. *A monster like you doesn't deserve a life-mate.* "I am a monster. I agreed to Lori's initial plan to steal your inheritance. I think she planned to kill you all along, but I refused to see it."

"But you defended me." Renee shook her head. "And

we're not married. How would killing me now make the ranch Lori's?"

"She was going to forge the marriage papers and claim the ranch in probate. When I found out, I refused." The plan still made Black sick to his stomach. He didn't mention that Saul had considered the deal. After all, his uncle had thrown himself at Lori and given Black time to grab Renee and try to escape. Black still didn't know what had made his uncle change his mind, but he would be forever grateful.

Lori curled her lips. "I'm the only one strong enough to do what's best for the herd."

Renee's mouth became a thin, pale line, and in spite of her diminutive height, she seemed to stand ten feet tall. "Best for the herd? You have no idea what that even means." She looked at Black, eyes burning with dark fire, then swiveled to address the crowd. "I don't know most of you, but I'm going to assume you're good people. Black's people. This woman murdered my grandfather and Black's grandmother—your previous leader. What's the herd punishment for murderers?"

To Black's surprise, the shifters dipped their heads in respect. He had to admit, the commanding force radiating off Renee at the moment rivaled that of his grandmother. *Grandma.* Lori had killed her. His veins felt sluggish with ice, reliving the loss.

One of the bachelors spoke up. "Banishment is customary."

"Banishment?" Renee drew up straighter and crossed her

arms. "So she can find another herd to terrorize? I don't think so."

Black wanted to string Lori from the nearest tree, but that punishment would be better than she deserved. She'd murdered two people. Terrorized the herd. And tried to kill his life mate. He wanted a punishment that would make her suffer. He glanced at her shattered leg and realized she'd already done that to herself. "Her days of running with a herd are over."

Lori's face paled to a chalky white. She stared at her leg as if only now realizing the break was real.

"Because of her leg?" asked Renee. "Can't she just have surgery?"

"She could." Black knelt next to Lori, his vet instincts breaking through his anger. The break looked even worse up close. "But the bolts and other hardware used to fix it would detach the first time she tried to shift. She'd be worse off than she is now. And without surgery, she'll be crippled for life. In both forms." Black kept his gaze on Lori, trying to find satisfaction at the thought of her crippled. It wasn't enough, but it would have to do.

Renee's eyes brimmed with tears, but the hard lines on her face told him she was angry, not feeling empathy. "I don't know if that's enough. But this isn't only about me." She spoke with that same note of authority she'd used when she'd asked about punishment earlier. She looked at the people around her, making Black take notice of them, too. Bachelors.

Elders. Mothers. Teens. His herd. She said, "You lost someone, too. And it sounds like there's still a choice to be made. Does she have surgery or not? How does the herd vote?"

"Wait!" Lori begged the watching shifters. "My plan could still work. There's no one here but us. Just say the word—"

A bachelor walked past Lori without sparing her a glance and placed a hand gently on Renee's shoulder. Then he turned to face the watching shifters. A gray-haired elder stepped closer and took Renee's hand. Slowly, the entire herd moved to surround Renee and Black in the kind of acceptance only a herd could give.

Pride blossomed in Black's chest. They were affirming his life-mate. Not even Old Man Toliman had received this kind of acceptance. He'd been respected, and the herd loved him, but he'd always been an outsider. A benefactor, not a peer. Renee had just become both.

An elder woman raised her voice. "She doesn't deserve an equine form. I say surgery."

"Take her to the human hospital."

"Put in pins."

"You can't!" Lori screamed as two bachelors stepped forward, grabbing her by the arms. "They won't operate without my consent!"

One of the men shook his head. "Not if you arrive unconscious."

Her face creased into ugly lines. "I'm your lead mare! I was only looking out for you!"

The men dragged a screaming Lori from the pasture. They'd handle her from here, and Black was relieved to be free of the duty. Most of the shifters followed in human form. Others shimmered to horse form and departed toward the pasture.

Black only had eyes for Renee. He rubbed a hand over his hair, missing the comfortable weight of his cowboy hat. "How's your leg? I can carry you home if you don't mind riding bareback."

She looked at him through her lashes. "Mmm. Riding a cowboy bareback. I like it."

He chuckled, pleased to see his flirty little filly back. Kneeling next to her, he helped steady her as she lifted her injured leg over his flanks. Once she was settled in place, he rose. Her warmth settled against his spine, and her legs wrapped his withers with a comforting pressure he'd never expected to feel with a rider. Shifters talked about how humiliating it was to carry a human, how uncomfortable and heavy. But he rather liked how close it drew Renee against him. She wrapped her arms around his chest and settled her cheek against his shoulder with a sigh, her breath wafting across his bare skin.

He eased into a level trot, heading toward the ranch. Her knees tightened around him, ignoring the pain from the bite. "I want to feel the wind. Will you run for me?"

His blood thrilled at the words. "Are you sure?"

Her cheek nodded yes against his back. "I love you like this."

He bunched his hind quarters and took off at a canter. Renee clung tightly to him, her body moving with his, melding against his, in an act as intimate as sex.

They passed Lori, who spat obscenities at them, but Black kept going. Renee cried, "Faster!"

"Don't let go!" He yelled back.

"Never!"

He veered left, skirting the fence, and kicked it up to a gallop. Her thighs pressed his flanks, her breath hot on his shoulder. He'd never felt so free. So alive. He let out a whoop of joy, echoed by her laughter behind him. Taking a wide arc, he headed back to the house at a trot. If he never had anything else in this world, he had this moment, this inkling of belonging to someone, and he'd nurture the feeling the rest of his life.

14

*R*enee played her fingers across Black's chest, traced her lips over the line of his shoulder as he trotted over the darkened pasture. Crickets sang their nightly serenade from among the rocks where they'd first made love. She delighted in his sweet hay scent and this land.

Her land. Her ranch. The idea was still so new, she sometimes woke thinking she must've dreamed the whole thing. She'd been here over a week, overseeing everything from daily stall-mucking to a secret shifter meeting beneath a midnight moon. So much of her dad's misconceptions about her grandfather made sense now. Maybe she should reach out to him now that she was settling down…

Black reached back and brushed a hand up her leg. "You okay?"

He somehow knew what she was thinking and feeling

almost as soon as she did these days. She didn't understand how he could know her so well in such a short time, but she knew she was happy here with him. Whole.

"I'm good," she said, rubbing her cheek against his back. Whatever was going on inside her, she hadn't figured out how to talk about it yet.

He seemed to know that, too, and continued on, his hooves thudding softly against the earth, steady as a heartbeat. Renee realized that what had been dancing around in her mind had nothing to do with her father, her mother, or even her grandfather. What she needed to talk about was right here on the ranch. Right here in her arms. *Life-mate.* They hadn't talked about it since he first told the herd. As though he knew it scared her more than any thrill-seeking she'd done with Steph.

But now she was ready to jump.

Taking a breath, she tightened her arms around Black's ribcage. "Will you marry me? For real?"

Another corny line, she realized, too late to take it back.

Black stopped and craned his neck to look at her, his lips crooked in a sideways smile. "You're not just playing me, are you?"

She grinned impishly. He really did understand her. "I've never been very good at pick up lines, so I figured I'd cut to the chase. Besides, you did call me your life-mate, right?"

His face turned solemn. With one deft move, he lifted her from his back and set her gently to the ground before shimmering back to human form. "You are my life-mate, Renee. I love you. I have nothing to offer you but myself and a promise of undying adoration and protection. But if you'll be my bride, I pledge myself to you freely and fully, until death steals my last breath."

Renee took a step closer. "I don't know how you did it, but you changed me." She swallowed. "I love you, Black."

He looked down into her eyes. "You changed me, too."

Sliding one hand around her neck, he cupped her head and drew her into a kiss. She linked her hands around his waist and pressed her heartbeat next to his. She'd finally found the one thrill she was willing to die for. And the only one she wanted to repeat every day for the rest of her life.

I hope you enjoyed visiting Montana with Renee! Next up is a seductive djinn who promises pleasure. Turn the page and keep reading!

THE DJINN'S DESIRE

A STEAMY FANTASY ROMANCE

THE DJINN'S DESIRE

Can she make her wish come true? Or will evil get the better of her?

Tanika must keep her djinn from killing again. How? By refusing to complete the wish she made as a child, a wish for a loving mate and happy family. As long as that spell is incomplete, the demon can't move on to claim another soul.

Enter Ophir, a sultry man who promises to sweep her off her feet. She wants to resist, but she craves his kisses. Needs his touch. Yearns for his embrace. A little taste of pleasure doesn't mean she's committing to a future, right?

But Ophir has a secret she never expected, and Tanika finds herself on the wrong side of a magic she didn't know she possessed. Not only is her heart on the line, but the very thing that makes her human - her soul.

anika Skye jiggled the lock on the accordion grate protecting the salon and gave it a good hard kick before the bolts slid free. Using her full weight, she shoved the screen aside. On the cracked plate-glass door, the Seance Salon's logo had been hand-painted in bright pink letters around a rendering of a gold crystal ball with a comb and pair of scissors. The remaining glass on both the door and the large window had been painted black to hide the interior from prying eyes.

She picked up her basket of towels and entered the dusky shop, a small bell above the door frame jingling. The overheads flickered on with an annoying electric buzz, revealing two beat-up hairdresser chairs and their accompanying plate mirrors, a pair of folding chairs next to a magazine rack for waiting customers—which she never had—

and a small area at the back surrounded by a threadbare velvet curtain where she did psychic readings. The scent of permanent-wave solution cloyed the air, directing Tanika's gaze to the hair sink; Birdie had once again neglected to wash the hair-rollers from her last client.

Or the water'd been shut off. Either was possible.

Much as Tanika loved this place, sometimes she wondered exactly what she was proving by keeping it open. Dropping her basket of clean towels into Birdie's station chair, she moved to the sink and turned the faucet to hot. To her relief, a solid stream of water emerged. She checked the black-cat wall clock Birdie had bought on a whim, saying it fit to have a witchy bit of decoration in the salon. Seven-fifty a.m. If she hurried, she could get the rollers cleaned before her first reading this morning and air out the stink. The chemicals didn't mix well with the scented candles she used during her readings.

The soft jingle of the store's bell drew her attention, and she turned, hoping for a walk-in. No one was there. She pressed her lips together and returned to washing the rollers. Sometimes if she ignored his antics, he went away. The water she was running sputtered and turned icy. *Dammit.* Cringing, she kept washing.

Then the lights went out.

With a sigh, she settled back and glared at the dark wall in front of her. "Fucking poltergeist."

In response, the lights flickered back on. The nearby velvet curtain rippled, and a scrawny, bare-chested man stepped through it. Not around it. Through it. His voice sounded just as emaciated as his body. "I told you not to call me that."

She dumped the curlers into a strainer and turned to face him. "Then stop fucking acting like one."

He tilted his head, the craggy lines on his face attempting a pleasant smile. "You know how to get rid of me."

"Nope. I keep telling you. You die with me." She'd been saying this so many years, the words no longer even gave her a twinge of regret.

His visage turned into a snarl, purple djinn magic sparking in his eyes. "What do you care what happens to me? Your wish has already been paid for. Just embrace it and live out your happy little mortal existence while you still have time."

Tanika's stomach churned, just as it did during each of these interactions for the previous fourteen years. In truth, she wanted to do exactly what he suggested. Create a stable home with a family to love. A little girl's dream. One she'd eschew forever if it meant the demon—he called himself a djinn, but to her he'd always be a demon—living in her mother's locket could never terrorize anyone again. She turned away from him, busying herself refilling the shampoo. He usually went away if she ignored him long enough.

He glided to a stop directly in front of her, his amorphous lower body bisected by the rim of the sink. "How about I swap it out for a new wish?"

She shook her head, refusing to look at him.

He slid closer and leered in her face. "You're going to lose the salon."

Her upset stomach tightened into a rock, hating that he was right. Every time she tried to settle into one spot and build a life, something went wrong, and she was certain her demon had a hand in it, much as he denied it. She'd grow comfortable, make a few friends, then somehow everything would get ripped out from under her. If she wasn't going to embrace the fulfillment of her wish, he'd take away anything that might pass as a surrogate.

Most recently, her landlord had raised the rent on her crappy little lease, hoping to edge her out and demolish the aging building to make way for a new hotel. She and a handful of fellow tenants were putting up a good fight, but it wasn't a battle she was likely to win. And finding a lease she could afford elsewhere in town would be next to impossible.

The bell tinkled, this time for real, and the apparition of her demon popped out of existence. "I'll be right with you!" Tanika called, drying her hands on a nearby towel.

Instead of her first client, Mr. Daniels stood at the door, his white apron smudged with what looked like chocolate. "I brought you an éclair, Tanika. Before they're all gone."

"Oh, Mr. Daniels, you didn't have to do that." Her hips were curvy enough without his constant feeding. Not that she was going to say no to a chocolate éclair.

"It's nothing." The white-haired old man took her hand

and placed the cream-filled delight in her palm. "I still owe you for cleansing my place of that pesky spirit."

Heat crept up Tanika's throat. The pesky spirit had been her demon, and once she'd figured out he was making trouble after hours, she'd moved her mother's locket off-site to a safe deposit box. Now the djinn could only materialize through the connection of her unspent wish, keeping his power limited to her direct physical vicinity. "You don't owe me anything, Mr. Daniels."

"I tell all my customers about you." He looked around at the shabby interior. "I don't know why you and Birdie can't get more business."

She shrugged. "Not many people believe in magic. Why do you think I'm cutting hair on the side?"

"You don't read the bumps on people's heads?"

Phrenology? Damn. Why hadn't she thought of that? She'd need to add it to her list of services. "Uh, yes. Yes, I do."

He glanced at her wall clock. "I'd better get back to the cafe, my dear. Have a good morning."

Although it was barely after eight a.m., Tanika plopped down in her hairdresser chair and took a big bite of éclair. With no telling what the future might bring, she was going to enjoy every moment of what she had right now.

2

*O*phir laughed as his convertible took the corner with a squeal of rubber. These modern human inventions almost made living on Earth bearable. Almost.

He pulled into a parallel parking spot along the row of run-down storefronts. Whenever he came to a new town, he liked to hit the oldest neighborhoods first, searching out the antique shops for any sign of his kin. Over the centuries, he'd caught whiffs of portals, but always arrived too late to pinpoint the source. After so many failures, his search had become more of a habit than an intent.

Getting out of the car, he paused on the sidewalk, trying to decide which persona to adopt for this mid-America Main Street kind of town. Although he couldn't change his six-foot-three height, bone structure, or skin color, he'd become quite adept at altering his clothing, posture, and voice to affect anything from geeky college student to wealthy billionaire. Today he decided to choose the latter, but in a low-key sort of way, magically fitting himself with a pair of Givenchy jeans and an untucked button down shirt.

The door of the dive cafe he'd parked next to swung open, letting out a waft of fresh baked goods along with a young woman carrying a white paper bag. He smiled at her and she drew up short, her mouth hanging open. He was quite used to this reaction from women, especially in this persona. "This place any good?" he asked.

"Yes," the woman said in a breathy voice.

"Thanks." He winked and moved past her to the door. He'd developed a fondness for sweets, discovering that an infusion of sugary carbs staved off the weakness he experienced being away from his home dimension. If he carb-loaded, he could sometimes even manage the more exhausting spells without being laid out for days afterward. The energy burst was nothing compared to the energy a djinn acquired upon harvesting a soul, but carbs were easier to acquire.

Inside, the cafe's cheery interior surprised him. Buttery yellow walls with white trim made the place seem larger around the three small wood tables. A hand-written sign at the door said WELCOME, PLEASE ORDER AT THE COUNTER. At the back, a large glass case displayed rows upon rows of freshly-baked cookies, breads, and pastries.

Moving past the tables, he stood behind a man in a charcoal-gray suit placing his order. At the register, an old man in a white apron greeted the customer by name and quickly took his order, handing him a cup of coffee to sip while he waited for his food. Ophir stepped up to the counter, eyeing the sumptuous desserts in the case. "What do you recommend?"

The old man's eyes were red-rimmed and tired, but he smiled and pointed to a chocolate-glazed eclair. "I only make these once a week, and they go fast. If you're in the mood for something to stick to your ribs, we're offering free-range turkey club sandwiches today."

"I'll take three eclairs," Ophir dug into his pocket and pulled out his wallet. "And what the heck, a sandwich, too."

"Something to drink?"

"Coffee with ten sugars."

Raising his brows, the old man produced the coffee plus a white bag with the eclairs. "There's sugar over there." He pointed to a small ledge near the exit that held a tall white sugar dispenser and a carafe that presumably held cream. "Sandwich'll be just a minute."

Ophir poured his sugar then took a seat against the wall. The door jingled, and an older woman entered. Her plain cotton-print dress screamed poverty, but she wore antique cameo earrings and paid in coins out of her vintage sequined coin purse. *Stingy widow but spoils her grandkids.* He once would've used his people-reading skills to play on a human's greatest fears or deepest vices, encouraging them to make a wish that would expend their soul. Now he only read people out of curiosity.

Closing his eyes, he tipped his chair back against the wall, breathing the buttery-yeasty-cinnamon-chocolate-vanilla air. Oh, so many delights to sample. He'd have to remember this place while he was here in town. The scent of anise drifted his direction, and he inhaled deeply.

His eyes popped open.

Anise?

The scent lingered around the woman who'd just entered. His chair clattered sideways to the floor as he launched himself at the woman. She took a step back, one hand fluttering to her heart. "Excuse me?" she asked.

His nostrils flared, eyes scouring her from head to toe. The scent was on her, but not *from* her. It trailed toward the door like perfumed breadcrumbs. Spinning, he dashed for the exit, yanking the door open so hard the glass rattled.

"Sir! Your sandwich!"

Ophir didn't bother with a response. On the sidewalk, the trail led to the right. He shoved past a wide-eyed passerby. The scent was fresh and sharp, guiding him as surely as a leash.

He passed a bicycle repair shop, a vacant storefront, a photo shop. The scent ended as suddenly as it began, and he realized he'd overshot. Veering around, he slammed open a blackened glass door and entered a shop curiously devoid of appeal. Two shabby hairdresser chairs sat to the left, their accompanying mirrors hand painted with the names Birdie and

Tanika across the tops. A ceiling-to-floor velvet curtain cordoned off an area at the back next to a small door marked "restroom." No one was in sight, but the anise scent filled the place like heat in an oven. It coated everything with an oily magic that would make a mortal's eyes slide away in disinterest. *Interesting spell choice for a place of business.*

Ophir's gaze cut right through the glamour. A portal had been used here for at least a few, solid years to have left behind this thick residue.

From a small door at the back, he heard a toilet flush, then a woman emerged, her dark curls a tangled mess on top of her head. Dark eyes, olive skin, cheeks still rounded by youth. Gypsy ancestry. She wore a billowy blouse that floated over her hips in a feather-light caress but still managed to show off the rounded curves of her breasts. Despite his urgency to find the portal, his cock stirred.

Her face broke into a genuine smile. "Welcome to the Seance Salon! How can I help you?"

"I'm... looking for someone." He shifted his gaze around the room, trying to pinpoint the source of the magic. But the portal had apparently been here so long, opened and closed so often, it was impossible to pick out a single location.

"Oh." Her smile faltered, then resumed in a more plastic fashion. Her voice had lost its perky hopefulness. "I'm afraid I'm the only one here. Perhaps I could interest you in a reading?"

He narrowed his eyes, trying to read her, but the oily

magic was causing interference. He'd only encountered a handful of humans with a hint of their own magic during his many centuries on Earth. Most genuine magic came from a human passing off a djinn's powers as their own. She must know about the portal. Perhaps during her "reading" she'd reveal its location. He forced his shoulders to relax and smiled. "I think I'd like that."

She blinked. "You would? I mean… of course! Come this way."

Leading the way, she pushed aside the worn velvet curtain to reveal a table draped in a cheap red tablecloth flanked by two folding chairs. He stepped inside the cramped space, senses alert for any sign of the portal. The curtain dropped behind them, plunging them into semi-darkness, and she moved to the opposite side of the table. A match grated to life, polluting the anise scent with burning sulphur, followed by a candle smelling of bay leaf and vanilla.

He frowned. "Do you have to burn that?"

She paused, flame hovering over a second candle. The flickering light reflected from her eyes. "It helps me center my psychic energies."

Being this close to a portal was making him antsy. If he could touch her, he could at least determine if she had the portal on her. Maybe even cut through the magic to gauge her fears and desires. Clenching his jaw, he thrust a hand across the table. "You read palms?"

She blew out the match and gave him an uncomfortable smile. "I'm afraid I have to ask for payment up front."

He stifled a laugh. Of course she wanted money. She was a gypsy. Who needed magic to read this kind of human? Digging out his wallet, he pulled several hundred dollar bills free and let them flutter to the table. He had no time to haggle. "Enough?"

Her dark eyes went round, and she nodded tightly, sweeping the bills toward her. "What's your name?" she asked.

He thrust out his hand again, laying it palm up on the table. "Ophir."

"Ophir." She rolled the word around on her tongue, and he was surprised to find himself wondering what that tongue might feel like running over his cock. "That's an unusual name. Ancient."

"I know," he growled, trying to stay focused. It had been a long time since a woman had exerted this kind of influence on him. *Find the portal, then you can dally.* He wriggled his fingers insistently.

Without touching him, she leaned over the table to look, her breath tickling his flesh. Above the gaping neckline of her shirt, her cleavage seemed to scream for his attention. She studied his open hand, still without touching. What was she doing? He curled his fingers into a fist, hiding his palm.

She looked up to meet his gaze, her dark eyes like vortexes in the candlelight. "I can't read it if you don't show me."

He swallowed, mouth suddenly and inexplicably dry. "Don't you need to touch me? To trace my lifeline?"

"I prefer not to influence the reading with my own aura."

He flared his nostrils, quickly running out of patience. Slowly he uncurled his fingers, curious what line of bullshit she'd feed him about his future.

She stared down again, her gaze lingering for what felt like an eternity. When she finally looked up, her brows were furrowed. "I'm not... your lines are all there, but they read like a textbook. Like they were drawn on instead of emerging from your soul."

Ophir jerked his hand back as if burned. He looked into her eyes, pulling threads of his magic around him like cloak, unsure if he should run away or move closer. Had he actually found a human who could touch his realm? She'd definitely seen something of the truth, but didn't understand. And he had no idea what that meant.

She chewed one corner of her upper lip, her gaze shifting to her lap. Slowly, she brought the money he'd given her back into view. Shoving the bills across the table at him, she said, "I'm sorry."

He stared at the money, stunned. The paper meant nothing to him. He could conjure more whenever he pleased. What surprised him was that she was giving it back. And very little about humans surprised him these days. Shaking his head, he said, "Tell you what. You let me read your palm, and you can keep the money."

Her gaze cut to him, suspicion flickering in her eyes. "You want to pay me to read my palm? Why?"

He shrugged and held out his hand in request. "Call it a whim."

After a moment, she lay the back of her hand against his open palm. Her face remained completely serious. "Okay. But if this is a gimmick to ask me out, the answer is no. And I'm still keeping the money."

Chuckling, Ophir wrapped his large hand around her smaller one and drew it close. Her knuckles were slightly chapped, but the rest of her skin was soft and warm. A fresh, citrusy smell rose from her flesh, and he breathed deep, seeking the sharp anise bite of djinn magic. It was there, ingrained within her flesh, as if her very cells were infused with the power.

And he still couldn't read her.

He caressed her wrist with his thumb, sensing the very mortal pulse beneath her skin. There was something more within her, something of his own world. Something djinn. Certainly she wasn't the *source* of the magic? A portal had to be metal.

"So what's it say?" she asked, interrupting his thoughts.

Keeping his face serious, he leaned forward over the table. He wasn't sure what was going on here, but he knew how to find out. "Believe it or not, it says you're going to go out with me."

～

*F*rom where the stranger's fingers wrapped around Tanika's wrist, a shiver ran up her arm and seemed to settle in her chest. More unexpectedly, a heated longing began to pulse deep in her core. She got asked out on a regular basis, but always said no. Dating meant emotion. Attachment. A longing for family. The one thing she could never have. To allow such a thing to come true would release her djinn, and she'd sworn to do anything it took to take him to the grave for what he'd done.

At twenty-seven years old, she was still a virgin, and planned to be until the day she died. Yet this man, this strange and sexy man, gave her the urge to break her rule, just this once.

"You don't even know my name," she said, her heart thundering in her ears.

"Mmmm," he said, screwing one coffee-brown eye half-closed and peering at her palm. He had lashes a supermodel would be jealous of. "I'm going to say your name is… Tanika."

She gasped and jerked her hand away, her heartbeat turning from excited to fearful. Her mother'd had the sight much stronger than Tanika, but even she couldn't guess a person's name by looking at their palm. "How on Earth could you see that there?"

He grinned and jerked a thumb over his shoulder.

"Normally, a magician doesn't reveal his secrets. But your name is painted across the mirror out there. I took a chance that you don't look like someone called Birdie."

Tanika relaxed into her folding chair. He was just a player. That, she could handle. *Tit for tat.* Reaching out, she retrieved the bills still lying on the table and tucked them into her pocket. With these, she'd be able to stave off eviction for at least another month. Putting on her most mysterious smile, she looked at him through her lashes. "I'm afraid I don't date. But if you'd like to come back for another reading tomorrow after my psychic energies have renewed themselves, I'd be happy to look into your fortune again."

He leaned his broad shoulders back against his chair, folding his hands in his lap, his eyes dancing with mirth. "How do you know I have a fortune?"

Flushing, Tanika put a hand to her neck. "I didn't mean… I was only offering…"

"Oh, now my sweet little gypsy girl's all flustered." The sultry depth of his voice reminded her of a tiger about to pounce, and his perfect white smile threatened to dazzle her. No one man deserved to have so much sex appeal.

"I don't want you to think I'm after your money."

"Well, aren't you?"

She blinked, unsure how to answer. Of course she was after his money. Just not in an underhanded sort of way. "I'll give you your next reading for free."

"I'd much rather you simply went out with me."

"I already said no."

"I believe in second chances."

She licked her lips, wondering what a date with this man might be like. She'd never been on a date. Not once. Although she hadn't been able to read his fortune, she'd had a lot of experience reading people in general. Ophir seemed like the kind of guy who'd treat a girl like a princess, at least for the short duration he was playing her. Plus he was sexy as hell. She shook her head, squeezing her thighs together. Sex wouldn't fulfill her wish, but her djinn would do anything he could to make her wish come true, even turn a player into a devoted husband. Yet... how would it feel to kiss Ophir? To even *say* she'd kissed a man like Ophir?

The bell at the entrance rang, and Birdie's familiar mincing footsteps clicked across the linoleum, bringing Tanika back to reality. She rose and pushed the heavy velvet curtain aside. "I'm sorry. I just can't."

Ophir stood as well, moving closer to her than he needed to exit. His impressive height made her dizzy as much as the masculine scent surrounding him. Was that Polo? He leaned down close to whisper in her ear. "You will. I'm a patient man."

With that, he turned toward Birdie. "You must be Birdie! Perhaps you could find time to give me a trim?"

Tanika watched as the petite woman flushed to her platinum blonde roots while Ophir took a seat in her chair. She shot Tanika a glance as if asking for permission. Tanika shrugged and nodded. Let him move his attention to another woman. No skin off her nose.

Yet as Birdie trimmed his hair, chattering about inane things like the weather, Tanika found herself looking for tasks to keep her nearby, her gaze straying to Ophir's handsome face far too often. And worse, catching him looking back at her—far too often—the sexy hint of a dimple at the edge of his mouth.

Unsurprisingly, he gave Tanika a broad wink, paid in cash, and sauntered out the door without a backward glance.

Birdie collapsed into her chair. She kicked off her high heels and fanned herself with the hundred dollar bill he'd left. "Where'd that hunk of man come from?"

Tanika blinked at the door, still feeling dazed, then returned her attention to the curlers she was sorting for the third time. "He just walked in here off the street. Said he was looking for someone."

"Lordy, he can look for someone in my seat any time he likes. Or under my seat, if you know what I mean." Birdie sat up and tucked the bill into her bra. "Why didn't he ask you to trim his hair?"

Shrugging, Tanika carried the curlers back to the plastic storage shelf. "Spreading the wealth? I gave him a reading. Or tried."

"What do you mean?"

She shook her head, remembering the strange, rubbery resistance when she'd focused her sight on him. "It was weird.

Like he'd been coated in plastic or something. I could see the surface, but not the real man underneath."

"Ohhh, mysterious. Maybe now someone'll finally pique your interest, eh?"

Tanika snorted. "Yeah, right. Like he'd be interested in me."

"The way he kept looking at you in the mirror, I don't think he heard a word I said."

"No one hears a word you say, Birdie. You talk about the weather."

"What'm I supposed to talk about?"

"I don't know. Juicy stuff."

Birdie hopped out of the chair and grabbed the broom, sweeping up the nearly non-existent traces of Ophir's hair. "Not all of us have the sight to find the juicy stuff."

Tanika placed a hand over her heart. "I never use my gift for evil."

"Mmm. Well, maybe you should once in a while. At least to get us more customers like that."

Sighing, Tanika went to fetch the dustpan. Any more customers like that, and her demon might just get his wish.

3

*O*phir returned to the bakery to find the eclairs sold out. Disappointed, he bought a huge blueberry muffin and three cookies instead and sat at one of the tables, watching customers come and go in the small cafe. Over the centuries, he'd gone through periods of indulgence—food, drink, sex, even some of the interesting drugs created by humans. His immortal body could be drowned in pleasures the same way a mortals could. But unlike mortals, a saturation of vice always ended in boredom rather than death.

The luscious gypsy was an interesting conundrum. A way home, or something else? Perhaps she carried a whisper of djinn blood. It would explain the tingle of magic rising from her skin. His blood heated at the thought of her skin. *All* her skin, naked, lounging on a bed of silk pillows, her glossy black hair spread like a fan around her head. How long had it been since a mortal had intrigued him? He hadn't allowed himself to become interested, let alone attached, to one of the short-lived creatures since Emelda had been taken from him.

A raw spot deep inside him threatened to open again, and he shook his head to clear it. No time to fall into that pit now. A portal was nearby. Home was nearby, full of fellow djinn with lives long enough to matter. No more living among these painfully short-lived humans. He only had to figure out how to convince Tanika to open up.

Licking crumbs from his fingers and sipping his coffee, he watched a small boy press his forehead against the cafe's display case while his mother paid for their order. Mortals. They were made to die; the young were especially vulnerable. Yet somehow the race pressed on as if they were doing something that mattered. He'd watched generation after generation refuse to learn from previous mistakes.

Well, he'd learned from his. No getting attached to mortals.

Tanika was mortal, therefore his only interest in her must remain only a means to an end. Like any mortal with access to a djinn, she'd keep that knowledge close. He'd need to seduce it out of her. But she'd already made it very clear she wasn't interested. She'd stood firm against him, his money, even his subtle come-hither magic. At first he'd thought it was the glamour magic he'd detected throughout the salon interfering, but Birdie had reacted as expected. Only Tanika was immune. He'd have to seduce the sexy gypsy the hard way, with charm.

The cafe owner approached Ophir's table with a pot of coffee in one hand. Flour dusting his forearms, walking with the care of someone on sore feet, but Ophir sensed the fellow loved his shop, loved the community he felt it built. "Refill?" the man asked.

Ophir nodded and slid his cup forward. This persona was by far one of his favorites. Both women and men responded favorably to a tall, handsome, and obviously rich man in his prime. "Thank you."

The man poured steaming, fragrant coffee into the cup. "I haven't seen you here before. You new in town?"

"I am. The name's Ophir." He held out a hand to shake. "You seem to get a lot of regulars in here."

"Only way I'm keeping the doors open. Gregory Daniels."

"Seems to be tough times around here." Ophir exhaled a small trust spell at the old man, hoping to glean more information. "You know Tanika? At the salon?"

The wrinkles in Mr. Daniels's face creased into a smile. "You a friend of Tanika?"

"Just met her, actually. I'd like to ask her out."

"Oh, she's a gem. Works way too hard. Here." Daniels retreated behind the counter and emerged with a small bag. "Take this to her. She has a soft spot for sweets." He winked.

Soft spot for sweets. Good to know. Ophir bowed his head gratefully. "You're too kind."

"Be good to her. She doesn't go out much."

"I'll do my best." Ophir dropped a hundred dollar bill on

the table, and headed for the door, thinking of just how good he'd like to be to her.

On the sidewalk, the late afternoon sunlight reflected off the pavement while the rumble of passing cars filled the air. A homeless man sat with his legs stretched across half the sidewalk, calling after a woman who scurried past. "Marry me! Marry me!"

Flicking out a spell to encourage the man to sleep, Ophir stepped around him. No wonder these businesses were struggling. He headed to the salon, breathing deeply of anise. Inside, Birdie hovered over an elderly lady in her chair. She looked over her shoulder toward the door. "Why, hello, again!"

Scanning the small area, Ophir held up the small bag. "I have a delivery for Tanika."

"Oh, no! She just left." Birdie's brows scrunched into genuine regret, and he found himself liking her despite himself. She licked her lips and glanced at the wall clock. "I don't think she's coming back tonight."

Ophir opened the bag and looked inside. A glossy chocolate eclair lay cradled in frilly paper at the bottom. He chuckled. "That old baker told me he'd sold out."

"You mean Mr. Daniels?"

"I understand Tanika enjoys pastry." Ophir cocked his head. He might as well begin practicing coercion without using magic. "Any way you can let her know I'm here?"

Birdie grinned. "Atta boy. Why don't I call her? You can wait if you like."

"I would much appreciate it."

While she hurriedly dug out her phone and dialed, he strolled back to the curtained area. Might as well use this time to search for the portal. Leaving a djinn talisman unattended would be a novice mistake, but then, Tanika *was* human. Her race had been making novice mistakes for millennia.

He ran his fingertips down the velvet curtain, across the rickety table, and to the chair where Tanika had sat. The entire salon stank of hair chemicals and scented candles, but beneath it lay the remnants of magic, both old and new. Glancing toward Birdie, who was talking into her phone and looking at him through her lashes, he nonchalantly sat in the psychic's chair and ran a hand beneath the table. Nothing there. He set the bag down and let his gaze roam the walls. A cheap plastic clock shaped like a cat and an old framed photo were the only decorations besides mirrors. Rising, he moved to the photo, bending slightly to look at the weathered faces of two women glaring back at him as if they hadn't wanted a picture taken. Their dark curly hair reminded him of Tanika. Relatives?

Birdie called across the salon, "She'll be here in a few minutes."

Moving to Tanika's chair, he sniffed for magic while he lowered himself onto the worn pleather. Still nothing. The old lady in Birdie's chair beamed at him. "Aren't you a strapping young man?"

He smiled politely, itching to search the counter and mirror. He could have cast a shielding spell to allow him to do just that, but for some reason the idea of going about charming Tanika without magic had a strong hold on him, and he wanted to "play fair," if only in his mind. Instead of using magic, he sat and stared at each item as if it might start speaking and reveal all the salon's secrets, and hopefully some of Tanika's. Several envelopes sat on the counter, the topmost one stamped with a big, red OVERDUE notice. Cans of hair spray and mousse. Several plastic combs and brushes. Along the left edge of the mirror, photos of random, smiling people overlapped each other in a collage he didn't understand. Nothing old. Nothing metal. Nothing *portal*.

After a few minutes, the bell over the door jingled, and Tanika entered, face slightly flushed and full breasts heaving. Her brows were knit with concern, but the moment her gaze met his in the mirror, she seemed to relax. She glared at Birdie. "You said I had an emergency client."

"This guy's hot enough to set of the smoke alarm." Birdie waved her scissors without looking up. "I call that an emergency."

The lady in her chair covered her laugh with her fingers.

Ophir rose, languidly stretching knowing the effect his body had on most women. "It's an emergency eclair, actually. Mr. Daniels sent it for you. It's the last one, and I'd hate to let it go stale overnight."

Her face softened. "Mr. Daniels? I see. Well, thank you."

"He said you'd split it with me."

She raised one eyebrow at him, a tiny smile toying with the corner of her mouth. "I don't split my desserts. Can't you tell?"

Ophir let out a melodramatic sigh. "Well, then I guess I'll have to eat the rest of it."

"The rest of it?"

He shrugged. "I was hungry."

"You ate my eclair?" She blinked at him, as if she truly couldn't believe his words.

He smiled his best, sexiest smile. It'd been eons since he'd had to rely purely on wits and charm, and he felt a little rusty. The challenge was delicious, especially with someone as stubborn as Tanika. "Let me make it up to you with dinner."

She crossed her arms, face hardening. "I said I'm not going out with you."

"Give me one good reason why not."

Birdie spoke up behind him. "She doesn't date."

Tanika glowered in her direction.

Perhaps a previous heartbreak had made her wary? He took a breath and changed tactics. "I'm not asking for a date. I'm repaying you for the eclair."

The old lady's wavering voice chimed in. "Give the fellow a chance."

"Surely you eat dinner?" Ophir asked.

"I said no," Tanika gritted between her teeth.

The woman was more than a challenge. She was

impossible. How could he charm her without magic? He recalled the overdue bills on the counter. Perhaps he could find another way to engage her. He let out a melodramatic sigh. "I'd hoped to be more subtle about this, but I guess I'll get right to the point. I want to invest in your salon."

The room went silent, even the snip snip of Birdie's scissors going still.

"Do you think I'm stupid?" Tanika asked. "Nobody would want to invest in this place."

He held up both hands, palms out. He'd finally hit a nerve. But he'd have to play this carefully or she'd toss him out on his ear. "You're the first genuine psychic I've met. An honest to God human being with a hint of real magic," he said. The truth of his words stirred his blood. If he never found a portal home, she might be the closest thing to his kind he'd ever find. He moved forward and put a hand on her elbow. The soft skin beneath his fingertips sent an unexpected thrill of pleasure up his arm. "Can we talk about it over dinner?"

For a brief moment, she resisted the pressure of his hand.

He curled his fingers around her inner arm, stroking his middle finger over the tender crease inside the bend. A tiny shiver rippled across her skin beneath his fingertips, and a flush infused her cheeks. He smiled and in a low, intimate voice, asked, "Please?"

To his delight, she allowed him to guide her to his convertible.

4

*T*anika fastened her seatbelt, still in a daze as she watched Ophir round the front of the bright red Ferrari convertible to get into the driver's seat. *Holy shit, he drives a fucking Ferrari.* If she hadn't already been under some sort of hormonal haze from his touch on her arm, she's have been swooning in her seat. From the moment he'd first walked in the salon door, she'd been having X-rated fantasies, and now she was on a date with him. In a Ferrari. Or the closest thing to a date she'd ever have.

It's only a business dinner, she reminded herself. But she couldn't keep her eyes off the broad cut of his shoulders or the way his ass looked in those undoubtedly expensive jeans.

He slid into the seat and looked over at her. "Top down?"

All she could think about was flashing him her breasts. Her nipples hardened at the thought of his gaze lingering over her flesh. Fingers brushing the sensitive rosy tips. Maybe that sensual mouth of his...

She jerked back to reality and nodded, highly conscious of his masculine cologne from where she sat. He started the engine. In mute fascination, she watched his hand move to the gear stick, ease the car into first. So close to her left knee it sent a shiver of pleasure up her leg, pooling low and hot in her belly. She fought the urge to open her knees and make contact with that hand. She was a virgin, but that didn't mean she couldn't imagine what it might feel like to let his palm move over and slide up her inner thigh...

Jerking her gaze away, she squeezed her knees together and forced herself to stare out the windshield.

He pulled into traffic and quickly sped up, taking them sharply around a corner and shooting for the ramp to the freeway.

Her stomach quivered at the acceleration. He darted around a lumbering box truck, sailing past a line of traffic on the right. She grinned, her curls whipping about her face.

He glanced at her. "You like speed?"

"Oh, yes," she gasped, throwing her head back as the car surged forward. Speed was delicious.

He shifted gears again, sliding between two sedans before easing into the slow lane. Then they throttled up again, the convertible's engine throbbing deep in her bones.

All too soon, they reached the exit, and he slowed to a more reasonable pace for the side streets. They glided to a stop outside Bottega Soleil, the fanciest French restaurant in town. The place was supposedly booked solid months in advance. Hadn't he said he was new in town?

She pushed her hair out of her face with both hands, breathless from his seduction of speed, and reached for the door handle. He already had the door open for her, a hand extended to help her rise from the low seat. How'd he done that? This was beginning to feel more and more like a date. Perspiration prickled beneath her arms. She accepted his offered hand, her skin tingling at the contact, and rose from the bucket seat. "You know you can't get in here without a reservation?"

"Don't worry." He smirked. "I'll get us a table."

He cupped her elbow, making her heart race, and guided her to the door. The maître d looked up and smiled at them—well, at Ophir. His disdainful gaze swept over Tanika's cheap black slacks and peasant blouse and refused to look again.

"Wait here," Ophir said, and sauntered toward the man. After a few short words and a generous tip, the man ushered them back into the subtly lit dining area. A string quartet played softly in one corner of the room, and burgundy tablecloths fell in perfect pleats from all the tables, each place setting gleaming with crystal and silver. Single white rosebuds served as centerpieces, and the guests wore pearls and ties. To her surprise, the maître d held her chair back for her, shook her napkin and placed it on her lap.

"Thank you," she murmured.

The waitress arrived on the maître d's heels, setting a basket on the table and handing them each a menu. She smiled brightly at Ophir, fingers toying with the top button of her blouse as she handed him a wine list. "May I start you off with a drink?"

Ophir took the list without looking at the woman, his gaze solidly on Tanika. "Do you prefer red or white?"

Tanika's skin tingled under his attention, pooling deep in her core. Never in her life had she experienced a reaction like this to a man. Everything he did seemed to have a sexual connotation, albeit only in her own mind. He made her... giddy. There was no other way to describe it. Shaking her head, she folded her hands in her lap. "Water's fine." Best to keep a straight head around this guy.

Ophir handed the list back. "We'll start with fresh fruit and cheese, plus two glasses of house red."

The waitress bobbed her head and sauntered off. Tanika remained ramrod straight in her chair, her gaze on Ophir. "Let's keep this professional."

He lifted his napkin between two manicured fingers and flicked it open before laying it across his lap. "How am I not professional?"

"You ordered wine."

"You've never had wine at a business dinner?" He raised a brow.

Tanika suddenly felt three inches tall. "I've actually never been on a business dinner."

A sexy smile caressed his mouth. "*I've* never met such an honest gypsy."

Her chest tightened. Her mother'd called herself a gypsy. Tanika's first eight years of life had been spent on the road. Her wish for a husband and family had arisen out of a desire for stability. Hands bunching into fists in her lap, Tanika replied with a whisper she wasn't even sure Ophir could hear. "I'm not a gypsy."

He cocked his head, as if listening to something deeper than her words. "I suppose you're not, at that."

The waitress returned with two glasses of wine and left. The string quartet began to play a familiar waltz, each note thrumming the air like a heartbeat. Ophir picked up his wine glass and sipped, his deep brown eyes regarding her over the glass. Uncomfortable, she stared at her own glass, but didn't touch it. "Why did you bring me here, really?" she asked.

A moment passed. "I really do want to invest in you. You see the future?"

Taking a breath, she thought about how to put her gift into words. "Not so much the future. More like... a person's desire."

"And you exploit that."

"No!" Her mother had used her sight that way. Gauged a client's deepest desire, and then loosed the djinn on those most willing to pay. The client would get their wish, Mom would get her money, and the demon would gain another soul. "I never use my gift to exploit. Only empower."

"Well, there's your problem. You undersell yourself. Sounds like you need a business advisor."

She looked away. Birdie always asked her the same thing. The truth was, she didn't charge enough. Sometimes she gave out advice for free. Her clients were often lower-income, and needed a shoulder to cry on as much as anything. How did this stranger know so much about her? "My clients don't have a lot of money."

"I assume most of them wish for wealth. Can't you... guide them... toward that?"

"Most people say they want money, but if you look deeper, you'll find they actually want something else. Something they think money can buy them. Usually it can't. I help them focus on the things they want that are right in front of them."

A small platter of cheeses, grapes, figs, and melon seemed to appear on the table before them, almost as if by magic. Ophir selected a plump grape, popped it into his mouth, and chewed slowly. Did every move he made have to be so damn sexy?

"And besides." Tanika reached for a bite of melon, inhaling the sweet, dewy scent before nibbling on it. "If I knew how to get my hands on a load of cash, don't you think I would have by now?"

He laughed. "I thought that's why you're talking to me?"

Tanika smiled, refusing to take his bait. "You're the one who insisted on taking me to dinner. Are you saying you're my wish come true?"

"I can be if you'd like me to be." The low rumble of his voice and the intensity of his gaze made her insides quiver.

She looked away, studying the other guests while she regained her composure. Nearly all couples. One family in the corner had a small child. Who could afford to bring a child to a restaurant like this? Another couple nearby sat looking deeply into one another's eyes, the wife's pregnant belly pressed into the lip of the table. She couldn't hide the bitterness in her voice as she said, "You have no idea what my wish is."

The waitress appeared again, and Tanika realized she hadn't even opened the menu. Without batting an eye, Ophir ordered for both of them, and the waitress whisked the menu boards away. "I'm fairly good at guessing a woman's desires," he said, his voice sultry. She sucked in a sharp breath as he leaned forward. "Give me your hand."

Without thinking, she offered him her palm, assuming he was going to play at reading her again. His long fingers wrapped gently around hers and he rose from the table, pulling her to her feet. "May I have this dance?"

Without giving her time to respond, he pulled her toward the quartet. A small dance floor sat between the players and the tables, but no one used it. She spluttered, hyper aware of every eye in the restaurant following them. Her pulse in her ears drowned out the string quartet's song. "I don't know—"

At the edge of the parquet, he swiveled, pulling her to him with one fluid twitch of his muscular arm. She found herself pressed against his chest, his hands at her waist, his feet guiding her as if they'd been performing together for years. Up close, his masculine scent made her mouth water.

She smoothed her trembling fingers up the hard planes of his chest to settle on his shoulders, allowing herself to be swept along. The watching restaurant guests faded to meaninglessness. This moment was exactly what she'd always dreamed her prom would be. Or her wedding dance. She tilted her face up to look at him. Dark stubble dusted his angular jawline, and the ring of lashes around his eyes almost made her think he had to be wearing makeup. What would it be like, to have just one night with a man like this? Even one kiss?

He smiled down at her. "You look lovely when you blush."

The heat that had crept across her face during the walk to the dance floor intensified at his words. But she didn't let go. She hadn't had a drop to drink, and yet there it was, the dizzy, giddy swimming sensation of being swept off her feet. "Do people dance together at business dinners?"

His lips grazed her ear, and his low voice shot straight to her core, melting her knees. "If they don't, they should, don't you think?"

He squeezed her tightly against him, spinning a small circle that left her even more lightheaded. Her body thrummed with desire from her scalp to her toes. She clung to him as he settled into a steady rhythm that had her thinking of other rhythms she'd never experienced. Oh, God, was that his hard on she felt pressed against her? The heat of it threatened to burn her clothes right off her body.

Closing her eyes, she turned her face toward him, the scrape of his stubble along her cheek as thrilling as any car ride. She'd never been this close to a man. Probably never would again. A small voice inside her urged her on. One kiss, just to try it. They were in a public place, so what could go wrong? His breath fanned against her, flaming her passion higher.

Then his lips met hers in a blaze of light.

5

*O*phir had intended the kiss to be quick, almost chaste. A test of her desire. Instead, he found himself devouring her lips, every atom of his being striving to join hers as his tongue explored her mouth. His pulse kicked up when she moaned, soft and thrumming, melting into his arms as if she, too, felt the need to entwine their souls. He matched her growing passion. It was impossible not to. A slow burn spread through him the longer they kissed, still rocking in time to the string quartet, and he fed the fire with each rolling thrust of his tongue. He'd never felt so hungry. So crazed with lust. Desire hooked into every thread of his being with a force as intoxicating as if he'd claimed her human soul.

Yet here she stood, alive and well, her lush body aligned with his, nipples hard against his chest. Her fingers dug into his shoulders, pulling him closer, as if she were afraid he was going to disappear.

He had no intention of disappearing.

Tilting his hips, he pressed his rock-hard cock against the softness of her belly. A rippling shudder rolled through her, and he gripped her hips firmly. Her passion was more than a drug. It was like magic. He craved more.

She pulled back with a gasp, breaking the contact of their lips. "I don't think this is a good idea."

He leaned closer, brushing his lips against her cheek. "You taste of magic, Tanika. I wish for more."

She exhaled a waft of anise-sweet breath against his neck and tilted her face away, exposing her neck. "We can't always have what we wish for."

Rather than taking it as a rebuff, he took it as an invitation, and lowered his face to the crook of her throat, brushing his nose along her satiny skin. He opened his lips slightly and took a deep breath, tasting her pheromones along with the magic. Great Allah, he wanted her. Wanted to pour his energy within her. To see what might come of a union with this mortal. The desire shocked him.

He pulled away to look into her eyes. Not even Emelda, with her harem training, had ignited within him a lust this primal, a desire to become one. Tanika was an intriguing blend of innocence and worldliness he'd never before encountered. And the sweet anise scent of her skin spoke of more than mortal blood. Yes, of course. That was the driver for his intense reaction. After so long away from his own kind, the magic coursing through her blood was triggering his instincts. His cock throbbed painfully and his balls felt weighted with iron as he thought of claiming her. Portal be damned, he needed this woman.

He slid a hand up her back to cup the nape of her neck. "Sometimes wishes change."

Her brows scrunched. "Not mine."

"Tell me what you wish for."

"It doesn't matter. Especially to a man like you."

A man like me. How did she see him, exactly? Narrowing his eyes, he cast an obscuring spell about them and pulled her off the dance floor toward the kitchens. Waiters moved out of the way without even realizing, and soon he had her past the cooks and dishwashers to a narrow hall leading to a small, dimly lit manager's office.

She'd followed him dazedly until this moment. At the office door, she pulled back. "I'm not going in there with you."

"Why not?"

"I barely know you. And I'm not the kind of girl who does it in back alleys with strange men. We should go back to the table and talk about the salon." She attempted to duck under his arm and retreat to the bustling kitchen, but he planted his palm against the wall to block her passage. The idea of doing it in a back alley with her—doing it anywhere with her, everywhere with her—raised the flames of his desire to new heights.

"This isn't a back alley," he breathed against her ear, her scent making his mouth water. He was close enough to taste her skin. He resisted. "And we're not done. Not yet. You need to answer my question."

"Which question?"

"About me granting your wish."

She turned squarely to face him and placed her hands on her hips. "Like I haven't heard that line before."

He grinned, feeling very mortal. Vulnerable, even. For some reason it felt good. "Did it work?"

Standing on tiptoes, she pressed her mouth to his ear. "No." She dropped to her normal height. "Our food's probably getting cold."

Instead of moving aside, he grasped her hips and backed her against the wall. His mouth muffled her gasp as he plunged his tongue between her lips, kissing her with deep, rolling thrusts. His hands molded to her waist, but he kept a breath of distance between their bodies, letting her know if she struggled, he'd back off.

She didn't.

To his satisfaction, she grew pliant and leaned into him. Threading her fingers into the curls at the back of his neck, she returned his explorative kisses. Her essence filled him, melded with his magic. Widening his stance, he steadied his legs and thrust a thigh between her legs, pressing her more firmly against the wall. She tilted her hips against him, the heat radiating from between her legs threatening to burn through his pant leg.

As their tongues danced and rolled, the urge to have her grew stronger. Her tiny moans of pleasure acted like quicksand—to resist or struggle would only sink him faster. Every inch of his skin tingled with desire to feel her naked against him.

He shoved the edge of her peasant blouse upward, skimming the satin-soft skin beneath with his palm. *More.* He needed more. Sliding his hand around to her lower back, he dipped inside the waistband of her leggings to cup her ass over her cotton panties. He lifted her against him, kneading her flesh.

She gasped, legs rising to hook around his waist, ankles crossed at his lower back. Damn, she was sexy.

Pulling her off the wall, he carried her inside the office, kicking the door closed behind them. No one would bother them with his spell in place. In the back of his mind, he knew he was making a mistake. The woman kissed him as if she were starving. As if she was a djinn herself, about to consume his soul. The unknowns of her nature chilled him. And yet Tanika was the first female he'd met who stirred his elemental nature. More than just sex, she aroused the pure, raw instincts that drove a djinn to mate.

Mate? The idea frightened as much as drew him. Djinn did

not take a mate lightly. Sex was simply release. Mating was binding, as dangerously unbreakable as the magic to grant wishes. And she'd burn out in the blink of an eye.

Don't think about mating. You just need to have her to get her out of your system. Then you can move on.

He carried her to a leather sofa against one wall, wanting to savor her. To make her feel the same intensity of desire he now had coursing through his bloodstream. Lowering her to the cushions without breaking the kiss, he knotted one hand in the curls of hair behind her head to cradle her descent. He settled against her, kissing her deeply, on and on until her legs parted and she looped her free leg behind his knee. His hips settled against her, his throbbing cock pressed hard against her sex. She whimpered, her hands clawing at him, pulling him closer into the kiss as her hips tilted upward against him.

Breaking the kiss, he trailed his mouth along her jaw to nibble at her ear. A shudder ran through her body at the sensitive touch. He slid one hand down over her leggings to caress her inner thigh from knee to groin, thumb pointing a line straight to the apex of his desire.

"What're you doing?" She tightened her grip on his shirt, balling the material in her fists, but she didn't push him away.

"Touching you."

He waited a moment, giving her a chance to deny him, then inched his hand higher, cupping her cloth-covered sex. Heat and dampness met him.

He groaned. The instinct to rip her clothing from her body and plunge himself deep inside her gripped him. She'd fit him perfectly, he could sense it. His cock jerked, taking on a life of its own, and pre-come dampened his boxers. How easy it would be to lose himself in her. He needed to possess her, and nothing was going to stop him.

Propping himself on an elbow, he gazed down at her. It would be too easy to go too fast, to take without concern for her needs, and he wanted her to need him as much as he needed her. Her half-lidded gaze was drowsy on him, her lovely mouth swollen from his kisses. "You enjoy being touched, don't you?"

She swallowed hard, but didn't respond. And he so needed to hear her voice.

"Answer me."

"Yes," she whispered, closing her eyes.

He slid his hand up to her waistband and once again tunneled his fingers beneath the fabric. Easing his fingers under the waistband of her panties, he threaded through the soft curls covering her mound. She sucked in a breath.

Great Allah, he wanted inside. To feel her heat wrapped around him. The excited yet hesitant way her hands clutched his shirt while her stomach trembled made him wonder exactly how experienced she was. From the way she'd kissed, he would've said she'd been around the block. Maybe he'd guessed wrong?

He slipped his fingers deeper, splitting her open. She cried out, buttocks tightening in response to his touch.

"You're wet, Tanika." He stroked the swollen nub of her clit with his middle finger, letting his other two fingers massage her outer lips. "So wet. I like that."

"I shouldn't…" Her bottom squeezed tighter, lifting her toward his touch. "Oh, God. We shouldn't be doing this."

He curled his finger through her folds, probing her opening. "Do you want me to stop?"

"I should say yes." She met his gaze, her irises open windows to her lust. Her upper lip was clamped between her teeth while she panted, telling him of her conflicted desire.

"I won't do anything you don't want me to do." But he didn't give her a chance to reconsider. He tugged her pants down around her hips, exposing her tawny olive skin to his gaze. "I only want to give you pleasure."

"We barely know each other."

At this moment, he was ready to bare his soul to her. Reveal his nature. Grant her every wish. He lowered his face to kiss her exposed hip bone. "We will. I promise you."

She panted, her belly trembling beneath his cheek. "We're in a public place."

"That's why we came back here." He flicked his tongue against her skin, sliding his fingers along her slick folds.

"You planned this?" She panted.

"Not exactly." Teasing her opening, he slid one finger into her tight, wet heat.

She let out a shuddering cry, her velvet core convulsing around him. "Oh, God, that's good."

He pressed a second finger to her opening, and met physical resistance. *She's a virgin?* He nearly lost his rhythm. The knowledge shocked him and raised a protective feeling inside him he hadn't felt for centuries. A need to cherish and nurture. To honor her. Since Emelda, he'd avoided those kinds of feelings at all costs. But now he didn't think that was possible. Tanika was... special.

Continuing to use only one finger, he gently stroked her quivering inner ridges, massaging her clit with his thumb. This woman was becoming more and more intriguing. More and more *his*. "I'm going to make you come until you can think of nothing else."

She let out a throaty groan, and he grinned, dipping his face between her legs and clamping his mouth around her clit while his finger continued stroking. Her flavor flooded him, sweet, salty, and tinged with magic. He thrust inside her as deeply as her tightness allowed, adjusting the speed and angle of his penetration to match her quivering desire.

When he thought she was ready, he masterfully eased another finger inside her, stretching her until she stiffened. Then he curled his tongue around her clit until she bucked against him for more. Again and again, he eased her open, until both fingers pumped in and out of her. Her arousal soaked his hand, and her quickened breathing pressed her pointed nipples against the thin fabric of her blouse. He thrust and licked until her legs were quivering.

"Ophir, please." She rocked against his hand, words full of desperation and need.

He slid his free hand under her bottom, lifting her toward him, and buried his face in her short, wet curls. The fingers pumping into her hooked to reach her G spot, which he'd avoided until now, wanting to bring her as high as possible before sending her over the edge.

This woman was his. Every atom of her, inside and out, belonged to him. When the slight change in the muscles of her core told him it was time, he clamped his mouth over her clit and sucked.

Her body convulsed, her pussy tightening around his fingers with excruciating ecstasy. She cried his name as he tasted her release.

Once she sagged against the cushions, he crawled up and took her mouth in a deep kiss. She sighed, tickling her fingertips along his ribcage to settle on his lower back, pulling him closer.

Such a simple move. And yet it bound him as completely as any portal ever could. A tiny voice in the back of his mind screamed at him to run away, even as a sense of rightness settled over him, like he'd finally come home. He wanted to curl himself around her and hold her for all eternity.

He warred with memories of the last eight hundred years, all the mortals he'd seen come and go. No matter how long they walked the earth, humans eventually passed on. They could be injured. Got sick. Grew old and died. One moment they could be alive and healthy. The next, gone.

And there was a damn good chance he'd just become addicted to this mortal.

6

*J*anika felt as boneless as a jellyfish, eyes heavy with sleep. She would have succumbed if it hadn't been for the weight of the man lying atop her. His breath heated the curve of her neck while his fingertips skimmed the edge of her breast through her blouse. Her body was too tired to react. Or protest. If he'd wanted to take her right then she wouldn't have objected.

"Why didn't you tell me you're a virgin?" Ophir's voice rumbled close to her ear.

She stiffened, reality crashing down and stealing her breath. *What am I doing?* She shoved against his chest. "Get up."

He lifted himself free and sat back on his heels. She disentangled herself and rolled off the sofa, crawling a few feet away before getting to her feet. Her legs were like rubber bands. *It's only a one time thing. Nothing can come of this.* But her heart ached with the enormity of what had just happened. She wasn't the kind of girl who could treat a heated make-out session like it was a leisure activity. That's why she'd avoided this kind of connection so long. Already she could feel the heartbreaking constriction in her chest at the thought that this man—this gorgeous, thoughtful, sexy-as-hell man—could never be a part of her life.

Scanning the floor for her leggings, she spotted them on the back of the sofa behind Ophir. Rather than brave being near him again, she held out one hand. "Please hand me my clothes."

Without taking his gaze off her, he reached behind him and retrieved the clothing. "Why are you afraid?"

She swallowed, heart thundering against her ribcage. Her muscles ached as if she'd just finished a marathon, and a surprisingly delicious burning between her legs served as a reminder of the heights she'd just reached. Grabbing her pants, she met his gaze. The connection between them pulled her toward him as if only he could alleviate the trembling deep inside her. A longing for passion, affection, and partnership. He made her want to tell the truth. She jerked her gaze away, stepping into her panties. "You'd never believe me."

He swung his legs around to face her, settling his backside into the sofa as if he was about to watch a football game. Except the only entertainment was her struggling back into her clothing. He said, "Try me."

Her stomach dropped. Back at the salon, he'd said he believed in magic. That's what had started this entire thing. Could she confide in him? Would it ruin her chance to save the salon? Or worse, drive him away? This man had just chosen to pleasure her while taking none for himself. The thought of never seeing him again hurt. Settling her waistband around her hips, she took a deep breath and faced him. "Did you really mean it when you said you believe in magic?"

"I do."

"And that's why you want to invest in the salon?"

"Yes."

She pointed a finger back and forth between them. "This can't happen again."

"I can't promise that." The hungry gleam in his eyes made her swallow down her own lust and longing.

"It'd only end in trouble. Believe me."

"How do you know?"

She clenched her teeth. "Because I do."

"Convince me."

Standing there glaring at him, she was torn. The need to justify herself had never felt so strong. *If I tell him, what's the worst that could happen?* He'd think she was crazy and run away forever. Which would probably be a good thing, even if it meant losing his business backing. Still aware they were in a public place but needing to finish this conversation for good, she moved around the desk. She needed something physical in between them to carry on. She'd never talked about her wish with anyone. She wasn't sure why she wanted to now. But Ophir seemed more genuinely interested than anyone she'd ever met. She stared at the stacks of receipts littering the desk, only half-seeing. "My mother and grandmother died when I was eight." She twisted her fingers tightly together, trying to keep the horror that haunted her dreams under control. "They gave their lives for me."

She glanced up, and his attention threatened to burn a hole straight through her. He asked, "That's their photo in the salon?"

She nodded, neck stiff. "It's one of the few things that survived the blast. Besides myself. I survived without a scratch." Her skin prickled with remembered heat, and her blouse stuck to her skin uncomfortably. "The official report said our motor home's propane tank was leaking. But..." She looked at him through her lashes, bracing herself for disbelief and ridicule like she'd received as a child. "The real cause of the explosion was our demon."

He narrowed his eyes. "Demon."

It wasn't a question. It was a statement. What was he thinking? Was he afraid? Did he think she was batshit crazy? Her pulse thrummed in her ears. "I know I sound crazy, but he's real. And you don't need to worry. He's not dangerous. Not anymore."

The demon had taunted her during her early years, telling her to grow up fast so he could be free of the obligation tying him to her. Apparently he hadn't realized her unfulfilled wish would block his greater powers. That he wouldn't be free to harvest more humans until her wish was complete and she was settled in with a loving husband and family. By her eighteenth birthday, when the wish could be granted, she'd resolved to reject it.

Ophir asked, "Is he... still with you?"

Her hand automatically went to her chest, where the pendant had hung for years until she'd discovered the dampening power of the safe deposit box. Ophir's gaze followed her move, then returned to meet her eyes. She chewed her lip, uncomfortable under the scrutiny. "He's restricted to minor magic until he fulfills my wish." She tried to lighten the mood. "I call him a poltergeist, but he hates that."

"I'll bet he does. He probably doesn't like to be called a demon, either." Was that amusement dancing in his eyes? He relaxed back onto the sofa. "So let me get this straight. You made a wish, and you believe your mother and grandmother paid for it?"

"I'd already made the wish when my mom found me, and a wish can't be broken. But it can be renegotiated, so she and Grandma bargained their two souls for my one. I watched them make the deal."

"I'm sorry." His brows drew together in what seemed to be genuine regret. "What did you wish for?"

She swallowed, wondering how he was taking this all in stride, but on the other hand she was glad he wasn't making telling it any harder. Especially now that they were at the point of this confession—the reason she couldn't be with him. Couldn't allow herself to fall for him, not even a little. "To have a loving husband and family and live happily ever after."

He cocked one eyebrow. "Ah, a delayed wish. That makes more sense. You no longer want the wish?"

Tears burned the back of her eyes and she set her jaw, the longing ache within her stronger than she'd ever experienced. "I don't deserve it. It's my responsibility to make sure he never hurts another human being again. If I allow him to fulfill the wish, he's free. If I die before then, he dies with me." She grit her teeth, helpless anger welling up within her. "I'll destroy that evil creature if it's the last thing I do."

"I see." He rose suddenly, his eyes impossible to read. "We'd better get back to our table. I don't know about you, but I'm starving. And we have a business deal to conclude."

Her heartbeat was painful inside her chest. He had no more questions? She hadn't known what she expected, but complete acceptance of her situation—indifference, even—wasn't it. She'd told him she had a demon, for God's sake!

He waited by the door, then escorted her from the office, one hand familiarly on her lower back. Tingles ran up and down her spine at the contact, but he seemed unaware of his effect. The kitchen staff went on about their business, oblivious to their passage, and she wondered if he'd paid them all off. Planned this entire thing. But if that were true, why hadn't he taken full advantage of her? She stumbled back into the dining room, more confused and torn than she'd been during his seduction.

Maybe he really *was* only interested in the magic? Seducing her was merely a side amusement. *Or he stopped because he found out you're a virgin.* That made more sense. She had no skills or abilities in that department. Of course he'd lose interest in her.

She told herself that was fine as long as he still wanted to invest in the salon, which it sounded like he did. After all, he'd said they had a deal to conclude. If he could save the salon, she could harden her heart and forget what had happened. *Or hold onto it forever.* The one and only date she'd ever have. Best make the most of the memory. Signaling the waitress, she said, "I'd like to see the menu again, please."

Damned if she wasn't going to order the most expensive thing on it.

*O*phir swirled his wine and studied Tanika over the rim of the glass, so many thoughts warring within him, he didn't know where to begin. She'd called her djinn a demon. A creature. And she wanted him dead, even at the expense of her own deepest wish. That was powerful magic in and of itself. An unfulfilled wish explained so much; the magic embedded within her cells, the reason he couldn't read her like he could other humans. The attraction pulled at him stronger than any portal ever had. Stronger than even another djinn had any right to pull. The attraction only a mate could wield.

A mate who wanted to kill djinn.

He grew dizzy with memories of Emelda, who'd carried djinn blood within her, although she was unaware of it. Believing she might be worthy as a mate, he'd courted, wooed, and eventually revealed his true nature to her. She'd been a devout Muslim, and confessed his secret to the Imam, who in return incited a riot against Ophir's master. The outcry was explosive, for the master was disliked throughout the kingdom. Deep under the influence of the poppy, the master slept while the rioters set his chambers on fire. His ring-portal melted and his bones charred to ashes. Ophir could only stand amidst the flames and watch, unable to act without his master's orders. He'd closed his eyes against the volcanic intensity released with the destruction of the portal. Shuddered as the fire raged throughout the palace. And walked away as the flames spread over the rest of the city like a tsunami.

No one in the palace survived.

He blinked away the memory as the waitress removed his half-empty bowl of lobster bisque and set a plate fanned with enormous prawns before him. Loving a mortal was folly. He might as well fall in love with one of these shellfish. But fate seemed intent on driving him forward. Tanika was irresistible.

She'd ordered a prime rib with fermented garlic cream. He found it amusing that she'd decided to order her own meal after their intimacy. As if she, too, wanted to resist the extraordinary connection between them. She licked her lips and eyed his plate as if regretting her entree decision.

"Would you like to try one?" he asked, stabbing a succulent prawn with his fork and holding it out to her.

"Oh, I don't want to take away your dinner."

"Please." He stretched the fork across the intimately-sized table toward her mouth.

She hesitated only a moment, her gaze never leaving his, then leaned in to accept. The fork held too much for a single bite, and when he continued holding it toward her, she grinned delightedly, finishing the morsel off. "Thank you. That was amazing."

"I didn't say it was free." He cocked a brow at her.

She looked at him wide-eyed and frozen, like a deer in the headlights.

Damn, her innocence was sexy. He pointed his fork at her plate. "I want a taste of your prime rib."

"Oh!" She laughed nervously and pushed her plate toward him. "Oh, sure. That makes sense."

He looked down at the plate then back at her. Smiling in a way he knew women couldn't resist, he opened his mouth expectantly. Wooing her might be folly, but he couldn't help himself. She was so lovely sitting there across from him, refreshing in so many ways. His honest gypsy. He didn't have supernatural hearing, but he swore he could hear her heartbeat racing like a mouse's. Making her uncomfortable was a delightful game.

"Oh!" She hurriedly cut a slice of prime rib and lifted it with her fork, hand trembling.

"You're adorable when you're nervous." He allowed her to shove the too-huge bite in between his lips. The beef was quite nice, tender and flavorful and seasoned with a hint of lemon.

"Is *this* normal for a business dinner?" She stared at her fork as if it were a foreign object.

Still chewing, he shook his head slowly, eyes never leaving hers. She'd known the answer before she'd asked it, of course. Mortals couldn't help playing the game.

A series of emotions contorted her face, as if she wasn't quite sure which to settle on. Brows pinched and lips pale, she cleared her throat. "Listen, I know we kind of got off on the wrong foot. But like I told you, what happened back there," she twitched her gaze toward the kitchens, "can never happen again. I can't be in a relationship. I want to talk about the salon. Business."

So they were back to this. Business instead of pleasure. She was a stubborn one, for sure. Her rock-solid refusal to fulfill her wish must be driving her djinn insane. He realized he was jealous of this unknown djinn having access to her any time, day or night. "Okay, then. I want you to be my personal psychic. On-call twenty-four seven."

Her brows drew even closer together. "But I couldn't even read you."

"Exactly." He bit into a prawn, chewing slowly. "So when you do see something, I know it'll be real. That's worth a lot to me."

Tanika narrowed her eyes. "I don't believe you."

This woman might be innocent when it came to men, but she'd obviously had a lot of experience with her djinn's trickery and double talk. He picked up an asparagus spear. No relying on a trust spell. No charming her with a come-hither. Perhaps right now the truth would serve him best. Yet the truth had cost him Emelda, and he didn't want to repeat that cascade of horror. A partial truth, then. He set down the asparagus and wiped his mouth with his napkin before proceeding. "What if I told you I can free you of your djinn?"

He'd been thinking about this ever since she'd revealed the unspent wish. Everything with djinn came at a price, and Ophir had wondered from time to time how he might convince a kinsman to allow him passage, since he had little to offer. Tanika's wish provided a unique opportunity. After decades trapped by an unfulfilled wish, her djinn was probably desperate to return home. Enough that he'd relinquish his claim on the portal if Ophir assumed the wish's debt. Tanika could not only be rid of her djinn, but Ophir could remain at her side. At least for the remainder of her short mortal life.

Tanika let her fork clatter to her plate. "I don't want him free. I want him dead."

The venom in her voice sent a chill through his immortal blood. The death of a djinn was a rare thing. More fierce in its repercussions than the destruction of a portal. Even the power-hungry djinn who hunted those weakened after procreation were cautious in their methods. What would she think if she ever found out Ophir was a djinn? He cleared his throat, vowing to himself not to let that happen. "I can send him away. Humans will never have to worry about him again."

She regarded him through narrowed eyes. "How do you know so much? How do you even know he's a djinn?"

His breath caught. He'd let that slip. She'd never called him a djinn, only a demon or a creature. "I've been drawn to magic my entire life," he said. "I've studied centuries of arcane knowledge. As soon as you said there was a wish involved, I knew."

Her shoulders relaxed a fraction. "He took advantage of a young child. Killed my family. Has basically held me hostage for almost two decades. I want him to suffer. "

"He won't be free. He'll be trapped in his own realm once again. Believe me, he'll suffer." The djinn was already suffering, his magic slowly draining away the longer he held the wish open, yet he was unable to close it. Djinn magic was a lawful thing, even though djinn nature could be chaotic. An agreement could be twisted, reinterpreted, even renegotiated, but never broken. Her djinn would return home a weakened thing, susceptible to other djinn.

She licked her lips, obviously still skeptical. "You could really banish him from Earth? Forever?"

"I can't promise forever, but he'll be weak. At the mercy

of other djinn, and believe me, they are cruel. The likelihood of him acquiring another portal is slim."

"And what would happen to my wish?"

He scratched behind his ear, uncertain how to answer her. He had every intention of fulfilling her wish. And yet a part of him felt dirty that he'd use the wish to requite his own desire to mate her. She was mortal. Fragile. Finite. Ultimately, he'd be the one to suffer, left behind when she passed on. Djinn magic could not grant her immortality. A wish required a soul, and becoming immortal was contrary to the cost. "Wishes never go away. Whether or not yours comes true would be up to you."

Tanika stared past him a moment, her eyes glazed as if thinking about something. Her throat rippled as she swallowed. Then she rose so fast her chair clattered to the floor behind her. "I have to go. Now."

Spinning, she ran from the restaurant.

Ophir was on his feet, confused by her sudden turn of emotion. And then a familiar scent from behind him made him stiffen. "I wondered what had my little human in such a tizzy."

7

*O*phir spun to face the voice. The scent of djinn magic assaulted him, but not the sweet anise coming from Tanika. This was a bitter acetone stink, the kind that came from a starving djinn. The bare-chested man standing in the middle of the restaurant gathered no odd looks, his magical glamour forcing the servers to skirt him without realizing why. He slid directly toward Ophir and took Tanika's seat at the small table. Age lines creased his face, a feature rarely seen on djinn, yet he still moved with the lithe confidence of one who had no fear of physical harm.

Slowly lowering himself back into his seat, Ophir faced his kinsman. Their kind seldom came face-to-face here on Earth, and when they did, it was often because warring masters caused them to clash. He hadn't been in the presence

TAMSIN LEY

of another djinn in almost a millennia, and he found himself surprisingly misty-eyed with emotion.

His new table companion snatched up Tanika's wine glass with one gnarled hand, downing the contents in a single gulp. "Ah, I miss having a master who appreciates the finer things."

Picking up his own wine, Ophir sipped, keeping his face neutrally amused, despite the rapid pulse in his temples. "Greetings, kinsman. I'm called Ophir."

"Elim." The djinn waved a hand over his bare chest, conjuring an outdated dress jacket and cravat, then signaled the waitress for more wine. "You'll have to forgive me, Ophir." The djinn cut into Tanika's prime rib. "I have very limited time here, and am seldom near the pleasures of such fine cuisine."

Ophir wondered exactly how this djinn had come to be here, since he'd detected no portal on Tanika's person during their intimate encounter, and a djinn could not travel far from that point. But it wasn't a question he could ask outright. Talking to another djinn required finesse. A careful attention to detail so as not to be trapped when an inevitable deal was brokered; all interactions with djinn resulted in a deal. "Does she treat you so badly?"

The waitress appeared with a bottle and filled Elim's glass to the brim while he chewed in ecstatic delight. After swallowing, he met Ophir's gaze, brows lifting suggestively. "My voluptuous mortal offers all manner of decadent opportunities."

Possessiveness flared inside Ophir's chest, and he wanted to leap across the table to throttle the djinn for daring to hint at any sort of intimate knowledge of Tanika. Then he realized what Elim was doing—tempting him, possibly with an intention to trap him. Elim had to be looking to escape the deal with Tanika.

Smirking, Ophir pushed the bread basket across the table toward the hungry djinn. "She calls you her poltergeist."

Eyes hardening, Elim upended the bread onto his plate and sopped up the meat juice with a slice. "I see," he spoke around a mouth full of food. "Did she tell you her wish, then, too?"

Ophir nodded placidly.

"Interesting. No matter." He washed down his mouthful with wine. "The mortal's biological clock is ticking. I'm confident I can bring her around soon. Perhaps you can tell me why you might be skulking around another djinn's master?"

Ophir sighed and set his glass down, dabbing at his mouth with a napkin. It was too soon to reveal he had no master. That he was seeking a portal. Revealing his desire made it a target, easy leverage, just as Elim's predicament was leverage right now. Yet it wasn't enough. Ophir needed to strengthen his own position and make Elim more insecure. "It's good you have your master under control. These humans have such fickle desires, don't they? So short-lived and unaware of what they truly want, especially the young. How old was Tanika when she made her wish?"

Gaze narrowing, the djinn paused, his teeth buried in a

hunk of bread. He set the morsel down and slid a glance left, then right. "I don't feel the pull of a portal nearby. Where's your master?"

Blood thrumming in his ears, Ophir narrowed his eyes at the other djinn. "I could ask the same of you."

"You need to be on your way." Elim stuffed a full slice of bread into his mouth, making his withered cheeks bulge.

"Is this your mistress's territory, then? Is she sultana of the realm?" Ophir chuckled, imagining Tanika enrobed in a translucent silk kaftan and bejeweled head-to-toe. He might have to facilitate that fantasy once this was all over. "I do not envy you, beholden to such a master."

Rising, the djinn flared his nostrils. "Are you saying you have no master? What sort of power have you found?" The djinn's body rippled and began to fade. With an indignant huff, he scowled down at himself, snatched one final slice of bread from his plate, and was gone, taking with him the bitter acetone scent of his magic.

~

Tanika didn't look back as she fled the restaurant and her gleefully grinning djinn. All she could think about was dragging the monster as far away from Ophir as possible, thankful he could only appear in her near proximity since she'd put him into the safe deposit box. If she moved fast enough, perhaps Elim couldn't even get a clear picture of who she'd been dining with. How many people had he twisted and warped in an attempt to make them suit her wish? This was why she didn't date. Why she stayed away from men. Why did her demon have to ruin everything?

During her early years, her demon had only appeared to annoy her, but upon her eighteenth birthday, and her rejection of her initial suitor, he'd begun causing real trouble. Her first apartment building had experienced electrical shorts and constant outages, with his constant reminder that all her troubles could end if she'd only accept the wish. The next place she lived had to be condemned when they found black mold. A duplex she rented had burned to the ground. Then there were the tricks he'd played on poor Mr. Daniels, putting weevils in the flour and replacing the sugar with salt.

Reaching the sidewalk, she realized darkness had fallen, and the street lights cast deep shadows across the cars parked along the curbs. She dug out her cell phone and dialed a taxi, giving it an address several doors away. A year ago, after the incident with Mr. Daniels, she'd marched to the bank and rented a safe deposit box, hoping to restrict her demon's access to her neighbors through distance. Renting the box had cost every spare penny she had, but she was nervous enough about letting the pendant out of her sight. She wanted to ensure it was as safe as she could make it. Elim had laughed at her plan, threatening to override the security systems and allow thieves into the security vault. With great pleasure, she'd reminded him that even if he did end up in another's hands, he had nothing to offer a new master; he could grant no wishes until hers had been fulfilled.

Ahead, she spotted a yellow taxi pulling to the curb and ran to meet it. Clambering into the back seat, she gasped out her home address to the driver, still recalling the moment she'd sealed the safe deposit box over the pouch with the necklace. Elim had been standing beside her, cursing. Then his voice had ceased as if she'd flicked off a radio. He'd disappeared as if he'd never existed.

For months, she'd believed herself free of him.

Then he'd reappeared in her kitchen, snarling with fury and breaking every dish she owned. Apparently, the metal box interfered with his ability to use the pendant as a gateway. As dishes crashed all around her, and his hot breath fanned her face, he informed her he'd not be shut away so easily.

The taxi dropped her off outside her condo and she headed through the narrow courtyard. At least the demon's power had been diminished by the safe deposit box. He could only appear in her immediate vicinity, and couldn't tarry long enough to cause trouble. At least, not much trouble. It also took him time to recuperate between appearances, so she knew she had a little breathing room now. But running out like that had probably ruined Ophir's confidence in her as a business partner. She should've known this would happen. Sooner or later, the demon always discovered her plans and found a way to pollute them. She was a fool to hope any of her dreams might come true.

Opening her front door, she was surprised by the demon clucking his tongue. "Naughty, naughty girl. You certainly like to dance with the devil. What would your mother think?"

Her stomach roiled. Somehow he always knew how to make a bad situation worse. Usually by invoking her mother. Well two could play at that game. He was always complaining she kept nothing in the house worth eating, hurling her rice crackers and diet protein powders to the floor like a petulant child. The sumptuous restaurant must have driven him crazy jealous. "How long did you get to smell the food before you faded away, poltergeist?"

For once, he seemed unruffled by her jab. "Tell me, what did Ophir offer you?"

Shit. He'd managed to talk to Ophir long enough to learn his name. Had he managed to change him, too? To bend him to suit her wish? Now she could never trust another interaction with Ophir again. She stalked past Elim to the kitchen without answering, leaving the lights off in case he decided to start smashing light bulbs.

"Send him away." Elim trailed behind, feet making no sound on the scratched linoleum. "I'll beat whatever he's offering. Do you know how rare it is to be granted a second wish?"

"I don't want anything from you. Ever. You're a monster and I'll see you in hell." She wanted to make tea, but didn't feel like having boiling water nearby if Elim got angry. Opening the fridge, she searched for a diet soda.

"Yet you'll deal with *him*?"

She didn't understand the venom in his voice, but she liked making him angry. "We're in negotiations."

"Over what?" His voice was harder than usual. Clipped. Dare she say nervous? Ophir had said he could banish the djinn. Could it be true? This was the first time she ever recalled Elim asking her to send someone away, especially an eligible bachelor.

In the yellow light streaming from the open fridge, she took in the exaggerated lines around his eyes and mouth. Did he look more craggy than usual? His hands were balled into fists at his sides. Whatever Ophir'd told Elim had frightened him enough to make him discount a potential husband. *Good.* She smirked and took a long drink of her soda. "He wants to invest in the salon."

"Invest?" The flesh around his eyes twitched. "What does that mean?"

"I imagine he'll be spending a lot of time around here. He wants to become a partner and help the salon start making money."

The demon began to chuckle. "He told you he wants to make money?"

She blinked nervously. Ophir hadn't said he wanted to make money. He'd asked her to be his personal psychic. *In spite of the fact that I couldn't read him.* Distrust flared again. "Why, what did he tell you he wanted?"

Elim laughed harder, his wide mouth revealing blocky

white teeth. "You don't know, do you?" He leaned in closer, eyes filled with deep purple fire. "Ophir is a djinn. Just. Like. Me."

The floor seemed to sway beneath Tanika's feet, and she groped for a dining chair to steady herself. "Wh-what?"

But her demon didn't answer. His laughter faded along with his body, and she was left standing in a dark kitchen wondering if she should cry or laugh hysterically.

A djinn? Really? What the fuck? Was she some sort of evil magic magnet?

She fisted her hands into her curls and screamed under her breath. She didn't need the neighbors calling the cops again. They had often enough while her demon was throwing one of his tantrums. Everyone in the building assumed she was schizophrenic, having violent domestic squabbles with herself.

Flopping into the kitchen chair, she threw her head back and stared at the ceiling. Ophir had arrived at the salon looking for somebody. For Elim? Did djinn make house calls on other djinn? She had no idea. Then there was his insistence that she go out with him. She pressed her thighs together as she remembered his hands all over her body, the wave after wave of indescribable pleasure he'd elicited in her. Was that merely part of some elaborate djinn scheme? For what? To convince her to become his personal psychic?

She laughed out loud, leaning forward to lay her head on the kitchen table. *A psychic for a djinn. Hilarious.*

Then she bolted upright. Maybe that was double speak for

him asking her to be his master? That's kind of what Mom had been for Elim, using her psychic abilities to sell his wishes to the highest bidder while abstaining from making any wishes herself. Had Ophir been proposing the same kind of deal? A ball of dread enveloped her stomach. No way in hell would she ever agree to that.

But he hadn't asked for anything like that. He'd offered to banish her djinn. Was that because a person could only be a master for one djinn at a time? Her mom would've known. But Mom was dead. She realized she was panting and took another swig of soda, trying to calm her heart. Perhaps not all djinn were like Elim. What if her demon—her djinn—was, like, a djinn felon, or something? Ophir might be a sexy djinn cop, out to capture his man and sweeping the girls off their feet along the way.

She shook her head. *You've been reading way too many romance novels, Tanika.* If Ophir was a djinn cop, he would've captured Elim at the restaurant. *Unless Elim faded too fast?* She had run away fairly quickly.

Dammit. It was time to stop arguing with herself and make a plan. For all she knew, Elim was lying about the entire thing, and Ophir wasn't a djinn at all. Her demon could be trying to use reverse psychology on her, to trick her into fulfilling her own wish. It wouldn't be the first time he'd attempted that tactic. She needed to talk to Ophir again. Give him the opportunity to explain his side of things.

Unfortunately, she'd just fled from a date with a guy she

knew nothing about. Not a phone number, an address—hell, not even his last name. What kind of idiot was she? Taken in by a set of broad shoulders, sexy chocolate-colored eyes, and a lightning-fast Ferrari. He was probably long-gone from the restaurant by now.

Looking around to be sure she was alone, she opened the cupboard and pulled a box of rice crackers from the back shelf. Beneath the cardboard-flavored disks, she'd hidden a bag of miniature peanut butter cups from Elim's prying eyes. If Ophir was indeed a djinn, then good riddance. And if he was still interested in investing, he'd return to the salon tomorrow.

Sitting down at the table, she unwrapped the first one of the night and put the entire thing in her mouth. Chocolate solved everything right?

8

*U*nsure of exactly what he was after, Ophir tracked Tanika down. The task proved quite easy, even without magic. Her name was unusual enough that a quick Google search, cross-referenced against the city's DMV records, yielded her home address. Why rush to go back to more companions like Elim when he'd just found a woman like Tanika? Now he stood at her door with a bag of takeout in one hand and a fresh bottle of wine in the other. He pressed the doorbell and waited.

Footsteps vibrated behind the door, then a long pause, as if she was considering pretending to not be at home. No doubt Elim had already informed her of the situation, poisoning her against a fellow djinn. *She wants to kill her djinn.* The reminder should cool Ophir's blood, but Elim was kind of a dick—most djinn were. *Plus she's mortal.* None of it mattered. He couldn't talk himself out of seeing her again.

Holding the bag of take out in front of the peephole, he called out, "We never got to finish our meal."

Another beat of silence, then the bolt clicked and the door swung open, stopping short on the security chain. Through the crack, Tanika's eyes were round, and her ample breasts heaved a little too quickly. Elim must've indeed told her, and now she was afraid. Ophir decided honesty would be the best approach to win her over. "I'm sorry I didn't tell you."

She seemed to wilt, like a fresh-cut flower in the sun. "So you are a... a djinn?"

For the first time in his long existence, Ophir wished he could answer differently. He had to resist the urge to take her into his arms and apologize. "Yes."

"Why are you here?"

Again he held up the bag and grinned. "To finish our meal." Her lips thinned, and he realized he'd been too playful. He dropped his arm, allowing his expression to become serious. "I apologize. I'm here to talk. I swear to you I'll tell the truth. Whatever you want to know."

"Why. Are. You. Here?" she repeated.

He took a deep breath, shooting a glance up and down the courtyard before answering. "I came here looking for a portal." The portal might be what had brought him here, but it was no longer the reason he sought her out. If djinn weren't immune to their own magic, he might've wondered if a wish had brought them together.

The shielding in her eyes faded. Deep within her gaze, he thought he detected a hope that matched his own. "You don't have one of your own?"

"I'd really prefer not to have this conversation standing in the courtyard. Do you mind if I come in?"

She licked her lips, hesitating only a heartbeat. Then she loosened the chain and held the door wide for him, pointing down the short hallway. "The kitchen's through there."

"Thank you." He brushed by without touching her, forcing himself to be satisfied with only a deep breath of her citrus and anise aroma. Inside, he examined the small apartment. The place was oddly devoid of furniture and decoration other than an overstuffed couch loaded with fluffy pillows and a flat screen TV bolted to the wall. He sifted the air for magic, seeking signs of Elim's portal. The apartment smelled of anise, just like the salon, but it hadn't been coated in an oily glamour to dull its appeal.

The kitchen proved to be similarly plain, holding only a small folding table and two folding chairs. On the table sat an open bag of candy, empty metallic wrappers rolled into little balls and piled to one side. One cupboard hung open, revealing two cans of soup and a box of rice crackers.

Setting the takeout on the table, he asked, "Are you moving?"

"What?"

"This apartment looks… barren."

"Oh. Things just… tend to get broken a lot here at home."

He clenched his jaw, hating the thought of anything she valued being broken. No wonder she called her djinn a poltergeist. He opened the Styrofoam carton, allowing the rich aroma of butter chicken to fill the air. "I hope you like Indian food. There was a little hole-in-the-wall place along the way, and it smelled so good, I had to stop."

She remained standing. "Please, just tell me what you want from me."

Right to the point, then. The time for pleasantries was over. His heart broke a little that the intimacy they'd developed at the restaurant was over, but perhaps if he regained her trust, she'd let him back in. First things first, however. Once again he sifted the air for Elim. "Is he here?"

She narrowed her eyes. "He's locked away. Why?"

Her words sent a chill down his spine. Just as contact with metal disabled his casting, a portal completely surrounded in enough metal could be rendered inert. No wonder the other djinn had looked so gaunt. Ophir had assumed it was merely the drain of an unfulfilled wish held open for so many years. Now he realized it had to be because Elim had not only been unable to broker more wishes for energy, he'd not had enough food to replenish his corporeal body. He was literally burning his own magic reserves like a human burned fat. "How did he come to the restaurant?"

"He uses the wish connecting us like a conduit." Her skin

looked a little green at the words. "But he says it takes a lot of energy. Twice in one night is a lot. I doubt he'll be back again soon."

Ophir'd never heard of such a possibility; Elim must be a very powerful djinn. Thinking about Elim using her like that made Ophir's blood run hot. "Is he hurting you?"

She cocked her head, arms crossed. "I believe you said you'd answer my questions. So far I'm the only one answering anything."

"Fair enough." He took the other seat and placed a second plastic fork on the empty side of the table in invitation. "I'm looking for a way home, and Elim's is the first portal I've come this close to finding. Probably because your wish is keeping the portal ajar."

"What happened to your portal?" Her brows furrowed.

"Destroyed." He put a bite of chicken into his mouth, but she was looking at him with such concentration, he hardly tasted it.

"So you're free?"

He swallowed. "Free? I suppose so. I'm not tied to a portal. But I can't get home, either."

She perched hesitantly on the opposite chair and shifted her gaze to the empty countertops. "Do you grant wishes?"

He watched her obviously forced nonchalance. Was she searching for a way to break Elim's bond? "I can't negate one wish by granting another if that's what you're asking."

"That's not what I asked. I want to know if you..." Her breath shook as she finished her sentence, "harvest souls."

Wariness settled hard against his breastbone. She wasn't hoping for another wish, then. She was searching for a reason to hate him. His djinn nature urged him to spin a vague answer that could be interpreted multiple ways. She'd asked in present tense, so he could honestly answer no. But that wouldn't be the real truth she was looking for. And he'd promised to tell her the truth. He felt as bound to that promise as if he'd made a deal for a wish. *You've been among mortals too long*, he thought to himself, even as he said, "Not anymore."

After a short pause, she asked, "But you used to."

"I will not lie. I did." He watched her lovely face for signs of hatred. Instead, he saw guarded curiosity.

She fiddled with her hands in her lap. "Why did you stop?"

He cleared his throat. This was another question that had both an easy answer, and a difficult one. He decided on a halfway point. "After eight hundred years, I no longer feel the addictive pull."

She seemed to consider. "What you really mean is you can't."

He had to appreciate her intelligence. She'd obviously had much experience with her djinn's double-talk. "I can perform small magic to suit my own purposes. However, the heavy magic required to grant a wish is beyond me."

"Because you lost your portal?"

"A portal provides a connection to the deeper magic, yes."

Once again she crossed her arms, gaze so intense it threatened to ignite anything flammable it touched. "That's why you need me. You want to use my djinn's portal and resume trading wishes for souls."

"No," he denied, although his mind spun with contradictions. He'd been searching for a portal so long, he'd forgotten his motivation. Was it to resume his previous life? Or was it to escape the eternal grief of losing those around him to mortality? He hadn't really thought about what would happen after he located a portal. All he knew at this moment was that he wanted Tanika to be happy. "I want to help you escape the trap you find yourself in."

She laughed, her face lined with derision. "You're basically a djinn forced into in rehab. Why should I trust you? Or for that matter, why should you trust yourself? Drug addicts think they're free, as well, until they have the opportunity to use again."

Ophir stiffened, once again shocked by this mortal who could see things more clearly than anyone—djinn or human— he'd ever met. Was he simply an addict? The long ago memory of souls he'd taken, the dramatic rush of energy and power, washed over him in a way he'd not experienced in a very long time. A remembered hunger almost impossible to fight. The absolute euphoria of consuming a mortal soul.

And he realized it paled in comparison to the way he felt around Tanika.

~

*T*anika's nails bit into her palms as she waited for Ophir's reaction to being called an addict. With all her heart, she wanted to believe not all djinn were like Elim. But Ophir had admitted to harvesting souls, and the way Elim talked about the experience made her believe it must feel like a giga-hit of meth. How could any djinn who'd experienced that reject an opportunity if it came along again?

Ophir's features clouded, and he seemed lost in thought. Then he bent over the butter chicken and inhaled, eyes closed as if in meditation. "The combination of spice in this dish is like nothing found on my world." Opening his eyes, he wrapped his long fingers delicately, almost reverently around the carton. "When I am surrounded by sensations like this, I feel... almost human."

She remained frozen with her arms crossed, almost afraid to move. The sensual way he enjoyed the aroma made it difficult to concentrate on his words. The conversation was serious, yet all she could think about was the way his big hands caressed the carton.

"My time here among mortals, who can't take a single day for granted, who manage to create wonders in spite of their limited individual existence, has changed me." He released the carton and leaned back in his chair. "Djinn are only creative in deal making. We don't produce things, don't innovate solutions. From the phone I used to Google your address, to the convertible I drove here, there are no limits to human imagination. You excel over and above my race. Taking even one of you before your time is finished is a waste of potential."

God help her, she wanted to believe him. But he still hadn't actually answered the question, and she knew from her dealings with Elim how tricky words could be. "That's just like saying how pretty a cake is right before you cut it."

That elicited a laugh, not the gloating kind she was used to from her djinn, but one of pleasure, eyes squeezed shut while he shook his head. "You are truly delightful, Tanika. Both charming and quick-witted. And you are correct. Let me say in plain words what I mean." He met her gaze, his dark eyes filled with intense purple light. "After eight hundred years among humans, I find the thought of taking a human soul repulsive. I personally don't ever want to do that again."

She took a deep breath, considering what he'd just said, looking for loopholes. Elim would bend words, but he prided himself that he never lied. Apparently truthfulness was a djinn value or something. She couldn't find any wiggle room in what Ophir said. Hesitantly, she offered, "Promise me you won't harvest anyone again, and I'll believe you."

His gaze remained steady. "I will not harvest a mortal soul ever again."

Shoulders relaxing, she realized she could finally take a full breath. "All right. Then why are you looking for a portal?"

The purple light infusing his gaze flickered. "I… don't know that I am."

She frowned, uncertain all over again. "Isn't that what you claimed when I let you though the door?"

"It is. But you've made me rethink that goal."

Her belly tightened with anticipation. What goal might a djinn have, other than harvesting souls? Unless… "Wait, I know what's going on." She thrust up a hand. "Elim's cast a spell on you to make you complete my wish."

"Impossible." Ophir shook his head. "Djinn are immune to each other's magic, at least here on Earth."

A wave of relief flooded her. She wanted Ophir's attention to be real, not the product of some charm. "Are you sure?"

He smiled. "I'm sure. I'm here to save you from your djinn."

Maybe he is with the djinn police. "How?"

"Elim's wasting away under the wish's burden, and would probably do almost anything to be free of his debt."

She sneered. "He would. He's offered to renegotiate our deal many times." Her temper flared at the thought of all the things he'd suggested. "But like I told you in the restaurant, I don't want him free. I want him dead."

Ophir cocked his head. "That won't bring back your mother."

His words hit her like a blow to the stomach. "I know that. But I can at least be damned sure that monster never harms another human being." She fought back self pity. She'd resolved to follow this path years ago, and wasn't about to let another tricky djinn talk her out of it.

"You're not only refusing your wish, you know. Elim'll torture you until the day you die." Ophir leaned forward with his elbows on the table. "Did you know he's put a glamour on the salon? He's dulled it to make it less appealing to customers."

"Bastard." She slumped back in her chair and scowled, hands going limp on the table. "I knew he'd done something, but he'd never admit it."

"What if I send him back to my dimension? Permanently? So he can never return to this realm?" He reached across the table and enveloped one of her hands with his. "Would that satisfy your quest to protect humanity?"

His touch set her blood on fire. *Focus, Tanika.* "You said you can't access strong magic without a portal. Plus he's immune. How do you plan to beat him?"

"The way all djinn deal with one another. A deal."

"What kind of deal?"

He licked his lips. "I believe I may be able to assume his debt."

Her heart stopped beating for a moment. "As in... you become my djinn?"

"I'd take up ownership of the portal, yes."

"I knew it!" She jerked her hand away, betrayal burning through her.

"I meant it when I promised to never harvest another

mortal." His gaze remained locked with hers, but he withdrew his hand. "But I can't think of another way to break Elim's hold on you."

She was still coming to grips with meeting a second djinn, let alone trust his motives. And yet some part of her wanted to trust everything about Ophir. The way his touch could make her brain turn to pudding was uncanny. Suspicion blossomed in her chest. "Are *you* casting a spell on me?"

"I am not. In fact, I can't." His response was long, drawn out, and sexy. "I've never met a human like you."

Her breath fluttered in her throat. "What do you mean?"

He leaned forward, the cheap folding chair creaking as he shifted. "It could be the magic of your wish infusing you, or perhaps you carry a trace of djinn blood."

"As in, a djinn was my ancestor?" Her stomach flip-flopped, the chocolate she'd eaten earlier churning uncomfortably in her stomach. The idea of having ancestral ties to a djinn made her physically nauseous.

He shrugged. "It's possible. During the early years of our ventures to Earth, before it was discovered that mortal souls could be consumed, a few djinn found human mates and bonded. After so many millennia, however, the remaining bloodlines are very thin."

Even more than the prospect of being part djinn, talking to Ophir about mates and children made her uncomfortable. She swallowed, squaring her shoulders. "So I'm a special snowflake or whatever. That still doesn't explain why you care so much about my happiness."

He rose, his body slow and languid, and moved around the table to stare down at her. "Consider it selfish. I don't want you running away from me every time I look at you because you're afraid of a wish."

If she'd been standing, her knees would've buckled under his hungry gaze. His cologne had been masked by the butter chicken earlier, but now he was standing close enough to bump her knees, and his masculine scent filled her with heady desire. With one hand, he pushed the folding table aside, the rubber-capped feet squeaking against the linoleum, and moved into the space it had occupied. Squatting, he placed one hand on each of her knees.

Captured by his intense stare, she couldn't form words. A long, heart-stopping moment passed. Slowly, he pressed his body between her unresisting thighs, pushing them open until his breath fanned her face. He teased his tongue along the seam of her mouth, sending a shiver straight to her navel. Quivering, she felt her lips part to accept him.

Heaven help her, this man turned her very thoughts to jelly, not to mention her body.

He nibbled her top lip first, then her bottom, as if sampling her for the first time. Her hands crept to his shoulders, slid up and caressed the back of his neck. A tilt of his head, and his mouth captured hers, tongue running along her teeth before stroking long and firm inside her. She clung to him, letting him lead her in an erotic dance, his hands sliding up her thighs to rest at the bend of her hips.

A hungry noise escaped him, telling her how badly he wanted her, sending rockets of anticipation deep into her core. She hooked her ankles around his waist, thrilling at the rigid length of his erection pressing against her sex. He tilted forward, grinding himself against her clit and deepening the kiss. Remembering the way he'd coaxed an orgasm from her at the restaurant made her core quiver with excitement. What they were doing was dangerous. Forbidden. It only made her want Ophir more, to experience all he had to offer. To accept his promise of freedom.

"Tanika," he groaned against her lips. Sliding both hands under her bottom, he rose, keeping her entwined about him like a starfish. His muscles rippled as he moved, sure and secure even with her added weight. As if he'd been to her apartment a million times, he easily carried her through the living room to her bedroom, nudging open the door with one foot and lowering her to the bed. All the while never breaking contact with her hungry lips.

The sound of someone clearing his throat froze them both.

"Looks like I got here just in time." Elim's voice grated through the room like breaking glass.

9

Ophir straightened to face the other djinn, his nerves on fire with magic. The food must've bolstered Elim's reserves. Tanika scurried to the bedside lamp and clicked it on, revealing her djinn with his arms crossed, deep scowl lines cut into his face.

"How are you here again so soon?" she said breathlessly.

"I was worried for you." Elim's voice dripped sarcasm. "I am, after all, indebted to your happiness."

"If that were true, you'd keel over and die," she spat out.

Rolling his eyes, Elim turned his attention to Ophir. "This is not the situation I expected to find you in. What are you playing at, Ophir?"

Ophir chuckled, stretching his neck side to side and smoothing his shirt across his chest, thinking carefully about his words. "You hinted at Tanika's... pleasurable...

opportunities when we spoke at the restaurant. I was curious." He sat on the bed, bouncing slightly as if testing the springs. "Since I'm immune to your magic, I thought I'd offer her pleasure with no strings attached. Now if you'll excuse us, we'd prefer not to have an audience."

To his surprise, Tanika didn't balk at his crudeness. She pointed to the door. "Yes, Elim. Leave."

Elim's body seemed to vibrate, rippling as he leveled his glowing, purple gaze at his master. "You're not the kind of woman who can have a one night stand and walk away without regrets."

Tanika sniffed. "How would you know?"

"I saw to that with the way you were raised. Loving, moral adoptive parents. A family to teach you how to achieve your wish." His eyes glowed with purple embers. "I took care of you."

Ophir laughed. "Took care of her? More like you were nervous. That must've cost a lot of energy, reinforcing the wish's hold on her."

Elim's eyes narrowed, turning their purple glow to slits. "A poor deal, I admit. We've all made them. And she refuses to renegotiate." He licked his lips and cocked his head slightly. "You could help me. Convince her to complete the wish."

Ophir yawned as if growing bored with the conversation. Yet inside he was thrilled. Elim was making this deal so easy. "That would be a costly bargain, my friend. She's quite adamant she wants you dead."

"Everyone has a price." Spittle flew from Elim's lips. "Just find out what hers is."

"Mm. Your predicament *is* intriguing." Ophir rolled his head to look at Tanika where she still cowered by the lamp, her olive skin ashen. "What would it take, Tanika?"

She visibly gulped, her gaze meeting his. A heartbeat passed. Then ten. Finally, she shifted her attention back to Elim. "I want you to leave Earth and never interact with another human again."

Elim's nostrils flared. "That's no kind of deal. You get what you want and I get nothing."

"Nothing?" She stomped forward as if she was going to attack, but stopped at the corner of the mattress. "You took my mother and grandmother! You already had your payment!"

Ophir rose, joining her. She was magnificent when she was angry. He wouldn't be surprised to see a flicker of lavender light in her eyes. He smirked at his fellow djinn. "She's right, Elim. I'd take her deal."

Eyes blazing, Elim curled his lips and took a deep breath. Weak as the djinn might be, he still seemed to swell with power. "What's in this for you, Ophir? Why are you here? Not merely for a piece of mortal ass."

A rumble of warning rose from Ophir's throat. Before he could speak, Tanika elbowed past, glowering at her djinn. "You're just angry I've found myself a friend with benefits, and there's nothing you can do about it."

The bedside lamp popped and went out, leaving the room

lit only by the flames in Elim's eyes. "Do not mock me, mortal. I've been patient until now."

Tanika seemed to be on a roll, though. "What're you going to do, poltergeist? Dull my scissors? Swap the colors on my hair dye? You have no real power left. You're just a shell of whatever monster you used to be."

Elim roared, throwing his hands out as if to strangle her. Tanika reeled, throwing her hands up before her while the djinn roared, "I'll burn down the salon with Birdie inside if that's what it takes!"

Ophir lunged, knocking the djinn aside. Elim wouldn't actually harm Tanika, not with the wish hanging between them, but Ophir refused to allow her to be intimidated. He stood nose-to-nose with Elim, his breath ragged. "Not as long as I'm around."

Elim's eyes grew wide. Then his mouth spread into a leer. "She's not just a piece of ass for you, is she?" He stepped back and put both hands on his scrawny hips, a chortling laugh rolling out of him. "I thought mating humans was a thing of the past for our kind, yet here you are, proving me wrong. You do realize she's mortal, right? You're tying yourself to a mate who will wither and die."

The room suddenly felt devoid of air. Elim was right. Tanika was destined for death, just like every other human being Ophir had ever met. Just like Emelda. And no wish could ever change that. What kind of fool djinn was he to fall in love with a mortal not once, but twice? Hadn't he learned his lesson the first time?

He glanced at Tanika across the shadowed room. New terror gripped his soul as he realized the truth of it. He no longer cared about the portal. No longer needed to escape Earth. All he wanted was Tanika, to have and to hold for the rest of her life. Then he would gladly take Elim's place beside her in the grave. No matter what else happened between now and eternity, Tanika was his. He didn't want to think about the what-ifs. He only wanted her. She was his, for her lifespan and beyond.

Still laughing, Elim flicked his hand in dismissal. "But who am I to judge if you want to do my job for me? Have at it, lovebirds. I'll be waiting."

With that, the djinn popped out of sight.

~

Tanika remained utterly silent, staring into the dark at the spot her demon had just vacated. She felt light-headed. First she'd been reeling from finding out Elim'd orchestrated her adoptive parents, which completely upended her interpretation of her childhood. Then she'd slammed up against another loss when the demon physically threatened Birdie, which meant that to protect her friend, she'd have to sever yet another relationship. And finally, this business about Ophir wanting her for a mate.

That one was hardest of all to believe. Mate sounded a heck of a lot more permanent than husband.

Hesitantly, she moved to the wall switch and flicked on the overhead light. The stricken expression on Ophir's face told her he was in as much shock as she was. Her heartbeat felt weak and thready as she whispered, "What's he talking about?"

Ophir sat on the edge of the bed and then fell backward as if he could no longer hold himself upright. Staring at the ceiling, he said, "For eight hundred years, I've seen mortals come and go. Learned to distance myself from caring. All I've dreamed of is going home, of leaving this realm of mortality and death for good." He turned his head against the comforter to spear her with his gaze. "Yet now I find I cannot bear missing one microsecond of your very short life."

His words exposed her heart to an unfamiliar rawness— hope. She held a brief mental image of a house and a yard, Ophir playing ball with the kids, family picnics. A life of joy. He might as well have just uttered wedding vows.

She shook her head violently, trying to rid herself of the daydream. What was she thinking? Djinn probably didn't even have weddings. "Please don't. I can't. You know I can't."

He sat up again, face hard as steel. "You can if we destroy the portal."

Her mouth dropped open. For some reason she'd believed destroying a portal was impossible. But Ophir was proof it could be done. "Won't that just free him like you are?"

"Not if you destroy it while he's on the other side."

"Couldn't he find another portal and come back for revenge?"

"Portals are extremely rare. I doubt Elim will ever find a way to visit Earth again."

She bit her lip, considering. Was it enough to banish the demon? How much longer could she hold out against her wish, especially with Ophir seducing her by his mere presence? Ophir's plan meant Elim couldn't bother humanity for a long, long time. Possibly forever. It also meant destroying his only way home. She shook her head. "I can't ask you to do that."

"You're not asking me. I'm asking you. Marry me, Tanika."

Her knees began trembling, the room spinning around her. She stumbled forward and sat, hard, on the mattress beside him. Pulling her toward him, he cleared a tangle of curls from her cheek with gentle fingertips. "I know this is sudden. It's sudden for me too, but a djinn knows when he's met his mate. If you'll have me, I'll be yours for the rest of time."

Tears filled her eyes, and she blinked furiously to clear her vision. She didn't want to lose sight of this gorgeous, amazing man who was more than she'd ever hoped for in a husband. Except for one thing—he wasn't human. He'd just reminded her he was over eight hundred years old. She knew djinn were immortal, but she'd never thought about the fact she and Ophir could never grow old together. The consequences of that fact took away her breath. "You mean for the rest of my life. When I'm gone, you'll be trapped here on Earth, alone."

He shook his head. "Djinn only mate once, and mates are bound much the same way you and Elim are now."

Either her ribcage had shrunk, or her heart swelled, because there didn't seem to be enough room inside her chest. "You mean you'll die?"

He shrugged and looked away. "Yes."

"No!" She sat up, cupping his angular cheek. He immediately cradled her knuckles, turning his face to kiss her palm. His breath was warm on her skin. Alive. More than alive. He was immortal. Something humans dreamed of. Schemed for. Nausea rose up inside her as she scrambled for her options. "You grant wishes. Can't you make me immortal?"

Lips still pressed to her palm, he smiled, but his eyes were pinched with sadness. He pulled her back down against him so her cheek rested against his chest. "Granting true immortality is beyond my power. The closest thing I could do is extend your life over and over." His voice grew brittle. "Assuming you could find a willing a mortal soul to pay the price."

She stiffened, remembering her mother's sacrifice. Nausea roiled within her. "Have you granted such a wish before?"

"No." He squeezed her in reassurance. "I knew the possibility existed, but I never mentioned it as a solution when a master requested immortality."

Twisting, she looked into his face. "But you just told me."

His melted-chocolate eyes met hers. "I'm not concerned about you pursuing such a deal."

She swallowed, the urge to kiss him making her mouth tingle. His heartbeat was strong beneath her cheek. He knew her well, in spite of the fact they'd just met. She could envision spending the rest of her life with him. But she couldn't ask him to give up immortality. He'd regret it in the end. He needed to think about what he was losing. "Tell me about your home world."

Brow furrowing as if he was struggling to remember, he said, "It's impossible to describe in human language. A place of shifting ether and ebony ribbons of plasma. Djinn are beings of energy. We follow the plasma like gypsies on houseboats. We shift and deal, trading in energy. Our dimension is a realm of souls, if you will. A portal allows us to experience corporeal existence."

"To have a body, you mean?"

"Yes."

"Why would you want that?"

"Energy is like a drug to my people. Moving from matter to energy and back again is the most potent experience we have. Absorbing a human soul is indescribable bliss." His face flushed and he looked away as if ashamed to meet her gaze. "Once we discovered Earth, had a taste, it was impossible to go back. I think... I think I've been lucky to be here long enough to break the addiction. To become human."

She realized he meant it. He didn't want to go back to the

way he was. She whispered, "Once the portal is gone, you'll be trapped here."

He pressed his lips to her forehead. "I can't recall a day I didn't long for a portal, and now you couldn't force me through if you tried." Pulling back, he lifted her chin, looking into her eyes. "A mortal life with you, Tanika, would be worth every moment."

His intensity made her nerves jangle. She'd lived so long in denial, she was uncomfortable with the idea of her wish being fulfilled. "What if I say no?"

He scrunched up his face, and then gently nipped her nose, turning her anxiety into laughter. "You're not getting rid of me that easy. I have to stick around and keep you out of trouble, whether you'll have me or not."

She wrapped her arms around his waist and squeezed, the hard planes of his body pressed against hers. The tips of her breasts ached where they crushed against him.

He slid his hands down along her spine and cupped her bottom, adjusting her to bring her even closer. The familiar touch on her body made her insides thrill. She was going to do this. She was going to accept her wish.

Moving her hand to the hem of his shirt, she slid her hand beneath to the rippled muscles of his back, shocked by her own brazenness. His skin tremored in response, and she felt the surge of his cock against her belly. Her core tightened in response. Anticipation. Primitive emotions roiled within her, and the spot between her legs grew unaccustomedly warm.

Lowering his face to hers, he claimed her mouth, his lips demanding. One hand gripping the back of her neck, he thrust his tongue deeply inside her, rolling it and tangling against her insecure responses. She worried she might do it wrong. What if she wasn't able to please him? She'd never even had a childhood boyfriend to practice with.

Ophir didn't seem to mind. His roving hand cupped one of her breasts, massaging her aching flesh while he kissed his way across her jaw and down the column of her throat. The contact sent jolts of desire down her spine and stirred butterflies in her stomach. His hand left her breast and smoothed its way down to her hip. In one swift move, he'd lifted her blouse, raising her from the mattress to sweep the garment over her head. Cool air tingled across her skin.

Now his hands had full access to her torso, the warmth of his touch branding her. His fingers teased little gasps of pleasure every time he cupped a breast or dipped beneath the waistband of her leggings. His teasing fingers circled around her back and unhooked her bra. The sudden release of the elastic band felt like it might set all her butterflies free. She loved it. Wriggling out of the straps, she prickled beneath his hungry gaze.

"Beautiful," he murmured, and rolled her to her back. He swooped down, swiping across one nipple with his wide tongue.

Sparks ignited, her areola tightening her nipple to an impossible peak while the other breast cried out for equal attention. He suckled, flicking the sensitive tip, and a pulse of pure pleasure skittered downward toward her core. He moved to the other breast and gave it the same treatment, until she was arching her back for more.

Then he pulled away, and she felt nothing but the weight of his stare for a few heartbeats. She opened her eyes and met his. The lust there was undeniable. Yet he didn't move. Only knelt above her, his legs straddling hers. Anticipation built. Was she supposed to do something? She shifted her gaze downward to his crotch, and her insides thrummed at the bulge in his jeans.

His sultry voice reached out to her. "Do you want something, Tanika?"

"Yes." She couldn't hold back her desire.

"What? Tell me."

She flicked her gaze up again, meeting his eyes. He wanted her to ask? To beg? To take?

"You never said yes. I want to know you're sure." His voice wrapped around her like a caress.

Oh. She licked her lips. "You. I want you."

He smiled a sexy, naughty grin. Slowly, his long fingers unbuttoned his shirt, exposing his hard pecs and molded abs. His skin was smooth, except for a fine line of hair below his belly button, pointing the way into the waistband of his jeans. He tossed the shirt aside, a waft of masculine cologne filling the air, and then he was hovering above her, his naked chest brushing her peaked nipples. She made an unintelligible noise, barely able to breathe.

Supporting himself on his elbows, he cupped her face and kissed her, tongue delving deeply as her hands explored his exposed skin. Her legs were still trapped between his knees, and she flexed her hips upward, like a flower straining to open. He clamped his legs tighter, as if telling her to wait, and continued to kiss her, exploring every millimeter of her mouth.

Slowly, he began rocking, ever so slightly, rubbing their naked chests together. Each teasing abrasion across her nipples made her squirm. A need was growing inside her. A deep, undefinable desire for his attention all over her body. But the kiss was so mesmerizing, she didn't want it to end.

As if sensing her frustration, he lifted one knee and pushed it between her legs. She grunted in surprise and then delight as he ground his thigh against her clit. It pulsed and throbbed, and she clamped her thighs over his leg and rocked her hips. He increased his rhythm to match her desire, bumping against her. One hand left her face and cupped her hip, holding her steady, strengthening the contact with her clit. Her need grew. Rose up over her like a physical thing. Quivered on the edge, and crashed down over her.

Moaning, she rode her orgasm, legs quivering. Before the wave fully subsided, he moved to her breasts, running his tongue in circles around first one areola, then the other. The bundles of nerves there sent electric shocks of pleasure to her already pulsing core, drawing out the cascading orgasm like a sigh.

His mouth trailed from her breasts down her belly, leaving damp kisses to prickle in the cool air. He dipped his tongue into her belly button before moving lower. Her leggings slid from her body, taking her panties along with them, and she lay completely naked before him. He knelt and blew warm air across her clit. She shivered.

"Ophir," she moaned, not sure what she meant by it. He took it as a question.

"Yes, my love?" He kissed her inner thigh, sending more electric tingles rocketing to her core.

She parted for him, his hands gently easing her thighs apart and up, claiming complete access to her. The brush of his touch on her curls left her quivering. Then his tongue split her lower lips, swiping upward from the well of her desire over her clit, circling before dipping downward once again. She held still, panting, waiting. He circled her clit once again, then clamped his lips over the nub and sucked. She arched, a moan of pleasure escaping her. God, he knew how to work her body. She pushed her sex more firmly against him, begging for more.

He groaned, and pressed his face into her, penetrating her with his tongue. Lost to him, she grabbed fistfuls of his hair and bent her legs higher to accept him. His palms massaged her thighs, thumbs circling the sensitive space where her ass met her legs and into the crease along both sides of her pussy.

He sucked and nipped until she couldn't focus on anything except the need to come again.

One of his hands left her thighs and he pressed a finger into her, sliding in and out until her core tightened around him. She whimpered and squirmed, unsure if she needed to get away or beg for more. He thrust harder, deeper, adding a second finger, sucking hard.

Another orgasm whipped through her, waves traveling from deep inside to take control of her entire body, wracking her with convulsions of pleasure.

Still it wasn't enough. It was incomplete. Panting, she reached for him, wanting, wanting everything. "Please. Fuck me."

His lust-filled gaze captured hers as he knelt above her. With one wave of his hand, his jeans winked out of existence, and he was before her in full naked glory, cock pulsing high and thick. A moment of fear engulfed her. He looked so big. So hard. But then he was lying atop her, the line of his erection teasing her wet cleft while he once again soothed her with his kisses.

She tightened her grip on his shoulders, wriggling. His cock was so heated, so hard. And she wanted it. She wanted all of it. The smooth round head poised at her entrance, pressing but not penetrating. She arched into him, her body tight with anticipation and need. So close. And yet he remained frozen. Panting.

"You sure?" he asked.

"Yes," she gasped. "Please."

He kissed her at the same time he thrust forward. She gasped, the sharp burn both surprise and relief. He felt impossibly large, and yet impossibly right. He filled an emptiness inside her, completed her in a way she'd never imagined possible. Her heart raced and she gasped for breath.

"You feel so good." He pulled back and rolled his hips to work more of himself inside her. "Am I hurting you?"

She shook her head and sighed, accepting him, wanting him, fitting him. She reveled in the burn as more of him slipped inside her. He paused, only partially joined, and stroked his tongue slowly along her lips. Rocking, he stretched her, eased into her, each thrust pushing him deeper. The assault on her senses was impossible to resist. She spread her legs as far as she could, welcoming him. With one more steady push, his hips settled against her with satisfying finality.

"Perfect," he hung his head and panted. "Everything about you. So perfect."

She wrapped her arms around his shoulders and held him close, relishing the indescribable sensation of their joining. The awe of holding him inside her only lasted a moment. Then he pulled back and thrust again. The burn was less, now dominated instead by lust. His slow strokes ignited her in a different way than his mouth or his fingers. A fuller, more complete sensation.

In and out he thrust, as she flexed to meet him until his

skin was slapping against hers. She groaned every time he embedded himself inside her, and his panting drove her to a frenzy. Her core tightened around his cock, all burning and pain long forgotten. Dizziness consumed her, and every nerve seemed stimulated. He pushed her higher than she thought possible for the human body to experience. She couldn't breathe. Couldn't move. Her body seemed locked on the edge of her orgasm.

He groaned her name and somehow filled her deeper. She teetered, waves rolling through her, up and down her body, setting her trembling. With a grunt, Ophir thrust once more. Hot bursts of his release filled her, each pulse of his cock sending another rippling contraction through her body. The rolling waves seemed to go on for an eternity, their joint release ending only after he'd given her everything.

The world came into focus again around her. Ophir's hot, slick skin pressed to hers. His panting breath in her ear. The reassuring weight of him on top of her. Her breathing slowed. Peace filled her. Contentment. What they'd just shared was nothing short of amazing.

"My beautiful, perfect Tanika."

She let out a tremendous gasp. "That was… that was…"

"Bonding. That's what that was. I'm sealed to you. Now rest and let me hold you."

She did rest, safe and at peace for the first time since making her horrific wish.

10

*O*phir rolled off Tanika's body, and the loss of her warmth was sharp. Immediate. He tugged her against his chest, reclaiming the comfort he'd found in her arms. She murmured and snuggled her luscious backside against him. He wanted to stay here forever. But they had one last thing to do.

He whispered in her ear. "Wake up, my love. We have a portal to destroy."

She curled herself tighter into a ball. "Now?"

He reached down and pinched her ass, hard enough to elicit a yelp of surprise, but not enough to truly punish. "Yes, now. Your wish is complete. He'll take the first chance he can to hand the portal to a new master."

She bolted upright, the curve of her breasts illuminated in

the faint glow of dawn outside her bedroom window. "But the bank is closed."

"No better time to break in, then, is there?"

With a gleam in his eye, he rose and conjured his clothes back into place. She scrambled for her own, and he smirked, watching her slide her feet into her leggings.

"You could help, you know," she grumped.

"And miss out on your divine curves? I think not."

She flushed as rosy as the sunrise outside.

Once they were both clothed, he led them to the convertible, settling her into her seat before asking for directions.

"We have to go to Redmond."

He squeezed her knee and drove them to a nearby doughnut shop.

"Why are we stopping?" she asked.

"I'm going to use a lot of energy to create a crucible hot enough to melt the portal. Carbs loading'll help." While the tired young man behind the counter filled two coffees, Ophir picked out a dozen doughnuts. "What's your favorite?" he asked Tanika.

"Oh, none for me, thanks."

Tipping the young man a hundred, he handed the pastry box to Tanika so he could douse his coffee with sugar. She took a deep breath of the box top and moaned. "Just holding this is going to make me gain twenty pounds, you know."

At the passenger side door he held out the keys and relieved her of the box. "Will you drive so I can eat?"

Her eyes lit up. "Drive? Me? This is nothing like my Ford Escort."

"You'll do fine." He bit into a Bavarian cream, tangy sweet cream flooding his tongue, and pastry melting in his mouth. He held it close to her mouth. "Try this. Just a taste."

Licking her lips, she hesitated, then leaned in and took a demure bite. "Oh, God." She closed her eyes and let her head fall back against the head rest. "That's delicious."

He shoved the rest into his mouth and reached for another, feeling the slowly building energy settle into his bones.

"Are you really going to eat all of them?"

He waggled his eyebrows and nodded, amused by her censuring tone.

"Lucky." She put the car into drive, eased out of the parking spot, put on her blinker and looked both ways before pulling onto the nearly empty street.

He laughed around a mouthful of jelly doughnut. "You don't have to be so cautious."

"About the car? Or the doughnuts?"

"Either." He held the doughnut toward her, and this time she took a big bite. Raspberry filling dotted the corner of her perfect mouth. He leaned over to lick it off, thrilled at the way she turned into him to transform the move into a kiss. After a long moment, she pulled back and took a breath, waggling a finger at him.

"Don't distract the driver." A smile adorned her face as she stepped on the gas, lurching them forward.

They reached Redmond in record time, where the bank's two-story brick building cast a long shadow across the pavement. Tanika pulled into the parking lot, stopping in a far corner under a huge oak tree. Cutting the engine, she looked around. "Someone is going to notice this car."

Ophir gave her the last bite of a maple bar, then kissed the stickiness from her lips, savoring her flavor as much as the doughnut. "Don't worry about it." He opened the door and got out. "You can even leave the keys. Only the people I want to see my car see it. Come on."

Taking her hand, he strode to the front door, flicked his fingers, and the locks released. He'd disabled the security cameras and alarms the moment he'd seen the First National sign. Luckily all these were small spells. He was going to need every reserve once they reached the portal.

"What about the guard?" she asked.

"Sleeping." Holding open the heavy glass door, he allowed her to lead the way. Putting the guard to sleep had been a bit of a heavy lift, but a necessary one.

She crept forward, darting looks left and right, making him smile. Not bothering to hide the echo of his footfalls on the marble floor, he lagged just far enough behind to admire her sexy ass twitching as she took one cautious step after another. Past the teller stations with their antique wrought-iron cage fronts, down a short hall decorated with crown molding, and around a corner to the steel vault door.

Pausing, he asked, "I need to know how big the portal item is and what it's made of."

She looked at him, deep worry in her eyes.

He reached out, smoothed a hand over her cheek, and pulled her into a kiss. "It'll be fine. I'm going to create a crucible. All you have to do is drop the portal in."

"That's all?"

He nodded. "It'll melt the metal and ruin the crystalline structure that gives it power."

She took a shaky breath. "A gold pendant. About the size of a walnut." With a small voice, she added, "Please tell me this will work."

Her words touched him. He bent and kissed her again, gently, reverently. "I will never let you down."

Letting her go, he placed both hands on the wheel lock and twisted until there was a clunk. The door swung open silently. Inside, rows and rows of lockers lined the walls.

Tanika walked straight to the left wall and pulled out her key. "It also requires a bank manager key."

"Never mind. Just point me to the correct box."

She did, and he breathed a release spell at the lock. His heart was thundering in his ears. Everything hinged on getting this done before Elim realized what was happening. "You don't need your key. Be ready to open it. I'm going to conjure a crucible now."

Closing his eyes, he summoned the whirling pool of energy from the pit of his stomach and focused it at waist level in front of him. Heat filled the room, radiating outward from the glowing pinpoint floating there. Opening his eyes, he stared at the growing circle of light, willing it to become a tiny, blinding sun. He flicked a glance at Tanika and nodded, every ounce of his attention on the brewing heat.

Tanika yanked the box outward and fumbled with the flip-top lid. She pulled out a black velvet pouch and let the heavy box crash to the floor. He could feel the portal's energy, smell the anise-sweet scent of its magic. But that magic no longer had any power over him. Ophir breathed through his nose, pouring all his strength into the crucible. Sustaining this much energy output could cause him to collapse. Tanika had to hurry. She struggled with the pouch's drawstring, and he shouted, "The whole thing."

Understanding lit her features, and she tossed the entire pouch into the whirling heat. The velvet went up in a puff of dark smoke. In the center of the crucible, the pendant darkened for an eye blink, glowed red, then golden white.

When he was sure the structure was melted through, Ophir cut the energy flow. The melted gold continued to hover a moment longer, still caught in the force of residual energy. Then it fell like a giant teardrop to the floor, landing with a splat.

Tanika jumped backward to avoid the volcano-hot spatter.

Ophir stepped forward, worried she'd been burned. He might be immune to the heat, but he should have warned her. He'd taken no more than one step when his legs gave out and he fell face first onto the hard tile, the world going dark around him.

11

*T*anika believed she was strong. A big girl. She ought to be able to drag a man across a perfectly flat, smooth floor. But no. Ophir's big frame might as well have been an elephant. Her ballet flats refused to find purchase on the highly-polished marble, and she was forced to remove them, praying the police couldn't ID a person from their toe prints.

Even in bare feet, it took her forever to slide him as far as the vault door. She paused to rest, staring into the room of safe deposit boxes. Globs of hardened gold adhered to the marble, and a crack marred the tile her metal box had hit. The box's lid was bent, but she'd managed to force it back into its slot while waiting for Ophir to regain consciousness. When he didn't, she'd had no choice but to move him herself.

She knelt next to him, smoothing her fingertips over his

brows. She hadn't thought a djinn could be rendered unconscious. Was mortality already creeping up on him? Her stomach churned with regret. He was hers, and now it was her turn to take care of him. They had to get out of here before the bank opened in...she glanced at her phone. Forty minutes. *Shit!* She grabbed his wrist and pulled again, inching him along the floor until he cleared the vault's threshold.

Stepping over him, she moved his legs aside and pushed the heavy metal door shut, spinning the locking wheel. What would the employees think when they got here? She shook her head. She had to trust Ophir could cover their tracks—was somehow *still* covering their tracks. At least there'd been no alarms so far.

Grabbing his wrist, she pulled again, progressing to the corner of the short hall leading to the main lobby. Ophir's hip snagged on the corner as she attempted to round it, and she had to tear his belt loop free of where it had caught on the baseboard's ornate brass corner plate. *Stupid, fancy bank.*

Sweat trickled between her shoulder blades. She tugged harder, all too aware of the ticking clock echoing in the lobby. Someone would be arriving to open the bank at any moment. Dropping to her knees next to Ophir, she patted his cheeks. "Ophir, wake up." She smacked him harder. "Wake up!"

His eyes rolled beneath his lids. Then his lashes parted the barest millimeter. He mumbled something unintelligible.

"We have to get out of here. The bank's about to open, and I can't drag you the rest of the way fast enough."

A shiver rippled along his skin and seemed to reach into his bones. Then he rolled to his side, pushing upright on wobbly feet. Relief made her own knees weak. She wedged one shoulder under Ophir's arm and led him toward the doors. Down the steps. Into the bright morning sun.

Across the street, a man jogged behind his leashed dog. A pickup truck zipped past, country music twanging from the open windows. No one seemed to take any notice of two people limping across the empty parking lot.

Cursing her choice of parking spot, she helped Ophir limp across the vast stretch of pavement to the convertible. The top was up, and she frowned, not remembering Ophir putting it up. But she'd been so frightened, he could have walked on his hands into the bank and she might not have noticed such a detail. As they neared the car, the soft top accordioned back, exposing the interior.

Elim sat in the driver's seat.

12

*T*anika let out a half scream, and Ophir nearly fell at the sudden loss of her support. He forced his bleary eyes to focus, catching himself with one hand on the top edge of the convertible's windshield. Tanika was repeating, "No, no, no…"

Elim grinned at him from behind the steering wheel, his perfect white teeth as menacing as fangs. His face had lost its craggy lines, and the subtle fire in the depths of his eyes glowed with djinn health. "Where are we going next?"

Ophir somehow found the strength to straighten, glaring down at the djinn. "How the hell are you here?" He'd felt no flow of magic from the portal between the time it had emerged from the box until the crucible rendered it useless. "This shouldn't be possible."

"My dear mistress's stubbornness taught me a few things." Elim leered at Tanika. "One of which being that I no longer need a portal to move between realms."

Still reeling from energy depletion, Ophir tried to focus. He'd known the crucible would cost him, but he'd counted on not needing much magic immediately after finishing the job. And never considered he'd pass out completely. Poor Tanika'd dragged him out all on her own. He turned to her. "Are you okay?"

Her lips were still formed around the word "no" and her skin was ashen. "You promised he'd be trapped on the other side."

Guilt gnawed at his chest. "He should be. I don't understand." His guilt turned to anger, giving him strength. He squared his shoulders and faced Elim. "How are you doing this?"

Like a racecar driver, Elim lifted himself up and swung his legs over the car's door, keeping the vehicle between himself and Ophir. But he didn't act afraid. Instead, he pushed his shoulders back and shook his head as if enjoying a sea breeze. "The tiniest connection to an Earth-bound djinn is enough of an anchor, it seems."

Outrage filled Ophir. He hadn't felt any shifting of power, but this method of travel between dimensions was new to him. "You're using *me*?"

Tanika sank to her knees on the pavement.

"I wonder what my range will be?" Elim turned his back and took a few steps away from the car.

Tanika started sobbing.

Ophir stalked around the hood, his legs protesting the movement. He needed to come up with another deal, and fast. "Wait. I have questions."

Elim paused and looked over his shoulder, a slight smile on his lips. "What do you offer for answers?"

Dammit, he wasn't ready for this. Not mentally or physically. If he only had something—anything—to use as leverage. Stopping his advance, he stared intently at the djinn. "Do you have access to full power?"

Laughing, Elim faced away and resumed walking. "The wish has released me. Now, if you'll excuse me, I believe the police have arrived, and I don't want to be caught up in your mess. I have quite a few lost years to make up for."

Elim winked out of existence as flashing lights appeared at the end of the street, headed in the bank's direction.

Ophir wobbled back toward Tanika and pulled her toward the car. His glamour would make police look the other way—a useful spell for driving, and doubly useful now. He expended a tiny fragment of energy to strengthen the magic, fighting the nausea that swept in as a result. Was his extraordinary weakness from more than just creating the crucible? He'd have to think on that, but later. He shoved Tanika into the passenger side door just as a police car squealed to a halt at the bank's front steps. The rumpled guard greeted the officers at the glass door.

Ophir sagged in the driver's seat, Tanika equally wilted in the passenger seat. He closed his eyes and let his head fall back against the headrest. "That went horribly wrong. I'm so sorry, Tanika."

Her shaking breath suddenly huffed to anger, and she began beating his shoulder with her fists. "You said he wouldn't be able to come back!"

"I had no way of knowing." His heart broke as he realized how badly he'd betrayed her. How much he'd underestimated Elim's power. He grabbed her fists, self-recriminations making him feel like he weighed a thousand pounds. Love had made him impulsive. Reckless. He should've thought his plan through better. After essentially losing his portal, Elim had used Tanika's unfulfilled wish to access Earth, so it should be no surprise he could find yet another thread to follow. A thread Ophir provided. Ophir swallowed, an idea forming. A horrific idea, but one that should work, using the only leverage Elim had provided.

He hugged Tanika's balled fists against his heart. "I believe we can still banish Elim from this world."

She stared at him, her breasts heaving, tears coating her cheeks. "How?"

He pressed his lips together, hesitant to speak the solution aloud. A solution that would finally grant him his eight-hundred-year-old wish. The wish he no longer wanted. "If I go back, he no longer has a channel."

Her mouth fell open. "You can't! You said you'd stay with me forever!"

"I know." He stared sightlessly out the windshield. Every molecule in his body ached at the thought of leaving her. "But we can't allow him to stay."

In the rearview mirror, he spotted a police officer squinting the convertible's direction. Dammit, their suspicion was too strong. Even the glamour could only hold up against certain levels of attention. Elim was probably watching from some nearby tree and laughing. Grinding his teeth, Ophir started the engine, slammed the car into drive, and peeled out, tearing up an edge of the grass between the sidewalk and street. As soon as he was several blocks away, he slowed again and pulled into an empty driveway.

Turning to him with knit brows, Tanika said, "I see a major problem. Didn't you say you needed a portal? You can't go back without one."

He'd considered this when he first decided on this course. "The weakness I experienced is due to more than merely creating the crucible. I think it's because of Elim. He used me as an anchor between Earth and our realm. I should be able to trace the path back to the source. Back to... home." The word felt like poison on his tongue.

Still barefoot, Tanika jumped out of the car and started

walking. He climbed out after her and jogged to catch up. "Where are you going?"

"I don't know. I just want it all to go away."

He stopped, letting her pull ahead. "I promised you I'd free Earth of his presence. And I mean to do it."

Her steps faltered and her shoulders slumped. "It's not fair. I only just found you."

In three strides he was next to her, his heart in full agreement. Yet he couldn't stay here with her, not with a potentially vengeful djinn stalking her. The only way to protect both her and the rest of humanity was to go back. "I have to do this. He's a danger to you and every other person he meets."

"Isn't there another way? Would a wish break the connection?" She looked at him with hopeful eyes.

He shook his head. "We're immune to each other's magic, remember?"

She shoved both palms ineffectually against his chest. "I don't want to have to choose between you and him! I lose no matter what!"

He opened his arms, relieved when she fell into them, pressing her cheek hard against his chest. Resting his chin atop her head, he breathed deeply of her sweet anise and citrus scent. "I'm so sorry."

There was really nothing more to say. So he held her while she cried. He looked at the achingly blue sky overhead, took a deep breath of the morning breeze, full of the scent of cooking bacon and the rose bushes climbing a trellis on a nearby house. Ran his palms along Tanika's bare arms, enjoying the velvet skin beneath his touch. All these things he would lose when he once again became pure spirit.

She turned her chin to look up into his face. "There's no other choice. You have to go, don't you?"

He nodded, and brushed his lips gently against hers. Her beautiful face crumpled into tears once again, and he crushed her tightly against him, never wanting to let her go. The world seemed to stand still around them, time losing all meaning, and yet barely any time at all passed. He would hold this in his memory for all eternity. Finally, he pushed her away, holding lightly to her arms.

"Now?" She whispered.

He wiped moisture from beneath her eye with a thumb and put it to his lips, tasting salt. Even the sad things he'd miss. "Before he has a chance to trick another soul."

She stepped back, body rigid, eyes tight. The tendons on her neck stood out with repressed tears. Holding up her right hand, she regarded the palm. "I only have one heart line. Unbroken." She held it out for him to see. "I love you, Ophir. I will until the end of my days."

His chest was so tight, he wondered if it might not be possible to die right then and there. "And I will love you through all eternity."

With that, he closed his eyes and focused on the tiny thread he now knew had always been there. The one that allowed him to do small magic, yet had never seemed large enough to allow a soul to pass. He pulled deep from what little energy remained within him, feeling for the djinn in his realm to anchor him, as Elim had suggested. There were plenty there to choose from. He stretched himself thinner than he ever thought possible, felt his cells vibrate, his molecules dissolve... and his consciousness become energy.

13

anika stared at the spot Ophir had stood only moments before. She'd seen her djinn dematerialize a million times. It had always been a relief. Now, watching Ophir fade from existence, it felt like the world had cracked in two, leaving nothing but an empty shell. She stared at her palm again. The strong and unbroken heart line. The lifeline following the long curve of her thumb.

She walked to the car and climbed in, numb. Drove back to the salon without knowing quite how she got there. The security gate moved aside without complaint, as if sensing her inability to argue. Inside the familiar, dark space, she paused, staring into nothingness.

What was she doing? What could she do? Her life had no meaning left. No wish to live for. No wish to live *against*. Elim was gone. Ophir was gone. Her purpose was gone. Sure, she had an awesome new car, but it meant little to her without the sexy man who drove it.

Still in the dark, she flopped into her chair, staring at her shadowy outline in the mirror. Her wish had been granted. But not fulfilled. Didn't that mean something? Didn't Elim still owe her?

Some spark deep inside her ignited, like a fire against her breastbone. Narrowing her eyes she glowered at her reflection. Two pinpricks of lavender light had her spinning the chair around to look behind her. "Hello?"

Her heartbeat thundered in her ears. Rising, she scurried to the light switch and flooded the room. She was alone. She looked at the mirror again. Her grief-stricken eyes stared back. She must have been imagining things.

Shaking her head until her brain rattled, she decided to ready the shop for opening. It was all she had left. She wondered if Elim's horrible spell still tarnished the place, and looked hard at the folding chairs near the darkened window and the shabby velvet curtain in the back. She'd never seen the taint, so she wasn't sure why she expected to see it now. Well, if nothing else, she could try a cleansing, just to be sure.

By the time Birdie arrived several hours later, Tanika was airing out the last of the sage smudge and hand-scrubbing the floor. Birdie had to raise her voice to be heard above the Zen piano concerto playing loudly from Tanika's phone. "I know you're an early riser, but this is going a little overboard, even for you."

Tanika sat up on her knees and wiped an errant curl from her cheek with the back of her forearm. She didn't feel any better. All she could think about was finding a way to reach Ophir. A seance. A lucid dream. There had to be a way. "We needed cleansing."

"If you say so." Birdie clicked over the newly clean floor in her kitten heels and stopped the music. "This have anything to do with your date last night?"

Last night? Had it only been one day since she'd met Ophir? How could so much have happened? She felt like she'd been struck by lightning, and every emotion had been seared to ash. She dropped back to all fours and resumed scrubbing. "I found my soul mate."

Birdie gasped and rushed over, slapping Tanika's shoulder. "Get out. Your soul mate?" When Tanika kept scrubbing, she bent and snatched the sponge away. "Up. Now."

Unable to summon the will to fight, Tanika rose and stumbled to her chair, her knees aching and damp. Once again she flopped, this time not facing the mirror. Birdie fisted one hand on a hip and raised both brows. "You don't drop a bombshell like finding a soul mate and then say nothing else. Now tell."

Tanika shook her head. Birdie would never believe the truth. Yet a lie was an impossible task. "He can't be part of my world. So he left."

Birdie's mouth hung open in shock. "He left? You let him leave? Why?" Her gaze narrowed. "Is it because he was loaded?" She walked over and spun Tanika's chair to face her own, then plopped down to look at her. "Did he leave you, or did you leave him?"

The barrage of questions would normally have made Tanika laugh. Today, it only made her jaw quiver, and her chest grow tight.

"Oh, girl, I'm sorry." Birdie jumped up and raced over to pull Tanika's shoulders into a hug. "I shouldn't be so nosy."

"It's okay." Tanika sniffed, leaning her head against her friend's comforting warmth. "Everything is just too complicated to explain."

"Why don't I do your hair? You seem like you could use a little pampering."

Tanika nodded. Perhaps some physical comfort would help relieve her ache. At this point she hadn't much else left. She rose and followed Birdie to the wash sink, leaning her head back and allowing the hot water to soak into her scalp. Birdie's fingers massaged fragrant suds into her curls, and Tanika closed her eyes, allowing tears to leak toward her hairline. If Birdie noticed, she didn't say anything, just hummed under her breath and continued scrubbing.

The spray of rinse water was a blessed white noise Tanika found surprisingly soothing. Hypnotic. Birdie wrung her hair, and worked conditioner into the ends.

The salon bell jangled, and Birdie's fingers paused a moment. "I'll be right with you!"

Her bright voice jarred Tanika from semi-meditation.

"Thank you, Birdie. I can finish myself. Go take care of our client."

"I can wait." A man's voice said.

Tanika's entire body tightened. She bolted upright in the chair, blinking runnels of water from her eyes. Standing just inside the open doorway was Elim.

Her words choked her, filled her throat and cut off her air without emitting a sound. She clutched her middle. How could he be here?

Elim glanced her up and down as if she was inconsequential, then turned his brilliant smile toward Birdie, one hand extended as if to shake. "You must be Birdie. I've been dying to meet you."

"No!" Tanika shot from the chair, intercepting his outstretched hand and smacking it aside. She rounded on Birdie. "Leave. Immediately."

Birdie's face paled with shock. "Is everything all right?"

"Please, Birdie. No questions. Just go."

Gaze darting between Tanika and Elim, Birdie scurried past. "Should I call the police?"

"No. Just get away from here as fast as you can. Far away. Don't come back until I call you."

Birdie fled.

Tanika squared her shoulders and advanced on Elim until she was nose to chest, looking up into his face. "How the hell are you doing this?"

"You thought my connection to Earth was through Ophir?"

He clucked his tongue and turned away from her, surveying the salon as if seeing it for the first time. "You cleansed in here. I wondered if you'd ever notice."

"You said your connection to another djinn gave you a portal."

"No, I said my connection to djinn blood was enough for a portal."

Her stomach fell. Djinn blood. Ophir had believed she might have a trace within her. "He went back for nothing?" Her words scratched from her throat.

"Oh, my poor Tanika. So lost without a man."

Her cheek twitched, and the fire she'd felt earlier against her breastbone blossomed once again. "I'm lost without my *soul mate*." She stalked toward him once again, punching a finger into his chest with each word. "You owe me a wish."

His face paled. "Now slow down. You—"

"My wish was for a mate."

He back pedaled, holding both hands up, palm out. "I'll find you a new one. Just give me some time."

"I already have a mate. A mate for eternity. What I don't have is my happily-ever-after." A sudden realization hit her. He *couldn't* fulfill his end of the bargain. Ophir was immune to his spells. What did that mean in the world of djinn, with their rules about truth and deal brokering? "You took your payment up front. And now I'm calling your deal."

"I can show him how to come back."

"He won't. We decided it was more important to be rid of

you than it was to stay together. As long as you're alive, we'll deny ourselves." She crossed her arms, her victory a bittersweet bile in her throat. "I think the term in chess is checkmate."

Two overhead lights shattered, and he swelled like he had so many times in the past to intimidate her. "I didn't have to show myself to you. My range is quite far, now. I only returned to be sure you were all right."

"You returned to gloat," she gritted between clenched teeth. "And I want my wish."

His figure began to shimmer, the purple spark in his eyes guttering like a candle at the end of its wick. "You can't. Tanika, I beg of you. You don't understand."

"I'd ask you to bring back Mom and Grandma, but you can't revive the dead. So there's no way for you to repay your debt to me except with your life." She bared her teeth at him. "I want it. Now."

His eyes grew wide, the flame shrinking to minuscule pinpricks. He shook his head and opened his mouth, but no sound emerged. Instead, the oval formed by his lips grew. And grew. Impossibly huge, it consumed his face. Opened into a pit of nothingness before her eyes, as if he was swallowing his own body backwards. Larger and larger the oval grew, drawing him in, shrinking him. Swallowing him. Sucking down with a whoosh into a florescent purple globe of light.

It hovered there, the flames within it flaring and swirling

in patterns like galaxies being born. She stepped closer, mesmerized. She'd won?

The globe shot forward into the burning spot in her chest, slamming her backward to the cold, hard floor.

～

*T*anika woke to gentle fingers on her brow. Without opening her eyes, she assessed every square inch of her body. Every nerve tingled, and she could feel the blood coursing through her veins. Breathing was a magnificent experience, the sweet licorice scent of anise filling her nose. She opened her eyes to meet a chocolate brown gaze.

Ophir's face spread into a grin. "Wake up, my love."

She sucked in a breath. Blinked. Reached a hand up to trace the hard line of his jaw. Solid. Warm. Her head was cradled in his lap, and the salon's flickering florescent bulbs backlit his hair like a halo. "Am I dreaming?"

"If you are, then so am I." He gently slid from beneath her and rose, holding a hand down to help her up. "Are you well enough to stand?"

Gripping his hand, she stood. Easily. Lightly. She felt more alive than she'd ever thought possible. "I'm... confused."

Ophir pulled her close, enveloping her. "Oh, my brilliant Tanika. You don't know what you've done."

She shook her head, wrapping her arms tightly around his solid waist. "I really don't. Please explain?"

A chuckle rumbled through his chest, filling her with joy. If this was death, it was the happiest thing that had ever happened to her. He kissed her hair, then her forehead, then pressed his mouth close to her ear. "You caught Elim in the bargain of bargains. An impossible debt." He pulled away just far enough to look down into her face. "A debt that could only be repaid with every ounce of his being. You are now immortal, my lovely bride."

Her legs suddenly refused to hold her, but Ophir was there. Catching her, he carried her to her salon chair and set her down. She stammered, "Immortal? What does that mean?"

"We can be together for eternity."

The hope swelling her heart threatened to burst. She shook her head, sure she must be dreaming. Or dead. "I thought no wish could ever make me immortal."

"A regular wish couldn't." He grinned at her. "A human soul doesn't carry enough energy for such a wish. But the soul of a djinn is a different matter."

The memory of that purple globe embedding itself within her rocked her again. She shook her head in disbelief. "He gave me his immortality?"

Ophir nodded. "Not gave, exactly. More like made restitution. It was the only way he could fulfill his bargain."

Tears overwhelmed her, and she buried her face in her hands. "I can't believe it."

He cupped her head with both hands, showering kisses over her hair and the hands covering her face until she lowered them and accepted his touch on her eyelids, cheeks, and lips. He breathed against her, a life-giving sensation. Grabbing handfuls of his shirt, she pulled him closer, kissing him for real. Lips hungry against his as if this one kiss had to last forever.

After a long moment, she pulled away. "But how are you here?"

"Our mate bond drew me as surely as any portal."

When he said it, she felt the connection between them, like an unbreakable ribbon around her heart. "Bound." Excitement made her nervous. Unsure where to look or what to do. She had her happily-ever-after? For real? "Can we have children?"

"Of course." He smirked. "But one thing at a time, my love. We have a very long honeymoon to enjoy first."

The jangle of the shop's door drew Tanika's attention. Birdie burst into the salon with Mr. Daniels and a police officer close behind. Birdie stopped short, her brows knit as she took in Ophir kneeling next to the salon chair. "Oh!"

The police officer moved into the room, looking around with a concerned eye. Tanika felt a shimmer of magic ripple from Ophir. The tension in the room relaxed. Mr. Daniels winked and said, "Glad to see you two lovebirds getting along." With that, he left.

Tipping his hat, the police man left as well.

Birdie wiped a tear from the corner of her eye and fanned herself. "Oh. My. God. I knew he was meant for you the moment I saw him."

Tanika nudged Ophir. "Don't do that to her."

"Do what?"

"Make her all gushy."

He laughed and rose from his knees. "I'm not, believe me. Birdie is gushy all on her own."

One hand fluttering over her heart, Birdie rushed to the chair across from where Tanika sat. "You two are perfect together, just like I thought." She settled into her chair and looked expectantly between them. "I want to hear the whole thing, from start to finish. A love story right here in our Seance Salon."

Tanika beamed at Ophir, her heart light as she thought about their future. Their very long future. "There's really not much to say. He came back for me. That's all that matters."

Ophir smiled back. "Soul mates are meant to be together, bound for eternity."

Tanika threaded her fingers into Ophir's, the chaste touch warming her as surely as his fiery kisses. "I'm so glad you found our little salon."

"And I'm so happy to have finally found home."

Happiness surrounded her like she'd never imagined possible.

14

Tanika smiled as Birdie made another silly face, and the chubby toddler she held up to the mirror bubbled with laughter. Tiny handprints marred the glass along with a few slobbery spots where Theon had kissed himself. He was the spitting image of Ophir, with dark hair, fathomless coffee-brown eyes, and even the hint of a dimple at the edge of his mouth. And if Birdie was any indication, he was already killing it with the ladies.

"Come on, Theon." Tanika reached for her son. "Aunt Birdie has work to do."

"I'm never too busy to spend time with this little cutie." Birdie blew a raspberry against the boy's cheek before releasing him to Tanika's grasp. "You don't bring him around enough these days."

"I'll try to be better." Theon's weight settled into Tanika's arms and his familiar, sweet-baby scent filled her with joy. He flung his arms around her neck and gave her an open-mouthed kiss on her cheek, and the woman getting her hair cut at the station beside Birdie's cooed in appreciation.

The salon buzzed with activity, thriving since the glamour Elim had placed over it had been removed. The once tiny shop now took up most of the block and had fourteen hair stations as well as a spa section in the back. Birdie ran everything almost single-handedly, allowing Tanika to focus on her new family. Tanika only came in to give an occasional psychic reading with one of her old clients. It was too bad her absorption of Elim's power hadn't given her a djinn's ability to grant wishes, but that didn't mean her previous ability to read auras was any less real. She often wondered when and if Theon would develop powers, and if they'd be like hers or more substantial like his father's; Ophir said the child might not develop powers at all.

Shifting Theon's weight to one hip, Tanika looked her petite friend up and down, noting how thin she looked. "You should take a vacation."

"Soon as I find a hot guy like Ophir to rub me down with sunscreen." Birdie winked.

Tanika flushed, the vivid memory of her most recent trip to a remote beach with Ophir washing through her. There were definite perks to being married to a guy who could snap his fingers and take you anywhere in the world at any time.

The phone rang, and Tanika waved goodbye as Birdie

picked it up. Ophir was at the cafe, probably glutting himself on pastries. She stepped out onto the sidewalk and hurried toward the scent of cinnamon, sugar, and chocolate.

Ophir met her part way, a large, bright pink box in hand. "All done?"

Theon squealed and reached for his father. Ophir traded Tanika the box for the the child and settled Theon comfortably in the crook of an arm. She loved seeing the two of them together.

"Open that." He nodded at the box. "Mr. Daniels had a big selection today."

She lifted the lid, the aroma of buttery sweet goodness rising from inside. An assortment of doughnuts, brownies, big soft cookies, and two eclairs were arranged in pretty papers. She picked through the delectable treats as Ophir carried Theon to the car and settled him into his car seat. Although Ophir could take them anywhere and give them anything, they mostly lived a regular human life.

And she loved every minute of it.

Finally settling on a brownie, she sank her teeth into the creamy, ganache coating, flooding her tongue with dark chocolate. She gave a groan of dramatic pleasure.

Theon stretched a hand out, making grabby motions toward the treat. Ophir plucked a cream-filled doughnut from the open box, handing it to the child. Whether Theon ever developed powers or not, he obviously had full control over Ophir's heart.

With his chubby fists clamped around the doughnut, Theon smashed it against his open mouth, spewing Bavarian cream down his front.

"You're giving him that whole thing?" Tanika said around a mouthful of chocolate. "That's going to be terrible to clean up."

Ophir smirked and snapped his fingers, making the dribbles vanish. Then he closed the car door and turned to pull her into his arms, leaning backward against the windows.

She settled against his hard chest and tilted her face up to his with a smile. "Cheater."

In the reflection of the car's windows, she watched a group of young women pass by on the sidewalk behind her, gazes fixed with longing on her and Ophir. She took a deep breath of contentment. *My days of longing are over.* Who would've ever guessed her wish could turn out this way?

Using the pad of one thumb, Ophir wiped frosting from the corner of her mouth. "You're almost as bad as Theon."

She caught his hand and licked the frosting clean. His eyes darkened with desire. Without breaking his gaze, she sucked the digit into her mouth, twirling her tongue around it suggestively. Between their bodies, his erection surged to life, and a matching heat grew between her thighs.

He made a low sound in his chest. "I think I've been a bad influence on you."

Tanika smiled around his thumb and released it, kissing

the tip one last time. "I think I like having a genie at my beck and call."

He wrapped an arm around her lower back and pulled her closer. "Your wish is my command, my love."

Lowering his head, he claimed her mouth with his. The kiss flooded her with more than desire. It filled her with happiness. Contentment. Love. She'd finally reached her happily ever after. And she was ready for eternity together.

I hope you enjoyed this trio of hot, mythical monsters. Make sure you sign up for my VIP newsletter. There's an exclusive deleted prologue from The Djinn's Desire *waiting for you right now! Members get exclusive giveaways, sneak peeks of future books, and bonus scenes. Sign up here:*

https://books.bookfunnel.com/m4m-deleted-scenes

If you're craving more sweet and steamy paranormal heroes, you'll love my Alaska Alphas series! Start the series with Accepting His Mate, *a sizzling Alaska double feature! Shifters Kepler and Adrian aren't looking to be tied down. But when they each stumble upon their fated mates, their instincts roar to life.*

Tap the cover to buy now or keep reading for a sneak peek!

EXCERPT FROM ACCEPTING HIS MATE

AN ALASKA ALPHAS DOUBLE FEATURE

The bear dropped to all fours and charged toward her with unbelievable speed, feet thumping against the earth like a drum.

Darcy screamed again, feet churning uselessly against the rocks. She grabbed a handful of pebbles and threw them as the bear broke from the shrubs a few feet away. Flinging her arms up to cover her face, she glimpsed a golden shape streaking in from the side.

It slammed into the bear, bowling it sideways and tumbling into the bushes. A wide swath of brush flattened in their wake. Darcy lowered her arms, gaping at the entangled creatures. The second beast was almost as large as the first, its long, golden tail lashing as it snarled and clawed the other predator. *Do we even have mountain lions in Alaska?*

The animals circled each other, fangs bared, ears laid back.

Lunging forward, the bear struck with one giant paw. The big cat sprang straight up, out of the way. He landed on the bear's shoulders, sinking his fangs into its neck.

With a deafening bellow, the bear reared, shaking the lion off. The lion twisted and landed on its feet. Facing off, they circled again, snarling and lunging.

I have to get out of here. Darcy pushed upright, palms stinging and sticky with blood from where she'd fallen against the rocks. A jolt of blinding pain shot up her ankle, and it suddenly refused to take her weight. Breathing shallowly, she leaned one palm against the cliff and hop-stepped back the direction she'd come.

The mountain lion appeared to be driving the bear away, pursuing it toward the trees at the other end of the slope. Darcy had no idea how she'd been lucky enough to have two predators decide to duke it out with each other instead of have her for a snack, but she wasn't about to complain.

She tripped over a root, collapsing to her hands and knees. The sound of battle had ceased, and for a moment, she held still listening. Was it too much to hope they'd forgotten she was here? Maybe she should just crawl away so they wouldn't see her over the bushes. She lifted her head, aiming for the tree line.

Her gaze connected with the tawny golden eyes of the mountain lion. He crouched less than an arm's length away, muzzle stained crimson and one ear torn. She jolted backward, toppling onto her backside like a crab. This is it. The end. No one would even find her body because the lion would drag her off and eat her.

The lion prowled forward, a deep purr vibrating the air. His golden eyes mesmerized her, and her heart thundered so hard, she couldn't breathe. She found herself unable to look away.

He stepped forward slowly, gracefully, until his front paws straddled her. She was forced to lie back to avoid bumping noses. Barely breathing, she lay beneath him, the heat of his body radiating against her.

"N-nice kitty," she whispered.

He continued purring, lowering his face to rub his cheek against hers.

She cringed, expecting fangs. Only the rough prickle of his whiskers rubbed her skin. With trembling hands, she pushed his head away, the tawny fur lush and soft against her palms.

The big cat responded by purring louder. His golden eyes held an intelligence she hadn't expected. Why wasn't he tearing into her? Could he be somebody's pet? She dug her fingers into the thick fur and the tight fear in her chest eased a bit.

A long rough tongue snaked out to taste her throat, sending a surprisingly sensual shiver through her. She lay perfectly still as the lion moved down her body, snuffling and licking and rubbing. Was he marking her? She knew nothing about mountain lions.

He lifted a wide paw and placed it on her belly, kneading

gently without baring his claws. Her skin quivered under the touch. He nudged his head up the inside of her thigh until he reached her center, hot breath penetrating her jeans.

She gasped, belly tightening around unexpected butterflies. Oh, God. She'd never had a fetish for animals, but this lion…

The cat lifted his head, intelligent gaze connecting to hers. He seemed to be considering. After several heartbeats, the air between them shimmered. The cat's features grew hazy, muzzle flattening and ears receding. The furry hide smoothed, and the limbs lengthened. Within moments, the beast was replaced by a tawny-haired, golden-eyed man kneeling between her legs. His hands were planted on the ground on either side of her thighs, every naked square inch of him rippling with muscle.

In a voice like a roll of thunder, he asked, "Why do you reek of catnip?"

Click here to buy ACCEPTING HIS MATE and keep reading now!

Bewitched Shifter

Midnight Heat

Wild Child

Kirenai Fated Mates (Intergalactic Dating Agency)

Kirenai Fated Mates Boxset (Includes first 3 books)

Arazhi

Zhiruto

Iroth

POST-APOCALYPTIC SCIENCE FICTION WRITTEN AS TAM LINSEY

Botanicaust

The Reaping Room

Doomseeds

Amarantox

ABOUT THE AUTHOR

Once upon a time I thought I wanted to be a biomedical engineer, but experimenting on lab rats doesn't always lead to happy endings. Now I blend my nerdy infatuation of science with character-driven romance and guaranteed happily-ever-afters. My monsters always find their mates, with feisty heroines, tortured heroes, and all the steamy trouble they can handle. I promise my stories will never leave you hanging (although you may still crave more!)

When I'm not writing, I'll be in the garden or the kitchen, exploring Alaska with my husband, or preparing for the zombie apocalypse.

Interested in more about me? Join my VIP Club and get free books, notices, and other cool stuff!

www.tamsinley.com

www.ingramcontent.com/pod-product-compliance
Lightning Source LLC
Chambersburg PA
CBHW070733190726
48292CB00002B/250